CW01664266

THE PEOPLE OF THE HORSE

THE PEOPLE OF THE HORSE

Mary Mackie

GUILD PUBLISHING
LONDON

Copyright © Mary Mackie, 1987

Printed and bound in Great Britain by
Adlard & Son Ltd, The Garden City Press
Letchworth, Herts

This edition published 1987 by
Book Club Associates
by arrangement with W. H. Allen & Co. Plc

This book is sold subject to the condition that
it shall not, by way of trade or otherwise,
be lent, re-sold, hired out or otherwise circulated
without the publisher's prior consent in any
form of binding or cover other than that
in which it is published and without a similar
condition including this condition being imposed
upon the subsequent purchaser.

For Chris

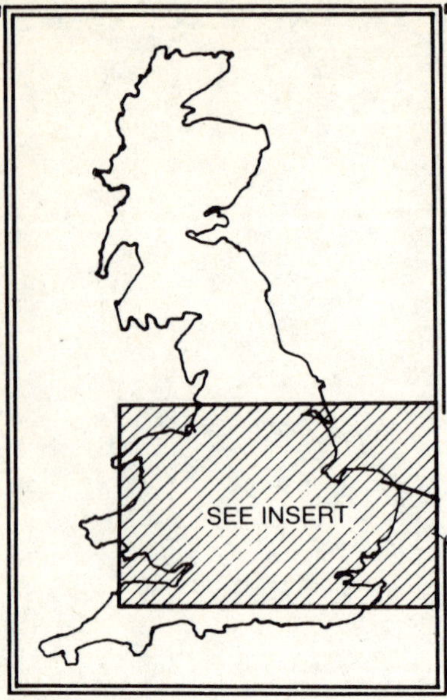

BRITAIN

1st Century A.D.

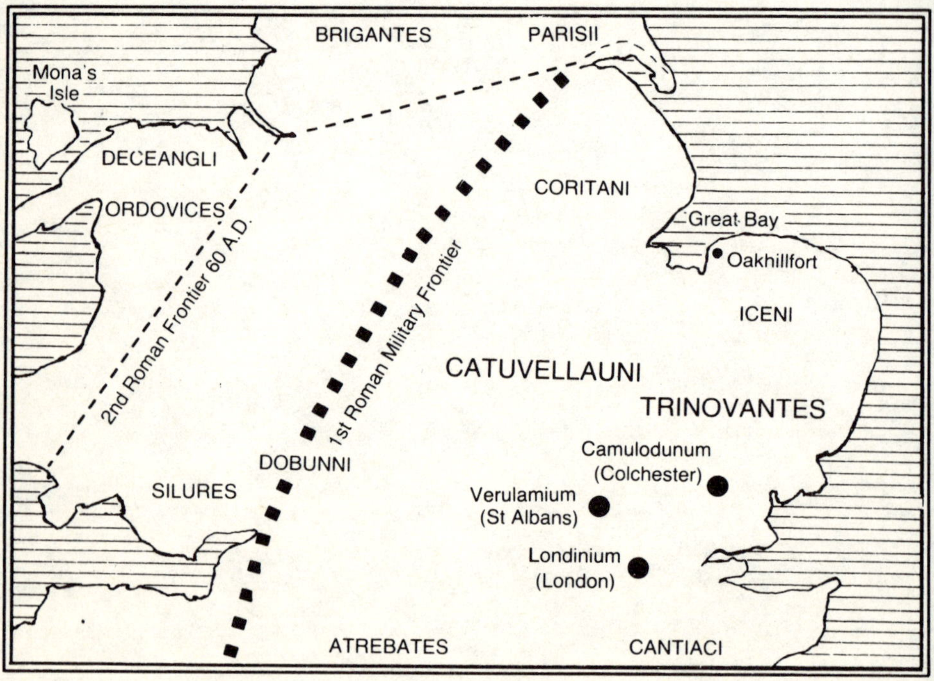

THE MAIDEN'S SONG

Furze fires quenched by ivy dew;
White, and scarlet, and midnight blue.
In willow days the hawk will fly
To hunt the hare through evening haze
And seek the night-dark trees that stand
Gathered to guard the sacred place.
The moon in artless beauty rides
Twin-horned above the alder blooms,
To breathe a sigh among the reeeds
And whisper, Willow, he comes, he comes.

Furze fires quenched by ivy dew;
White, and scarlet, and midnight blue.
Now comes the Maiden, purified,
Drawn by the note of him who trod
The primrose path, all clothed in green,
Mortal, with footsteps of a God.
In Night's deep cloak and silence dread
Folded, the rites of love they sing;
Not of themselves, Immortal rapt,
As has been, as is now, as shall be again.

Furze fires quenched by ivy dew;
White, and scarlet, and midnight blue.
He sleeps, as with the ebbing tide
She leaves – the Maiden, oak and wren
Threefold beneath the bone-white moon
Who, smiling, hides her face again.
Then full in manhood comes the sun
With fire and tears; his power shall move
A wind to stir his singing head
And chant, Awake, Albina's grove!

BOOK ONE

Queen and Maiden

One

He came from the teeth of a winter storm, tossed naked onto a beach of smoothed stones at the edge of the Great Bay. His long hair was strewn about his head like seaweed and his flesh was pale as death. Above him grey clouds shredded as the wind tore at the sky.

A fishermaid found him and called her three brothers, who were mending nets by the salt pans. They sidled cautiously closer until the oldest drew near enough to poke the body with a wary toe. The stranger did not stir. He lay on his belly, his bearded cheek turned against the stones with his long hair straggling across his face. Raw wounds bleached by the sea gaped along one thigh and across his shoulder.

The lads peered at him, noting the strange design of the tattooing about his waist and on his buttocks, and the carved pink quartz in the ring he wore on his thumb. The ring would fetch a good price, and so would the fine sword he still clutched in his lifeless hand.

The oldest fisher brother – by name Bledrew, a youth of seventeen summers – stepped boldly forward to claim the sword for his own, but as he touched the blade the man growled deep in his throat. Bledrew sprang back, filled with superstitious dread – no mortal man could return to life from drowning – only Gods and heroes had such powers. The stranger might be a son of Llyr, the sea-god.

Then from his eye corner Bledrew glimpsed a movement that made him look up at the wooded rise that backed the beach. A dog had appeared there, followed by others – fierce brindled hounds such as were kept by warrior nobles for hunting. Behind the dogs, riders now came into sight, a party of ten or so all dressed in bright-dyed wools and furs, with their weapons slung behind their shoulders.

At the centre of the group rode a girl no older than Bledrew. Her hair was a rich chestnut-red, flowing over a cloak of beaverskin, beneath which she wore trews and tunic of striped red and green wool. Seeing the stranded man, she kicked at her pony and let it pick its way among the stones, her companions following. Beneath her rich cloak Bledrew glimpsed the gleam of a gold torc at her throat.

Until that moment, awe had kept him frozen. Now he hastily backed away from the half-drowned man, trying to protect his brothers and his sister behind his outspread arms. For the girl was Boudicca, queen of the Iceni – queen, and Maiden, Chosen of the Goddess – and with her rode her older brother, Mocuxsoris, and other young warriors both male and female. They came from the high chief's village up at Oakhillfort, on the knoll that dominated all this part of the coast.

The young queen halted within easy speaking distance of Bledrew and his siblings, her green eyes steady on the lad's pale face. Behind her, her companions gathered in an interested half circle, glad of the diversion after an unsuccessful morning's hunting.

'Who killed him?' Boudicca asked. 'Did you?'

'L-lady!' Bledrew stammered, spreading his hands to show her he possessed no weapon. 'Me? No! The storm . . . the storm left him here. And . . . he's not dead. When I touched him, he groaned.'

Her brother slid down from his shaggy mount and, drawing a jewelled dagger from his belt, approached the stranger across the crunching stones. He squatted beside the limp figure, a hand reaching as if to turn the man onto his back.

'Be careful, Mocuxsoris,' the queen said.

He glanced back at her, a grin showing white through his red moustache. 'I'm not afraid of a half-drowned slave. I wonder where he escaped from – and whose sword he stole along the way?' He bent closer, peering at the weapon clutched in the stranger's hand. 'It's a fine sword – expensive. Look at the jewels on the – ho!' He lunged backwards, losing his footing on the stones as the apparently lifeless figure suddenly sprang to its feet. Mocuxsoris sat down with a thump and the naked stranger whirled, stiff-muscled, to stand at bay. His teeth were gritted in a snarl behind his thick beard, and chill light stroked along the blade of his sword as he held it ready to strike.

Bledrew and his family backed off even further, eyes wide as they stared at the spectacle. The warriors had all hoisted their spears ready to throw and Mocuxsoris leapt to his feet, taking up a fighting stance, his dagger in his left hand. Only the queen remained still, surveying the stranger with bold, assessing eyes.

Though his skin was blotched from the cold, his nakedness revealed him to be in the prime of youthful manhood. The Great Mother had blessed him with a strong, shapely form and long limbs. Beneath the wet hair and unkempt beard Boudicca saw a pleasing face that made her curious about the man. She also saw the brow tattoo of the all-seeing eye, which marked him as a blooded warrior of the nobility.

His whole body was shuddering uncontrollably with the cold but he glared at Mocuxsoris and said through clenched teeth, 'The sword is mine. Two men have tried to take it from me – both are dead. Do you want to be the third?'

Mocuxsoris drew breath to reply, his eyes glittering under the tangle of red hair on his brow, but slowly the tension went out of him. He stood up, threw back his head and laughed. 'By the wren! This wraith from the sea-foam thinks he can kill me before a spear can reach him! What shall I do with him, sister? Slay him, or call him brother for his audacity?'

The stranger glanced at Boudicca, evidently surprised to hear Mocuxsoris defer to her. 'Is she your leader?'

'She is my queen,' Mocuxsoris said with a mocking bow. 'And my sister. Through her runs the royal blood of the Iceni, passed from mother to daughter.'

'Iceni?' The stranger's tone sharpened. 'Are you the children of queen Veda?'

Mocuxsoris regarded him with more interest. 'Who asks?'

The man from the sea turned his attention to Boudicca. As if his legs would no longer hold him he fell to his knees, his sword arm sagging. 'I am Huan, son of queen Diavixa and the high chief Muirmenn, of the Caledones. Your kinsman, lady. Blessed Bran, my thanks! My journey is ended at last!' With which, he pitched onto his face on the stones and lay still.

*

As Huan revived, his nostrils twitched to the scent of stewing pork. He lay warm and comfortable among soft furs and he could hear a quern grating, stone rubbing on stone to grind flour. It was only when he tried to move that he discovered the stiffness in his muscles. Pain shafted through his injured shoulder, forcing from his lips a muttered curse that made a soft hand fall on his arm.

He opened his eyes, alert at once, and found himself staring into the green eyes of the young queen. Her pale face was framed by rich red hair coiled in an intricate style that left one swathe to fall across her shoulder, and though she returned his look unflinchingly a faint flush stole into her cheeks and the tip of a pink tongue moistened her lips. The two small boys behind her – identical fair-haired imps – giggled and threw back their hands to their mouths.

Huan swallowed with difficulty, coughing to ease the taut dryness in his throat. His voice was a mere husk of sound. 'I remember you. On the beach. You're the high chief's daughter.'

'I'm Boudicca,' she answered. 'Queen of the Iceni since my mother died two summers ago. My father is the high chief Antedios.'

'And these?' he asked. 'More brothers?'

'Cousins. Kin.' As the twins' giggles increased, Boudicca got to her feet and shooed them out. They ran, tumbling over each other, tossing aside the curtain that covered the doorway and knocking into the old woman who was coming in.

She began to remonstrate as they darted by, then her glance fell on Boudicca and her eyes narrowed in her lined, tattooed face. 'What are you doing here?'

Boudicca's flush deepened but she held her head high, her hair almost brushing the hazel wattle of the sloping roof. 'I came to see if he was recovered. It's my duty to care for a guest in my house. Sometimes you forget who I am, Saille.'

But the priestess returned her glare. 'Queen you may be, but you're Maiden, too – Dia's Maiden. The service of the Goddess comes before every other duty. Remember that!'

'I have not forgotten. I shall fetch some ale, and some food, while you tend his wounds.'

Tossing her long red hair, Boudicca ducked beneath the curtain and the old woman clucked to herself as she bent to throw back the furs and unfasten the binding on Huan's thigh.

His wounds had been freshly dressed with herbs and unguents by the time Boudicca returned bringing a beaker of ale and a hunk of bread. With her came her brother Mocuxsoris, amused and interested. His presence seemed to give the old priestess leave to depart.

With her own hands, Boudicca lifted the stranger's head and helped him take a few sips of ale. He thanked her with his eyes, noting the fresh flush that stained her fair skin as she knelt beside him breaking off pieces of bread, and dipping them in the brew before feeding them to him.

Mocuxsoris sat on the other side of the pallet, his back against the painted wattle of the wall. 'My father the high chief says he's heard of Chief Muirmenn,' he told Huan. 'We're kin, somehow. According to Alvran, our bard, who studied with the Druids, you Caledones trace your ancestry back to the sacred queen, Brecca, as we do.'

'That's so,' Huan agreed. 'We're blood kin, but our ways parted long ago.'

'And the Caledones ended up in the far north,' Mocuxsoris said, scratching his head. 'So how did you get here? Swim?'

'By long, twisting fateways,' Huan said with a wry smile. 'Some day I'll tell you all my journeyings – one night in hall when I've had enough ale to loosen my tongue. But lately I've been held as a slave among the Brigantes. They took my sword and set me to work like a yoked ox, but I escaped one night, stole back my sword, slew the man who robbed me and fought my way to the coast where I found a boat – a coracle, not meant for winter seas, but it was all I could find. Then the storm came. My paddle was swept away. The coracle overturned. But Llyr brought me to Icenia.'

Boudicca was watching his bearded mouth as he spoke. No man had made her feel as Huan did, sharply conscious of herself, of him, and of the stir of new emotions in her breast. She was convinced that it was not cold Llyr who had sent him but the Goddess – the Goddess in her incarnation as Andastre the passionate.

With a start she realised that Huan was watching her, aware of her interest and responding to it. She offered him another piece of ale-soaked bread and watched the way his even teeth closed over it, his lips just brushing her fingers. A fleck of foam trembled among the reddish hairs of his beard, exciting her beyond reason.

'I was fated to come here,' he said in a low voice, his eyes on her face. 'Before I left the islands my mother the queen Diavixa laid a *geis* on me – to be an exile from my own land, to journey five long years in search of a bride, to find at last my Kinsmen of the Horse, and discover my destiny among them.'

This man was too bold, Boudicca thought, unsettled by the bright, intimate expression in his blue eyes. He had no right to speak so openly to her about finding a bride, not yet, not while she was under the Goddess's command.

As she withdrew from the room she heard Mocuxsoris say with a laugh, 'Now you've offended her. You'll need patience, friend. My sister's dedicated to Dia – tabu for all men – at least until the Great Year ends.'

Among the People of the Horse – the Iceni – the high chief held greatest authority, but he gained this power through marriage to the queen. The ancient royal blood of Icenia, in direct line from legendary Brecca, herself a daughter of the Goddess, passed down from each queen to her oldest daughter or nearest female relative, whose husband would in turn assume the role of high chief.

Therefore a queen's sons had to find their own fortunes. Some, like Huan, chose to travel and seek a bride among other tribes; some rebelled and were sent to the pit to await the fire; others – a very few – contented themselves with a place among their sister's guard. Mocuxsoris had not yet decided what to do with his life.

Boudicca's brother came frequently to visit Huan as he recuperated, though after that first day the girl-queen herself remained aloof. The two young warriors swapped tall tales of their adventures; they spoke of women, and inevitably they talked of war.

For some years now, a neighbouring tribe had been making frequent incursions into the borders of Iceni territory. These Catuvellauni were now ruled by two brothers, Togodumnus and Caratacus, who were evidently intent on enlarging their territories at the expense of any neighbour who stood in their way.

'They've overrun the Trinovantes, our neighbours to the south,' Mocuxsoris told Huan, 'and they've forced the high chief of the Atrebates into exile. Our Druid, Eogan, says cries for help have been sent to Rome. He's not pleased about that.'

'Rome?' Huan was startled.

'Well, you can see the reasoning behind it. The Catuvellauni are getting above themselves. They ought to be stopped. My father's biding his time because for the moment we seem to be safe enough, apart from a few nuisance raids – at present, you understand, the Catuvellauni are more interested in pushing deeper into Albion, away from us. But the trade routes are hazardous and some things are getting scarce. Like wine, and gold. I ordered a new armband for Huctia – my woman, you must meet her – but every time I go over to the goldsmith's he just wags his head and says he can't get the gold.'

'And you think the Romans are the answer? Are you mad? Haven't you heard what they've done in Gaul?'

Mocuxsoris hunched his shoulders, pulling at an end of his red moustache. 'The elders say it'll be different with us. We're allies of Rome. We've had trade treaties with them for years. But this . . .' He spat onto the pounded clay floor and stared gloomily down at the dark spot he had created. 'I'm not so sure. If they bring their legions over here, we might be hard put to get rid of them again. I say it's up to us to fight our own battles.'

'I, too,' Huan said. 'When I get back my strength, we'll go after these brothers and challenge them. You and I together. Togodumnus for me, Caratacus for you. Agreed?'

'Agreed!' They laughed fiercely at each other, clasping hands in confirmation of a bond of brotherhood.

As winter's grip eased on the land and ploughs went out into fields cut in the shallow soils of the undulating heath, Mocuxsoris and his new companion had their chance to meet with the Catuvellauni. A call for help came from the Iceni chief who ruled the border lands: the Catuvellauni were marauding in his territory.

Antedios, high chief of the Iceni, gathered warriors from

all clans of his tribe and set forth to do battle with the invaders, taking with him Mocuxsoris his son and their distant kinsman Huan. They took their light battle chariots, and fierce dogs collared with spikes. Their leaving made a brave sight, though some women wept.

Boudicca didn't weep; she railed at being left behind and paced the heights of the defensive banks until the war party was gone from sight along the winding track through gentle hills that led to the Way. She had wished to fight beside Mocuxsoris and her father – and Huan. The waiting behind would be intolerable.

But Saille came to her, reminding her that her first duty was to the Goddess. It was a necessary duty. If the rites were not observed, disaster would ensue: the heavens would fall, the earth split under them, the sea overflow. Boudicca had to be patient and play her part. Afterwards she would be free to pursue her life as she chose.

To her joy, not many days passed before the warriors rode home again, elated by their triumph over the hated Catuvellauni. Several of them brought the heads of enemies impaled on their spears. Muddied from the long ride, many of them displaying bloody bindings over wounds, they rode into Oakhillfort shouting greetings to the loved ones who ran out to meet them. A few familiar faces were missing: among them Erainna, one of Boudicca's closest friends; the chariot commander, grizzled veteran Uccus; and Gomer the chief of the border fort. But Mocuxsoris was safe. His bold grin caused Boudicca's heart to lift as she waved at him and saw Huan there by his side, smiling at her in a way that hinted at shared secrets. And her father . . . her heart almost stopped as she saw him sagging on his horse, barely able to stay upright because of the pain from a speartip that had broken off deep in his shoulder.

'I'm all right!' he chafed when she fussed over him. 'Just get me Eogan. He'll be able to cut it out.'

That night Boudicca attended the celebration feast in the great hall, where much ale was drunk, old songs were sung and tall tales of heroic deeds were woven out of happenstance. She listened to the boasting – most of which came from Mocuxsoris – with amusement and pride. She had already learned of the heroism of her brother and of Huan, both of whom had fought naked in single combat and bested Catuvellauni champions. Unfortunately both of the Catuvellauni chieftains had been absent from this particular battle.

'They had heard that Huan and I had sworn to take their heads!' Mocuxsoris claimed. 'They were afraid to face us.'

In the days that followed, Antedios lay sick for long night after long night. Boudicca tended him anxiously. Eogan the Druid had cut out the shard of iron but the resultant wound festered and would not heal despite all the ointments and spells that Saille applied, and despite the prayers that Eogan intoned to the stars.

But at last Antedios rallied, though his wound still refused to heal cleanly. He insisted on sitting with the council to deliberate the matter of the vacant chieftainship of the border fort. Several claimants came forward, but the elders elected Mocuxsoris the king's son as the new lord of the border lands and guardian of the Way – an honoured position that satisfied his pride and his desire for action.

Mocuxsoris selected a guard of warriors to go with him to the border lands, and before they left he and the warrior-maid Huctia were married in the sacred oak grove along the knoll, with feasting and celebration and the ritual purification of leaping over fires.

Boudicca missed her brother, but she found consolation in the fact that Huan of the Caledones had declined to accompany Mocuxsoris. Huan had other plans for his future; he had been elected a member of the high chief's guard and had settled into the life with ease, welcomed for his courage and his good humour. Though no word had been said between them Boudicca was warmly aware that she figured centrally in his plans. When her duty to the Goddess was done, she was sure, Huan would speak his heart.

And the time was fast approaching: Eogan the Druid and Saille the priestess read the stars and foretold that the wheel had turned over the required nineteen summers; the present Great Year was ending. The season of the Maiden would come with the following spring.

As the year turned preparations were made for the festival of dark Samhain; cattle and sheep were slaughtered and put down to salt, a few of the fittest animals were brought to pens inside the high banks of Oakhillfort to overwinter and breed again come spring.

On a day when a wind whipped dead leaves around wattle and thatch, the Druid Eogan sat beneath the sacred oak and tossed a handful of bones and pieces of flint from which to read the portents. A drum called the people to gather for the choosing of the new Green King. All within earshot left their chores and made their way to the central meeting place.

A slave laid a bearskin rug for Antedios to sit on and the high chief emerged from his roundhouse leaning on the arm of his daughter. He had aged during the past moons. His wound still wept; his shoulder was stiff and painful, and he had become aware of aching joints and wandering thoughts.

Boudicca stood behind her father, her breast a tight knot of excitement and apprehension as the ceremony began.

The eligible warriors – those who had attained manhood but were yet unmarried, with among them Huan of the Caledones – squatted in a circle around the sacred oak, their eyes fixed on the Druid as he hunched with his half-shaven head bent over his runes muttering under his breath. Eogan wore an ancient cloak of a fur so muddied and matted by weather and rough-sleeping that it was hard to tell what animal had supplied it; but his fingers were heavy with rings, weaving mysterious patterns over flints and bones.

He leapt up suddenly, throwing his scrawny arms to the sky and crying aloud in a wordless bellow that made people start, some of them exclaiming in awe. A child started crying and was hushed by its mother, as from under his cloak Eogan produced a wicker bottle, its neck just wide enough to admit a hand. He shook it and the ritual glass pebbles rattled and rolled inside the container.

Slowly, Eogan walked around the circle of young warriors, offering the bottle. Each man in turn dipped an eager hand into the container and drew out one of the glass pebbles, holding it hidden in his fist.

Hardly daring to breathe, Boudicca saw Eogan stop finally in front of Huan, who straightened to his full height and smoothed his auburn-fair moustache. He shaved his chin daily, as did most of the younger Iceni, but he had kept his long hair and wore it bound tightly back into a thick, intricate braid. It showed off the fine contours of his face, the strong nose and high cheekbones, and his brow where the Warrior's Light was tattooed.

He stared into Eogan's eyes as he reached inside the bottle and brought out a pebble, holding it tight in his fist as the Druid stepped back to the centre of the circle, saying, 'Now!' Each man opened his hand palm upwards and glanced to see what fortune was his.

Most of the glass pebbles were coloured white, but the coveted one was clear, and at its heart there was a drop of scarlet, said to be blood from the breast of the robin. Boudicca saw Huan stiffen. Across the circle his eyes met hers, his strong teeth showing in a grin as he hoisted a clenched fist and yelled aloud for pure joy.

The Goddess had chosen him to be the new Green King.

At dawn the following day, all the young warriors gathered for the traditional boar hunt that marked Samhain. The old Green King, who had stood proxy for the God at festivals the previous year, set off alone, wreathed in yew. It was his task to raise the first boar and lead the others to it. Somewhere in the forests, the yew wreath would be swapped and Huan would then lead the triumphant huntsmen home with their catch to the feast which marked the beginning of his reign as Green King.

'Hunters!' Eogan cried. 'Your quarry has fled to the woods. The ancient rites of Samhain demand his death. Fetch him home. Fetch him home to the fires!'

They set off merrily, noisily, and returned at dusk weary but singing with two boar slung on poles. When the hunters had refreshed themselves, they joyfully joined the dance that twined around the fires at the oak grove along the knoll.

At the feasting the following day, Huan's gaze lingered openly on Boudicca. The great hall filled with drunken noise and chins ran with grease from the succulent pork roasts. Through the smoke and clamour, she was constantly aware of Huan, her glance drawn again and again to where the young warrior sat among his friends. She was wrong even to think about him, but she couldn't help herself.

Her father retired early to bed, plagued by pain in his injured shoulder, and soon afterwards Boudicca left the hall as brawling broke out. The warriors were required to hang up their swords when entering hall, but they still had fists and teeth. She left them to enjoy themselves as they would.

As always at that time of year, fires burned outside each door to warm the honoured dead whose ghosts gathered at Samhain. Flickering light licked under thatched eaves and across flint-bedded pathways and one or two men lay snoring in heaps, having come out for air only to be felled by their first good breath.

Shivering, Boudicca drew her cloak more securely around her as she made for the largest house, the queen's house, whose high roof bit a curving conical shape out of a starry sky. Then behind her a step sounded on the stones and she glanced round to see Huan coming after her through firelight and shadow, wearing only a linen shirt and leather breeks, evidently inured to the cold by the mead and ale he had imbibed.

He paused in front of her, staring into her face. His breathing sounded hoarse and shallow. 'Lady . . .'

'What is it you want?' she asked in a haughty undertone despite the excitement beating in her blood. 'I'm not to be followed, Huan. Go back to the hall.'

'I'll go when I'm ready,' the reply came gruff and his big hands fastened on her shoulders. 'But first – '

Before she could protest he dragged her to him. His mouth fastened on hers and though she bunched her fists to beat him off her muscles refused to obey her will. She leaned on him, her body responding to him with a hunger that dazed her. How long she had waited for him. How long!

Then someone came out of the night – Eogan, and some of the elders. They forcibly parted the pair, dragged Huan stumbling away and left Boudicca blinking. Dimly she heard Huan laugh out loud as if the prize had been worth the punishment, and then she realised that old Saille was there, staring at her, and with her the sharp-eyed acolyte Morica.

'Are you mad?' Morica hissed. 'Couldn't you wait? You'll destroy everything. Wait a few moons and – '

'No!' Saille exclaimed, her face grim in the firelight with its tattooed eyes and straggle of white hair. 'Boudicca . . . child . . .'

'What will they do to him?' Boudicca asked, struggling to see the receding shadows that were Huan and his captors.

'He'll be thrown into the punishment pit, for a night, or maybe two. And as for you . . .' Saille's hand clamped viciously on the young queen's arm, making Boudicca look at her. 'Did he do more than we saw? Has he ever done more?'

Face burning, Boudicca drew herself up to her full height, towering over the bent priestess. 'How dare you ask me that? I would not dishonour the Goddess. I know my duty.'

'But not well enough! From now on, Morica will stay with you night and day. Until Beltane. You must come to the Mysteries a virgin. You must! Or will you force us to choose another Maiden?'

The threat cooled Boudicca's temper. No, there must not be another Maiden. Her people were relying on her, their queen, to fulfil the rites and ensure the safe continuance of the tribe. She could not betray her sacred trust. She would avoid Huan from now on, however hard it proved – at least until after Beltane.

Two

Throughout that winter, Morica was a constant presence at the young queen's elbow. Her watchfulness irritated Boudicca, who came to hate the thin face and gleaming eyes of the priestess. She was never allowed within arm's length of Huan and if she let her eyes linger too long on him she was subjected to a lecture on duty and obedience. Nor did the young warrior's attempts to break through the taboo meet with any success. He too was watched, by the high chief and by the elders. Everything conspired to keep the pair apart.

But the endless winter did pass. At last spring spread its green fingers among the trees. The white hawthorn began to bloom. With it, came Beltane.

On the first night of the new moon, all the young people gathered at the gates of Oakhillfort carrying sputtering torches, with the older folk in groups on the high, grassed banks to cheer them on. Dressed in white, garlanded in willow, and accompanied by Morica and old Saille, Boudicca brought a wicker cage containing a hare. Huan, decked in oak and holly leaves to honour the twin Gods, and carrying a spear, waited with the others. He sent a smiling glance at Boudicca but she replied with a hooded look; she knew well enough what revels occurred in spring-scented woods during the long night of Beltane Eve. The Green King would be gone with the rest. She, still under a vow of virginity, must stay behind.

A mood of excitement and levity surrounded the youths and maids and as Boudicca released the hare a great whoop of delight broke from the crowd. The hare bounded away, fleeing the noise and the light of spitting torches. Youths and maids ran after it to stream along the chariot track and out among the fields, headed for the woods. The 'hare hunt' would probably last all night.

As Boudicca wondered which of her maidens would find herself in Huan's arms under the young moon, Saille and Morica stepped up behind her. A soft cloak was laid on her shoulders and the two women took her arms to lead her away into the night.

Fear laid a cold hand on her. 'Now?'

'You must prepare,' Saille said.

'But . . . tomorrow . . . the races . . .'

'The races are for the others. For you there are more important duties. Come, Boudicca.'

The men who had been watching the start of the hare hunt seemed to have melted away. Only the women remained, beginning a soft chant as they formed a procession behind the Maiden to escort her down through the woods to the priestess's hut among the alders by the river, where she spent the night.

Boudicca slept fitfully, wondering what the coming day held for her. She knew the ritual in outline; it was told in the Maiden's song. She must meet with the God in the rites of love. Now that it was about to happen, the thought terrified her. But there was nothing to fear. Other Maidens had met with the God in the Great Year ritual. The last one, nineteen years ago before even Boudicca was born, had been a kinswoman of queen Veda – a gentle, sad-faced woman who had met her death in the frozen marshes one year when the ice gave way. That was long after she had served the Goddess in the Mysteries. What was there to fear?

At dawn, Morica and Saille roused the queen and the three women set out across the river toward the marshes where the tangles of growth on a wilderness of islands was interspersed with streams and pools, here narrow, there broadening into lakes. They travelled mostly by coracle, following a course familiar to Boudicca, who had been shown the ways of the marshes by Saille during her training. She knew now where they were going. She could picture the place with its shadows and its tree-stump altar thick with dried blood.

It seemed to her that an uncommon hush lay over the watery landscape, as if even the wind had halted to await the coming of the Maiden. In a silence broken only by the splash of a paddle, her heart beat loud, pulsing in her throat like a captive frog.

They travelled slowly, in awful silence, fasting and praying, all three of them mentally preparing for what was to come. This was the most sacred service they could ever perform for the Goddess, a rite enacting Dia's coupling with the God who was at the same time Her lover, Her son, Her sacrifice.

Some time after noon, when a faint mist hung over the waterways, they came to a narrow island where Morica beached the coracle and instructed Boudicca to undress and bathe in the deep, cold pool of purification. The two priestesses meanwhile built a fire and laid out the garments Boudicca was to wear – a white tunic and cloak streaked with silver thread. They dried her with reverent care, doused her body in sweet perfumes, and combed out her hair until it was shining, all the time instructing her in her duty.

They gave her a hot drink whose aroma was familiar and she sipped it steadily, her hands tight around the cup. It was rich with a drug that would help her forget her fear. Over the past years she had become used to its effect. Sometimes it brought visions; sometimes it dulled her senses; sometimes it brought forgetfulness. As the cup emptied she began to feel the first effects – the light-headedness and the euphoria.

Easing her aching back, old Saille sat down beside Boudicca, taking from a fold of her cloak a long, thin knife in a bronze sheath hanging from a leather thong. The hilt was crusted with dark blue quartz – the death colour. Her mind numbed by the intoxicant she had taken, Boudicca tilted her head as Saille slipped the thong over her hair and round her neck. It hung sweetly between her breasts, emphasising their thrust against the thin linen of her robe.

'With this you mark Him,' the priestess said, lifting Boudicca's chin to stare into her eyes. 'Do you understand me? When He has sated His lust, you will give Him a drink from the jug you will find behind the altar. It will make Him sleep. And then . . .'

'Am I to kill Him?' Boudicca asked, her eyes wide and dark.

'No! It's part of the ritual, to remind Him of the time His folly caused the Goddess to punish Him by taking His head. She could do it again when He lies defenceless, but She is merciful. You will merely mark Him – a cut across the base of His throat, so!' She demonstrated with an arthritic finger. 'And then you will leave and return here to us. The light from the fire will guide you.'

All at once, so it seemed, dusk had crept across the marshes. Exultation beat in Boudicca's blood as she saw the pale outline of the new moon, the Virgin Goddess, hanging in the sky over a bank of alder and willow that marked the sacred island where the God would be waiting. While there was still just enough light to pale the water's surface, she set out in her coracle, understanding now why Saille had brought her here so many times: it was in order that she might find her way in near-darkness with her brain muzzy and her veins filled with what felt like hot wine. She felt herself enveloped by the Goddess, swept up in Her desire for a union with the God, essential female moving to a coupling with essential male.

Deep among the undergrowth that crowded the sacred island she saw an orange gleam. Someone had lit a fire there. Someone was playing music – the plaintive notes of a reed pipe called to her across the darkening marshes. The God! Her coracle brushed against reeds and bumped on dry land. She jumped out, pulling the boat after her until it was clear of the water; then she turned to follow a path outlined by the pale faces of primroses. She felt as though she were floating, light as a butterfly, moving through mist towards beckoning firelight in a clearing that opened abruptly before her.

A man sat by the fire, naked, on a bed of fur blankets. He was blowing on a reed pipe. As she stepped into the firelight he looked up and she knew him, even through the mists across her mind. It was the God – the God in the shape of the Green King. The Goddess had been kind. Or perhaps She too wished to experience, through Boudicca, the pleasures to be had in the arms of Huan of the Caledones.

Huan had been tutored, too, by Eogan the Druid – tutored and drugged until, waiting for the Maiden, his lust had become a throbbing, intolerable pain. When she appeared on the edge of the firelight he got to his feet, every conscious part of him centred in his fierce erection and the need to bury it in a woman. He knew who she was – Boudicca, the girl-queen whose eyes and curves had lured him from the moment of their meeting until he was near mad with desire. Now, she dropped her robe and stood before him, naked but for her cloak of red hair. The sight of her white breasts with their dark, taut nipples, her slender waist, full hips and the brush of hair between her thighs brought a growl to his throat.

He strode forward and seized her, half expecting her to fight him, but instead she met him with open arms, clasping him tightly as he bore her to the ground and took her without gentleness. She cried aloud as his tumescence broke her maidenhood, and then she stared up into his face with wide dark eyes and her body began to move beneath him, grinding against his. Her voice urged him on. Her nails scored his back, her teeth sank into his shoulder. She answered him with a passion and lust as great as his own, exciting him beyond anything he had ever known.

Twice he took her, and then a third time. At last, sated and exhausted, they sank back into the crushed grass gasping for breath.

'You're leaving?' he asked, a hand on her arm to detain her as she rose.

'No, not yet. Hush, be still.'

On the edge of the clearing an old tree-stump squatted, black in the light from the dying fire, with the moisture glistening across its crown and down its bark – moisture that was blood from an earlier sacrifice, she guessed. Behind this altar she found a silver jug full of wine, and with it an ornate cup. These she took back to Huan and offered him a drink.

He gulped thirstily and lay back smiling, a hand caressing her hip. The drug in the wine was a strong one; within seconds Huan was deeply asleep.

Obeying her instructions, Boudicca lifted his head and rested it over her knee so that it lolled back and exposed his throat. Then she took the knife with its blue quartz hilt and, to honour and obey the Goddess, drew the sharp blade lightly across the base of Huan's throat. Blood pricked out like tiny beads on a necklace, meeting to form a thin trickle that ran down the side of his neck onto her leg. She felt its sticky warmth as she bent to kiss his unresponsive lips. Then she withdrew her knee, laid his head down carefully and stood up.

For a moment she let her eyes dwell on the shadowed glory of his naked body, his manhood as limp as the rest of him now, sleeping in peace. But she must leave: the rite demanded it.

Gathering up her robe and cloak from where she had dropped them, she retraced her steps down to the coracle, stepped into it and pushed off toward the distant gleam of a fire on the islet where Saille and Morica waited.

Huan woke with the sun in his eyes and a vicious headache that squeezed at his temples and made him groan as he flung a hand to guard his aching brain from the bright light above. Then a shadow fell across his face and when he looked up, through squinted eyelids and slitted fingers, he saw Eogan looming over him. The Druid was smiling, showing his teeth in fierce satisfaction.

'You met with the Goddess, Green King.' His bass was sonorous even when he spoke quietly. 'You took your pleasure of Her, and yet She spared you. She has left Her mark on you as a sign. You did well.'

Huan fingered the sore line at his throat, where blood was thinly crusted. It was little enough to pay for the pleasures of the night.

'Where is she?' he asked.

'You'll see her again. But not yet. First there's hunting to be had. Your companions are waiting for you. It's the hawthorn month.'

During the hawthorn month no men were allowed inside Iceni villages except the sick, the very old and the prepubescent. For a moon after Her spring rites, in the time most sacred to Her, the Goddess demanded chastity of all Her people: the women stayed at home, the married ones tending to their chores while the warrior-maidens stood guard. Young males went hunting in the forests; the high chief and the elders rode abroad among the settlements to hold court with other chiefs and oversee the land. Only a few men remained near the fort in case of urgent need; they camped near the enclosures in the woods, where the horses were kept, and guarded the approaches to the settlement.

The Maiden too was kept from going home in that Great Year. Through the hawthorn month she stayed in seclusion in the marshes with old Saille. Their shelter was a bower of branches, and they were brought food sometimes by Morica and more often by the unseen hands of the fenfolk, who came gliding in their coracles at night under the moon and left their offerings on the bank of the stream. As the moon waned to Her darkening, the absence of Boudicca's regular menstrual flow made it fairly certain that she was with child.

'It's a miracle!' Saille breathed, her lined old face shining with devout joy. 'You're truly blessed, lady. The Goddess has answered all our prayers.'

And so the Maiden returned to Oakhillfort and to her people, her Beltane duty done.

Her reunion with Huan, at first shy and uncertain, became a thing of joy for both of them. Where before everyone had kept them apart, now everyone contrived to aid the cause of love when their queen and the young Caledone warrior sought solitude. Neither of them questioned this change; they accepted with joy. They came together frequently, of their own free will now, their passion unaided by drugs, their love for each other deepening with each meeting.

As a pledge, Huan gave to Boudicca his thumb-ring with its stone of rose-quartz. Since it was too large for her own thumb, she wore it on a thong round her neck, along with the flint amulet that declared her to be an initiate in horsemastery.

So the weeks passed in a joyous haze of love and hope for Boudicca, toward the special festival of the Great Year Solstice.

The moon was a thin crescent in the sky, spreading a pale glow over the Great Bay and the expanse of the eastern sea. The susurration of waves came soft on cool night air scented with the smoke of extinguished fires.

On the top of low red cliffs, the women of Icenia trod their ritual spiral, swaying and stamping in the slow rhythms and chanting in low voices as they kept vigil through the brief night of the midsummer solstice. Among them the young queen danced, her hands caught in the clasp of old Saille on one side and her acolyte Morica on the other.

Boudicca smiled to herself as her feet pounded the earth in the slow cadence of the maze dance. Huan's child was inside her. Her body felt ripe and firm beneath a loose red robe that whispered across her skin like a lover's fingers. Though her eyes were closed she could feel the moon's light on her upturned face as she had felt it through the alders on the sacred willow islet in the marshes, where He had come to her – He, the God.

Tonight they would be coupled again: Maiden and Green King, acting out the ancient story of the Gods; queen and warrior, carving out the destiny of their people; woman and man, delighting in the pleasuring of each other.

Boudicca had no doubt that soon Huan would go to her father the high chief and offer for her hand in marriage. The council could not refuse such a worthy claimant. Of all men, Huan of the north was most fitted to be the husband of the queen and therefore chief of chiefs among the Iceni.

The stars had only just brightened when the eastern sky showed grey with the first false dawn and the men returned, walking to the solemn beat of a drum. At their head strode Eogan, wearing the newly-flayed skin of a sacrificial stallion, the head with its wild crested mane set on his own head. Blood dripped down the Druid's face and body, which was naked but for a leather apron.

The sun had grown to manhood and his power would now be waning; therefore, the God had been slain in the form of a stallion – the most sacred animal of the People of the Horse

– and parts of his flesh had been eaten to honour Him. As light increased, it showed that most of the men bore the red stain of the holy rite.

The drum's beat sent a thrill of religious fervour prickling across Boudicca's scalp as her instinct responded and her eyes sought out the figure of Huan, in his role as Green King. He stood as a human symbol of the God. This solstice, his fine body was clothed in ritual nakedness and wreathed with holy oak. With him walked twelve young men of the tribe, the Green King's traditional companions. Among them was Mocuxsoris.

On the edge of the cliff a log of oak had been prepared. Now Huan and Mocuxsoris knelt to kindle the need-fire, twirling an oak branch vigorously to make sparks appear. Eogan in his bloody cloak of skin, made taller than ever by the stallion's head, faced to the east and lifted his arms, praying aloud to the God. In answer, the first bright ray of light peered over the edge of the sea and the Green King's companions added dry moss to the sparks of the need-fire so that a tiny flame appeared. Eogan cried loudly in triumph and the celebrants prostrated themselves as the Druid chanted the ritual words.

Lying prone with her face buried in her hands, Boudicca felt the light growing around her and experienced a familiar shiver of awe. The Gods remained faithful: the wheel of the heavens and the wheel of the seasons would continue to turn.

Throughout the day the celebrations continued with competitions at arms, with races, and feasting and drinking around the great fires which had begun with those first sparks at dawn. The Green King held the champion's place at the feast, waited on by his companions as if he were truly the God, and Boudicca felt herself responding to the rites as she quenched her thirst with wine and barley ale, and sank her teeth into wedges of venison. Tonight, she told herself, she would lie again with Huan under the stars. She was growing impatient for the darkness to fall. The heat of the Goddess was on her.

At last, as the sun sank to the west, the Green King left his place at the feast and, chased by his companions, took the path down the red cliff to splash into the sea and purify himself. Howls of drunken laughter floated back to where the celebrants danced around the sacrificial fires, weaving the spiral symbol of immortality. Boudicca was among them, her head spinning, her senses all heightened by the drugged wine the priestess had given her.

She saw Eogan returning, clad again in the stallion's skin as he walked to the edge of the cliff and the sun sank to a fiery rim. He raised his arms and cried out in a voice that brought silence over the feast and everyone paused to watch the young men come up from the beach stamping in rhythm and singing raucously. They were carrying the Green King over their heads. They had bound him in branches. His head trailed back between their upraised arms, exposing the thin red scar at the base of his throat, where Boudicca's knife had marked him on the sacred isle at Beltane. His long hair hung loose, dripping water.

The sight reminded Boudicca sharply of the day she had found Huan on the beach, half drowned, washed up on the shores of her queendom by decree of the Goddess. The Goddess, the All-Wise, the Enigmatic, the Unpredictable . . . Suddenly, apprehension clutched at her breast.

The drums increased their beat until the air on the clifftop throbbed with the sound. Boudicca felt her heart thudding in response until she could hardly breathe. Her hands crept to her throat as she tried to think through a fog of intoxication. What was happening? Why did the air feel heavy with menace? The ritual was only symbolic. At least . . . it had been symbolic every time she had watched it. But this was the Great Year Solstice. The Great Year . . .

The young men came near the fire and knelt with their captive held above their heads. Huan was cognizant; Boudicca saw that his eyes were open, and calm, regarding from upside down the tall figure of Eogan as the Druid in his bloody cloak of stallion skin approached, lifting high a curved knife.

Huan was smiling.

The drums stopped. In the sudden, shocking silence, the knife flashed down.

A gush of blood obscured Huan's face. His head lolled further from the grinning wound in his throat and a sighlike groan escaped the throats of the watchers. Beneath that sound came the death gurgle of the human sacrifice.

The knife chopped again, severing the head. The Druid held it by its long hair while blood pumped over his legs and feet to splash into a golden jewelled chalice that Saille held.

Boudicca seemed to feel nothing. It was as though the Night Mare had sent her a vision from which, terrible as it was, she knew she would awaken before long, unharmed, to find everything as it had been before. The familiar unreality granted by the ivy drug numbed her and she watched unblinking as Eogan took the chalice from Saille's hands and sprinkled blood to the west and the south, crying, 'Thus dies the God, to be born again; that the seasons may turn, the earth be fecund, the people faithful. Thus He dies, to ensure the continuance until the next Great Year. Caridwen take Him. Arianrhod guard Him. Latona give Him rebirth.'

He drank from the chalice. A great cry rang up as the body of Huan was laid on the altar stone between the fires and the Druid raised his knife again to carve the sacred right haunch, for which the Green King's twelve companions fought like starving animals.

Trapped in her own swimming unreality, Boudicca saw her brother Mocuxsoris stagger drunkenly away from the fire, wiping his mouth with the back of his hand. His moustache, his chin and his hands were smeared with blood and he was grinning – until he met Boudicca's eyes: her expression seemed to sober him. He stopped, staring at her. She turned away.

That night, something in Boudicca died. She felt it dwindle and blink out, leaving a tight cold knot in her gut that remained with her for the rest of her life.

Three

That year heavy rains made the harvest difficult and the farmers took pains to dry and parch the grain before it was stored, though even so some of it rotted in storage pits and granaries. The rains continued, past Samhain and into the winter, weeks of mild, unhealthy weather with thick fogs rolling in from the Great Bay to isolate Oakhillfort in damp grey blankets.

No one ever spoke the name of Huan of the Caledones.

Boudicca went about her life like a shadow, hardly speaking, never singing, and prevented from hunting by her condition: the priestesses refused to let her do anything strenuous, for fear she might harm the child she was carrying – the child of the God. She was still the Maiden and would be protected until her child was born.

'A girlchild,' Morica kept intoning, her eyes glittering. 'You must bear a girlchild for Dia.'

That seemed to be all that concerned the priestesses – that the child should be female.

The mild, inclement weather carried off more than one of the older folk with lung disease and sweats. One of those who died was old Saille, the priestess, who was found at her hut by the river still clutching her figurine of the Triple Goddess. No one had realised how ill she was. Perhaps no one had really cared – especially not Morica, who at once assumed the old woman's role as wisewoman and seer.

Antedios, too, fell ill with a hacking cough that on occasion nearly choked him. His straining opened up his shoulder wound, which began to fester again. He kept saying that he felt the call of the wild geese, enticing his soul away.

The high chief spent most of his time huddled in blankets and furs by the central fire in the queen's house where smoke-blackened hazel wattle supported the thatch. Underneath it hung joints of smoked meat. The high, curving roof was supported by a ring of timber pillars carved elaborately and painted in colours dimmed by time and smoke. Each pair of pillars supported an embroidered curtain which gave privacy to the low chamber behind. Tall bronze shields and ceremonial swords belonging to members of the queen's household hung from roof and timbers, adding their own richness to the scene. Among those swords was one which had belonged to Huan.

'You must take a husband,' Antedios said to Boudicca as she stood weaving blue thread across yellow on her loom. 'I can't die in peace without knowing who's going to come after me. What if the Catuvellauni attack again? Who's going to lead the warriors? The council will have to make a decision. Have you any preference?'

'No, father.'

Her voice was colourless and he shot her a look from his

eye corner. 'Your fancy would be taken into account, you know. It was your mother that picked me out for herself. Though of course, I was pretty much the only candidate.' He hunched his fur blanket more warmly round his aching shoulder and sank further into a huddle by the fire, his face twisting as he tried to contain another fit of coughing. When he spoke again his voice rasped in his chest. He was lost in memories. 'I was a sturdy warrior in those days. My father was chief in the forests and sent me to be fostered here by the high chief and the queen – your grandmother. A champion, I was. No man could wrestle me to the ground. Swiftest with a spear, skilled at the reins, strongest with a sword. I recall a raid when Parisii sneaked over the Great Bay to take women for slaves. We went after them – right into their own territory – and killed them all. There was one – a great brute covered in scars, tall as an oak. I split him in two – crown to crotch. The pieces just fell apart and lay there.' He laughed, and the laughter brought on another racking fit of coughing.

Worried, Boudicca sent a slave to warm some mead to ease his chest but when she bent over him in concern he waved her away. 'Don't fuss me, girl. There's nothing you can do. Except birth that babe you're carrying and turn your mind to the future instead of brooding on the past. There must be some young man who pleases you. Think about it.'

Boudicca straightened, a hand to her aching back. She felt the child stir inside her, kicking strongly – Huan's child. But she mustn't think of it that way. In common with all children conceived during sacred rites, it would be accepted among the tribe as a child of the God. Perhaps that was the only reason Huan had been sent to Icenia – to become the father of this sacred child. Only the Goddess knew.

After the winter solstice, the cold came. Ice gripped the rivers and the water in the well; the ground was hard beneath padded feet and fires crackled, sending sparks up to a sky full of bright cold stars. The birch month passed. The rowan month began.

In the birthing hut – the priestess's hut by the river – Boudicca knelt over a cushion of sealskin rugs, gripping the hands of her kinswoman Tadia, naked but for the short robe that was her only protection against the chill. Her body strained, pain wrenching through her womb as the child struggled to be born. Sweat dripped from her chin to trickle down between her breasts, and nausea choked the back of her throat, bitter from the taste of the potion she had been given to hasten the birth. The child must be born before the moon set, or the portents would not be good.

The drugs caused her mind to wander amid fearful images: fire, blood, and a raven perched on the back of a great white sow. And Huan, welcoming her into his arms, smiling as his throat was slit. She was only vaguely aware of firelit shadows looming around the birthing hut, and of the stamp of feet as the women swayed and chanted.

The air reeked from the stench of black smoke that writhed from mutton-fat lamps. And through the smoke loomed the watchful figure of Morica. Lank hair fell to the shoulders of her wolfskin cloak and in the flickering light her eyes were bright from the ivy intoxicant she had taken. Blue tattoos around those eyes gave her face the appearance of a skull.

Beneath the prayer-chant of the women, the priestess hissed, 'A girlchild, daughter. Give me a girlchild for Dia.'

The phrase sent a shiver through Boudicca. What would follow if the child should be a boy, or if it should die? What if, like Tadia, she should be delivered of twins? No one had been willing to answer when she asked such questions. The child had to be a girl. Anything else was unthinkable.

In her delirium she fancied she saw Eogan keeping vigil outside in the snow, bundled in furs and with his beard icing in the wind. She must not fail in her duty to the Goddess. For five years now, since her womb wept with its first sacred, lifebearing blood, her life had been directed to just one purpose. Now the moment had come, and behind the eyes of Morica she saw the Goddess Herself waiting to witness the birthing.

She must think of that; she must forget Huan. His part had been to supply the seed, and then to give his blood to the earth. His soul was among the blessed; he would be reborn to honour. The meaning of it was part of the Mystery.

'Andastre!' the cry broke from her as the pangs ripped at her body. 'Help me! Hear me!' She bit her lip, tasting the acrid tang of her own blood. She was pure animal, driven by the need to expel the thing that pained her.

This time the contraction grew until with a final vicious thrust of agony the baby's head burst through. Morica gave a low cry and bent to receive the babe, while Tadia murmured encouragement. Panting for breath, Boudicca waited for the next contraction to grip her womb; as it grew in intensity, she screamed the name of the Goddess and expelled the child's slithering body from her. Morica's hands were there to hold it, a swift knife severing the cord, with scarlet thread to bind it. Then the priestess lifted the baby and slapped it sharply. The child gave a high wail.

'A girl?' The question merged with Morica's laugh of triumph.

The priestess nodded, her eyes glittering like those of a she-wolf. 'A girl. Small, but complete. She'll live. Blessed be the Great Mother!' She straightened, lifting the baby over her head. 'Behold the child born of the God!'

A cry from the women echoed up to the setting moon as they tossed pine branches onto the fire, filling the hut with scented smoke and a crisp, crackling sound. Aware of intense relief and pride, Boudicca lay back on her pallet, feeling sweat cool on her body. Tears trickled down her temples into her hair.

Tadia bent over her, bathing away the blood and mucus from her thighs. 'She's a fine girl. What will you call her, cousin?'

'The name is chosen!' Morica snapped. 'She is Rhiannon.'

Too weary to object, Boudicca watched the red darkness of fire-light through closed eyelids. Rhiannon of sweet singing birds, she thought. She hoped it was a good omen.

A shadow came between her and the fire and she looked up. Morica loomed over the pallet, holding the child close in her arms. Over its tiny head she stared down with burning eyes. 'Your duty is done. Well done. Now the Goddess grants you the future. You must make sacrifice in thanksgiving, daughter. You have given us a new Maiden.'

A chill ran through Boudicca. 'A new Maiden? You mean the child?'

'The child.'

'No!' The denial shuddered out of her on a breath of horror.

Morica's smile stretched her lips, showed her teeth, but left her eyes cold. 'Yes, lady. Dia wills it so. The last Maiden failed Her. The last Maiden failed to conceive. So you were chosen, by signs and divination. It was a good choice. The Goddess ordained it. And this time She has granted us this blessing – the Maiden Rhiannon, born of the God. We will raise her, you and I, to serve Dia in her turn.'

One more rite had to be performed before Boudicca resumed her life. She travelled with Morica deep into the marshes, to the sacred pool where the Goddess Herself bathed annually in order to renew Her virginity. Here Boudicca immersed herself in the freezing water and emerged shivering, shuddering, but purified and ready for her role as wife.

Antedios sat propped on a mound of hay covered in furs, his back against one of the carved wooden pillars that upheld the roof of the warriors' hall – the communal meeting hall. Each breath brought agony to his lungs and when he coughed he brought up blood. His shoulder was a constant numb pain, the wound weeping afresh every time it was dressed. It had begun to stink of putrefaction.

But the thought of death no longer frightened him. He was ready for it, eager for the Otherworld where his spirit would find its youth and strength, amid verdant woods where game was plentiful and a warrior could ride the finest horses. Perhaps Veda would be waiting there, fair as the day he had first met her. His thoughts were more of that shadowy country in the land of the Glass Castle than they were in the present. He could not concentrate on the argument flowing among the council.

In a circle around the central fire the elders deliberated, with Morica's sharp voice occasionally stabbing above the rest and Eogan brooding by the door leaning on his gilded ash staff. The oak seer disliked being enclosed by walls; his domain was the oak grove and the forests, among wild things who shared his vagabond existence.

They were discussing whom to choose as their queen's husband and next high chief.

Boudicca herself stayed in the queen's house, aloof from the gathering. She was tending her child, crooning to the babe as it suckled at her breast, its tiny hand fisted against the white curve of her flesh. She felt towards it a fierce, protective love such as she had never known. Partly, that love was an echo of what she had felt for Huan, and partly it was a result of her trust in the Goddess. However obscure it seemed at the moment, there must be meaning to what had happened. Everything had led to the birth of Rhiannon. The child was special: she was the Maiden. The thought of it both thrilled and terrified Boudicca.

As a means of shutting out thought of the future, she immersed herself in motherhood, sharing the domestic preoccupations of her kinswoman Tadia, whose youngest daughter Cameira was only a few moons older than Rhiannon. Tadia's eldest, Ferna, was thirteen now and the mischievous twins, Ylas and Matuac, had six summers behind them. Besides these, Tadia had borne three other children who had not survived. It was the will of the Goddess. But Rhiannon would survive: she was strong; and she was under the special protection of Dia.

Boudicca tried not to think of what was happening in council. Little she cared which man they chose as her husband. She had never loved before she loved Huan; she doubted she would ever love again. She was a toy of fate, first as Maiden, now as queen. Her hopes of having a life of her own had been mere childish folly.

Many men had been mentioned as candidates for her hand, warriors from all branches of the Iceni, and some noble sons of neighbouring tribes, though few of these remained. The incursions of the Catuvellauni had destroyed many chiefs and their families; those that were not dead had fled into exile, to Rome. Togodumnus and Caratacus grew daily stronger and bolder. How long could Icenia hope to remain safe from the marauding Catuvellauni?

The same thoughts preoccupied the council. For the troubled times ahead, the Iceni would need a strong, wise chief. It was no good choosing some hot-blooded youth, or a man who thought with his belly instead of his brain. Slowly the list was shortened, runes were read, a sacrifice made and portents taken from its death struggles. Slowly, the name of one man came clear.

'Prasutagus?' Boudicca pronounced the name as if she had never heard it before.

Tadia nodded eagerly, her glance darting about the queen's

expressionless face. 'Prasutagus. Chief of Eldergroveplace. They say he's a wise, thoughtful man. And in his youth he was a fine warrior.'

'You mean he's old now?' Her mouth curved wryly. She recalled the man – tall, thick-bodied, with lank fair hair and beard turning to grey. He must be twice her age. He had been married once, so it was said, but he had no children. Since his wife died, he had dedicated his life to ruling his clan, a task he achieved through cunning and strategy rather than brute force. He was a quiet man, not given to excess of any kind. But it was rumoured that his anger could be deadly.

On the brisk winds of the ash month, Prasutagus and his guard of warriors arrived at Oakhillfort, fully armed and dressed in their best colourful clothes and wealth of adornment. Men on the banks blew welcoming blasts on great curved war carnyxes as the party rode up the track from the fields, with farmers' children running out to greet them with shouts of glee, dogs barking and slaves pausing in their work to watch. Warriors of the queen's kin, glinting with gold and bronze ornament, rode out to meet them and escort them home.

Prasutagus stood tall in his richly-decorated two-wheeled chariot behind a handsome young reinsman – his foster-son Garanhir, fair and muscular. The chief's striped cloak had its hood thrown back so that spring sunlight lit his fair-grey head and though he was near forty-summers-old, he was still erect; his flesh firm, his shoulders broad. As he was driven down the main track into the village he ignored the staring people who gathered on either side. He kept his head up, his eyes fixed on the royal party who waited by the sacred oak.

The high chief Antedios was there, lying on his pallet, and around him stood his bodyguard of twelve warriors both male and female. All of them were richly dressed in gaudy colours, wearing brooches and armlets and gold and silver chains about their necks. Boudicca stood beside her father, clad in a red-striped gown and cloak with a golden girdle at her waist. Her hair was curled up at her nape and braided down her breast, thick with beads. Gold ornament bedecked her arms, and her clothes and the great electrum torc of Icenian queens lay bright and heavy about her throat. Beside her hovered the watchful Morica, with Eogan at the other flank of the group.

As the visitors drew nearer, Boudicca searched the face of her husband-to-be, seeing a humorous cast in it, as though the ceremony amused him. Then she realised that it was the old scar across a corner of his left eye that gave a deceptive lightness to his expression, leaving his eyebrow and the corner of his eye permanently atilt. In fact, his expression was unreadable, his face as immobile as if carved in stone. In that first meeting of glances she felt as though she had encountered a palisade that walled off his feelings.

A few paces away he stepped down from his chariot and strode forward to give her a formal salute with a fist to his brow touching the Warrior's Light tattooed there, symbolically obscuring himself before the greater glory of his queen.

'Lady.' The deep, soft voice caressed her before he turned to her father, saluting again, kneeling to be more on a level with the high chief whose breathing sounded stertorous. 'Lord . . . You do me much honour. May Vron grant me worthy of your trust.'

At the festival of the spring equinox, the marriage was celebrated at the oak grove along the knoll from Oakhillfort. Newborn lambs were sacrificed on the single huge flint, brought from the forests of the north-east of Icenia, that formed the altar. Fires burned on the hillside in the shape of a horse's hoof to commemorate the time when, in ages past, the White Mare Goddess had stamped Her foot here and marked it as Iceni ground.

Together, Boudicca and her new husband leapt the fires to purify themselves in the smoke. Then with great ceremony the high chief Antedios took his great gold torc, whose ends were shaped as owls' heads, from around his neck and gave it into the hands of Eogan. As drums beat and people chanted, the Druid placed the torc of Iceni high chiefs around the neck of Prasutagus, whose long hands moved up to finger the smooth gold and the enamelled eyes of the owls, as if he still could hardly believe his good fortune. Then he accepted the white rod – the symbol of chieftainship.

Afterwards, while folk grew merry and bawdy with ale and feasting, an exhausted Antedios was carried home to lie in his room at the queen's house. The short journey brought on one of his coughing fits and when it was done blood flecked his grey beard, his skin was tinged blue and the Warrior's Light which once had shone on his brow was wrinkled with his flesh behind a fringe of thinning grey hair. Now that a new high chief reigned, Antedios felt free to give up the struggle for life.

Boudicca knelt beside him, aware of the tall figure of her new husband behind her. 'I must stay with him,' she said.

'Of course. He needs you.' Prasutagus laid a hand on her shoulder and when she turned her head to look up at him questioningly his mouth smiled as if to comfort her. He touched her cheek, smoothing its soft contour with the backs of his fingers. 'I am not an impatient youth, Boudicca. I can wait.'

Everyone waited, for the six nights that Antedios lay dying. It was time enough for a message to reach his son Mocuxsoris, who rode in haste from his border lands. Boudicca clung to her brother's hand as they shared their grief and sat with their father until at the last he smiled and spoke the name of his beloved Veda, as if he saw her waiting for him. Then with a sigh the breath went up from his body.

For three nights the body of the high chief lay on his ceremonial chariot in the death hut. Eogan squatted on his heels, casting runes and praying. The high chief's best weapons lay with him, his great ceremonial sword and his ornate spear crossed on his chest, his belt holding a dagger in an enamelled sheath. People made their way to visit him, taking a path between deep ritual pits to the low palisade and the square hut where mutton-fat lamps sent out an oily smoke. They brought gifts to help him in the Otherworld: a jug of mead, a loaf of bread, small figurines of clay. Boudicca herself gave two bronze horses to pull his chariot, and she laid beside him a set of imported glass counters and a board, so that he could play his favourite game.

He was buried as befitted a high chief, in an earthen chamber dug close to the Way, with braziers of charcoal at his head and feet to warm him. He lay on his chariot in all its finery, with his weapons and death gifts piled about him. When all was done, his people piled his grave with flint pebbles until it formed a bold mound that travellers along the Way might see and remember Antedios of the Iceni.

Soon afterwards, Mocuxsoris left to return to the border fort and Boudicca felt herself truly alone but for the tall, grave husband who was still a stranger. She was queen, but she felt like a lost child as she wept that night in the darkness of her room.

A flicker of light made her sit up clutching her furs across her breasts as Prasutagus ducked in beneath the curtain at the low door-way, bringing with him a small lamp that he placed on a shelf on her wall. His wry left eye gave him the appearance of levity, but his real expression remained inscrutable.

It was time for him to claim his prize. The thought caused a kick of awareness deep in her womb as she remembered Huan and the sweet, secret pleasures of coupling. Perhaps it could be the same with Prasutagus. Perhaps, in time, she could grow to love him.

Brushing the tears from her face, she pushed aside her fur blankets and lay naked beneath her husband's gaze, watching the way his eyes slowly feasted on every pale curve. He began to undress, his movements deliberate, unlike the passionate haste with which Huan had thrown off his clothes at the same time kissing her, embracing her, caressing her: with Huan there had been joy and laughter in loving.

With Prasutagus there was nothing but cold duty. It took him a long time to be ready for her. Then he came to her quickly, spilled his seed into her, thanked her gravely, and went back to his own room.

Lying dry-eyed in the darkness, Boudicca knew that she had been wrong to think he was coming to claim his prize. The prize he most wanted had been claimed on the day of their marriage, when Eogan the Druid had placed round his neck the great owl-headed torc of Iceni high chiefs. It was the power of the chieftainship that Prasutagus most prized, not the woman through whom he had claimed it.

Four

Under the brightness of the rising sun, a harbour in north-west Gaul seethed with activity. Merchant ships lay at the wharves, their masters haggling with buyers, and along the shore fishing boats were putting out with ready nets, skimming among the troop ships of the fleet waiting to sail with the next tide. The broad road leading down from the walled town was busy with traffic, servants carting loads of logs for the local governor's bath-house fires, Imperial officers on horseback, rich merchants riding in litters to examine their cargoes, and Gaulish peasants about their chores. But all gave way before the marching ranks of legionaries who came from the heath where their temporary camp had been erected toward the harbour and the waiting troop carriers.

Many among those marching soldiers of Legio VIII were prey to misgivings about the coming voyage. Despite the bravado of fluttering pennants and the sheen on leather armour, all of them had heard the tales of this Western Ocean, said to be the most treacherous in the world. Many a sailor had returned to Rome with stories of sea-monsters and sudden, inexplicable storms of supernatural violence, which had driven their ships onto the gloomy mist-ridden shores of Britannica, called by its inhabitants Albina's Isle, where lived weird creatures of hideous aspect and ferocious temperament. Britannica, here on the edge of the world, had long been a place of dread.

Such thoughts held no cheer for men now bound for those haunted shores, though their sergeants had reminded them of the divine Julius's victory there near a hundred years ago. And there was some consolation in knowing that four legions had recently landed safely and won more victories beyond this narrow but terrible channel. Now Claudius Caesar himself had arrived, personally to supervise the surrender of Albion's barbarians to the civilising influences of the Empire. If the lame and inarticulate Emperor was willing to undertake the voyage, not one of his soldiers dared show reluctance.

Marching feet trod a steady rhythm across the quayside, under the general noise of voices, creaking timbers and crying gulls. Not far away a grain-ship was unloading. One of the amphorae had been dropped and shattered, spilling its golden contents. A slave was being whipped for clumsiness and a cloud of screaming gulls had come swooping to enjoy the unexpected feast.

A slight boy some seven-summers-old watched the fun with bright blue eyes. At first sight he might have been taken for the son of a wealthy Roman with his close-cropped dark hair and clean tunic, but the white bronze brooch at his breast was of strange and ancient design and around his neck a light torc of twisted gold spoke of his Celtic heritage. Today, if Neptune favoured the voyage, he would see his native land for the first time.

Part of him rejoiced in the fact and it was that part he let show; he took care to conceal the bewilderment and apprehension of a child taken far from the only home he had ever known. For he was Farann, son of Vindorex, son of Addedomarus the exiled high chief of the Trinovantes whose lands lay in the east of Britain. And a prince of the Trinovantes did not allow himself to indulge in fear.

As he watched the sun glint on the wings of the clamouring gulls, he saw a lad about his own age dart from behind a pile of bales to kneel by the spilled grain and scoop it up with a leather cup, eyes darting furtively. Across the glitter of white wings, their glances locked and the ragged urchin froze, though his look was more defiant than fearful. A strange empathy flashed between them and for the first time Farann dimly understood his father's forebodings. This lad was a Celt, too, but his people were a conquered race forced into submission and slavery by the Roman eagles. The lad was thin and obviously hungry, obliged to snatch food where he could, even fight for it with seagulls. Was that the fate Vindorex saw lying dark across the future for his own tribe?

But before either of the boys could do more than stare they were both distracted by a loud, discordant trumpeting from the town. Cries were heard, and people scattered at a run as four elephants were led up behind the ranks of soldiers, tended by tall black Nubians. Farann glimpsed the superstitious horror in the other boy's eyes as the young Gaul straightened and backed away, a yell breaking from him before he turned and ran as if he had seen demons.

His fear reminded Farann of what his father had said when it became known that the Emperor intended to bring elephants on this journey. 'Elephants – of course, elephants. To amaze and bedazzle the stupid barbarians. That's all we are to him – uncouth illiterates to be used for the greater glory of Claudius Caesar.' Vindorex's voice had been full of bitterness, though he had spoken low, to the few loyal warriors left to him. Farann had not understood the mood among the men. For some reason, the nearer they had come to their own land, the deeper had grown their distrust of the Romans.

'Farann!' the voice called across the furore and when Farann spun round he saw the slave Crico, his tutor, gesturing at him. 'Come, Farann! We're going aboard now.'

A fresh south-easterly from Gaul filled the sails of the troop ships as they headed out into the Western Ocean. In the prow of the Emperor's own galley, a small knot of people gathered around a litter where lay an old man. Most of them were straining their eyes for the first sight of the home they had not seen for many years. Now at last, after delays and frustrations, their tribal lands would be restored to them and their exile ended.

It might be too late, though, for the old chief Addedomarus. His breathing sounded hoarse even above the plunging of the waves and the creak of the timbers. Sightless eyes stared at the bright September sky as he asked for the tenth time, 'Do you see her yet?'

Her – as though the land of his birth were a beloved woman. The thought caused a quiver of grief and rage to run through Vindorex, the old chief's son, and he knelt swiftly near his father. 'Any moment. She's there, waiting for us just beyond the horizon.' He glanced up at the gathered attendants, his gaze scanning familiar faces. Some of them refused to meet his eyes, others returned his look with sympathy and sorrow. Addedomarus had waited so long for help, trusting in the old treaty with the first Caesar, but the Romans had delayed and prevaricated for so many years that even now the old man might die before he could set foot on his own soil again. A curse be on the Romans, Vindorex thought; they made easy promises but moved only when it best suited their own purposes.

'There!' someone exclaimed, and a hand pointed. Vindorex leapt to his feet as all eyes turned forward to see the dark bulk of land on the horizon, appearing and vanishing as the sea heaved the ship from crest to trough.

'You see her?' came the croak from the litter as the old man lifted himself, seeing visions against his inner darkness. 'Ah, yes – there she lies. Albina's Isle. And Camulodunon. Soon. Soon.'

Aware of a disconcerting lump in his throat, Vindorex glanced down at his son as the boy strained on tip-toe to see. Vindorex bent and swept the boy up into his arms, pointing to where minute by minute the land showed clearer. 'There it is, Farann. *Home.*'

The wind lifted Farann's dark hair as he peered against the sea's brightness. Though he smiled and made brave show of sharing the excitement, apprehension lay heavy behind his eyes, causing Vindorex fresh concern. Until now, Albina's Isle had been just a name to the boy, a place of which his father and grandfather spoke with longing. All Farann had ever known was Rome, where he had been born and educated in Roman ways; his mother had been a noble Roman, braving the outrage of her family to marry a foreign exile. For love of Vindorex, she had become an outcast among her own people, and then she had died before he could reward her loyalty by bringing her home to where power and wealth were his, where she might hold her head high as the wife of a Trinovante chieftain. He would never forget, or forgive the Roman system for what it had done to him, but he promised himself that he would raise his son, and his baby daughter crying now in the arms of her nurse, to be proud of their true heritage among the forests and marshes of Trinovantia, and though they might be beholden to Rome they would never bow to Caesar or worship at the shrine of Roman gods.

As they drew nearer to landfall, his thoughts grew darker and more bitter, coloured by fear for his father, who seemed to be dying in front of his eyes. Blindness had robbed him of the hope of seeing familiar sights again, and every heave of the ship made Vindorex fear that his father might not even live to feel the firmness of Albion's ground. Still, to judge by the radiant joy on his aged face, the old chief would fly with a happy soul to the back of the north wind. For him, the immediate future was simple enough.

For Vindorex, and the other chiefs of Britain, there would remain the problems of the present. He knew well enough why Claudius had sent his legions to destroy the Catuvellauni – not to revenge the Trinovantes, or the other tribes who had cried for Roman help against the aggressor; no, the legions had marched at last in order that Claudius might write his name in the annals of history, alongside that of Julius Caesar, as conqueror of Britannica.

This time, Vindorex was sure, when the Emperor departed, the legions would remain.

On the night before she was to leave for the great gathering at Camulodunon, Boudicca found herself unable to sleep. A high wind blustered across the land, finding every crack in the wattle walls and moaning as if in pain. Eventually, the young queen pulled on a pair of deerskin trousers and a loose tunic, picked up her sling and pouch of stones, and went out into the sleeping village. A dog barked softly and, recognising her, came sniffing to be patted. Boudicca rubbed his ear, speaking soothingly to him.

The night was warm, with a full moon shining down on round roofs of thatch. The tide sighed as it swept in across the sands of the Great Bay and the mild, mischievous wind darted here and there, swirling and tugging. It made Boudicca feel unsettled and in need of reassurance.

Going to the gates, she persuaded the watchman to open for her. She found herself on the winding path that snaked between the high defensive banks, and then she was out in the open, breathing deeply as she strode down the tree-clad slope of the knoll to the woods where warriors would be guarding the horse enclosures. She avoided the guards, making deeper into the wood near the river, seeking solitude.

A patch of brightness through the trees drew her on to a clearing where the moon swam overhead in a pool of sky. She fell to her knees and lifted her arms in supplication, upturning her face to the white moon as she prayed,

'Andastre, hear me! Guide me! Mother of All Living, Spinner of Fates, do not desert one who has served you well.'

But a drift of cloud sailed across the face of the moon, causing Boudicca to despair. It had been the same since Rhiannon had been born. She felt alone, discarded. Had the Goddess turned Her face away from one who had been Maiden?

A stick cracked behind her and Boudicca whirled to her feet, instinctively fitting a stone to her sling as she strained to see through the shadows. Someone was coming from the direction of the hillfort. The moonlight fell on pale hair draped lankly either side of a thin, bearded face. She recognised Prasutagus.

He paused on the edge of the clearing, spreading his hands in a gesture of apology as his deep voice came soft under the sighing of the wind. 'Forgive me, I had no wish to disturb your devotions but I heard you leave. I too find sleep elusive.'

'You?' The word jerked out of her.

'Even I.' His voice was heavy with irony. 'Do you think I never suffer from doubt?'

'Doubt of what kind?'

'Of many kinds. Why are you troubled, Boudicca?'

She thrust her sling back into her belt. 'The wind unsettles me.'

'You're uneasy,' he amended, moving slowly towards her. 'And not because of the wind.'

Turning her shoulder to him, she folded her arms about herself, saying, 'I would feel better if Mocuxsoris was with us.'

'So should we all,' he agreed. 'For the Iceni to be divided at such a time is . . . unfortunate.'

He was being tactful, but still she felt obliged to defend her brother. 'Mocuxsoris is not alone in his misgivings. There were other dissenters in council. And Eogan said – '

'Eogan is afraid!' he cut in, angered by mention of the Druid. 'He thinks like the Druid he is. *I* must think like a high chief.'

His hands came on her shoulders, his fingers savouring the touch of her heavy silken tresses. He liked to touch her, but only as a man might touch a beautiful wood carving or an artfully worked sheath of bronze, with admiration and pride of possession; she often wondered if her husband had ever felt real desire for any woman.

In a quiet voice that had iron at its core, he said, 'You were there when the council cast its vote. It fell to my argument. The decision is made, Boudicca.'

The moon shone clear again as she peered at him, resenting his tone. But she wished he would not dismiss her misgivings – and those of her brother – so lightly.

Taking her silence for acquiescence, he laid an arm around her shoulders. 'Come, let's go back. We both need sleep.'

On their way back to the knoll they passed one of the guard. Shadow on shadow, the warrior touched fist to brow in salute.

'All's quiet?' Prasutagus asked of him.

'Yes, lord. Only wild things are stirring tonight.'

'Wild things,' the high chief repeated, his voice warm with affectionate amusement. 'Including the queen and myself, Garanhir?'

'Lord – ' Garanhir sounded embarrassed and Prasutagus laughed, laying a hand on the young man's arm.

'Watch well, Garanhir.'

'I shall, lord.' He stepped back, saluting again, and Boudicca knew his eyes were on her in the darkness. She was aware of a quickening in her blood, a tautness behind her breast. The feeling was as unwelcome as it had been since it had begun two summers past, when Garanhir first came to her notice as reinsman and favourite foster-son to her new husband.

Long after she and Prasutagus had returned to their separate rooms she remained wakeful. Her husband had spoken of doubt, but he was never tormented, as she was, with yearnings for things without name, with hopes unfulfilled and certainties turned to quagmire under her feet. She had seen twenty summers, and for eighteen of them she had known where her destiny lay. But since Rhiannon, her daughter, had been born everything had changed. It seemed to Boudicca that the Goddess, having used her, had cast her aside to drift with the wind.

She prayed devoutly for guidance, her whole being tensed to hear the slightest breath of an answer. And at last it came, borne on the blustering wind that buffeted through the thatch and made her nerves vibrate to its message. Be content, the Goddess breathed along that wind. You are young yet. Your time will be again. Only have patience.

Comforted, Boudicca slept.

The following morning they left Oakhillfort and set out along the Way for the borders of Icenia. Boudicca and her husband rode in their ceremonial chariots. These were light and speedy, an oak platform set between two tall spoked wheels rimmed with iron, and with a shaft pole set centrally to support the double yoke. A pair of chariot-trained horses was strapped to each yoke with harness hung with gold and enamelled-bronze ornaments. The vehicles themselves were richly decorated: wheelhubs and rims were edged with bronze engraved and polished until it shone like gold; embroidered cloths with fringes of gold braid draped the woven wicker sides of the chariots; and all the wood was stained red and green from alder dyes to honour dark Bran, the Raven, Lord of the Otherworld.

Boudicca had her young kinswoman, Ferna, as her driver. Given a choice, the queen would have preferred to take the reins herself as she did so often while hunting or on the training ground, but protocol demanded that for this occasion she ride with regal decorum. She stood erect, her legs braced to ride the jolting and a supporting hand lightly on the curved handle that protruded from the basket-weave side guard. Her loose red hair fell cloak-like about her.

Beside her, Prasutagus rode in his own jingling chariot, with Garanhir at the reins. Their escort was the traditional royal guard of twelve warriors, both male and female, mounted on the sturdy horses bred in Icenia, and behind them walked slaves leading a string of packhorses.

They followed the ancient track along the chalk ridge until a traders' route diverged from it, heading south through thick oak forests toward Trinovante territory and Camulodunon. At night, they made camp beneath the canopy of oaks, with the horses tethered nearby and guards set.

On the second night, Boudicca woke suddenly to full awareness. The night seemed to be alive with supernatural forces that warned of danger. Deep in the forest, wolves howled at the first full moon of autumn. A wind was rising, rippling the skirts of the queen's rough hide shelter and sighing through the trees like waves on a shore. The tethered horses shifted and tossed, whinnying nervously until the horsemaster, Vranaun, rolled with a curse from his blanket and went to quieten them. Several of his companions stirred, too: Iceni warriors, far from home, slept lightly.

Something was amiss. Boudicca sensed it in every prickling nerve of her body and wondered how Prasutagus could still be snoring gently beside her. Instinctively, she felt for the sword that lay ready at her side.

The first yell brought her to her knees. One bound took her to her feet outside her shelter, where in the faint moonlight she saw her warriors scrambling from their blankets. Wild shouts split the night. Vranaun's voice was raised in warning. The horses stamped and screamed in fright.

Then came the clash of sword on sword. Figures moved in shadows among the milling horses. Brigands after the livestock!

'Behind them!' Boudicca's clear voice lifted in command. 'Cut off their escape!'

Her warriors obeyed, lithe shadows running and leaping to vanish in the forest. Boudicca herself made straight for the centre of the commotion, where her guards fought off the horse-thieves. She saw her horsemaster stumble and fall. His assailant roared, lifting high his glinting sword for the final blow. But the roar died in his throat as the queen struck with her own weapon, using all her strength to send the razor-sharp iron shearing through animal skins deep into a brawny shoulder. He swayed like an oak awaiting the last axe-stroke, and Vranaun leapt up, driving his dagger under the man's ribs and straight to his heart.

Across the fallen body, queen and horsemaster exchanged a glance of mutual satisfaction and as she studied the glisten of moonlight on her bloodied sword blade Boudicca realised that she had taken command by instinct. And her warriors had obeyed. More than that, she had killed an enemy in battle – she had won the right to assume the Warrior's Light, the tattoo of the all-seeing eye of Dia. Now she was truly one among her warriors.

Elation filled her, and as she looked about she saw that the brief battle was over. The sounds of struggle had diminished.

Ponies were being herded back by warriors who called to one another in laughing triumph: the attackers were either dead or fleeing into the forest.

'Well done! Well done!' Prasutagus had appeared, sword in hand, in time to see the ending of it. Behind him, a clutch of slaves stared wide-eyed. 'Who were they, did anyone discover?'

'Tribeless brigands from the looks of them,' Coeling's voice came from the shadows. 'They probably took us for a party of merchants. What a surprise they got!'

The others joined in the laughter, some of them dragging off the dead bodies to leave them for predators to devour, others making for a nearby stream to wash the wounds they had received. Eventually the camp settled down again to sleep.

As the dawn sent misty light among the trees, the Iceni shook the sleep from their limbs. The warriors, both men and women, washed in the cold waters of a stream while slaves prepared a breakfast of cold meat, bread and ale. Chatting companionably, the high chief's escort stroked oil into their firmly-muscled bodies until their skin gleamed.

Today they would arrive at Camulodunon.

Boudicca herself drew apart to a sheltered pool with two slaves to attend her bathing. She dressed in a skirt of soft doeskin and an embroidered tunic of red silk fastened with a girdle of plaited leather worked with gold. A striped cloak of green and yellow was fastened by a wide brooch that spanned her breast, and around her neck she placed the royal torc of Icenia, made of many wires of electrum all twisted together, the ends fashioned into the likeness of hares' heads. It was a heavy reminder of her high birth. Over everything, slung on a weapon strap behind her left shoulder, she donned her sword with its hilt and sheath of decorated bronzework.

Returning to the camp, she looked on her warriors with pride. These were the flower of the People of the Horse, the strongest and boldest, most of them having less than thirty summers behind them. Her glance sought out Garanhir, taller than the rest, his body oiled and naked to the waist, scarred here and there from wounds got while hunting or raiding cattle. His fair hair was thickened and lightened by the traditional applications of lime-wash, and like the other men he wore it combed back in a crest from the Warrior's Light that adorned his noble brow.

He reminded her strongly of Huan.

Across the clearing their eyes met and she felt again the sexual awareness that flowed between them.

Turning away, she strode to where her kinswoman, Ferna, the oldest of Coeling and Tadia's offspring, was readying the chariot with help from the sturdy Cormax. Ferna was fifteen now, lithe and curvaceous, her long fair hair flowing free over arms and shoulders bared by a leather jerkin, and the way she smiled and moved told Boudicca that she was employing all her charms to enchant the young warrior. Cormax was so busy ogling the girl that he had got the heavy, gold-trimmed harness twisted.

'Is that task too much for you alone, Ferna?' Boudicca asked tartly. 'Perhaps I should choose another reinswoman.'

'I offered to help, lady,' Cormax said, swiftly straightening the harness so that the brightly enamelled head strap, glinting with red and blue, fitted more comfortably.

'Then you're a besotted fool,' Boudicca observed and saw him flush as she pushed past to stroke her ponies and offer them barley cake flavoured with herbs and wild fruit. The texture of their rough manes and muscled necks calmed her and made her wonder why she had spoken so sharply. Was she jealous of the obvious feeling between Ferna and Cormax, when she herself was denied such pleasures?

As the sun rose, the party of riders with their accompanying slaves and string of laden packhorses left the forests for more open land where heather faded and bracken blazed red beneath copses of aspen, scattered hawthorn and prickly furze. Ahead, and to either side, outriders rode alert for signs of danger. Boudicca stood in her chariot easily, legs braced and body relaxed as her narrowed green eyes scanned the horizon ahead, where gentle hills swelled against a blue sky.

A sigh escaped her, drawing Prasutagus's attention to her face. She found him watching her thoughtfully as he rode beside her, cloaked in fabric woven at the edge with gold thread. He too had put on his finest ornaments, engraved gold decorated with enamel, and around his neck he wore the great owl-headed torc which had been presented to him at the marriage ceremony.

Even as she wondered what lay behind his frown, her glance slid beyond him to where Garanhir was riding, a fine sight for a woman's eyes to light on. All at once she found herself questioning the laws that bound her to a man twice her age – a man who came to her in the night only on the infrequent occasions when need drove him. In the two years of their marriage, none of his seed had quickened in her womb.

She felt for the brooch that pinned her cloak, her fingers tracing the engravings of willow leaves, where stylised owls and hares hid. These were all symbols of the Goddess who had many faces, many names. To Boudicca She had revealed Herself most plainly as Andastre, Queen of Love and Combat; Her most ardent, passionate, fiery self. These aspects of Dia were mirrored in Boudicca's own nature. How long could she endure a dry, loveless marriage?

A high yell interrupted her broodings and speared her attention to the hill ahead. Down its ruddy brackened slopes a war chariot raced full tilt. The reinsman strained to control his galloping horses while his passenger whirled a sword over his head, left-handed, his cloak flaring out behind him. The light vehicle rocked dangerously, threatening to toss out its two occupants.

The Iceni stopped, outriders closing in to meet what appeared to be an attack. For a moment the air was tense with alarm as warriors positioned themselves to watch the lightly-wooded hills that lay around them.

Then: 'It's Mocuxsoris!' a shout went up. 'Mocuxsoris has come!'

Boudicca joined her own voice to the whoops that rang to the sky. Of course it was Mocuxsoris. His bold grin lifted her spirits with elation as the chariot careered to the bottom of the slope and slewed to a halt in a curve that nearly overturned it. Giving his reinsman an approving thump on the shoulder, Mocuxsoris bounded down from the vehicle and the other warriors crowded round, all talking at once, all glad to see the red-headed prince who had grown up with most of them.

He pushed past them, his smile broad as he strode to where Boudicca had stepped down from her chariot. He dropped briefly to one knee in homage before leaping up to embrace her, kissing her heartily through his red moustache.

'Sister! So. Here I am.'

Before she could speak through the joy that tightened her throat, Mocuxsoris had turned and was again on his knee, his red head bent before Prasutagus, who remained motionless, aloof and regal except for an instant when he glanced at Boudicca and she knew that behind his stern expression he shared her relief. His wry eye seemed almost to smile at her.

Voices ceased and a silence spread as all waited to hear what the rebel chief would have to say in his own defence. But it was Prasutagus who spoke first, saying, 'Mocuxsoris. Rise and be welcome.'

Mocuxsoris straightened, exchanging a frank look with the high chief. 'I am of the Iceni,' he said. 'I ride with the Iceni. If the council has decided for peace then I'll accept their judgement – with one reservation: so long as the Romans keep faith with us, I'm your man. But at the first sign of treachery I'll fight – and so will my warriors, to the last drop of our blood, if necessary.'

'So shall we all,' Coeling's gruff voice agreed, and shouts from other voices supported him. A mood of optimism now pervaded hearts lightened by the arrival of the lively prince.

Prasutagus lifted a hand for silence and drew a long breath. 'If there's treachery, my own sword will be the first to cry out for blood. But this is not the time to speak of failure. We go trusting in our allies. We go to treat for peace. Now that you're with us, Mocuxsoris, our hopes are twice as high. Where's your escort?'

'Waiting by the river in the next valley,' Mocuxsoris replied with a grin, 'along with Lanaccion and his contingent, come out of their gloomy forests like bears blinking in the sunlight. We're all with you, lord, all three branches of the Iceni together.'

'Aye!' the shout went up. *'Iceni! Iceni!'*

Five

Telling Ferna to double up with one of the riders, Mocuxsoris commandeered the reins of the queen's chariot and offered a hand as Boudicca stepped up beside him. She noted that her reinswoman swiftly accepted an invitation to ride behind Cormax. Mocuxsoris laughed and said, 'That's right, Ferna, warm his back for him. There's not much harm he can do with you behind him. It's face to face, belly to belly, that causes the trouble.'

Others joined in the teasing of the young pair, who replied with scorn. The joking went on, insults and threats being swapped in high good humour.

Eventually, Mocuxsoris glanced round at Boudicca. 'Do you wonder what made me change my mind?' he asked, low-voiced.

'I thought, for once, good sense had persuaded you.'

The gibe made him pull at his long red moustache to hide his smile, and his eyes were rueful; then all at once he was sombre again. In an undertone meant only for her hearing, he said, 'I came for you – for you, Boudicca my sister, Boudicca, queen and Maiden. I would not be the cause of a rift between us.'

She laid a hand at his waist in gratitude and he gave her a quick smile that made her heart swell with sisterly love. Childhood memories came swarming, warm with mutual affection, sharp with sibling rivalry.

'I'm glad you're here,' she told him.

'I, too,' he replied. 'How is it with you, sister? Are you well?'

'Perfectly.'

'And the child?'

'Growing, thriving, she chatters already.'

'And not yet two-years-old?' he laughed. 'A prodigy, by the wren!'

The invocation laid a shadow over her eyes. 'By the wren, indeed. She was got by the God, or had you forgotten?'

'No.' His expression said he had spoken thoughtlessly and was sorry to have raised dark memories between them. The ghost of Huan of the Caledones still lingered.

But Boudicca thrust the past aside and spoke of their journey and what might occur at Camulodunon.

'At least we'll show a united face at this gathering,' Mocuxsoris remarked. 'Unlike the Brigantes.'

'Oh?' curious, Boudicca leaned to look at him, a hand holding a blowing strand of hair. 'Are the Brigantes divided?'

'They say that queen Cartimandua is on her way to meet with the Emperor, anxious to make peace. But her husband and half of her warriors have remained in the north, standing defiant against Rome.' He grinned at her, the Warrior's Light bright blue against his stiff mane of red hair. 'A happy marriage, evidently.'

'Her husband's little more than a beardless youth, so I heard,' Boudicca replied, trying not to remember that it was Huan who had told her so – Huan who had been a captive slave of the Brigantes. 'She'll hardly be content to give way to the opinions of an untried boy. Eogan says she's a strong-minded woman.'

'No more strong-minded than you are, sister,' he observed with a twinkle, remembering squabbles of their youth. 'Wait a few summers and we'll see how you wind Prasutagus round your finger. He can only grow withered and old, while you're still an unfurling bud.'

The same thought had occurred to her, but for the moment she was content to wait, learning her own strengths. 'Years give him wisdom,' she argued.

'You mean he's past the age when a man's blood stirs to the call of the carnyx,' Mocuxsoris said. 'He prefers to sit and count his flocks and herds, like all old men.'

'Caution's no bad thing in a high chief,' Boudicca answered. 'Rashness only leads to trouble.'

'Rashness like mine?' His teeth showed, strong but crooked, through his shaggy moustache. 'Well, I'm come to heel, suitably cowed.'

This made her laugh. 'You've never been cowed in your

life! Nor repentant. You only give the appearance of it when it suits you.'

'True,' he agreed with merry unconcern. 'And it suits me now. If the Romans offer riches I'd be a fool to argue. Besides . . .' his smile died, leaving him intense again, 'I'm grateful to the Emperor and his legions for ridding me of Togodumnus and Caratacus. They were proving a nuisance harrying our borders.'

'Yes, I know.'

'Do you also know,' he said in a low voice, peering into the sun as they rounded the hill and saw the other warriors waiting beside a river banked with willows, 'that my instincts bid me join my old enemy Caratacus in outlawry, to fight against these Romans? The Druids want war. My heart agrees with them, Boudicca.'

Troubled, she watched his profile, knowing that her own heart was inclined to ride fetterfast with his. 'Prasutagus says the Druids should hold to religious affairs and not interfere in politics.'

'And Eogan?'

In her mind came a picture of the oak seer, wild of beard and hair, wilder still of eye as he raised his ash staff under the sacred oak, at his feet the bloody entrails of a sacrificial stag. His voice had sent a chill through the whole gathering as he prophesied.

'Blood,' she repeated his words in an undertone. 'Blood, fire, death and destruction – but that was before the Romans landed. His prophecy has already come true. Death and destruction did come – to the Catuvellauni.'

'Did he take omens for this meeting today?'

Slowly, she shook her head. 'We haven't seen Eogan since the council met. He's gone back to his forests to sulk – so Prasutagus says. But Morica made sacrifice and read the portents. She foresaw prosperity for us all, and great power for Prasutagus. In her trance she called him "king." '

'Then all should be well,' Mocuxsoris said, though his eyes held a different message.

Ahead of them now loomed the great complex of earthen banks, dykes and palisades with which the Catuvellauni had fortified their main stronghold. The defences stretched further than any arrow might fly, enclosing many scattered farms among a network of fields hardly relieved by any areas of woodland – Camulodunon had needed all its farmland to feed its mighty population. The banks and dykes also served as an extra defence for the town's guardian hillfort, set on a promontory above the river.

The Iceni were met by emissaries – an escort of legionaries under the command of a centurion of Rome, narrow-faced beneath the tall plumed helmet that gave him the illusion of height. Lacking knowledge of the island language, he indicated by signs that the newcomers were to follow him up to their allotted quarters.

On the slopes either side of the track, a scatter of thatched houses and outbuildings proliferated. Merchants had settled here, some from foreign lands, and craftsmen of all kinds had their quarters, their forges, their kilns and warehouses, their stacks of weathering timber. Children and dogs scampered about. The place was alive with activity, with smoke, the scent of hot metals and cooking pots. It was the greatest settlement in Albion.

Boudicca found herself impressed by the bustle. This, then, was once the stronghold of the hated Catuvellauni. It made Oakhillfort look like a village for fenfolk.

The Romans, too, were present in force. Beyond the double earth banks that surrounded the riverside hillfort, the bluff had bloomed with a city of red tents and waving pennants, among which armoured soldiers moved and horses could be seen. At the centre of the camp, a square palisade rose twice the height of a man, with wooden guard towers at each corner. Boudicca strained her eyes against the sun to see what was happening in the Roman camp, but her attention was diverted as her chariot wound its way around the entry track that twined between grassed banks and passed under a gate lintel bearing a plaque of greened bronze made in the likeness of the war god Camulos.

The Catuvellauni nobility had all fled, or been slain, or dispossessed in the aftermath of the Roman triumph. Now their houses were occupied by Trinovantes restored to their old lands, and by emissaries of visiting tribes. Warriors mingled among the roundhouses and the stalls of the market that had blossomed, impeding the progress of Boudicca's chariot. She barely noticed; she was enthralled by the spectacle. Enterprising merchants, beggars, conjurors and diviners had come to the great gathering in the hopes of making money. Among the throng she glimpsed the flicker of flame as a man swallowed fire.

As the sun sank toward evening on that first day, slaves bustled about the round-house which had been allotted to the Iceni. They had set a cooking pot on a chain suspended above the fire, where meat was stewing as the slaves set out their queen's belongings – the fur blankets and sealskin cushions, and the hangings to make private the section of the house where she would sleep.

Boudicca herself stood with Prasutagus at the doorway of the house, with Mocuxsoris and some of the warriors nearby. They were amused by the antics of a bright-eyed lad with a tray slung round his neck. On this portable platform he conjured with three cockle shells and a tiny white pebble, hiding the pebble beneath one shell, then shifting all around and taking bets on the whereabouts of the pebble. The lad's hands were swift and eye-deceiving: he won every time, to the mystification of his watchers and the annoyance of Duihno, who kept making fresh bets as if determined to outguess the lad before the game ended.

A movement drew Boudicca's attention to a path between some houses nearby, where a man was striding as if making direct for where she stood. By the gold torc around his neck, she judged him to be of noble blood, though the Warrior's Light on his brow was of strange design. Curious, she noted that the man had with him a boy of perhaps seven summers, their relationship proclaimed by the dark leanness in both of them, though where the father was tall and muscular the son was slight. They both had touches about their dress – the father's breeks, thonged with leather, and the way the boy's dark hair was cropped – which spoke of foreign influence.

Pausing before Prasutagus, the man saluted and said, 'Lord, welcome to Camulodunon. I am Vindorex, of the Trinovantes.'

'The son of Addedomarus?' Prasutagus asked.

'The same.'

This news further roused Boudicca's interest: Addedomarus, high chief of the Trinovantes, had fled into exile many years before, when this man must have been only a boy. They had lived under the protection of Rome since that time, constantly agitating for help in regaining their lands.

'I knew your father,' Prasutagus was saying. 'He and my father were sworn by blood. Is he here? I must speak with him.'

But a shadow crossed Vindorex's eyes and a muscle jumped in his jaw. 'My father is dead,' he said without expression in his voice. 'He fell sick as we journeyed with the Emperor from Rome and his breath mingled with the wind as our exile ended. But perhaps it was merciful. He did not see how our people have been treated like slaves under the Catuvellauni, nor learn the dishonourable end that came to some of his family. For that I can only be grateful to the Gods.'

Prasutagus shook his head in sympathy, thumb and forefinger smoothing down his long moustache. 'Indeed. Indeed. The Catuvellauni were ruthless. But they've been punished for it. I'm sorry to hear that your father's gone. Who rules now for the Trinovantes?'

'I'm my father's only surviving son,' Vindorex said, and a wry smile stretched his mouth. 'But before any decision can be made we must find enough elders to form a council. Even so, I'm here to extend a welcome to our neighbours, the Iceni.' He turned to Boudicca, his lashes flickering briefly as he swept her with his eyes from head to foot before meeting her gaze directly. 'Lady,' he murmured. 'Your presence honours us.'

His words and his tone of voice were deferential, but his eyes were those of a man who sees a woman he admires. Boudicca's instincts responded to that bold gaze and she took fresh note of strong arms and shoulders left bare by a leather jerkin, of his sturdy height, and the lean lines of a face from which blue eyes looked out with disarming candour. A pity, the thought crossed her mind, that he had been in exile when a husband had been needed for Icenia. Had Vindorex been available, he might well have gained the elders' favour. Though, considering the boy who stood beside him watching the scene with intelligent interest, perhaps he had a wife already. A Roman wife?

He was apologising for the little hospitality he had been able to offer, saying, 'The legions have commandeered most of the stores – even what lay in the warehouses by the wharf.

But let it not be said that the Trinovantes make poor hosts. Tomorrow, your warriors will be welcome to join us in the hunt. We'll make a feast to celebrate our homecoming.'

'A hunt?' Prasutagus said in surprise. 'Won't that mean a delay?'

Vindorex appeared not to understand. 'A delay, lord?'

'We expected to meet with the Emperor tomorrow.'

The Trinovante's smile was part grimace. 'The Emperor moves at his own pace. We await his pleasure. No doubt someone will warn us when he's ready to appear. It may not be for some days.'

'How long do they expect us to wait?' Boudicca demanded.

'Not all the tribes are here yet,' Vindorex said. 'We expect eleven of the chiefs, if all arrive who agreed to make terms. But the Emperor won't meet with anyone until he's finished consulting with his advisers and his officers, however long we stand waiting. Rome takes no account of inconvenience to barbarians.'

The dry cynicism in his voice made Prasutagus frown and say, 'Why are you bitter, son of Addedomarus? You and your family enjoyed the protection of Rome. Now you're home from exile. The Romans have restored to you the lands of your ancestors. Indeed, we all have cause to be thankful. The legions have destroyed the Catuvellauni.'

'Yes, lord,' Vindorex replied, a corner of his mouth twisting, 'that much I grant – they conquered the Catuvellauni. But they're still invaders. This time they won't be content to make treaties and depart. This time Claudius is looking for personal glory. He's here to make our island a part of his Empire. He will claim to be the first Caesar to extend his sway beyond the ocean.'

Mocuxsoris had been listening. Now he could contain himself no longer. He stepped forward, saying, 'Isn't that what I've always said?'

'Vindorex is stating an opinion, not a fact,' Prasutagus argued, obviously disturbed to find the Trinovante in accord with the outspoken Mocuxsoris. 'The Romans have come to us in peace, for mutual benefit. We'll meet them as equals. They may leave a peacekeeping force here, but it won't interfere with us. We'll retain our ancient rights. The emissaries promised it.'

Bending his head in diplomatic acquiescence, Vindorex agreed, 'That is our hope, lord. But while I lived in Rome I had the chance to observe their strategy. In return for aid they'll expect tribute – cattle and wheat to feed their soldiers, slaves for their work-parties and young warriors for their armies. If we're slow to obey, they'll be swift to anger. And as for those tribes who refuse to treat . . .' He hesitated, glancing around before leaning closer, saying in a lowered voice, 'There are now five legions in Albion.' He repeated the words as if to drive his point home: 'Five legions. Count them, lord – fifty thousand men, like trees in a forest, fully armed, fully trained, looking for glory and spoils.'

'What spoils?' Prasutagus demanded. 'The war's over. The Catuvellauni are defeated.'

'General Plautius won't be satisfied to leave enemies unchastised. It's his plan to move first against the west and destroy Caratacus, then to march on the Druid stronghold. And after that . . .'

Again Mocuxsoris broke in, this time laying an urgent hand on Vindorex's arm to gain his full attention. 'Did you say they plan to attack Mona?'

'They fear the Druids' political influence,' Vindorex replied. 'In Gaul, the legions have trampled through every sacred grove and killed every holy man they could find. Their commanders won't be content until the last oak seer on the Isle of Mona is destroyed.'

This, then, was why Eogan remained so virulent in his attacks on the Romans, Boudicca thought. If Vindorex was right, the Britons stood to lose the foundations of their way of life: the Druids had a voice in every council, they understood the correct form of sacred rites, and through the bards they kept the history of the people alive; they were the source of all knowledge and wisdom. Without the Druids, what would be left?

She saw that those of her warriors who had heard were thinking the same. Their faces were troubled as they looked at each other and muttered, and she caught the eye of Garanhir, who was watching her narrowly. Reading that look, she felt her cheeks burn as if she had stood too long in the sun. His expression was half reproachful, half sorrowful; he had noted her response to Vindorex and resented it. But he had no right to jealousy. Nothing lay between them. Nothing at all.

Beyond Garanhir, the beggar lad was still playing his shell game. Young Duihno bent by him staring down at the grubby, charlatan hands that had robbed him of every last coin in his purse. He must have decided on one last chance to regain his money. Boudicca saw the tautness in him as he glared down at the three moving shells on the lad's tray, and even as she watched Duihno lost again.

A snarl escaped him. Next second he had a dagger in his hand. His arm jerked faster than sight. The lad cried out and staggered back, spilling the shells from his tray, with blood seeping through the fingers of the hand he clapped to his slit cheek.

'He cheated!' Diuhno raged. 'It was trickery!'

'And you're a fly-brain, just asking to get tangled in the web,' brawny Nuadat chaffed him, but he flipped a silver coin through the air to the conjuror lad, who caught it deftly, scooped up his shells and scurried away. He would bear a scar for the rest of his life, but no doubt it would give him some stature.

At least the incident had broken the tension. Most of the warriors were amused by Duihno's gullibility. They crowded round him, poking fun, and as Boudicca turned away from the sight she found Vindorex's young companion staring up at her with bright blue eyes that returned her look with unchildlike gravity.

'Is this your son?' she asked.

Vindorex glanced at the boy, drawing him closer as he said with pride. 'Yes, lady. His name is Farann. He was born in Rome during our exile – as was his sister Cunovinda.'

'And his mother?' she enquired.

'Dead,' Vindorex said quietly, his hand tightening on the boy's shoulder as if to comfort him in their mutual grief.

'Was she, too, in exile?'

The blue eyes met hers as he said evenly. 'My wife the lady Julia was of Roman blood.' Evidently he did not intend to make excuses for that. 'Farann, this lady is Boudicca, Queen of the Iceni. Salute her.'

A small fist snapped to the boy's unmarked brow though his eyes never flinched from hers. He had the same direct gaze as his father, seeming to see her every thought, but where in the man this conveyed a sexual challenge, in the boy it was unnerving. A shiver raised the hairs along her spine – a shiver of foreboding. And as she tore her glance away she caught sight of a skein of birds winging from the woods beyond the river, flying a course from east to west in the shape of a ragged 'I', the death letter. Noting it, Boudicca wished that Morica had been there to interpret the portent. What did it mean? Danger from a seven-year-old lad? Or did the omen refer to this whole episode of the treaty of Camulodunon?

A night passed.

On the plain below the hillfort, Roman slaves and engineers came and went, working to build a dais on which the Emperor and his retinue would stand. Occasional groups of off-duty legionaries wandered in to examine the goods in the market and to stare at the giant woad-painted warriors in their gleaming armlets and brooches, their gaudy clothes and animal hides, their oiled skins and their manes of hair lightened by lime wash and swept back from tattooed brows. Some bartering went on, and much mutual curiosity, but in the main the mood remained warily friendly.

Among the gathered Britons, and surrounded by her own finest Iceni warriors, Boudicca held her head high, proud of her rank as hereditary queen. The only other woman who could claim such title was Cartimandua of the Brigantes, but when at last this ageing matriarch arrived from her territories in the north she stood defiant among her escort, scowling out at her neighbours. Presumably she was aware of the gossip that told of her quarrels with her young husband.

The hunt organised by Vindorex was successful, the ensuing feast a furore of eating, drinking and boasting that went on far into the night. Vindorex held the chief's place at the head of the feast, which took place in the open air, around fires where great spits held the roasts. Either side of him he invited Boudicca and Cartimandua, but evidently he found the Brigantian queen a dour companion for he gave most of his attention to Boudicca, answering her questions about Rome and about himself with frankness and a keen wit.

He had served with an auxiliary legion in the east before

being posted back to Rome, where his father had lived in exile. There, Vindorex had won his Roman wife against the prejudice of her family. Eventually, he had been drafted into the elite Praetorian Guard, the Emperor's own bodyguard, on a whim of the mad Emperor Gaius, also known as Caligula. With Gaius intent on making a glorious name for himself, Vindorex had come with the Praetorian Guard and the legions to the very shores of Gaul, within sight of his homeland, six years ago. The Emperor had planned an invasion of Albion. But such were the tales of the fierceness of the western ocean, and the strangeness of the island that lay hazed in mist across the channel, that the terrified legions had revolted and refused to embark. Caligula had screamed and stomped, to no avail, and had eventually saved face by ordering his troops to fill chests with sea-shells and beach pebbles, which he had proudly carted home to Rome, where he had claimed a great victory over Neptune.

The stories Vindorex told made Boudicca laugh. She had never met a man so well-travelled, so entertaining. But she was careful to keep Prasutagus included in the conversation rather than give him cause for complaint of her behaviour, and she feigned unawareness of the hooded glances Garanhir directed at her across the fires. She enjoyed the feast, enjoyed the reminders that she was still a young, beautiful woman. She felt like a tree in spring, starting to live again after the long winter of grief she had endured since the death of Huan.

But she had not forgotten her first and strongest love. She would never forget him. He had gone, but she wore his ring constantly at her breast, as a comfort and a reminder.

Many heads were groggy with sleep and ale-haze when at last, on the following morning, word came that the Emperor was ready to give audience to his Britonic allies.

Swiftly, parade gear was donned, faces painted with fresh woad, helmets burnished, horses harnessed, chariots readied. In an unruly stream, each group jostling for pride of place, representatives of eleven tribes of Albion left the hillfort to gather in front of the dais that had been built amid the fields of Camulodunon. On it stood a gilded throne, guarded by four members of the elite Praetorian guard who remained like men of marble as the chiefs and their warriors gathered with eager anticipation and curiosity.

The Emperor Tiberius Claudius, savouring a conquest that had been bungled, or balked at, by his predecessors for nearly a century, made the barbarians wait. The sun had climbed to the zenith before he announced his coming with the blare of trumpets and a phalanx of outriders winding their way from the encampment on the bluff. As the heralds drew nearer, their trumpets demanding attention, the crowd of Britons parted to make way and gape in awe at the trappings of Claudius's power: the uniforms, the fine horses, the shining parade armour.

Even the boldest Briton started at the sight of four huge grey beasts with flapping ears and legs like treetrunks, draped in gold and silks, led by tall black slaves wearing loincloths and leather straps worked with gold. The beasts plodded behind the litter which bore the elderly Emperor almost hidden from sight behind curtains of richest weave. And escorting their chief came line after line of dark-faced legionaries, all fully armed, all perfectly drilled, marching in the proud shadow of their gilded eagles.

'This is all show,' Mocuxsoris muttered to Boudicca, leaning from his chariot towards her while reinsmen and riders struggled to control horses that had got the strange scent of elephant in their nostrils. 'Monsters and a display of strength to frighten us. That's just what Vindorex predicted they'd do. I'm not impressed. Would their pretty lines hold still under a chariot charge?'

She made no answer, but she found herself looking again at the great grey beasts, and the legionaries in their armour and polished helmets, marching in disciplined might to beat of drum and call of curled trumpet, with banners and golden eagles swaying in the van. Small in stature they might be, but they trod over Albion's soil looking neither to right nor left, confident in themselves and the superiority of their civilisation.

When the treaty was made that warm September day, the limping, stuttering Emperor granted the Iceni total autonomy in their own lands, under the protection of Rome's banners. There would be no military occupation of Icenia, no billeting of troops or building of legionary forts. The Iceni were trusted, honoured allies. They would be awarded grants of money and goods to help them prosper.

For Prasutagus there was special honour – citizenship of Rome, plus elevation to the status of client king. King – just as Morica had predicted.

In return, he promised to pay the necessary taxes and to levy his quota of warriors to join the auxiliary legions – a small enough price for all the benefits he was gaining, so he argued.

Boudicca no longer knew what to think. As they headed back to their own lands by the Great Bay, she listened to the discussions around her. Most of the warriors had been impressed by what they had seen at Camulodunon, and by the promises of aid that would bring wealth to all of them. Even Mocuxsoris no longer voiced his doubts.

Boudicca was sure of only one thing – nothing would ever be the same for the People of the Horse.

Six

With the turning wheel of the seasons winter came and summer followed, with festivals in proper succession. Again snows fell, and spring brightened to summer, to harvest and then to autumn and the dark season of Samhain.

Solstice of the third summer following the meeting at Camulodunon found adults of the various clans of the Iceni gathered at their clifftop *nemeton*. Here they came every five years, and again at every Great Year when the celebration was most sacred of all. The timing was dictated by the Druids from their reading of the skies.

Fiery Audagas of nearby Seafort was present among the chiefs, with Lanaccion from the forests of the south, and fat Dagobit who had replaced Prasutagus at Eldergroveplace. Mocuxsoris had arrived with a contingent of his people late the previous night. He had brought his young wife Huctia with him; she was thickening at the waist again, with a third child – she and Mocuxsoris shared a happy fecundity.

The priestess Morica led the prayers and chanting which marked the women's vigil. She accompanied Ferna, who was that year's Willow Maid, and in the stamping line of dancers Boudicca swayed with closed eyes, the new moon shining on her upturned face and the Warrior's Light now blazoned on her brow. The rhythm of drum and pipes pulsed in her blood with unusual fervour. Perhaps the time was coming – the time long promised when her destiny would become clear.

Or was she sensitive to atmosphere because she remembered so vividly the last time she had been here, when Huan had died in place of the God?

Five years had passed since that time. Five years, and the treaty of Camulodunon. Foreign traders now came freely to the markets at Oakhillfort, bringing wine, jewellery, fancy trinkets, fine glazed red and black tableware and oil for the bronze lamps which now lit the king's house, smelling so much sweeter than the old mutton-fat lights. In exchange, the Iceni sold slaves, furs and skins, thick woollen cloth that was proof against weather, and tough, lithe hunting dogs bred to the chase. Prasutagus, his family and his nobles were learning that wealth came as a result of obedience to Rome.

But there was a price to be paid. Icenia was free of military occupation, it was true, but if no cohorts marched over Iceni soil, still the Roman presence was felt in visits from servants of the civil governor, the procurator. Assessors came prying into the affairs of the tribe, counting cattle, horses, sheep and other effects in order to calculate the taxes to be paid into the Emperor's coffers.

However peaceful the surface, no Briton could forget that Roman eagles flew over all of southern Albion now. And eagles, fine as they might appear at a distance, remained predators.

When the first grey of dawn misted the eastern sky, the steady beat of a drum marked the approach of the men, their hands and faces reddened with blood. Eogan led them, wearing again his crown and cloak of bloody stallion skin.

That year, it was Garanhir who had picked the blood-hearted glass pebble from Eogan's wicker bottle at Samhain, and now it was Garanhir who strode naked among his twelve companions with wreaths of oak twined around his youthful body. Watching him as the ritual fires were made and the festival progressed, Boudicca felt the lust-heat of the festival gather in her mind and in her womb.

She had begun to long for another child to be a companion for Rhiannon, but despite all her prayers and offerings the Goddess refused to grant her wish. Prasutagus seemed unaware of his wife's growing dissatisfaction. More and more she found herself thinking of lying with other men, younger men, lusty and full of life, and if sometimes the face of Vindorex the Trinovante came to her mind, more often it was Garanhir who filled her fevered dreams.

Garanhir . . .

The day wore on, with races, contests, feasting, drinking and dancing until by mid-afternoon the celebrants sank down on the grass to rest before the rigours of the coming night.

'So, sister!' Mocuxsoris threw himself down beside Boudicca, spilling wine from the curled horn cup in his hand. 'We've had no chance to talk. How is it with you?'

'Much as it was when we last parted,' she replied. 'And you?'

He grimaced, quaffing deep from his cup and wiping wine from his moustache with the back of his hand. 'The same. Too quiet for my taste. The youths go raiding after cattle, but there's no real fighting any more. We've no captives to set to the flames, only sheep and goats. Caratacus will make better offerings, if what I hear is right – he may have Roman hides to roast. I'll wager Eogan would relish the sight of a legionary or two staked in his fires.'

'No doubt.' She sent a hooded glance to where the oak seer was standing alone by a tree, a gaunt figure leaning on his ash staff, lost in thoughts of his own. 'He often speaks of Caratacus's valour.'

'With good reason. Caratacus has got the Romans running in circles. Why else do you think they've built their forts and made a military zone from Trent to Severn? – They're intent on keeping Caratacus in his mountains. As for the rest of us, here behind their lines – why, we've all meekly signed treaties and promised to keep the peace while the Romans move against the north and west. Compared with Caratacus, we're all gutless cowards.'

'You hated him once,' Boudicca observed.

'So I did, but at least he's true to himself. I used also to be proud of my Iceni blood, but it seems the Iceni have taken to striking at hares and so lost their courage.'

'It will return, when the moment comes.'

' "When"?' He regarded her with raised brows and a new alertness in his eyes. 'Do you foresee war, then?'

'I smell it in the wind. It will come, sooner or later. And we'll be ready. I still lead the chariots in training. And our younglings are still being taught the arts of war. Even Rhiannon can use a sling with fair accuracy, small as she is.'

She spoke with a mother's pride. Though only four-years-old, the child was already being trained, not only in arms but for the role she must fulfil at the next Great Year. The thought of it troubled Boudicca; she loved her happy, bright-haired daughter and prayed that Danu, the Great Mother, would not make the burden too heavy.

'And who will she fight?' Mocuxsoris asked. 'The Romans?'

'If necessary.'

'Is this what the king says?'

Boudicca glanced towards a bank of hazel bushes in whose shade her husband rested with others of the elders. 'He trusts in the treaty to protect us,' she replied, adding – because this was Mocuxsoris her brother, in whom she could confide without fear – 'You said once that Prasutagus was an old man. Perhaps you were right. He likes to count his wealth and sit in the sun. He . . .' she lowered her voice further as she spoke the condemnation, 'He can't even give me a child.'

'Then put him aside,' was her brother's answer.

She laughed bitterly. 'I wish it were that easy. Unfortunately, Icenian law doesn't count any more. My husband's a Roman citizen now, and it was the Romans who made him king. Their treaty was made with Prasutagus, signed by Prasutagus.'

Narrowing his eyes, Mocuxsoris stroked his moustache. 'We can't give them any excuse to discard the treaty.'

'Exactly,' Boudicca agreed with a sigh. 'They know Prasutagus to be a man of caution. They might not be so willing to see a younger man made high chief. Besides, the elders are with him. Under his leadership, they say, we've had only prosperity – and who can deny it? At present I've no choice but to remain his wife.'

Her brother shrugged, as if the discussion bored him. 'Then get a child with someone else; so long as you use discretion. Prasutagus won't dare refuse to acknowledge any babe you might bear, not if it means admitting his impotence.'

'I've thought of it, many times.' From under her lashes, she watched Garanhir sporting among his companions, clothed only in oak leaves. He would not refuse her, she knew.

'Then do it, sister.'

Feeling her blood flow hot with the wine she had taken, she said, 'Perhaps I will. Yes, perhaps the time has come.'

Many of the warriors at the feast watched her with covetous eyes. She had still the glowing beauty of youth, her red hair flowing unbound over a green gown threaded with silver as she gave herself up to sacred ecstasy in the dance. Mocuxsoris had been right: she could take her choice of virile men who would be proud to serve her, in any way. With every cup of wine she felt herself drawn more under the influence of the Goddess, being urged to follow Her example and take what she wanted.

Snatching up a horn mug, she held it under the amphora tipped up by a slave and watched the red liquid fill it to the brim and gush over. The wine ran down her hand as she approached the tree beneath which the Green King took respite in the shade with his companions.

Closest to Garanhir lounged the ugly, likeable Nuadat. He had a battered face that resembled the gnarled growths on an ancient tree and his broad body, roped with bulging muscle, was covered in scars. Beside him, Garanhir had a God's fairness of face and form. The two were rivals in arms, yet great friends, differing in nature as day differed from night. Garanhir was serious and thoughtful, where Nuadat exuded a merry carelessness that made everyone warm to him. Yet his was the strongest arm to wield a sword or throw a spear, and his was the deadliest accuracy. With these two at the head of our army, Boudicca thought with a spurt of ferocity, we could destroy the Romans.

Feeling the ecstasy of the Goddess on her, she drew near to the tree carrying the dripping cup of wine. Garanhir appeared to her as though touched by divine light; the oak leaves disguised little of his strong body. He was handsome, fair, thickly moustached as were most of the young men, and the Gods had blessed him with a hero's perfection of form, making him tall and straight. The Goddess Herself must feel Her loins loosen when She gazed on such a man.

Seeing her approach, he sat up, his bronzed skin gleaming over rippling muscle as he began to get to his feet.

Boudicca laid a hand on his shoulder, pressing him back down to the grass as she knelt beside him while his companions looked on with drunken grins. 'Your queen serves you, Green King,' she said, holding out the mug of wine and watching as a drop from her hand ran down his chest. She was tempted to wipe it away and explore the texture of his skin, or to remove the drop with her tongue, but there were too many witnesses. Even so, being so near to his unclothed form made her breathing shallow.

He accepted the offering and drank deep, wishing to please her. When only a few drops remained he upturned the horn and offered a libation to the earth. 'For the Goddess.'

'She will smile on you,' Boudicca assured him, adding in a low voice, 'I, who was once Her Maiden, advise you to be ready for Her favours, Garanhir.'

His eyes jerked to her face and for a moment they spoke without words before she straightened and walked lightly to where Prasutagus was now sleeping, refreshing his strength for the rites that were still to come. Not far away, Mocuxsoris lay flat on his back snoring beside Huctia his wife. Boudicca lay down beside her husband, staring at the bright sky, her pulse wild with anticipation, her head full of wine-induced mist.

As the sun went down over the Great Bay, the Green King and his companions ran down the narrow path in the red cliff to immerse themselves in the sea. Drumbeats pounded a slow rhythm as Morica took the hand of that year's Willow Maid and began the spiral maze dance, looping a pattern left and then right, slowly circling the fires on the clifftop. The other women joined in, Boudicca among them, her head heavy with the wine that prevented her from thinking, from remembering too much.

Wearing his skin cloak, Eogan walked steadily to the edge

of the cliff, the last light of the sun glinting on the gold-topped ash staff he held above his head. His bass voice thundered out in a great cry that brought silence as the Green King was brought up from the beach, bound tightly in branches, held aloft by his twelve companions with his fair head hanging down between their arms.

Boudicca caught her breath, chills rippling along her flesh, though she knew that, this time, the Green King would be destroyed only symbolically. The young men put down their captive and unbound the green branches from his limbs, throwing them onto the fire where plumes of smoke rose in the twilight. Garanhir stepped free, accepting a knife which Eogan handed to him as a young stag was brought up, also bound in branches, and he slit its throat; blood spurted into a cup held by the Druid. The sacred right haunch was cut and tossed to the twelve companions before the sacrifice was dismembered and thrown to the flames as Eogan intoned the invocation and sprinkled blood to the west and to the south.

'Thus dies the God, to be born again; that the seasons may turn, the earth be fecund, the people faithful. Thus He dies, to ensure continuance. Caridwen take him. Arianrhod guard him. Latona give him rebirth.'

The ritual completed, the Druid threw up his arms and another loud cry rang from him as the dancing and chanting broke forth again.

Night darkened over the clifftop where firelight played over whirling figures, most of them unclothed to draw nearer to the Gods. Couples began to break away from the dancing, some lying together in full view. Boudicca saw Ferna run off into the darkness with Cormax after her; those two must be married soon, she thought. She could feel the heat building in her own loins: she could wait no longer.

She caught the eye of Garanhir, knowing that he had been watching for her signal. He understood as she whirled and ran away from the circle of light, into the darkness of a hollow sheltered by hawthorn trees and hazel bushes.

She heard him breathing heavily behind her, panting from the exertion of the dance as she let fall her tunic and turned, naked, to see him in the starlight.

'Lady!' his voice came hoarse.

'Garanhir!' she answered, holding out her arms to him.

He embraced her, their mouths fusing in a kiss that sent flame running along all her senses before he muttered, 'The king – '

'The king's asleep, like all old men.' She pressed closer, tasting the sweet salt of the perspiration across his collarbone. 'Forget him. Forget everything. Garanhir . . . Garanhir . . .'

'Lady . . .' it was a groan.

'Will you deny that you want me?' she whispered as she laid hot kisses up his throat. She was exultant, delighting in the swelling thrust of his erection; he could not control his desire for her.

A shiver ran through him. His arms clasped her more closely and she felt the strong heat of him against her breasts, her stomach, her thighs.

'And if I get you with child?' he asked.

'I hope you do,' she said fiercely. 'To bear your child would give me great joy.'

It was true. She knew it as his mouth possessed hers and need raged through her, moistening her body in anticipation. Unable to wait longer, she drew him down to lie in the grass with her, feeling him slide inside her, answering the need that filled her. She rode with him, challenging him, clawing at him, begging him for a release which swept suddenly through her. She cried out in anguish and ecstasy as his seed flooded into her and he shuddered into stillness.

She lay wrapped in his arms, enjoying the closeness between them. Not since Huan had she felt such fulfilment. For the first time in five years she had not had to close her eyes and imagine herself in the arms of another man. For the first time in five years she was not left aching and empty.

'Lady,' he whispered hoarsely, 'the love I bear you is stronger than death. But if the king discovers what we've done, it will bring shame on us both. He's my lord. I owe him loyalty.'

'No!' She clutched at him, her nails digging into his flesh. She had drawn him on because her body burned with lusty needs that could be assuaged without shame in the heat of a festival. But having experienced him she wanted more. Much more. And frequently. She was young. She needed a young man's body to soothe the fires inside her. 'You owe me loyalty, too,' she said fiercely.

'You have it, as my queen. But in all honour we must deny the feelings between us. When this night is over, I beg you, do not tempt me more.' He withdrew from her, rolling to the grass beside her to stare at the paling stars.

For a moment she lay stricken, feeling the sweat turn cold along her body. 'This is a hard doom you lay upon us,' she said through chilled lips.

'To continue in shame would be harder,' Garanhir's voice came low. 'Ever fearful of discovery, ever hiding in dark places. It's no way for warriors to live.'

'I could command you to lie with me,' she reminded him.

He drew a deep shuddering breath and his answer came hoarse and slow. 'Lady, you could.'

'And you would obey, and grow to hate me. I'd have you willing, or not at all.' In this brief hour she had learned a great deal about Garanhir – and about herself. She had tempted him lightly, and now she was sorry for it. She lifted herself to look at him in the faint light, her fingers tracing the strong lines of his face, his tumbled fair hair and the moustache that grew thick on his lip. She spoke hoarsely, her voice shaking with passion. 'But know this, Garanhir, if it were in my power I'd put aside my husband and take you instead, before all the tribe. But it's not in my power. I'm queen, but the Romans make the laws.'

'Wed or unwed, lady, you've laid a *geis** on me,' Garanhir replied, his lips moving against her fingers as he stroked the long hair from her face and looked deep into her eyes. 'Though we never speak of love again after this night, this I vow by the twin Gods, Bran and Vron, Serpent of Wisdom and Star of Life: until the wild geese call me, I am yours.'

She trembled as he spoke that solemn oath. It was a vow unto death, more binding than any marriage ceremony. She was flattered by it, but it disturbed her; it sought to bind her, too.

His hand caressed her hip, smoothing the curves of her body, and she felt his desire mounting again as he bent over her, whispering against her mouth, 'But this night is not over yet.'

When she woke to full daylight and birds singing, Garanhir

* *geis – a spell of fate, impelling obedience; its breaking means death.*

had gone. Her head was heavy but the languor in her limbs felt sweet, even though a deep sadness clouded her thoughts. The Goddess could be kind, but She could also be cruel if the whim moved Her so. Twice now She had shown Boudicca the promise of love only to snatch it away. If she was fated to be denied human love, what other reward remained for a faithful Maiden?

Seven

The ceremonies over, the Iceni left their sacred place on the clifftop and started on the journey back to Oakhillfort, along the Way where countless feet from the dawn of time had worn a track. A firm ridge of chalk formed a strip of heathland fading into copses of mixed trees and bands of thicker oak forest as it headed southwesterly through gently rolling hills from the coast to the far borders of Icenia.

On either side of the Way outlying farms were set in hollows of the undulating land, their thatched roundhouses and granaries protected by deep ditches and hawthorn hedges. Their fields were scratched out of the shallow soil of the hillsides. And, dominating these rolling lands east of the Great Bay, the great defensive banks of Oakhillfort rose against the sky, set on a knoll. Midsummer had been celebrated at the oak grove here, too, among the old and the very young, though less elaborately than at the *nemeton* on the cliff.

A small group of youths and maids, old enough to ride but not yet past puberty and therefore forbidden from attending the greater rites of midsummer, kicked at their shaggy mounts as they rode noisily down the slope from the fort to greet their parents and kinsmen. Among them were the twins, Ylas and Matuac. Together, the merry party rode home, to the twining maze-like entry between the steep grassed banks and through the gateway that guarded the settlement.

Already traders had arrived, some of them tall, fair Celts of northerly tribes, who had sailed across the Great Bay. Others were shy, dark fenfolk, small of stature; they lived a simple existence in the marshes and brought for barter salt, fish, and the long marsh reeds so coveted for thatching. Soon the meeting place outside the great hall was busy as warriors jostled for the best bargain. Smoke threaded from the thatch of the roundhouses, geese waddled after scraps and a dog yelped as it was trodden underfoot in the crush of the market. Already the scent of cooking assailed the air as slaves prepared the feast that would take place that night.

In the queen's house, a cauldron steamed appetisingly above the fire and old Cauva the nurse was busy at her loom. None of her young charges was with her.

Striding in, prepared for a warm greeting, Boudicca glanced around for Rhiannon. 'Where's my daughter?' she asked of Cauva.

The old woman looked troubled. 'She's down by the river, lady. With Morica. I tried to prevent it, but – '

Boudicca heard no more; she was striding out through the passageway to the stone-bedded path. On the crowded area by the sacred oak, merchants and craftsmen haggled while warriors of various factions were arguing and posturing. There would be fighting before the market was over; there was always fighting at every market. Boudicca ignored the uproar and strode on down the track which led among roundhouses to the entry of the fort.

The high inner bank lay ahead, the sturdy gates bearing bronze plaques of the twin Gods, one wreathed in holly, the other in oak, while on the lintel another plaque depicted the Threefold Goddess, full face and in profile to left and right, girl, woman and crone.

Boudicca emerged at the spot where the land sloped sharply away at the end of the knoll, providing a commanding view. To her right, beyond a narrow stretch of woodland, the Great Bay laid its silver-blue expanse shimmering under the sun, while in front of her, beyond the river, stretching as far as the eye could see lay the watery wastes, lush growth and dark secret islands of the marshes.

Boudicca strode down the path among a light cover of hawthorn and bay willow, to a track worn stony by chariots as they raced at practice around the knoll. Beyond the chariot track, a further path wound through open woods to the priestess's hut by the river. There, beneath towering alders which overhung the water, the queen saw Morica with the pale-haired warrior-maid Erefwen, both of them crouched among banks of meadowsweet, with Rhiannon between them. The child was a tiny figure with pale red-gold hair curling over the shoulders of a green tunic. She pointed across the river, and her young voice came to Boudicca, crying, 'Look, look! The horse! The beautiful white horse!'

But the far bank of the river was deserted. Alder and willow grew there, over banks of blackberry and dog-rose, but if there was a horse it hid itself from Boudicca's eyes.

She saw the face of Erefwen first; the girl was kneeling by Rhiannon, holding the child's arm and staring at her with eyes dilated and darkened by drugs. The devouring adoration Boudicca read in those eyes made her angry and afraid. She strode forward and snatched her daughter away from the touch of the young warrior-maid.

'Leave her, Erefwen! Morica – ' The words choked off as she saw that Rhiannon too was dark-eyed from the effects of some potion, and deathly pale. She swept the child up into her arms, cradling her close as she glared down at Morica.

'What are you doing to her? She's too young to understand.'

'The Maiden is never too young,' Morica replied, eyes staring unfocused from their frame of blue tattoos. The priestess had grown gaunt, her cheeks hollow, her clothes hanging loose over her bony body, and in her hair a streak of pure white grew from above her right temple, straggling among wild, dun-coloured tresses. She appeared to be looking through Boudicca as she straightened to her full height. 'The Maiden must know the Goddess in all her guises: Virgin, Mistress, Death-bringer. Rhiannon must accept, when the time comes.'

'She will accept!' Boudicca cried. 'But the time is not yet, not for many summers. I forbid you to use her so! Already she dreams strange visions at night and cries out for me.'

The priestess nodded approvingly. 'The Night Mare visits her. That is to be expected. She sees the Mare by day, too. Did you not see her pointing it out to us? Already the Goddess is calling her.'

Troubled, Boudicca stroked her daughter's soft curls, pressing the little body close to her breast. Rhiannon seemed unaware of her presence; her eyes were still fixed on distances beyond the river. Boudicca herself had known hallucinations brought by the ivy drug, but Rhiannon was so young. Was she to be allowed no childhood, no merry play with her fellows?

'It's too soon!' she cried.

'It's necessary.'

'Why is it? My own initiation didn't begin until I reached puberty.'

'You were not born of the God.'

It was a charge Boudicca could not refute. She had been chosen as Maiden, not born to it. Nevertheless, she had to protect her child. 'I'll not have my daughter's young life spoiled!' she insisted. 'Leave her be, Morica. What she needs to know I can teach her, gently, as my own mother taught me.'

'This time must be different,' Morica said, clawing a strand of lank hair from her eyes. 'Comes the next Great Year, who knows what deep magic will be necessary? You forget the Roman threat. Eogan and I do not forget.'

Unnerved by that vacant blue stare, Boudicca felt premonition run like ants across her skin. She had no answer, nor did she understand what the priestess meant by 'deep magic'. She only knew she was worried, and at the moment her concern was for her daughter.

Turning on her heel, she carried Rhiannon away from that place of dread omens. The child was dazed, still gazing across the river with a hand reaching out in yearning. No, it was not right! Dia could not want her Maiden soulless, with no will of her own.

Wanting to protect her daughter until the effects of the potion lessened, Boudicca walked with the child in the woods, skirting the guarded enclosures where the horses were kept. Rhiannon loved horses; when she was older she would learn to ride the shaggy ponies, and then to yoke them and drive them, as her mother did. If she was to be queen some day, she must learn the ways of the chariots.

Beneath the trees in sun-dappled shade, Boudicca encountered Garanhir, his hips and thighs encased in leather breeks and a bronze neck-torc dark against oiled, sun-browned flesh. Leather straps slung crosswise round his torso supported a spear and the sword whose jewelled hilt showed behind his right shoulder. How fine he was, fair and bright with leaves moving behind him in a breeze. The sight of him made a pain move in her breast and her womb contracted with desire. There must be a way! she thought.

Their eyes exchanged silent messages as he saluted her formally and in the same moment she heard voices not far away – Nuadat conversing with the horsemasters Vranaun and old Nemmon, the three of them just visible behind swaying branches.

'Is the child unwell?' Garanhir asked with an anxious glance at Rhiannon's pale face.

'She was with Morica,' Boudicca said, and saw the swift frown that said he understood. 'I want no one to see her like this.'

He nodded to where his friend and the two horsemasters were yoking horses to a chariot. 'Nuadat has been challenged to a race by one of Audagas's men. If we go this way we can avoid them.'

Boudicca paused, watching him with smoky green eyes. 'We?'

'You should not be alone in the woods,' Garanhir said, his glance sliding away from her, 'especially when you have your daughter with you. If a bear attacks, how will you defend yourself?'

She smiled to herself bitterly. 'And who better for escort than Garanhir, the most honourable of our warriors? Not even my husband could object.'

At once his glance came up to her face, sharp and filled with pain. 'Are you mocking me, lady?'

'No.' Her voice caught in her throat. She felt the sting of tears behind her eyes as she let her fingertips caress the smooth silk of his chest, filled by an agony of longing. Then, realising what she was doing, she snatched the hand away and curled it at her breast, her eyes downcast. 'Forgive me, Garanhir.'

'Lady . . .' His voice shook on the word and when she looked up into his face she saw there a grief that matched her own. He made a movement toward her, stopped himself, and for a moment that stretched to eternity they spoke with their eyes, each searching the other's soul.

For him, the temptation was too great: when Boudicca stood before him with her pale face upraised and her eyes brimming with tears his love was stronger.

For her, there was only the desolation of her need of him – the need of one bright beam to light her life. Silently she pleaded her case: they would be careful, no one would know. What harm could be done?

Before they parted, they were agreed. The agony could not be endured. Neither of them was strong enough. Between them love was a clean fire that absolved them of all guilt. Few as the chances for consummation might be, they would take them, joyfully. One did not refuse a gift from the Gods.

Autumn came dark and stormy that year, with gales that sent leaves whipping across the heath, followed by cold rains that soaked the leaves into sodden drifts in the rubbish pits. The ivy month ended with heavy mists and wild seas that brought the grinding of pebbles to roar like the voice of the sea-god on the shores of the Great Bay.

The feast of Samhain, the celebration of the dying of the year before winter set in, when dark Bran took over from his brighter twin, was always surrounded by portents for the Iceni. The wind whistling dismally through the reeds along the fringes of the marsh was a harbinger of doom, as was the cry of screech owls sailing through the woods under a cold moon. All meant death – the death of warmth and light, and perhaps a death that touched closer to the hearts of the people: Waroch, champion of the tribe, lay mortally sick.

That year, Boudicca found the omens ever more black, though she was aware that her fears had much to do with her condition – she was carrying Garanhir's child. She suffered illogical fears on behalf of her lover, who must fulfil one more duty before his year as Green King was ended.

Wreathed in yew, Garanhir would go alone into the forests ahead of the others, to raise the boar, with the warriors following after him in a mock hunt of the old Green King. Somewhere along the way he would yield his wreath of dark leaves to the new participant, and the men would come home in triumph with their trophies to the feast. Long ago, so the bards told, the old Green King was really hunted and killed by his erstwhile companions, and even now such hunts often led to injury and, on occasion, to death.

In the absence of Eogan, it fell to Prasutagus to oversee the choosing of the new Green King. A warrior named Erthil won the coveted pebble and the right to lead the boar-hunt.

When the men set off in pursuit of Garanhir that dark dawn, Boudicca occupied herself with her chores, but her mind was off in the forests, following the hunt. She foresaw a tragedy. Subtle signs warned her she might lose her lover.

Towards evening, just before she set out to join the celebrations around the fires at the oak grove, she cut a lock of her hair and bound it in sacred scarlet thread. With this talisman secreted under her cloak she took a torch from outside the door and made her way through the darkness to the well. Here she set the torch on a pole while she nicked her finger with a knife and let the blood fall on the bound lock of hair. Under her breath she murmured a prayer.

'Queen of Heaven, protect him. Great Epona, give him strength. Caridwen, White Sow, choose him not as your mast. And you, Bran, Serpent of Wisdom, you are crimson-stained enough without his blood. Take mine in its place. Grant me this and I swear that the child in my womb shall be taught to bless your name above that of your brother.'

Then she touched her amulet to the flaring torch, setting the hair alight, and as the flame burned her fingers she dropped the blackened charm into the well and watched its last spark blink out as the ashes touched the water.

As if in response, the wind brought the sound of yelping hounds and within minutes the warriors were seen approaching, tired, bruised and muddied to the eyebrows. Duihno, who had always been foolhardy, had been gashed in the thigh by a boar's tusk, but his was the only real injury. The prayer of Boudicca had been granted. Garanhir was safe, his duties done, and the men were triumphant as they joined the dancing on the knoll: their labours had been rewarded by the capture of two full-grown boar, three sows, and five sucklings. The feast of Samhain, which would take place the next day, was secure.

All day slaves turned the great spits to roast the trophies of the hunt, and as the early night fell the people of Oakhillfort came to their great hall.

Each household had made its own fire, so that the settlement was lit by flames outside each door, to drive away the spirits of night and warm the sacred dead who were present in the form of dolls hung at each lintel. In the great hall, hanging up their shields and swords on the walls as they entered, the elders and warriors gathered with their families.

Wrapped in furs, her hood thrown back to display the circlet that bound her red hair, Boudicca led her daughter from the queen's house toward the hall, in a torchlight procession with the king her husband and their bodyguard of warriors. The night was ablaze with light, from the dancing flames of spitting torches and from the cooking fires over which the spits were being turned by sweating slaves. The wind teased at the flames, making them twist into restless spirals as smoke eddied and billowed, bringing the succulent scent of roasting pork.

Boudicca kept Rhiannon close beside her, under her cloak, partly to protect her from the cold and partly to keep her from Morica, who was prowling nearby.

'You see the boars roasting, Rhiannon,' Boudicca said as they passed by the cooking fires. 'They represent the bright God, Vron, whose time is done. Now his brother Bran rules over us to bring the darkest days and the winter. But with the winter solstice, the bright God will be born again and when he grows to manhood he'll chase away his dark twin and bring back the springtime.'

Springtime, when the child in her womb would be born. As she thought of it, the babe inside her flickered with life for the first time, making her rest a hand on her swelling stomach. Rhiannon looked up, asking in her clear treble, 'What is it, mother?'

'It's nothing, my love,' Boudicca smiled. 'Just your brother, anxious to be noticed.'

It was going to be a boy, she had no doubt – a fine boy to grow up strong and handsome like his father. Her eyes sought Garanhir, cloaked like the rest but distinguishable by his stature, and her heart swelled with pride in him. Since the night of the midsummer festival they had made love as often as they could, which was not often enough for her. But she tried not to be greedy, to be content with being able to share a soul-baring glance through the smoke of the hall and to know that, some time, when the Gods smiled, they would be together again. Sometimes it was almost too much to bear, but she bore it. She had to. She could not predict what might happen if her husband ever suspected the truth.

Prasutagus had accepted her pregnancy calmly, but this only troubled her. She couldn't tell whether he believed the child to be his or whether he guessed it had been conceived at the midsummer festival. It was the custom for such children to be looked upon as gifts from the Gods, but she had expected some reaction from so proud a man. Instead, he had merely nodded at the news and remarked that the new babe would be a companion for Rhiannon. His thoughts were hidden from Boudicca. Lately he had grown more distant from her, as though feeling that he no longer needed her to maintain his hold on power.

'Boars grub among the roots of the forest,' Morica was telling Rhiannon. 'They eat of the fruits of the trees. But the mast of Caridwen is the skulls of men. The boar is sacred to Her, the White Sow. We kill it only at Samhain, to honour Her.'

Boudicca drew her daughter closer to her side, casting an angry look at the priestess, who replied with a penetrating blue stare. Disturbed, Boudicca turned away and passed under the carved portals of the great door.

More fires burned in the centre of the hall and torchlight caught in the polished bronze of the weapons that adorned the walls. A shout of acclaim greeted the entrance of the royal family and their retinue, from throats already well lubricated with ale and mead.

Boudicca and Prasutagus took the place prepared for them at the head of the feast, on mounded hay covered with furs. The elders gathered on either side, squatting on their heels with the royal guard ranged near them – Garanhir, Nuadat, Ferna, Cormax, Duihno and the rest. Boudicca, holding the hand of her small daughter, sat down beside her husband. Neither of them looked at the other.

Jugs of ale, mead and wine went round and Alvran the bard sang the traditional song of Samhain which told of the continual struggle of the twin Gods for the love of the Earth

Goddess, first one supreme and then the other, causing the seasons to turn. As his harp plucked a final fading chord, shouts of approval came from the listeners, increasing in uproar as at last the doors were flung open and the roasts were brought in, still on their spits and borne by two slaves, each pig still whole but for its entrails, its skin browned and glistening with juices.

Lifting a hand for silence in the clamour, Prasutagus got to his feet, stepped to the middle of the room under the rise of thatch and raised his voice. 'The feast of Samhain is prepared. We mourn the passing of the God.'

'Aye!' came the chorus of reply from mouths drooling in response to the scents rising from the pork and most hands had already drawn a dagger, preparing to hack at the meat.

'We mourn also the loss of our friend Waroch, our champion, taken by a fever,' Prasutagus went on, to more shouts of agreement. 'Yet as the bright God will be born again, so a new champion shall be found.'

The people cheered, anticipating the announcement of contests to establish the strongest warrior of the tribe. It would be something to enliven the dark winter days.

'Garanhir!' Prasutagus summoned his favourite. 'To my side!' As Garanhir stepped forward, the king lifted his hands and stared around the circle of staring faces as if daring them to gainsay him. Despite the wry twist of his left eyebrow, his face was cold as the north wind. Something in his manner made Boudicca hold her breath as her husband started to speak. 'Bear witness, elders,' he declaimed with slow deliberation. 'Bear witness, people . . . I proclaim Garanhir the king's champion! The champion's portion shall be his.'

Raising his own knife, the king wrenched at the right hock of one of the boars, severing a chunk of the most succulent flesh from the haunch. This, the most coveted portion, he offered to Garanhir on the point of his dagger.

Boudicca shared the stunned surprise that mesmerised the hall, and from the faces around her she divined the trend of their thoughts. If anyone should have been made champion without the usual trial of strength, Nuadat was the obvious candidate, not only popular with everyone but a proven hero both in battle and at the hunt. However, unusual though the choosing might be, no precedents existed: the Iceni had been led by a high chief, not a king, when the last champion had been declared. Perhaps it was a king's right to honour his favourite in this way. After a few moments of confusion, people began to shout their loyal agreement. After all, Garanhir was a valorous warrior, known for his deep sense of honour; he would make a fitting champion.

Under cover of the clamour of approval, Boudicca saw Garanhir protest at the accolade, his lips framing the word, 'Lord . . .' Then he glanced at her and the agony in his eyes told her that if he became king's champion honour would bind him in total loyalty to the king – honour would force him to avoid all contact with the king's wife.

This was what Boudicca's prescient sense had feared – *this* was how she must lose him.

He dropped to one knee, accepting a title he dared not refuse, and through the dismay that filled her Boudicca glimpsed the gnarled face of Nuadat, scarlet with anger; the choosing of Garanhir before him was a mortal insult to his pride. He was about to challenge the choice, as was his right; any warrior who cared to try his strength might offer to meet the champion in combat – combat for the right to bear the title, for supremacy or for death.

Fear drove Boudicca to her feet, her green eyes blazing in a face gone ashen, and then she saw the bitter twist of her husband's mouth. The scar that tilted his left eye failed to trick her with its permanent sardonic lift; there was no amusement in him, only a chilling watchfulness.

He knew! The knowledge seared through her brain like a spear of ice, leaving her mind numb. He knew that she and Garanhir were lovers. This was his method of revenge, cunning and sly like the wolf he was: he had known that Nuadat would offer a challenge; he knew Nuadat to be the stronger; he would use Nuadat to take the life of a young man he had once loved as a son. It was Garanhir's life he wanted.

No!

Pride gave her the answer – pride that came boiling up in a cold fury of hate. Prasutagus had no right to declare a champion for his own personal ends. He was king only by decree of Rome. She, Boudicca, was queen of the Iceni. *She, Boudicca!*

Just as Nuadat moved to voice his anger, Boudicca cried sharply, 'Wait!'

Putting Rhiannon aside, she stepped forward and held up her hand for silence, knowing that she made an impressive figure with her head high and firelight playing over her red hair and her gold adornments. She took a breath and summoned a voice that surprised her by its depth and its power of command. 'The ceremony is not yet over. There is another boar – another champion's portion.' The words rang around the hall, stopping the final mutterings and making the people stare at her in wonderment.

She drew another long breath, savouring the moment, knowing she had the full attention of all her people and forcing them to wait for her to speak. Slowly, she drew her own sharp dagger from its jewelled sheath and held it aloft so that light slanted along its edge and drew all eyes. She was conscious of the power that flowed through her and with a thrill of awe she realised that the Goddess was with her, guiding her, even speaking through her.

Again she called up the compelling tone she had never used before that day. 'Bear witness, elders . . . Bear witness, all my people . . . We hail Garanhir king's champion, and worthy to be so. Now I, Boudicca, as is my ancient right, choose a *queen's* champion.' She paused and felt the relief that flowed around her. In time, the people would come to believe it had all been planned this way, a small drama to amuse them and enliven the feast. She would make sure they believed it. Across the firelit spaces her eyes met those of Nuadat and she saw the fierce pride in his ugly face even before she slashed at the unmarked boar, cutting from its right haunch a giant portion that she impaled on the point of her knife. 'Step forward to my side . . . Nuadat – Champion of the Iceni!'

'Aye!!' This time it was a roar that shook the woven hazel and thatch of the roof as Nuadat stepped forward to salute her and kneel at her feet, offering his life in her service.

Boudicca looked at her husband and saw him smile thinly as he sat down. She had saved her lover but she had also lost him; they would never dare to meet alone again, or speak of love, while Prasutagus lived. So be it. But if her husband had won a victory then so had she – she had found unexpected strength when she needed it. She had been reminded of who and what she was born to be.

Despite the heavy sorrow around her heart, new confidence surged through her, and her face was alight as she lifted her head, holding out her arms as if to embrace every one of her people.

'Let the feast begin!'

Eight

The queen's second child was born amid the showers and breezy winds of the alder month: another girl – a girl both fair and frail. From the first, Boudicca saw that her second daughter would never be a warrior. The Goddess answered prayer, but She was whimsical.

The babe was named Araunah and at the ceremony of her naming Prasutagus took her into his arms, acknowledging her as his own. Though he and Boudicca had never spoken aloud of the matter, a tacit agreement had been reached: he would forget her indiscretion; he was even pleased to claim paternity of a child, but in return she must never give him cause to doubt her fidelity, not ever again. If she brought shame on him, he would invoke Roman law to put her aside, and her lover with her, making them outcasts. And then, with the approval of Rome, he would have absolute power in Icenia.

This last threat hardened her determination. Garanhir was lost to her, she had known that from the moment he knelt to accept the accolade of king's champion. Besides, his sense of honour would have driven them apart before long; he had always hated to deceive Prasutagus. Every time they had been together Boudicca had been forced to plead and argue, playing the wanton. Her own pride would soon have rebelled. But if love was denied her she had found a new purpose – to thwart her husband's ambition to end the age-long tradition of matriarchy in Icenia.

Setting tiny Araunah to the breast of a wet-nurse, Boudicca

returned to the chariots and the training ground, leading the young warriors with increased vigour. Let her husband sit in council with the other old men and count his increasing wealth; if danger threatened, the Iceni would find they had a warrior-queen who would be well ready to lead them.

In the year when Araunah had survived her first full turn of the seasons, Ferna and Cormax were wed with ceremony in the oak grove along the knoll. Now that Eogan spent more and more of his time in the forests, Morica made sacrifice and declared the omens good before the families exchanged bride-price and dowry and the wedded pair leapt over the fires of purification. For Coeling and Tadia, the marriage of their eldest daughter was a proud moment, and Cormax's mother smiled on the young couple, thinking of chores that might now be shared.

The wedding celebrations went on far into the night, amid the usual drinking and brawling. But the ale must have put ideas into some heads, for when morning came most of the youths of the village had gone, along with horses from the enclosure down by the river.

Behind the curtain which separated her room from the central hall of the queen's house, Boudicca heard the discussion as she pulled on checked trousers and tunic and her slave dressed her long hair in rolls and braids.

'Gone raiding,' Coeling declared with satisfaction. 'And my twins with them. Those two are born warriors.'

'They're only twelve-summers-old,' his wife Tadia reminded him.

'Old enough,' said Coeling.

'Old enough to be led into mischief,' the voice of Prasutagus added sternly. 'It's Duihno who's behind this, I'll wager.'

The voice of old Vassedo joined in, defending his grandson. 'What else should we expect? Diuhno's been waiting too long to be blooded. His father won the Warrior's Light when he was fourteen-summers-old, and I took my first blood at fifteen. We were encouraged to be men in those days.'

'The days have changed,' Prasutagus said.

The king must have stalked out of the house, for after a silence Boudicca heard Coeling say bitterly, 'And it's the

Romans who've changed them. We live in fear of offending the Romans!' He spat loudly in disgust.

Waving away the slave who had been binding her hair, Boudicca swept aside the curtain and stepped into the circular hall. Furthest from the door, old Cauva sat watching Rhiannon, Cameira and other young girls working at their spinning. The wet-nurse dandled Araunah on her knee, while Vassedo huddled by the fire warming his thin hands. Coeling stood by the open door of the outer passage, a hand on his sword hilt, and Tadia was sewing listlessly, wearing a troubled look.

Coeling frowned at Boudicca, as if he had not realised she was still in the house. 'I speak my mind, lady.'

'You speak for more than one,' she replied. 'But the king is the king. I'll hear no treason, even from a kinsman.'

'Not even when you agree, in your heart?'

'I listen to my head, which is less inclined to rashness. As yet we've little cause to complain of the Romans. I haven't heard you refusing to use Roman oil lamps, or scorning to drink their red wine.'

Embarrassed, he fingered the enamel decoration on his sword hilt. 'It's not their merchandise I'm complaining about – though I could live without such luxuries. But what's happened to our honour? Where's our pride?'

She looked him in the eye, saying, 'Where it has always been – high in our heads, along with our courage and our wisdom. We're not defeated, Coeling. We're waiting – for the right cause.' Seeing that he had no answer to this, she glanced down at Tadia's worried face. 'And don't worry about your sons, Tadia. Young as they are, they have the blood of royal Brecca in their veins. They're warrior-bred. They'll return, tired and hungry, come sunset.'

At dusk, just as she had predicted, the youths returned with tales of bold deeds and enemies slain. Several of them were wounded, though none badly. As a trophy, Duihno bore the bloody, hacked-off head of one of his enemies.

Called to account for himself before the elders, the young man stood in the communal hall and boasted of leading his companions into deep forests, where they had encountered another band of wandering youths and engaged them in battle.

'Single-handed I slew three!' Duihno declared, holding up a blood-encrusted axe. 'With this weapon against their swords. Does anyone call me liar?'

Most of the youths around him shook their heads and Matuac, the older of Coeling's bright-headed twin sons, said, 'No, no. He did it. We all saw. Three of them. It was a bold fight. They came at him from all sides, but they were cowards. They feared his axe.'

'Enough!' Prasutagus rose to his feet, drawing all eyes to his pale face. He gestured to the wicker basket at his feet, which contained the head of a lad not more than eleven summers old. 'From what tribe did these youths come?'

'They were strangers,' Duihno said. 'Strangers in Iceni lands, and they attacked us.'

Prasutagus narrowed his eyes. 'From another tribe? Which tribe? Were they Trinovantes? Catuvellauni? Coritani? Which chief may I expect to come demanding justice?'

'Lord . . . we do not know.'

'I hope they were Catuvellauni.' This from Summac, a gnarled warrior with only a stump for his right arm and his left eye blinded – wounds got in battle with Caratacus and his warriors. 'Hah! Those sow-gotten bastards have still got a lot to learn.'

But one of the youths, who had been silent until now, spoke quietly, saying, 'They were Iceni, from Seafort.'

A murmur of disquiet rose among the listeners and Prasutagus fixed the boy with a glinting look. 'Audagas's clan? You're sure of this, Unthaus?'

'Yes, lord. One of them I recognised – Cadfan, the son of Audagas. I gave him a bloody nose at the market last midsummer.'

The incident was remembered by all. It had led to violence among the warriors. For all his youth, Cadfan had an unquenchable fire in his belly. But Audagas ruled a quarrelsome clan whose visits at festivals and markets seldom passed without injury or death for someone; he encouraged his sons to swift violence.

'They attacked us!' Duihno said hotly.

'Nobody doubts it!' the king replied with a gesture of anger.

'Not if they were youths of the clan of Audagas. But this – ' again he gestured at the basket on the ground before him – 'this was not well done. In battle one may claim the head of a sworn enemy, but in petty squabbles among boys . . . Elders, what is your judgement?'

The elders conferred, arguing back and forth until finally the majority decided that if Audagas came with complaints any fine he demanded must be paid by Duihno's kin, and the head must be returned. It was wrapped in cloth and placed in its wicker basket reverently in the death hut.

For once, Boudicca found herself in agreement with her husband. It was the way of youths to go out raiding after cattle and seeking a fight, to test themselves against time of real war, but this massacre of three beardless boys by Duihno's axe bespoke a wildness in the young man. Nevertheless, Duihno and the others – even the twelve-year-old twins – had truly been blooded: none could argue with that. They were awarded the Warrior's Light and wore the new tattoo of the blue all-seeing eye with satisfaction and much bragging of their valour.

Boudicca settled her sword belt more securely on her shoulder as she strode across the hall and through the passage to the outer door, onto a pebbled pathway which crossed the rubbish ditch. Children and puppies played among the roundhouses, or ran laughing across the grass in a game of catch which took them dodging round the sturdy trunk of the sacred oak. Women carried water from the well, or sat grinding corn in querns.

Erefwen, who had replaced the now-married Ferna as the queen's driver, was waiting with one of the training chariots. She was a slender girl with pale yellow hair; she made an excellent reinswoman, and she was devoted to young Rhiannon – perhaps too devoted, Boudicca had thought, which was why she liked to keep Erefwen near, where she could observe the girl's behaviour.

Boudicca mounted the chariot and, carrying herself straight and tall, balanced on braced legs with a hand lightly on the wicker side, was driven past the houses of warriors and of craftsmen. Near the tall gates the scent of hot metal came from the forge and Melliacus the smith paused to salute her, sweat streaming down his body to darken his leather apron.

The exit from the fort twined between staggered gaps in the double banks. It was the time of the red hawthorn blossom which Boudicca loved; it reminded her of Dia as Andastre – the full-blooded aspect of love and war. Denied love, Boudicca had turned her thoughts to war and as her chariot ran down to the trackway which circled the fort her heart leapt at the sight of young warriors already at practice. As usual, most of the older warriors were absent, gone hunting or trading, but a few always remained behind to assist their queen in training the youngsters.

Garanhir, with his young reinsman Gwyr small and dark beside him, drove up to meet her eyes without expression. 'Is it to be spears, lady?'

'Driving practice,' Boudicca decided, setting herself to look through him. 'Reinsmen alone.' She took the reins from Erefwen and bade the girl step down. 'I'll drive myself. Come, all of you. Who can stay with me? A race!'

Soon she was whipping up her horses, contending with Gwyr on one side and Nuadat's driver on the other while the rest trailed behind. She leaned back, knees flexed to cushion the jolting as the light vehicle bounced over the steep, rutted track, skirting the knoll. Beyond the woods, Boudicca glimpsed the distant gleam of the Great Bay, but her eyes remained on the ground ahead of her straining horses. Her ornaments and jewellery jingled along with the decorations on the harness, and from her eye corners she saw that she was drawing ahead of all but Gwyr.

As the chariots raced around the knoll, smaller children chased across the wooded slopes below the fort, cheering the warriors on; then as the vehicles jounced across more level ground outside the gates, some of the older children rode up astride shaggy ponies. Sensing the excitement, they kicked their mounts to join the race.

But one pony balked. It stood straddled and stubborn while its young rider kicked in vain, right in Boudicca's path. Vainly she sawed at the reins, trying to turn the horses, failing to see the rock that caught her wheel. The jolt tossed her into the air. She heard the upturned chariot splinter as it was dragged away and then the ground came up and jarred the breath from her body. She lay winded, her mind clouded. Shouting voices seemed to come from afar as anxious warriors crowded round.

'Mother!' the terrified cry came from Rhiannon. *'Mother!'*

The sound roused Boudicca. She stumbled to her feet, unaware of the blood seeping from a cut on her cheek, or of the dust that whitened her clothes and hair. The first thing she saw was the reddened, anxious face of Matuac, the cause of the trouble.

'Idiot child!' she raged at him. 'For all you wear the Warrior's Light, you'll never make a real warrior until you learn to control a horse!'

'Mother!' Rhiannon was running in among the crowd of chariots and unsettled horses, a leggy seven-year-old, heedless of her own danger. It was Garanhir who scooped her up into his arms and brought her to Boudicca.

The queen's eyes met his and she saw the fear he, too, had suffered. 'I'm unharmed,' she said. 'The Goddess protects me. Give the child to me.'

Thin arms tightened round her neck as she held her daughter close and summoned a laugh. 'Were you afraid? Ho, my love, I've had tumbles worse than that and so will you before you're done. Come, ride with me.'

'Lady . . .' Garanhir began but she quelled him with a look and deliberately turned her shoulder to him as she looked at the youthful driver nearest to her.

'Lend me your chariot, Unthaus. It's time my daughter learned the feel of a platform under her feet.'

Shaking away the clouds that threatened her mind, ignoring the pain that stabbed at her shoulder and hip, she set Rhiannon in the chariot, climbed up beside her and bade her hold tight as she clucked the horses into a walk. As the chariot trundled forward, Rhiannon gripped so hard on the wicker side that her knuckles showed white, but after a while she adjusted her balance, relaxed and looked up with a smile that sent a thrill of pride through Boudicca.

'I'll teach you to drive,' she promised. 'You'll be a warrior, Rhiannon. Like me.' But Rhiannon was also the Maiden, and the future queen of Icenia. What sort of life lay ahead for her?

As Boudicca's thoughts turned dark, the urgent call of a watch horn jerked her back to the present. She looked up to the bank where the watchman stood pointing away to the east. Far off beyond the trees, smoke plumed toward the sky.

'It's Urien's farm,' someone said. 'It's on fire! It must be a raid!'

Boudicca glanced behind her. Catching the eye of Matuac, she called him to her and the boy rode up, still red-faced and guilty.

'Take care of Rhiannon,' Boudicca instructed. 'I charge you with her safety. Nuadat! Garanhir! With me! All of you! Come!'

They were too late to save the farm. House and barns had been put to the torch and were still blazing. The attackers had fled, leaving the farmer's wife and family slain, though Urien himself lived long enough to whisper the name, 'Audagas.'

The council agreed that this time Audagas had flouted the law. He must be reminded that the Iceni were not barbarians; if he had a grievance, he must bring it before the council. Segovax, the law-giver, accompanied by a party of warriors, was sent to take this message to the sub-chief and bring back his reply.

Still stiff from her fall, Boudicca stood at her loom plying the shuttle and watching Rhiannon struggle to spin wool with a weighted spindle that seemed to have a mind of its own. It skipped between small fumbling fingers, producing a lumpy thread that as often as not ended up in a tangle. Eventually, Rhiannon gave a cry of despair and threw spindle and distaff to the ground.

'I'll never do it!'

Young Adalma, one of the horsemaster's children, moved in, picking up the discarded distaff. 'Of course you will. Let me show you again. In a little while you'll do better than Cameira. She never gives her mind to it. Think how angry she'll be if you show her up.'

Boudicca smiled to herself. How shrewd of Adalma to choose just the right incentive. Cameira, the youngest of Coeling and Tadia's brood, was a spiteful child and took pleasure in pinching the younger Rhiannon, who as yet had found no means of retaliation. Besting her at spinning might be a good way to begin, though Boudicca doubted it would work. Like herself, neither Rhiannon nor Cameira had patience with domestic chores. The chariots were in their blood. They were both warrior-bred.

Bursting into her thoughts, Nuadat appeared in the doorway, a fist snapping to his brow to obscure the Warrior's Light. 'Lady! Romans are on their way. A tribune and a handful of soldiers, from the office of the procurator. The king begs you prepare to welcome them.'

Boudicca sighed to herself, wondering what the visit could mean. More prying, without doubt – more counting of animals and personal effects to make sure the Iceni were paying their full share of taxes. Though the Roman presence was hardly discernible in Icenia, these occasional contacts were a sharp reminder of how much had changed.

She sent the children to play and ordered the slaves to prepare meat and drink for the visitors, so that by the time Prasutagus came in with the tribune and a sergeant, all was ready for them.

The tribune, like most of his people, was short and dark, dressed in a kneelength tunic with thonged sandals. A warm blue cloak hung long from his shoulders. He saluted Boudicca with a fist over his heart, but not before his eyes had widened at sight of her, taller than he with her red hair flowing about her and her green eyes unflinching as they stared into his.

'Lady,' he greeted.

'Quintilius Vitalis,' she repeated the name Prasutagus had spoken. 'Welcome. You'll take refreshment?'

'Perhaps some wine.' He sat down on the stool she had had set for him – for some reason the Romans always had to have seats instead of squatting comfortably on their heels. Prasutagus, too, had taken to using a stool, perhaps to follow the Roman fashion, though Boudicca fancied that with him it was old age and aching joints that begged comfort. The sergeant remained standing, gazing about with curiosity and occasionally frowning over a gesture or tone of voice; evidently he had no knowledge of the Britonic language.

Boudicca stood at her upright loom with stones holding the warp threads taut as she slid the bone shuttle back and forth, her fingers adjusting the edge of the cloth and her ears tuned to the discussion. She had little taste for polite talk with Romans and had difficulty concealing her dislike, so it was best to let her husband the diplomat conduct the meeting. However, she remained a close observer.

On most of these visits the procurator's emissaries were anxious to be pleasant, but Quintilius Vitalis seemed ill at ease, even shifty as his eyes roamed about the circular hall, lighting on the swords and shields hanging from carved posts.

He had, it seemed, heard of the burning of Urien's farm.

'A minor matter,' Prasutagus assured him with a wave of his hand. 'A squabble between factions of our tribe.'

The Roman frowned, partly over his difficulty with the Celtic tongue. '*Your* people?'

Prasutagus shrugged. 'Our youths have hot blood. If the procurator fears there is trouble brewing among the tribes, tell him to set his mind at rest. Under Roman protection, we fear no enemies. Besides, we're guarded by the blessing of the Gods.'

'You mean the Druids?' the tribune asked suspiciously.

'I mean the Great Goddess, the Guardian Queen, who gave us the Great Bay to the north, the marshy wastes to the west, ocean to the east and forests to the south.' He gestured with a long hand, turning his grey head as he spoke, then he gazed on the Roman with bland, pale eyes. 'The Iceni have long been protected by these defences.'

Quintilius continued to frown as if he suspected his host of using words to deceive him. The Romans hated and feared Druidic influence on the peoples of Albion, and Boudicca knew that if Eogan was anywhere in the village he would remain out of sight until these visitors had gone.

'What do you hear of Caratacus?' Quintilius asked of the king.

'Only that he continues to elude the governor-general and his legions in the mountains of the west.' Prasutagus shrugged, pulling absently at the bearskin mantle that draped one shoulder. 'What else should I know of an outlaw? You may assure the procurator – and the governor-general – that the Iceni hold no regard for such a man.'

Unable to remain silent, Boudicca murmured, 'We should hold even less regard for him if he were caught.'

'He will be caught,' the tribune assured her sternly. 'We shall subdue the west.'

She met his eyes, her own gaze deceptively mild. 'And the Druids on Mona?'

He hesitated, astute enough to know in what esteem the Druids were held. 'They, too, if they continue to encourage rebellion. It will be . . . regrettable, but necessary.'

'They are fools who resist the beneficence of Rome,' Prasutagus said with a glance that told Boudicca to desist.

Containing a smile, she returned her attention to her weaving.

As the conversation continued it became clear to her that the tribune had been sent spying. Caratacus's continued resistance had the Romans twitching. They feared that his successes might give ideas to others, which Boudicca had to admit was intelligent of them. Like her brother Mocuxsoris, she found herself admiring and envying the old enemy Caratacus. Catuvellauni he might be, but he was also a son of Albion; for five years now he had outwitted the legions of Rome and denied them access to the sacred isle of Mona. Other Britons might easily be entertaining similar ambitions.

So it was hardly surprising if the Romans had begun to feel uneasy: most of their army was concentrated on the front which stretched with a chain of forts from the river Trent to the river Severn, and their soldiers looked outward, to enemies in the north and west. Were they beginning to feel the cool breeze of rebellion blowing against their undefended backs?

However, whatever he was seeking, Quintilius Vitalis went away without finding evidence of unrest in Icenia.

When Segovax the lawgiver returned, he brought word that the sub-chief Audagas, in his fortress by the eastern sea, had openly admitted to leading a raid on the farm close to Oakhillfort in reprisal for the deaths of three youths of his clan and for seven more – including one of his three sons – wounded while on an innocent hunting expedition in the forests. He denied that his sons and their companions had instigated the attack.

'But if they had done so, he would not blame them,' Segovax reported. 'He says his youths are not bred like girls to sit at home and spin.'

'Insult!' old Vassedo cried, but Summac laughed and said that the youths of Oakhillfort had proved their supremacy by driving off Audagas's wild stallions. 'Our lads are well trained to arms, thanks to the queen.'

Shouts of agreement came from all quarters, gratifying Boudicca with their praise until Prasutagus called for silence and asked why Segovax had not brought Audagas back to tell his grievances to the council.

'He refused to come,' Segovax replied, causing mutters throughout the room. 'He says he has taken his revenge and will let it rest there, on condition that the head taken by Duihno is returned to Seafort at once for burial.'

'It shall be so,' Prasutagus agreed, seeming relieved to put an end to altercation among his people. 'But let Audagas be warned – my patience is not a boundless ocean. If he tries me too far, I'll sweep him away with the rest of the chaff.'

Nine

As the seasons turned, Caratacus of the Catuvellauni, now war-chief of the Silures and the western tribes, continued to harry and evade the Romans. Among the Iceni, argument about this news varied. The majority remained of a mind with the king: Caratacus was a fool who could not win, not against Rome. Others, more cynically, said that at least while Caratacus remained free in his mountains he was keeping the Roman legions busy and preventing them from bothering the tribes behind them.

But there were a few who regarded Caratacus as a hero, the only Briton to make an effective stand against the might of Rome; he was denying the enemy access to the sacred isle of Mona. Increasingly, Boudicca found herself agreeing with those who praised Caratacus's valour. The Roman yoke might be light as yet, but there would come a time when the reins bit deep and the goad would be felt. Eogan, Morica, and Boudicca's own prescient blood prophesied it.

Once again spring touched the land, though that year days

of steady rain prevented the ploughing and at the festival of the sun's manhood the furze fires across the heath burned fitfully, with much smoke. The cattle and sheep were driven out between the fires to rid them of demons, and at the sacrifice of lambs Prasutagus led the men in their leaping dance at the oak grove along the knoll, above the sacred pool. Eogan remained absent; of late he had been ever more elusive, some said on spying missions for his masters on Mona.

When all the fires were burned out, the children ran through the muddy fields scattering ashes to enrich the land, while farmers looked at the lowering skies and shook their heads. Despite their prayers, still the bright God hid his face. The crop would rot in such wet ground.

In the king's house, Boudicca watched with amusement as her own Rhiannon and Tadia's Cameira came home from the fields doused in mud and wet ashes, to be chafed over by old Cauva. The younglings were excited after their participation in the rites. They squabbled and squealed as they were stripped and plunged into a cauldron of water frothing with soapwort. Little Araunah looked on with wide bright eyes, clutching a doll to her breast, as the queen's slaves rubbed the two older girls dry on rough towels woven from nettle hemp.

This year would see Rhiannon's tenth summer. She was tall for her age, and straight, with a long mane of curling fair hair whose redness deepened with every season until it rivalled the colour of the red gold that formed Eogan's neck torc. As yet her body was a child's, pale and plump against the lither, darker contours of the older Cameira, but her eyes were disquieting, even to her mother. Calm, wide, watchful, at times those gold-flecked green eyes observed the world with unchildlike knowingness. In many ways, Rhiannon was older than her years, thanks to Morica's teaching. When the time came for her to take part in the Mysteries, the Maiden would be ready.

But in other ways, so her mother fretted, Rhiannon was very much a child still.

Often, Boudicca wondered what changes might have taken place by the time the Silver Wheel had turned in the sky and brought the beginning of the next Great Year and another Season of the Maiden. Eogan would be needed then. Would

Mona still be inviolate? At present Caratacus and his forces stood between the Romans and the sacred isle, but could they resist the legions for eight more years? What were the Druids doing – working on their magic to defend themselves? Eogan would never say, though he seemed to come and go as he pleased, passing his winters with his masters and somehow contriving to slip through the Roman lines to return again in spring to the forests of Icenia. He had a habit of appearing unexpectedly at moments when his advice was needed. The birds kept watch over the settlement for him, it was said; they took news to wherever he dwelt in the depths of the oak woods and so kept him informed.

Eogan appeared that year at summer's end, as the harvest was under way. Farmers, with their families and their serfs, bent in the fields with sickles, loading golden grain onto sleds that were dragged by oxen down to the winnowing sheds. Those who saw the oak seer coming out of the deep forests swore later that he materialised out of mist, and that three ravens had been seen circling round his head.

Stalking arrogantly with his wild beard and hair flowing in the wind, his craggy face expressionless, he came up the track leaning lightly on his tall ash staff with its gilded top, shaped in the spiral of immortality, catching hazy sunlight. His hair was shaven halfway back across his scalp, the rest left to grow unkempt, and he wore a gold ring dangling from one punctured earlobe. His tunic and trousers had faded to nondescript grey, and over his shoulder was slung a wolfskin on which were sewn the tails of other animals he had kept as friends – beaver, fox, stoat, wildcat. Around his scraggy neck he wore a torc of red gold, dug from the mountains of the west, and his every finger and thumb bore a ring with a gemstone. A dog ran howling away from him, its tail between its legs, and even Boudicca felt a sense of foreboding as she called her warriors to cease their spear-throwing.

She got down from her chariot, handing the reins to wraith-like Erefwen of the moon-pale hair as she stepped out to await the news Eogan brought. The Druid continued his stately progress until he was a stride away, looking her straight in the eye as one equal to another. Boudicca saw his grey eyes gleaming with inner fire and icy fingers seemed to walk up her spine, making her scalp prickle as his bass voice drummed from his thin frame.

'Caratacus has come out of the mountains. He has broken through the military line. The Romans are in disarray.'

This news made Boudicca catch her breath in admiration at Caratacus's boldness, and she heard a murmur of surprise and approval run among her warriors. 'What does he intend?' she asked.

'Perhaps to raise the other tribes to his banner,' Eogan said. 'Perhaps merely to alarm the enemy. His force is small. He may have to retreat to the safety of the west before the Romans close ranks behind him and cut him off. Who can say, lady? The Gods have not revealed the ending of it. But tell this to your husband the king . . .' He paused, raising his ash staff. In the sunlight, the stone set in the gold ring on his forefinger gleamed like blood, and when he spoke again his voice rolled sonorously in the ears of the attentive warriors. 'The day I foredoomed is coming! The Iceni will be forced to choose. Soon will the raven speak, the elder bloom, and the old moon rise in blood.'

The tiny hairs on Boudicca's nape and spine prickled, making her shiver, for he was prophesying death. 'For whom, Eogan?'

'For those who do not heed the warnings,' he replied with a flashing look. 'The message is given. Tell it to your husband, lady.' With that, he turned on his heel and began to stride back toward the busy fields.

She caught her breath at his insolence and injected a note of command into her voice, reminding him that she had power of her own as she called after him, 'Eogan!'

Three more strides he took before pausing to look over his shoulder at her. 'Lady?'

'The king will prefer to hear the message from your own lips.'

'No, lady,' the bass voice replied. 'The king hears only what he wants to hear. I am needed elsewhere.' But he turned fully to face the warriors, lifting his ash staff high over his head as he cried, 'Truth be in your hearts, strength in your arms, and fulfilment in your tongues!'

His voice still rang in Boudicca's ears as he paced away

down the slope. She had heard the blessing many times, but it had never sounded so awesome as it did on that day.

Boudicca found her husband indoors by the fire despite the warmth of the day. On his knee, little Araunah sat, enchanted by the magic he was working for her amusement, making a silver coin vanish and appear from her ear, or the folds of her tunic. She laughed up at him, teasing him by pulling at his beard until he retaliated by tickling her until she squealed. For this, at least, Boudicca was grateful to him – he had made a favourite of frail Araunah.

Putting the little girl down, Prasutagus watched her trot away to where her dolls lay scattered on a blanket among sleeping hounds. Only then did he give his full attention to his wife, hearing the Druid's message with impatience as he strode about the reed-strewn floor. 'Eogan speaks in riddles – as always. Why didn't he come himself?'

'He said you wouldn't listen. And it seems he was right!'

He swung on her, an arm flung out. 'Am I to pay heed to an old man's prattling? He spends too long in his forests. His mind is turning.'

'He prophesies death!'

'He always prophesies death!'

'Do you refuse to listen to a message from the Gods?'

His pale eyes pierced her with a look that warned her not to go too far. 'I refuse to listen to a message from Mona! The Druids are not the Gods, though they may think they are.' But, seeing that she was troubled, he relented and reached out for her. 'Boudicca . . .'

She recoiled from him, too angry to bear the thought of his hands on her. Seeing it, he tightened his mouth into bitter lines. 'So what is your will?' he asked. 'That we summon our warriors to war, to join Caratacus? Where shall we find him? What reason shall we give for our rebellion? And when we're defeated, as the Catuvellauni were so soundly defeated despite their strength, will you submit to being dragged in chains to Rome and sold for slavery?'

'I would die first! With a sword in my hand!'

'And your children?'

The question smote her to the heart. The children! Rhiannon, and helpless little Araunah . . . She glanced to where her younger daughter was playing with the dogs, long thin hair straggling across a thin cheek with skin so fair that blue veins showed through. The visions roused by Prasutagus's words made Boudicca feel chilled.

'Eogan would see us all dead before he gave up one handsbreadth of Mona,' Prasutagus said. 'Are you queen of the Druids, or queen of the Iceni, Boudicca?'

She stared at him narrowly, wondering what was in his mind. 'I'm queen of the Iceni,' she replied at last, her voice firm, her head high as she returned him look for look. 'I'm the daughter of an Icenian queen, and my daughter will be queen after me. The Goddess ordered it that way, from the time of blessed Brecca. No man can change divine law.'

This reply only made him smile, slowly and sadly, his scarred left eye drooping until it was almost shut. That happened when he was tired, she thought. Was he feeling his age? He said, 'You stare at me so challengingly, Boudicca. Do you really believe I want to usurp your place here?'

'Don't you?' she demanded.

He shook his head, searching every feature of her face. 'I only ever wanted one thing – to guard you. To care for you.'

To own me! she thought. 'You wanted the power you got through marrying me!'

For a moment he watched her sorrowfully, as if he had hoped for a different answer. Then he stroked his moustache with a thumb and forefinger, and turned away. 'Perhaps that, too. But never to replace you. Only to make sure you were strong enough to rule alone when I'm gone.' He glanced back at her, repeating the word, 'Alone. Or will you take another husband?'

Discomforted by the question, she felt her cheeks heat with blood. The image of Garanhir stood suddenly between them. It was a long time since she had allowed herself to think about her personal life. Now she discovered she was no longer so sure of what she felt and in an habitual gesture she reached for comfort to hold the pink quartz ring that hung on a leather thong at her breast. 'I'll consider that when the time comes.'

For a moment he watched her from his eye corner, then said quietly. 'I ended it for your sake. A queen should have the respect of her people. If they had known – '

'I have their respect!' she broke in, her hands clenched. She didn't believe him. He had separated her from Garanhir for reasons of his own. Was he making excuses now, seeking her understanding and perhaps her forgiveness? 'I have their love, and their support. They know I would die for them – as Garanhir would die for you.' The words spilled out of her. 'The fault was mine, not his.'

Prasutagus seemed to shrivel in upon himself as he turned away from her, his shoulders drooping, his back bent as if he were too weary to argue. 'I no longer blame either of you. It's done, Boudicca. For you, the future is what matters. You must take care. You'll need all the strengths you can gather to your side, if our daughters are to have anything left of their heritage.'

This was unlike him. Was he ill? He sounded almost defeated. But . . . 'our daughters' – the phrase made surprise twist inside her, mingled with a reluctant pity; neither of the girls was his child, yet obviously he thought of them as such, especially Araunah. Perhaps it was his way of coping with his impotence. All at once she knew that he was a lonely man behind his armour of pride, a cold man who wished himself otherwise, who longed for affection but was incapable of love. Had she been unkind to him? Had she misjudged him? Certainly she had never understood him.

She lifted a hand but hesitated before she could obey the impulse to touch him. Letting her hand fall to her side, she said, 'I shall be strong. I *am* strong.' But the thought of ruling alone was daunting; she wasn't ready for it. 'You're not ill, are you?'

'No. No. I'm only tired.'

She wanted to offer him some comfort but couldn't think of the words. 'I . . . I'm grateful. You've always been . . . kind.'

A breath escaped him – a sigh? a short, choked-off laugh? She couldn't tell. He straightened himself and looked round over his shoulder, his wry eye mocking her. 'Thank you, lady. I'm grateful for your gratitude. Now go back to your fledgeling warriors. Train them. Train them hard. When the storm breaks they'll be needed.'

'Storm?' she snatched at the word, her brow puckering as she stared at him. 'Do you feel it, too – a storm coming? The Romans?'

'Of course it will come! Too many people are itching for it.' He turned fully to face her, anger brightening his eyes and staining his cheeks. 'But while I live I'll stand against them, Boudicca. While I live, we shall have peace!'

Two moons after Eogan's visit, when the nights were lengthening and the days darkening toward Samhain, watch-horns announced the approach of a rider who beat with hands and feet at his weary, muddied mount. He was recognised as Iceni, a messenger from Mocuxsoris's clan, and the gates were opened to admit him. He rode shouting through the settlement, scattering dogs and geese as people stopped what they were doing and came running to see what was amiss. Near exhaustion, the man half fell from his sweat-lathered mount and grasped eagerly for the cup of ale that was brought to him as he sank to his knees on a carpet of crisp yellow leaves fallen from the sacred oak.

Boudicca emerged from her house and hurried to the meeting place, pushing between the people who were gathered to hear the man's news. He drank deep before looking wildly round at his audience with ale foam thick on his moustache. 'Lords . . . warriors . . . The Romans . . . they're coming to disarm us!'

A stir of disquiet moved among the Iceni as the messenger gulped the rest of his barley ale, and Prasutagus came from the hall with a group of elders. As the crowd parted to let them through, Boudicca cried, 'We have a treaty! They wouldn't dare be so treacherous. What reasons do they give?'

'It's because of Caratacus, lady,' the messenger gasped. 'Your brother sent me to warn you – they're going to take our swords so we can't join with Caratacus against them.'

'What nonsense is this?' Prasutagus demanded.

The man wiped the back of his wrist across his mouth, his eyes wild beneath a shock of tumbled hair. 'Mocuxsoris had word, from Camulodunon. It's true, lord! The governor-general has ordered his soldiers to come and take our weapons, for fear we might use them to help Caratacus. They're going to disarm all the tribes – all of us behind their frontier – and leave us with only spears for hunting.'

Coeling rasped his sword from its sheath, his face dark with anger. 'I'll kill any man who tries to take Blood-fury from me.'

Cries of agreement rose as several warriors drew their treasured swords, symbols of manhood and freedom, dedicated to the Gods and lavished with expensive decoration. Sharing their sense of outrage, Boudicca opened her mouth to speak, only to be stopped by a sharp, 'Wait!' from Prasutagus.

He stepped out from the group of elders, his hands lifted for silence. 'How do we know this news is true?' he demanded of the angry warriors.

'Lord!' The messenger raised his voice, kneeling with the cup clasped between his hands as he stared anxiously up at the king. 'By oak and wren, I swear it's the truth! They've already disarmed the Trinovantes at Camulodunon. The word came direct from Vindorex, the Trinovante chief. Prince Mocuxsoris begs that you rise with him to avenge this insult. He'll stand guard for Icenia and slay any Roman who dares come near our borders. But he needs more warriors.'

'We go to join Mocuxsoris!' shouted the voice of Duihno.

The king sought him out among the crowd, fixing him with a piercing glance. 'You, Diuhno – be silent! Through your rashness we lost Urien and his farm. None here will follow your lead, not for many moons. The council will debate, calmly. Disperse yourselves and await our judgement.' He spun on his heel, walking away towards the great hall with Boudicca and the elders around him.

Knowing that her heart agreed with the hot-blooded Duihno, Boudicca sat with the council and the two champions while argument raged. They brought in the messenger to repeat his tale more calmly, though its substance remained the same: having heard that the Romans were about to disarm the friendly tribes, including the Iceni, the furious Mocuxsoris was preparing to defy them.

'I don't believe this rumour,' Summac said, glaring with his one good eye. 'The Romans can't believe that we would rise at Caratacus's bidding. He's our sworn enemy.'

'He's a Briton,' Coeling argued. 'He's of our own kind. I believe this news. I'd believe anything of the Romans. Hasn't Eogan warned us not to trust them?'

Prasutagus drew a sharp breath. 'The Druids interfere too much in matters that don't concern them! They twist the truth into shapes that best suit their own purpose, which is to protect what they care for most – themselves and their sacred isle. The Romans are our allies. We have no reason to mistrust them. We must give them no reason to mistrust us.'

'They've given us much,' old Vassedo agreed, nodding his white head as he fingered the gold chain that hung long round his withered neck. 'I never thought I'd live long enough to be wealthy as I am now, though in my youth I enjoyed a fight. Even so, a man's sword is part of him, closer than a wife.'

Unable to contain her anger any longer, Boudicca leapt to her feet. 'Cowards! Will you turn us all into peasants and farmers? Without our swords we're nothing! Shall our warriors take to the plough? I say we go! We go to stand with Mocuxsoris my brother!'

'I, too,' brawny Nuadat declared, standing beside her just as Garanhir got to his feet and said, 'We go!'

Prasutagus looked at the three of them, stroking his beard. 'So speaks the youth of the tribe. Three votes for war. Three votes for a battle that will bring the Romans to tramp over us with iron-shod feet. Three votes to destroy all we have gained since the treaty at Camulodunon.'

'Four votes!' Coeling declared, rising to his feet.

There remained eleven council members, some who backed Prasutagus and others who were torn. Segovax the lawgiver, and Alvran the bard, both of them Druid-trained, decided for Boudicca and for battle, but the rest remained stubborn. They were enjoying their new wealth and the luxuries brought by the Roman peace; they were not ready to risk those things solely on the word of Mocuxsoris, who had long ago declared himself against any alliance with Rome. He had been waiting for an excuse, it was said, and now that a fortuitous rumour had come he risked bringing dishonour on all the Iceni, and probably death on himself and those who stood with him. To a Celt, his sword was not only a weapon but a sacred trust he held from the Gods, a symbol of his manhood; the Romans must know this. They wouldn't be so foolish as to insult their allies by taking away their manhood.

Furious, Boudicca stormed from the hall and paused outside in bright autumn sunlight, breathing heavily, aware of Nuadat and Garanhir behind her. She turned to them, her hands flung out. 'Shall we heed the old men?'

'Lady, we must,' Garanhir said, though his eyes told her

he disliked saying it. 'The council makes the law. If they decide for the king, who can blame them? He hasn't led us wrong so far.'

'So far!' But because this was Garanhir she held back her temper. 'It was bold of you – the king's champion voting against his lord.'

'In all honour, I had to speak out,' he replied. 'But now that the decision is made I'll defend it.'

'In all honour!' she mocked him, her fury turning against him. 'Nuadat, inform the warriors that we shall not be riding to join Mocuxsoris. Not yet!'

Saluting her, Nuadat strode away to where the warriors were waiting in groups near the oak. She heard their shouts of disbelief and disgust, saw them begin to argue. Only then did she look again at Garanhir and saw that she had wounded him. Some weak womanly part of her wanted to apologise. But she refused to listen. She was too angry. How dared he reprove her with his look, make her feel guilty? She owed him nothing. She was queen of the Iceni, but everything moved to frustrate her.

Only three days later, when driving rain kept most people under shelter, the cry of the watchhorn again drew Boudicca from the children and her loom. As she stepped to the doorway, she saw Unthaus riding in haste to slide from his dripping horse at the pathway of the queen's house. His hair was lank and wet round a young face marred by a scar that sliced from eye to ear. He had got the wound last Solstice in yet another disagreement with Audagas's warriors.

'There are men coming!' he cried, pausing to salute Boudicca, who gestured him to come into the house where Prasutagus was taking his ease with Coeling and others. His wet cloak brushed her arm as he passed and straightened to salute the king with a fist touched to the tattoo on his brow. 'A party of riders, lord. We met them on the road. Nuadat and the others stayed to keep an eye on them. They say they're Trinovantes, from Camulodunon. The leader calls himself Vindorex. He claims the right of friendship and the shelter of Oakhillfort.'

Startled, Boudicca shared a look with her husband, who rose to his feet a little stiffly, saying, 'I know the man. Let him come in. Shelter he shall have, at least until we discover his purpose. As to friendship . . . let us first be sure he brings no trouble after him.'

Wearing rainproof cloaks of thick, untreated wool rich with natural water-repellent oils, with wide hoods that kept the rain from their faces, Boudicca and her husband went out to meet the visitors. They rode in, flanked on either side by a line of watchful Iceni warriors returning from the hunt with their spoils. The Trinovantes were a sorry, sodden group, grim-faced and hungry-looking, as though they had endured a long and bitter journey. At their head rode Vindorex, wearing a leathern cloak with his dark hair flattened wetly to his head. Through rivulets of rain that dripped down his face, he stared with the eyes of a man who has learned to hate so bitterly that his soul has no room for gentler feelings. The change in him shocked Boudicca.

Drawing level with the Iceni king and queen, Vindorex slid from his horse, only willpower preventing his legs from buckling. He held himself stiff and proud despite his evident weariness as he turned aside and caught at the reins of a following horse, which carried two people – a youth and a younger girl. Boudicca recognised the boy as Vindorex's son, Farann, grown now to early adolescence but retaining that still watchfulness she had noted when they first met. The girl, who had the same dark hair, must be Farann's sister. How cold and miserable they both looked, hair wet, clothes damp. The girl's eyes were rimmed with red, as if she had wept for many nights. She stared fearfully at the people gathered about her, her unhappiness calling to Boudicca's maternal instincts.

Drawing the horse forward, Vindorex saluted Prasutagus, saying, 'Lord of the Iceni, these are my children. For them I beg the safety of your hall. And . . .' He hesitated, sending a tortured glance at Boudicca. 'I have news that must be told. We were riding to join Mocuxsoris but . . . we were too late. Long before we reached the fort we saw the great black cloud of smoke in the sky. The Romans had burst through the gates. They had set torch to houses and barns, smashed down everything they could find, driven off the livestock . . .'

Boudicca found her hand at her throat. She could hardly breathe for a weight of fear that pressed on her breast. 'And

Mocuxsoris?' she asked. 'What of my brother? And his children? His three young sons?'

Vindorex turned his shadowed eyes on her. 'Dead. Slain. All of them. Men, women, children . . . Lying in blood and ashes. There was nothing left, lady. Nothing that still breathed.'

Searching the bleak faces of his companions, and then the grim hard eyes of her own warriors, Boudicca found reflected there the truth she had to bear. Eogan's prophecy was fulfilled: Mocuxsoris was dead. Mocuxsoris the bold – Mocuxsoris her beloved, laughing brother, had perished by sword and fire, his wife, his young sons and all his people with him.

Ten

Though her eyes ached with unshed tears, hospitality demanded that Boudicca see first to her guests. Slaves were sent scurrying after food and drink, horses led away to be rubbed down, weary men taken to shelter and warmth. Boudicca herself carried Vindorex's daughter into the queen's house and left her in Cauva's care.

The girl's name was Cunovinda; she was almost of an age with Rhiannon. She had with her a jointed wooden doll that she clutched in her hand as though it were of great importance to her. Soon she was bathed, dressed in clean dry clothes and taken under the wing of a curious Rhiannon and Cameira, with little Araunah trailing behind. Cunovinda was young enough to be resilient. Whatever the hardships behind her, she would learn to adjust.

The boy, her brother, though, was different. Watching him among the youths of the king's household, Boudicca sensed his apartness, his self-containment. A proud one, this Farann, for all his small stature. In the first moments he managed to antagonise the twins, fifteen-year-old Matuac and Ylas, who came swaggering round him expecting the newcomer to match their boasting bluster. They were older and bigger than he, husky and fair against his dark slightness, but their overtures were met with a cold disdain that obviously baffled them.

They withdrew to a distance, heads together as they worked out a strategy with which to meet this new challenge.

Boudicca watched it all happening as if from behind a veil. For Mocuxsoris was dead and never again would she see his bold grin or hear him laugh and call her sister. His absence left a void that could never be filled.

Holding herself erect with an effort, she swept aside the curtain that guarded her own room from the throng of the main living area and sank down on her bed. Hands to her face, she rocked back and forth moaning, keening. Now she recalled that she had heard geese crying only last night, sounding like the spectral hounds of Gwyn the white rider leading the autumnal chase. The soul of Mocuxsoris must have been with them. He was gone, gone with the wild geese to the back of the north wind, gone to dwell in the Glass Castle of Arianrhod. Gone . . . Tears came now, hot and bitter, and Boudicca threw herself down to beat at her pallet and howl out her grief for her brother.

That night, Vindorex and his small band of warriors feasted in the great hall among the Iceni, and when the last bones had been gnawed and tossed to the dogs a demand arose for Alvran to sing the song he had made for Mocuxsoris. The bard strode to the centre of the hall and strolled round the fire plucking music from his lyre as he recounted the history of the queen's only brother, with all his deeds and honours. When he finished, hardly an eye in the hall had failed to mist with tears and Boudicca found herself weeping again. It would be a long time before she forgot her grief.

After a silence that spoke much of the tribe's high feeling for the lost prince, Prasutagus called for Vindorex to tell his tale at more length. The Trinovante, his face still bleak and dark, drained his horn of good honest ale – he had refused to touch Roman wine – and strode out to the centre of the hall, while Alvran the bard struck accompanying chords.

But if the audience expected poetry and tales of heroism from Vindorex, they were disappointed. He was no bard but a man of plain speech, a soldier, and his story was of defeat and depredation, of the slow disillusionment of his people as the Roman yoke tightened.

'Oh, yes, they made promises. We, too, had a treaty. But still they made our people work for them like slaves, to house and feed them; they took our young men for their armies, our girls as their whores; they cut down our sacred oak grove to build their fortress – and built it against our stronghold, inside the banks of Camulodunon; and then only a few nights ago they took our swords, our very manhood!'

'Then why didn't you fight them?' someone yelled. 'Why didn't you die like Mocuxsoris, defending your honour?'

Vindorex whirled on the man who had interrupted, and in his thin face his eyes flashed. 'Because we had no warning. They came fully armed, two centuries of them, right up to my hall. We had no choice but to hand over our swords. There was nothing we could do – which is why I sent word to Mocuxsoris, to warn the Iceni what was coming.'

'Cowards!' came the accusation.

This time Vindorex didn't deign to seek out the person who had spoken. Instead he drew himself up, lean and dark-visaged as Bran the Raven, and though his voice was low it shook with a passion that silenced every corner of the hall. 'Don't judge me in your ignorance! You know nothing of Roman treachery. I've seen it at first hand, in Rome itself. I've lived with it in my own lands for seven years now. At Camulodunon we're caught at the centre. Soliders and spies surround us everywhere. I send complaints to the procurator – he files them away. I go in person – he's too busy to see me. We're less than nothing to these arrogant "allies" of ours. Barbarians, that's all. You think you're safe because you signed a treaty? Fools! You're only safe until it's your turn for the boot on the neck, the sword in the ribs. The treaty protects them, not you! It keeps you quiet until they're ready to move against you.'

'Enough!' Prasutagus was on his feet, his face white with fury. Beside him, Boudicca saw the tightness of his clenched fist and felt him shake with the intensity of his emotion. Slowly the shouts of agreement died around the hall, but Vindorex turned defiant eyes on his host.

'I was asked to speak,' he said, low-voiced.

'Then speak,' Prasutagus. 'But I'll hear no hate-fevered war talk from a guest in my hall – or from my warriors!' As he spoke he glared fiercely about him, daring any man or woman to argue. 'With the example of Mocuxsoris before us we must all keep clear heads. He acted rashly. He may have sealed the fate of us all. The Romans know too much about war. How can we hope to stand against a race who have mastered the world? Is this why you've come to Oakhillfort, Vindorex – in the hopes of fermenting an uprising, so that we all might follow Mocuxsoris to the Blessed Plain of Forgetfulness?'

Vindorex's smile was bleak. 'No, Lord. I came only to seek your protection for my children, and weapons for my men. I've no place to go, except into the forests to live like a brigand – or to join the warband of Caractacus. My heritage is lost to me.'

'Explain!' the king rasped.

'I intend to, lord, with your leave. You may judge for yourself whether my grievance is just or not.' He took a breath and spoke in quiet, bitter tones. 'When they disarmed us, they told us they intend to take our lands for their own use. We must leave the place where Trinovante chiefs have ruled down the ages. Camulodunon is to be parcelled out as a gratuity to retiring veterans of the legions, who will build a town there and form a military reserve – a trained force to keep the southern tribes under control while the active legions patrol the frontier.'

Shouts of surprise, disbelief and alarm greeted this news and Vindorex let the noise run down into murmurs before he nodded grimly at those about him. 'These men, these . . . "veterans", have been gathering to make winter camp by our river. They're hard men, and they're sour at being forced to retire in misty Albion instead of going back to a place in the sun. Already we've had examples of the fate that lies in store for any Briton within reach of their bile.

'So – our capital is taken from us, but by gracious consent of the Emperor we Trinovantes are to be given a new home – a place that will have to be wrested from forests and scrubland and salty sea marshes. And that's not the last of it.' As the murmurs grew again he raised his voice, speaking louder and faster as bitterness spurted inside him, 'They've already named our new home. It's to be called Caesaromagus – in honour of the divine Claudius, who although he remains on this earth has been declared a God by his faithful sycophants. For him, a temple is to be built and dedicated at Camulodunon – a temple that must be served and paid for by us – by the grateful Trinovantes in thanks for their liberation.'

He paused, glancing round at his listeners, and as the shouts of horror and alarm grew among them he turned again to Prasutagus. 'So you see, lord, that I and my people have learned to be wary of Roman friendship. We, too, had a treaty. We, too, believed ourselves safe. But when they took our swords we learned the truth – too late. There was nothing left for us – nothing but the prospect of living cowed and defeated. My men and I agreed then that we would not submit.

'In guise of going hunting we left Camulodunon – with my daughter hidden under my cloak. By devious forest paths we came to the Way and the borders of Icenia, intending to stand with Mocuxsoris – intending to die rather than live in shame.' He paused, sighed, made a gesture of futility as his glance turned to Boudicca. 'Again we were too late. Lady, I regret it bitterly. I would have been proud to die with Mocuxsoris your brother.

'Now I have only my children, and my pride in myself, by which I've sworn to live free and to strive with fate until the Romans leave Albina's Isle or until the breath goes up from my body. I shall fight, lady, and my men with me. But someone must care for my children. Until the Gods grant me victory or death, I beg that you protect my son and my daughter. Will you do this, queen of the Iceni, for the only surviving blood of the royal house that bred Addedomarus?'

Boudicca rose to her feet as a hush descended and in the silence her voice was husky with weeping, not only for her brother now but for Vindorex and the younglings. 'The Goddess Herself must see that your cause is just, Vindorex. Your children have found a home here.'

'Your children,' Prasutagus added in a harsh voice. 'But you and your men must leave, Vindorex. If the Romans suspect we've given aid to rebels . . .'

A thin smile twisted at Vindorex's lips. 'We'll leave tonight, lord, rather than embarrass you longer. But we'll need swords. You might as well give them to us rather than to the

Romans. They'll be here in the morning – probably wanting explanations for Mocuxsoris's rebellion.'

'In the morning?' Prasutagus repeated. 'How can you be sure of that?'

'We had to make a detour through the marshes to avoid them. They were making camp along the Way when we passed.'

Vindorex and his men were gone before daybreak, but his warning proved true. That damp October dawn a daunting force of well-armed soldiers marched up to the gates of Oak-hillfort, four centuries of men under the command of a grizzled veteran, and with them an auxiliary regiment of deadly bowmen from Thrace. An unforgiving Quintilius Vitalis rode at their head.

Why had Mocuxsoris been allowed to rebel? the tribune demanded. Was this not a flouting of the treaty?

It took all Prasutagus's skill in diplomacy to persuade the grim ambassador that Mocuxsoris had stood alone, that the rest of the tribe had refused to rise with him. There had been no time to send warnings to Camulodunon; indeed, the Iceni had scarce believed the rumours that their allies were about to disarm them. Then, suddenly, it had all been over. The king regretted the incident, but would not be held responsible for the actions of one hot-blooded individual among his chiefs.

Vitalis declared that he believed the king, of course he did, but to be sure he must divest the Iceni of their weapons – before any more 'hot-blooded individuals' could disobey their council's advice and put the treaty at risk. Prasutagus could understand that, couldn't he? It was a matter for regret, but Vitalis had his orders. He must take away every weapon the Iceni had, except for their small knives and enough hunting spears to keep them in deer meat.

Under the tacit threat from overwhelming numbers of frowning legionaries and ready Thracian arrows, the Iceni had little choice. Stunned and demoralised by the loss of Mocuxsoris and all his people, the warriors gave up their cherished swords, with dark looks and muttered curses against those who unmanned them.

As an added insult, the legionaries searched the whole settlement to make sure no weapons had been hidden away from them. They roughly pushed into each house and barn, each roof and room, tossing over pallets, upsetting cooking pots and looms, frightening babies. Every action, every curse, every glance displayed the soldiers' contempt for those they regarded as conquered barbarians. Their brutality and their arrogance were noted by a people who were learning the meaning of resentment.

Boudicca knew she would never forget the day when common soldiers from a far foreign land shouldered her, the queen of Icenia, aside and searched every inch of her private chamber while her two daughters clung to her side, wide-eyed with bewilderment, and her warriors stood helpless under the threat of death. The Romans, to her distress and rage, even took the sword that had swung so sweetly in the hand of Huan of the Caledones. For that alone she would never forgive them.

Fortunately the intruders were too intent on looking for weapons to notice two dark-haired young Trinovantes among the youth of the queen's household. Vindorex's children were hidden as securely as new stars in the night sky, so obvious that no one gave them a second glance. It was a small triumph on a day of bitter defeat.

And Eogan had prophesised it, had he not? *The Iceni will be forced to choose! Soon the raven will speak, the elder bloom, the old moon rise in blood*. The Druid's prescient words of approaching doom rang through Boudicca's mind. Well, the Iceni had chosen, Mocuxsoris for his way, the royal house for theirs. One way had brought death, the other dishonour. Had there been a third course?

A further blow came to dampen the morale of the Iceni when they learned that bold Caratacus had at last been captured. He had come out of his mountains and sought refuge with Cartimandua, queen of the Brigantes, only to have that sour matron bind him in chains and hand him over to the Roman governor-general, along with his wife and children.

But though they had lost a great leader the people of the western mountains continued to harry and defy the Romans, denying them the road to the sacred isle of Mona.

An uneasy, sullen quietness fell over the south, but Albion's people were not, as Mocuxsoris had once said, come to heel suitably cowed; no, they were only waiting, for the moment Boudicca was still sure would arrive, however distant in time. Her instincts, and all the portents she read in the formation of clouds, the movement of horses, the flight of birds, told of a great struggle yet to come. She and her people must use this time of quietness to prepare.

Though Boudicca continued to grieve for her brother and his family, and for the other Iceni who had met their deaths at the hands of Rome, she began to see that Prasutagus had been wise, after all, to preach caution. Dearly as she had loved her brother, much as she understood how he had felt, Mocuxsoris had acted rashly; his rebellion had been too hastily conceived, with no real strategy but that formed in hot and angry blood. Even Caratacus, who had fought so long and bravely, had failed, in the end. Boldness and determination were not enough: to destroy the Romans would take coolness and cunning.

It was a lesson the queen of the Iceni learned well.

BOOK TWO

The Maiden Rhiannon

One

A light wicker chariot careered down the slope towards the woods, its two wheels bouncing, its ponies urged on at reckless speed by a girl whose long bright hair tossed in the sunlight. The boy beside her made frantic attempts to regain the reins, but though he was the older he was no bigger and Rhiannon easily kept him off with jabs of her sharp elbow.

Boucidda's older daughter was now twelve-years-old, tall for her age but still boyishly slender, her high cheekbones scattered with freckles to set off wide eyes of green flecked with gold. Bronze brooches adorned her fine linen shirt, which was dyed green and fastened with leather thongs, worn loose outside her spotted kidskin trousers. In the belt knotted about her waist she carried a sling, and a dagger in a richly enamelled sheath.

Though her arms and back ached with the strain of controlling the chariot her flexed knees effortlessly countered its bucking. She was hardly aware of the peril that threatened, or of Teyrnon's pleas that she stop. Her whole attention was fixed on the woods where, behind banks of white hawthorn blossom, glimpses of a white flank and the toss of a white mane lured her on.

'Rhiannon!' The boy's clear treble cracked on the name. 'Rhiannon, stop! Please stop!'

'No!' she cried, using her long whip though the horses were already plunging and snorting. 'Can't you see Her – the White Mare? The Goddess beckons me, Teyrnon. She wants me to follow.'

Again he lunged for the reins. Again she shouldered him aside with a strength that seemed more than her own. He lost his footing. Down on one knee, he clung on in fright, salt sweat biting at his eyes. Rhiannon seemed possessed.

Her skin looked translucent in the heat and her eyes were wide, the pupils expanded and dark, seeing visions. Her feyness awed and terrified him. She was the Maiden. If the Goddess was calling her, he, Teyrnon, had no right to interfere. But he could see no white mare. All he could see was the tangle of trees and undergrowth towards which the chariot was heading, seemingly intent on disaster.

'You must stop!' he yelled, grabbing again for the reins, shouting orders to the horses as he tried to bring them round in a circle short of the trees.

'No!' Her nails slashed for his eyes and as he swayed aside to avoid the blow the chariot jounced. A vicious lurch of Rhiannon's hip made him lose his balance. He was thrown out, but with an athlete's grace he twisted to make a good landing, somersaulted on the grass and gained his feet only slightly breathless as the chariot raced on without him. Rhiannon glanced round once, as if to assure herself of his safety, then she needed all her skill to steer the ponies into a gap among the trees, onto a faint hunters' track that seemed to open in front of her.

Branches slapped at her face and caught at her hair. The sun's glitter turned into a dazzle of gold and green like shimmers on a pool and sounds faded to a murmur. It was as though she had driven into deep, clear water and now was floating weightless.

With a jolt the chariot stopped. Rhiannon was thrown forward, between the horses. Pain wrenched up her arm as she flung out a hand to deflect herself from the central pole that held the yoke and her other hand grasped a handful of one pony's rough mane. For a moment she hung there among tall grasses and blackberry briars that scratched and pricked, her nostrils full of the scent of over-heated horse, her mind spinning.

Slowly, the enchantment faded. Heart thudding fast and heavy, she scrambled clear and stood easing her wrenched arm. She was deep in an unfamiliar part of the woods, alone but for the birds and her two unsettled horses, whose legs were tangled among blackberry briars. A fallen branch had forked itself against a spoke of one of the wheels – that was what had stopped their headlong flight. The ponies stamped uneasily, tossing their crested manes, sweat darkening their hides.

Now that her brain was clearing, Rhiannon recognised that she had been under a spell sent by the Goddess. Sometimes Dia came without warning and took over the thoughts and actions of Her Maiden. It was She who had persuaded Teyrnon to let Rhiannon handle the chariot. Poor Teyrnon was easy enough to cajole, half in awe of Rhiannon, half mesmerised by her. All he really understood was the handling of horses. Rhiannon felt guilty for the way she had used him. Had it really been the Goddess's doing, or was it her own wilfulness that had made her behave so recklessly?

Then she heard the snuffling. She spun round, a hand jerking the sling from her belt as the undergrowth rustled. With a sound that was half scream and half roar a great black boar pushed out from the shelter of a hazel bush where it had been grubbing and stood eyeing her. Rhiannon stumbled to the flimsy protection of the chariot. Her fingers sought in her pouch for a suitable stone to arm her sling while her eyes fixed in terror on the boar.

It was an enormous animal, quivering with hatred of humankind. Its tusks looked sharp as spears, jutting from its blunt and dripping muzzle; its eyes were glints of fury buried deep in folds of leathery skin from which thick bristles stood out. The horses began to scream in fright, plunging and tugging against the chariot until it threatened to shake Rhiannon off her feet.

She threw a stone. It bounced off the boar's snout, causing the beast to squeal and pause in surprise. She felt enthralled by its rage-reddened eyes, though her mind was working. Boars were sacred to the Goddess in Her most deadly aspect – Caridwen, the Hag, the Great White Sow, Dark Winnower of Souls. Had She sent this boar to claim the life of Her Maiden?

Before Rhiannon could move, a spear flashed in the sunlight, embedding itself at an angle in the boar's flank. The animal squealed with pain and fury, turning aside as a shaggy grey hound leapt into the clearing to the attack. The dog was young and unwary. A slashing thrust of deadly tusks bit deep into its flank and sent it spinning away to crawl into the undergrowth and let its lifeblood pulse out.

But in the same moment a guttural yell gave Rhiannon hope. A sturdy youth with a mane of thick fair hair appeared with knife drawn to defend her.

Her heart soared with relief at sight of her kinsman Ylas. As the boar charged, he leapt aside and grabbed for the trailing spear, but the animal twisted with startling speed and its bloodied tusk gashed Ylas's calf. He landed awkwardly, and fell. At once the boar was on him, slashing with its tusks. Rhiannon's scream split the air. Ylas tried to get up. The boar attacked with murderous cries. The youth toppled into bushes, the animal after him, blood flying . . .

Suddenly the clearing erupted with shouting warriors and barking dogs all intent on saving Ylas. Among them, in the confusion, Rhiannon recognised Matuac, Ylas's twin, and Unthaus with his grave, scarred face. The boar whirled on them, caught in a circle of barking, leaping, snapping hounds and razor-sharp iron that jabbed and feinted, keeping the animal at bay.

Maddened by fear and pain, the boar made a rush for freedom, straight for the chariot where Rhiannon stood. But a figure intervened – the Trinovante, Farann, a tall, lanky youth with dark hair and sun-browned skin. The boar charged at him, impaling itself on the point of his spear. Its weight sent Farann staggering backwards, against the chariot's spindly wheel. Rhiannon saw his muscles straining, his teeth in a rictus of effort showing white against his dark skin, but he held the boar, leaning into the spear until with a jerk the blade got past hard bone and plunged to the animal's heart. With a shudder, the boar stopped fighting, its legs buckled and it toppled onto its side with a thud that seemed to shake the earth.

As Rhiannon jumped down to the grass, she darted a silent message of gratitude at Farann, but beneath a tumble of thick dark hair his expression was hard and unreadable as ever. She turned away, a flush burning in her cheeks. Farann had always been an outsider; if he chose to remain so, letting his stubborn aloofness be a constant reminder that he was not of the Iceni, then so be it. Rhiannon was more concerned for Ylas.

Her young kinsman lay on the grass, blood oozing from wounds that seemed to cover his limbs and body; his face was pale, the blue all-seeing eye tattoo on his brow almost hidden under a coating of bloodied dirt and sweat. But he was conscious, and still grinning, if feebly, trying to cheer up his worried twin, Matuac, who bent over him like a mirror-image.

'Don't worry, I'll not die,' Ylas was saying, though his voice was weak and filled with pain. 'Look, here's Rhia. Ask her. She'll tell you the Goddess doesn't want *me* at Her Glass Castle, not yet.'

Matuac looked up at Rhiannon, his washed-blue eyes anxious in a face smeared with sweat and traces of his brother's blood. The twins weren't quite alike, she thought; though both were tall, sturdy, fair, with sharp noses and wide mouths, Matuac's expression was more guarded, his eyes swift to narrow and hide his thoughts, where Ylas was all open sunlight. 'Are you all right?' Matuac asked her first and, when she nodded, added, 'He's hurt, Rhiannon. He's badly hurt. What shall we do?'

'We'll take him home to Oakhillfort,' she said.

Matuac's eyes widened with dismay. 'In the hawthorn month?'

'Well, what else will you do?' she demanded. 'Leave him to die? Or is Eogan somewhere near? He could tend Ylas.'

His expression told her this was a vain hope, even before Unthaus said in his usual grave way, 'Eogan's far away. Ylas will die before we get there.'

'Then we must take him home,' Rhiannon said. 'You don't all have to come. One or two of you will be enough. I'll speak for you if my mother's angry.'

Though she was sick to the heart with worry, for Ylas had slipped into unconsciousness and his blood stained the grass all about him, Rhiannon tended him with leaves and herbs, stemming the bleeding as best she could and binding his wounds with strips from Matuac's shirt. Then the young men carried him tenderly to lay him in her chariot, which some of them had freed from its detaining branch.

By now, young Teyrnon had found them, his eyes asking for the meaning behind what had happened. Rhiannon couldn't explain it, even to herself. Her head felt heavy now, as it often did in the aftermath of an enchantment.

*

The sound of wailing brought Boudicca out from the queen's house to see the sorry procession riding slowly down the track. They were accompanied by a growing group of concerned women and girls and led by two stern-faced warrior-maidens of the queen's guard. Matuac and Rhiannon rode either side of a chariot which was being driven with great care by young Teyron. Behind them came Farann. Recognising the young man who lay bleeding and unconscious across the chariot with his legs dangling from the platform, Boudicca felt her stomach twist in apprehension.

With a cry of anguish, Tadia rushed past the queen to bend over her injured son and demand of his twin what had happened.

'Go and fetch Morica,' Boudicca instructed her staring slave, who set down the water jar she was bringing from the well and raced away with skirts flying. But the queen's gaze was fixed upon her daughter as the little party dismounted. Rhiannon looked pale, but she was composed and almost defiant as she met her mother's look.

'The Goddess called me,' she said. 'I was alone in the forest, drawn to a place where Caridwen sent a boar to me. Ylas thought to save me, but the boar was strong. Then the others came and saved us both. It was my idea to bring Ylas home, mother. He's badly hurt. What else could I do?'

'No harm's done,' Boudicca assured her. 'Matuac and Farann can be gone again by nightfall – that will suffice.'

Morica had not been far away. She came hurrying now, looking sharply at the two youthful warriors who should not have been there, not during the month when the Goddess demanded celibacy. But the Maiden herself had brought them to the fort and since the cause was worthy they would not be punished.

The priestess had Ylas taken to the queen's house and laid him on a pallet in the room he shared with his twin. She sent for herbs and charms and soon an acrid brazier burned by the foot of his bed to ward off dark forces as Morica tended Ylas's wounds with the help of Tadia his mother.

Boudicca, meanwhile, dismissed the crowd of inquisitive women and girls from the central hall of her house and then she demanded a fuller explanation from Rhiannon and the others. Matuac was angry now, blustering and bristling, mostly because he was worried about his twin; Teyrnon's eyes darted about him with fright as he confessed to having allowed Rhiannon to drive the chariot.

'But he had no choice,' Rhiannon insisted. 'I made him do it. The Goddess was with me. She willed it, mother.'

As for Farann, he remained silent, standing a little apart with his head high and his blue gaze fixed on distances beyond Boudicca's shoulder. She guessed that he had come because he, too, was concerned about Ylas, though he would never admit to such feeling.

The queen sighed to herself. This foster-son of hers had grown ever more difficult as he passed through puberty and came to young manhood.

'And what became of the boar?' she asked. 'No one has mentioned that.'

'Farann killed it,' Matuac said at once.

'He had to!' Rhiannon exclaimed.

Boudicca contained another sigh. How like Matuac to put someone else in trouble; he didn't do it maliciously, just unthinkingly. 'Farann?'

Now at last he looked at her across the smoky room, taller than she now that he was seventeen, but still thin, though the breadth of his shoulders told her he would fill out and become a fine man like his father Vindorex. His blue eyes met hers directly, as they had so long ago at Camulodunon and, as then, a quiver of prescience tingled along her spine. 'Yes, lady, I killed it.'

Perhaps that was why he had come – not out of concern for a friend but to confess to breaking the taboo. Boars were sacred to Dia, except at Samhain. And, prickly as Farann was, she knew him to be completely honest. 'You must make reparation.'

'Yes, lady, I will.' And he would, she knew – he would make an offering of something precious to placate the Goddess's anger.

Rhiannon, too, had to learn a lesson. Her claim of being drawn by the Goddess was spoken with the clear-eyed directness of truth, but it made Boudicca uneasy. Whatever the reason, Rhiannon had behaved irresponsibly: she had risked her own life, and that of Teyrnon, not to mention two valuable horses and a chariot. It suited Boudicca to put a stop to her daughter's freedom for a while.

Rhiannon was punished by being forbidden the chariots until she had spun enough wool to make a new curtain for her room – a penance that made the girl open her mouth to protest, only to subside with her lips set rebelliously. She had never properly mastered the art of spinning: it bored her and she hated the chore, as her mother knew full well.

In the queen's house as the hawthorn month ended, Ylas still lay sick and fevered, almost too weak from loss of blood to eat or drink. His wounds wept, angry with poisonous oozings that Morica dressed with herbal unguents and leaves, on his chest, his back, his buttocks and his limbs. Only Dia knew how the boar had missed tearing a vital organ. Perhaps Ylas had been right: perhaps Dia didn't want his soul yet; perhaps She had other plans for him.

Rhiannon sat by him with her spindle and distaff, absently twisting yarn while with half her mind she watched the flicker of the young man's lashes, and listened for any alterations in the rhythm of his breathing. In part she felt responsible for his injuries. As she cooled his burning face, her lips moved soundlessly in prayers that the Hag might spare him. Ylas was as dear to her as a brother.

From outside there came a clamour of greeting voices that told her her father the king, with the elders and warriors, had come home. Only moments later, there came a howl of anguish from a male throat and Coeling thrust the curtain aside as he entered his sons' room and threw himself down beside Ylas. He took one look at the youth and covered his face with his hands, rocking back and forth in an agony of grief, groaning, 'My son! My son!'

Concerned for him, Rhiannon tentatively laid a hand on the grizzled warrior's arm. 'He will be well, Coeling. I know he will.'

He turned his head sharply to look at her in faith and hope. She was the Maiden, closer to Dia than even the priestesses. 'Has the Goddess told you so?'

'Yes.' It was the answer he wanted, so that was the answer she gave. But in truth the Goddess's purpose remained an enigma, as it always was.

She saw the relief that flooded through him as he bent to smooth his son's damp brow. His faith in her prescience embarrassed her. Then as she edged a little away she caught sight of someone stooping in the doorway.

Her father the king was there, looking into the room with the curtain held aside. His pale eyes met hers with a piercing look, hard as pebbles on the shore. She knew that he had heard the story of Ylas's wounding, and that he held her responsible for it. Always he doubted her. He mistrusted the wilful streak in her nature. But she couldn't bring herself to be winsome and winning, as Araunah could. Araunah had always been the king's favourite child.

Prasutagus contented himself with that censorious look before he ducked out and dropped the curtain into place. Rhiannon stared down at the spindle in her hands, rubbing her fingers together, feeling the oil from the wool that softened her skin, and in her head tears pressed hard behind her eyes. She loved her father. All her life she had tried to please him, but somehow all her efforts went wrong, or were misconstrued. Try as she would, she couldn't seem to make the king love her as he loved Araunah.

Sometimes, Erefwen of the primrose hair came to tend the sick Ylas with the arts she was learning from the priestess. She liked to linger, to talk with Rhiannon, wanting to dress her hair and touch her clothes, doing honour to the Maiden – so she said.

But Rhiannon found Erefwen's presence disturbing. There came a day when the young woman's unsought attentions drove her away from Ylas's sick-bed to join her special friends, Adalma and the violet-eyed Cunovinda of the Trinovantes, Farann's sister. The three girls, along with Adalma's little sister Mina and pretty Pluma, old Summac's daughter, stood and gossiped high on the defensive banks surrounding the settlement, where they could work at their spinning while watching the young warriors at spear-practice on the chariot-track below.

Though their swords had been taken, and supplies of iron all but stopped by the Romans, over the years the Iceni had increased their store of spears enough to allow battle training to go on. It was the queen's command that her warriors should not grow slack. They must train, at the reins, with their spears, with axes and with wooden practice-swords. Because the time was coming when their battle-skill would be needed: the queen, and Eogan, foresaw it.

The chariots whipped by. Light glanced off oiled bodies and bronze-decked limbs; long hair streamed out, as wheels rumbled over hard ground, behind pounding hooves and tossing manes. Reinsmen rode intent on their horses, while warriors poised with throwing spears.

'Don't forget your yarn!' Cunovinda teased as Rhiannon's attention strayed and her fingers ceased their twirling for the tenth time.

Rhiannon sighed, spreading her hands in front of her. 'My fingers ache so. Look – blisters.'

'I've never heard you complaining about the calluses you get from chariot leathers,' Adalma observed.

Knowing she was being teased, Rhiannon pulled a sour face as she made her hands continue the tiresome chore.

On the track below, Boudicca's chariot approached, the familiar red hair flaming in sunlight that caught in gold armlets adorning the queen's poised right arm. She threw, swift and strong, and her spear cleft the air, flying in a deadly arc to thump into the centre of one of the straw figures set up as targets. Boudicca smiled in pleasure at her own skill as her driver brought her round to one side, where she could watch the target and cheer on her pupils.

Sturdy Matuac came behind her, driven by his sister Cameira, his face set in determined lines. Ylas's absence had inspired his twin to greater efforts on the training grounds, perhaps to clear his mind of fears for a while, or perhaps to even the standard of their mastery of arms while Ylas was laid low. In their sibling struggles, Ylas usually had the edge in fleetness and accuracy, while Matuac's talent was in his strength. But this time Matuac's spear flew home with a thud. A broad grin creased his sharp-featured face as he looked up to see if Rhiannon was watching.

She acknowledged his skill with a negligent wave of her hand even as she inwardly cursed the fate that kept her from the chariots and made her stand here spinning stupid yarn that had got itself knotted up yet again while her mind was elsewhere.

She turned to ask Adalma for help, only to see that her friend was entranced, her plain face alight in its frame of soft brown hair, her eyes wide and soft as a seal-pup's. Glancing at the warriors below, Rhiannon realised that it was Garanhir who had Adalma's attention – Garanhir, the king's champion, handsome, valiant and honourable, over whom many women had sighed in vain. Garanhir had no eye for women, it seemed. He lived only to serve the king – and, Rhiannon suspected, the queen too. She had often seen Garanhir watching her mother with open yearning when he thought himself unobserved. But many warriors had eyes for their queen. She was the most magnificent woman of the tribe.

Rhiannon shared a glance with Cunovinda, commenting silently on Adalma's hopeless passion for a man twice her age.

The practice below went on, and now chasing around the curve of the bank came Duihno's chariot, with Farann at the reins. Duihno was urging his reinsman faster, faster, drawing back his arm to launch his spear, when without warning a wheel splintered. The chariot sagged to one side, and Rhiannon's heart twisted in alarm even as she heard Cunovinda cry out. Duihno's weapon missed its target. He was sent sprawling half off the back of the platform as the horses pulled to the right, pivoting on the hub of the broken wheel. But Farann kept his feet and mastered the horses to a standstill.

Howling in fury, Duihno scrambled up and threw himself at Farann, grabbing the sharp-pointed goad from the younger man's hand. Farann threw up an arm to defend himself, and with that the muscular champion, Nuadat, was on them. One thrust of his massive arm was enough to send Duihno sprawling, though he leapt up again at once, his face contorted with hate as he flung curses at Farann.

'Son of carrion! Roman-bred dung! Filthy Trinovante peasant!'

Cunovinda caught her breath, her great violet eyes wide with pain in a face gone white. Insults to her brother were insults to her, too.

'Enough!' Boudicca's voice lashed across the stream of invective. She leaped down from her chariot, her face flushed with anger, so that even Duihno hesitated before his temper drove him to add:

'This outsider drives no more for me! I'll choose another reinsman. I'll have . . .' He glanced around the gathered drivers, picking out one of the youngest, to make the insult to Farann more keen, 'I'll have Cameira from now on. At least she's warrior-bred, not softened by suckling at the paps of a pampered Roman sow.'

At this, Farann threw himself on his older, stronger tormentor with such fury that Duihno was driven back. The two wrestled in the dust, fists, teeth and knees intent on doing injury. Then a knife flashed between them and Farann staggered back, a hand clamped to his arm. Duihno, his face contorted with rage, raised his dagger for the kill.

'Enough, I said!' At the cry from Boudicca, Nuadat intervened again, ducking beneath the raised arm, grasping Duihno's wrist and forcing him to drop his dagger. Boudicca, too, stepped between the angry pair, but before she could speak Duihno spat violently on the ground, said, 'If I'd had my sword, I'd have killed him!' and spun away to drag Matuac from his chariot and himself climb up beside Cameira.

From her place on the bank, Rhiannon couldn't hear what was said between her mother and Farann, but the youth stared beyond the queen's shoulder, stiff and remote with insulted pride. When Rhiannon glanced at Cunovinda she saw her friend's eyes blooming with tears. Then Farann turned away from the queen, his whole body rigid as he strode steadily towards the gateway, ignoring the blood that ran down his arm and left spots of dark wetness in the dust.

With a little cry, Cunovinda ran down the steps cut in the inner slope of the banks, among the wicker skeps where the bees made honey. Rhiannon followed, herself anxious about Farann. But his expression held no welcome. He might have stormed by if his sister had not set herself in his path, tears now streaming down her face as she said brokenly, 'Oh, Farann . . . Farann!'

Even Rhiannon divined the wealth of hopelessness that lay behind her friend's cry. No word had been heard from Vindorex for many moons; he might be dead, or captured like Caratacus and taken to slavery in Rome. No one knew his fate, not even the children he had left behind among strangers. What Farann felt was difficult to guess. He hid his emotions behind a palisade of aloofness. But Cunovinda missed her father and her home, often weeping bitterly at night when she thought no one could hear. She was terrified of losing her brother, too.

Laying an arm around her friend's heaving shoulders, Rhiannon looked into Farann's blue eyes and prevented herself from flinching at the hatred she read there. 'Let me tend your arm, Farann.'

'I don't need your help,' he answered roughly. 'Tend to Cunovinda. Leave me alone.'

Rhiannon gaped, then drew herself up, glaring with an arrogance that would not have disgraced her mother. How dare he speak to her so? She was the queen's daughter, and the Maiden. But Farann's lightning glance said he didn't care who she was, not at that moment; if she had been the Lady of the Nine Heights Herself he would not have let her touch him. All his Trinovante blood was roused and he told himself he hated every member of the tribe that had bred Duihno. Before Rhiannon could find words he had brushed by and was striding away with a stiff, angry gait.

The incident made Cunovinda withdraw into one of her silences, from which none of her friends could cajole her. At times such as these she felt herself an alien in Icenia, not only of a different tribe but of part-Roman blood. The mother she had never known was long dead, her father was out of reach, her brother sealed off behind hurts of his own. Cunovinda sought consolation from the White Goddess; at night when all was still she would creep out to sit under the stars and watch the galaxy wheel its pale glory across the sky – a sign of the Goddess as Rhea, She of the White Track of Stars, warm and womanly, yet ethereal – much as Cunovinda imagined her own mother must have been. And in the daytime, when the White Track was hidden, there was the human friendship of Rhiannon – Rhia – the Chosen One of the Goddess, to whom Cunovinda grew more attached as time passed.

Two

Again Rhiannon took her turn at sitting with Ylas, who seemed to be sleeping peacefully though he had grown thin and weak. His wounds were healing and last night the crisis of his fever had passed; Morica said she had done all she could and now it was up to him, and the Gods.

In that room with its twin pallets, its wicker storage baskets and its ledge where bronze figurines stood among a clutter of razors, jewellery and half-made carvings, Rhiannon watched over her kinsman. She worried over the shadows beneath his eyes, the hollows under his cheekbones, the damp fair hair lying unkempt against the grey-spotted sheen of sealskin cushions. The moustache of which he was so proud laid a golden shadow on his upper lip. He must live. He must!

As a bee fumbled by near the tied-up window flap that let light and air into the room, Rhiannon leapt to her feet to make sure the buzzing soul-taker didn't come in, but it droned by, intent on sweeter things. She let out her breath in relief, laughing a little at her own alarm. Ylas was strong. He wouldn't die now. Soon he would sit up, and then stand, and then walk, run, ride . . .

A movement behind her made her whirl in surprise to see Farann ducking under the embroidered curtain that guarded the doorway. As ever, the sight of her made him veil his expression against her as he returned her look with steady blue eyes.

'How is he?' he asked in an undertone.

'Sleeping.' She glanced at her patient as he sighed audibly and turned onto his side. 'He needs rest now. Don't disturb him.'

'It was you I wanted to see, daughter of the queen,' he replied.

His use of the formal title puzzled her. Humility rested uneasily on the shoulders of the young Trinovante. Very slowly, she drew herself up and let her cool glance move over him, from the dark hair past his broad shoulders, down a lanky frame clad in blue checked wool decked with bronze and gold ornament, and back again to meet his narrowed eyes. 'For what reason?'

'To make an apology. When last I spoke with you I was angry with Duihno, and therefore with all Iceni. It was impolite. I regret it.'

Her brow puckered as she tried to guess what was in his mind, though her heart warmed with pleasure; then she spun away from Farann as Ylas spoke faintly, saying her name. In a flurry of relief and joy she knelt beside him, seeing that his eyes were clear at last of fever and of pain. Weakly, he stretched his mouth in a smile.

'Hello, Maiden,' he managed.

'Ylas!' she murmured, and got to her feet feeling giddy with relief. 'Stay with him, Farann. I must get his mother, and Matuac and Cameira. Ylas is with us again.'

Everyone who heard the news rejoiced in it. Rhiannon ran here and there, telling anyone who would listen that Ylas was himself again and would be well. Her relief overflowed into wild happiness. She told the news to adults and children, she told the dogs that came wagging round her, the geese that waddled by, the tame hares her mother kept in pens by the granary. She told Melliacus the smith, sweating over his forge, and Adalma bringing water, and Cunovinda weaving a necklet of daisies.

'Now where are you going?' her friends called after her, laughing.

'To tell the horses!' Rhiannon replied.

Down in the woods she ran by the horse-enclosures leaping and skipping, calling out to Teyrnon to tell him the good news as he stood over a new-born foal with his father and grandfather. Old Nemmon looked up, his face grim as he waved her away from the scene – horsemasters were jealous of their secrets and the birthing of a foal was a special mystery not to be witnessed by the uninitiated.

Uncaring, Rhiannon whirled away and ran on among the trees toward the river, making a wide circle that would eventually bring her to Morica's hut, where she would bring the news of Ylas's recovery. But before she got there she saw two figures standing together in the shade beneath tall alders at the river's edge, a man and a woman whom she recognised with pleasure as the queen, her mother, and Garanhir the king's champion. She changed course, jumping lightly over thick clumps of meadowsweet as she called out to them, saying that Ylas had woken at last.

It was only later that she wondered why both her mother and Garanhir had seemed so startled to see her there, and why they had looked so guilty. They must have been very absorbed in whatever they were discussing not to have heard her coming. It was not the first time she had sensed a communication between them, covert and fraught with nuances she could not define. What had they been talking about so earnestly? She was old enough to guess, but she didn't care for the answer logic brought her.

Boudicca, too, worried about the incident. How the Gods loved to toy with human lives. For many seasons now, she and Garanhir had taken pains – and, indeed, it had been painful – not to meet alone; then when fate brought them together by accident, out of sight of any other, when for once they had allowed themselves to feel as human beings should, and when she had been on the brink of persuading him that their love had a right to exist . . . then, the Gods had sent Rhiannon, so innocent, so bright-eyed and merry – so perceptive.

But there was nothing for Rhiannon to know – nothing, except old wounds that ached at times and memories that would not let go.

That summer, Rhiannon spent much time down at the horse enclosures learning, along with Teyrnon, some of the skills possessed by Vranaun his father and old Nemmon his grandfather. For generations past, this family had served Iceni queens as horsemasters. They guarded their mysteries tightly, teaching them only to apprentices among their own kin and to certain favoured progeny of royal blood. So in her turn Rhiannon learned the rudiments of jading or drawing a horse by working on his keen sense of smell. A skilful horsemaster could make his control over the creatures appear magical to the uninitiated.

Around her neck now, slung on a leather thong, Rhiannon wore a small round flint with a hole in it. The token was worn only by initiates in horsemastery; it represented the all-seeing protective eye of the Goddess who among horsemen was called Epona, the White Mare. Because of her own affinity with Epona – she had seen visions of the White Mare since childhood – Rhiannon wore the flint with special pride.

In the heat of late summer, Rhiannon rode with her mother in the woods, with an escort of warriors riding idly behind them, guarding them but out of earshot. Boudicca saw how her daughter sat the pony with instinctive poise, as though it were part of her. The girl was truly warrior-born, which was well; it had occurred to Boudicca that the Roman threat might not come to a head in her own time. Perhaps it would fall to Rhiannon to lead the Iceni against the invaders, as queen of the People of the Horse.

As her mind turned broodingly on the future, Boudicca touched the flint horsemasters' amulet that dangled among gold chains at her breast. Alongside it, on the same thong, she kept a ring – a thick gold ring too large even for her thumb, with a stone of rose quartz.

'What *is* that ring?' Rhiannon asked.

Boudicca's hand snapped away from the stone of pink quartz; until that moment she had not realised she was fingering it wistfully. 'It's nothing. Just a ring. An amulet.'

Though they talked of other things, Boudicca's thoughts remained on the ring and the man who had given it to her. Perhaps she should have told Rhiannon about Huan of the Caledones. Rhiannon would be proud to know her real parentage. But how could she be told the story without also being told what fate Huan had met – the same fate that awaited the next man who came in guise of the God to meet with the Maiden at the next Great Year?

Whatever happened, Rhiannon must not guess the ending of that rite. It was a dread secret, a holy trust that all must keep. Each Maiden came unknowing. It had always been so. It would be again, when the time came. When Rhiannon was eighteen.

Already, to her mother's dismay, the girl was growing out of childhood. Her hips were beginning to round out and budding breasts showed under her shirt. Boudicca found herself prey to a conflict of emotions – a fierce protective pride, a deep maternal affection, and a growing concern for the demands the Goddess would make on the girl. The queen herself had faced similar demands, but Rhiannon seemed so much more vulnerable.

There was also within her, secret and despised even by herself, a gnawing envy of her daughter's youth, beauty and trusting innocence. Boudicca too had dreamed bright dreams, but they had been denied her.

'Soon you'll be a woman,' the queen remarked, her gaze on dancing leaves and sunlit glades that lay ahead of them amid gentle hills. 'You know what that will mean, Rhiannon. Tell me . . . among the young men, is there one for whom you have special regard?'

Rhiannon shrugged. 'No, not one I could name above the rest.' But in her mind rose a picture of the dark-haired, blue-eyed, enigmatic Trinovante, Farann, and beyond him sunny Ylas – happily restored to health though he would bear the whorls and welts of his scars for the rest of his life – and then grave Unthaus, inept Matuac, even Teyrnon.

A smile curved Boudicca's lips, though it hardly warmed her eyes. 'That is well, since you're dedicated to the Goddess. You must not allow yourself to grow too fond of any man – and you must let no man lie with you, not even at festivals. Morica will tell you the same. You must remain a virgin, Rhiannon.'

'For ever?' The gold-flecked green eyes widened in shock and alarm and Boudicca laughed under her breath as she reached to touch her daughter's mane of golden-red curls.

'No, not for ever. Just . . . until the right time.'

'Did you wait?' Rhiannon asked.

'Of course.'

'Until when? Until you married my father?'

Boudicca broke the disturbing contact of their eyes, pretending that her horse needed curbing. 'Until the Goddess called me.'

For a while they rode in silence, coming to a house guarded by a deep ditch and a tall palisade mingled with a hawthorn hedge. Smoke trickled from behind the hedge bringing the scent of hot metals to spread acridly through the woods. This was the home of Annamoris the royal goldsmith, who was famous for his skill in making elaborate gold torcs to adorn the necks of chieftains. But lately his raw material had been harder and harder to obtain – trade in gold had been restricted, along with supplies of iron ore that might have made weapons, by decree of the procurator in Camulodunon. Annamoris had been reduced to melting down gold coins from the royal treasury to make jewellery.

Three ferocious hounds came streaking from the shade of the hedge as the queen and her daughter rode by, but their baying ceased as Boudicca scattered something on the ground in front of them and the dogs turned and fled with tails between their legs. The queen smiled at her daughter, tightening the thong of a pouch that hung from her belt, from which she had taken the jading substance.

'It works with more creatures than horses,' she remarked. 'A pity you had none of this with you last spring. I've never tried it on a boar, but . . .'

They shared a confidential smile. Rhiannon, much as she had tried, had never managed to grow really close to her father, but with her mother there was a bond of affection, and an understanding forged by the fate they shared. Boudicca knew how apart the Maiden could feel, different from other children, part-feared, part-worshipped, wholly protected, and with a future that was kept obscure but for dark hints that were of little comfort. What did it mean, to be the Maiden?

Out of the turmoil of Rhiannon's misunderstanding, one thought rose to the surface.

'Were you forced to marry my father?'

The question made Boudicca draw up her pony and look closely at the troubled young face that confronted her. 'Forced? No, not forced. The council chose him as my consort. Their reasons were good and so I accepted him. I always knew I must marry for the sake of the tribe.'

'Because you were the Maiden?'

'Because I was the queen.'

'But was there love between you?'

Evidently Rhiannon was beginning to think of her own future. She was an intelligent girl and must know that her mother's marriage held no deeply emotional commitment. Boudicca considered her answer before she said, 'Not at first.

Now . . . a certain fondness binds us. And for you, my love, I'll make sure your own choice is considered.'

That was a consolation, but it was not her future marriage that coloured Rhiannon's thoughts, not at that moment. She longed to know more of her duties in the Mysterious rites of the Goddess, but the unknown frightened her and she shied away from the subject. 'Is that why my father doesn't like me? He doesn't avoid Araunah. Did she come after the fondness had grown between you?'

'No!' Boudicca edged her horse closer, so that she could wrap her hand round her daughter's thin wrist. Suddenly she was angry with Morica for confusing the girl, and angry that Prasutagus had not been more kind. Thinking to offer comfort, she said, 'You misunderstand, Rhiannon. Prasutagus the king is not your father. Before I married him, I too served the Goddess. You, my love, were born of the God.'

Rhiannon stared at her, searching her mother's face. There was pain in her wide green eyes, for she had learned to love Prasutagus as her father, distant though he kept himself; but there was also dawning comprehension. All at once everything became clear for her: this explained why Prasutagus preferred Araunah, because Araunah was of his own flesh. Children 'born of the God' were those conceived in the heat of festivals, when women lay with men as the Goddess moved them, when mortal flesh became Immortal-rapt.

'Do you know who it was?' she asked.

'Of course I know,' Boudicca said, looking into her daughter's clear, curious eyes and knowing she had to lie for the girl's sake. 'I told you, Rhiannon – it was the God.'

She wheeled her pony to start for home, ending the discussion. She had said enough, for now. There were still things Rhiannon had to learn – dark, holy, unspeakable truths that were better experienced without anticipation. When the time came, that would be soon enough.

But Rhiannon thought she could guess who the man had been: Garanhir. That would explain so much of the deep, secret feeling Rhiannon had always sensed between them. It pleased her to think that Garanhir was her father.

But which man would it be when the next Great Year wheeled the stars into place? Which man would she, Rhiannon, meet in the Mysteries?

*

Harvest was over, the stilted granaries and clay-lined storage pits crammed with grain, and the hills and woods had warmed with shades of autumn. One morning a band of Roman cavalry appeared at the gates of Oakhillfort, searching for Vindorex the outlawed prince of the Trinovante. They were greeted cautiously and kept waiting at the gate until the king came to speak with them.

The Roman officer said that Vindorex had been seen only a few nights before, when he and his dwindling band of followers had attacked a road-building party on the edge of Coritania. Their pursuers had followed them to the western extremity of the marshes, where the outlaws had managed to disappear.

If Vindorex knew of secret ways across the marshes, or if he could procure a boat, he might well reach Icenia – so the cavalry officer informed Prasutagus. In such an event, the Iceni would be wise to lay hold of him and throw him into one of their punishment pits until word could be got to the military authorities. This was what the wise queen Cartimandua of the Brigantes had done when the rebel Caratacus had gone to her for support. Of course, if Vindorex could be persuaded to surrender it would go better with him. He had proved his courage. A brave man could hope to be granted clemency – as was evidenced by the justice given to Caratacus when he appeared before the Emperor.

Looking for Cunovinda to tell her the news, Rhiannon was directed toward the granaries, near which were kept the tame hares; the queen bred the creatures for sacrifice and for giving of portents. Cunovinda was there by the wicker hare cages, and with her was her brother Farann. The young man leaned on a corner of the tall granary, his back to Rhiannon, his cloak stirring in the wind, while his sister crouched by an open cage in front of him. Evidently they had already heard the latest news of Vindorex their father.

'He'll probably have to pass the winter wandering in the marshes,' Farann was saying bitterly. 'Cold, hungry, friendless . . .'

'At least we know he's alive.' Cunovinda straightened, regarding her brother with shining violet eyes across the young hare she was fondling at her breast. 'He's alive, and a few days ago he outwitted a whole party of soldiers who were after him. That's something, Farann.'

'We know he's being hunted like an animal,' he replied, 'chased from bush to briar, and with his men being picked off one by one.' His fist struck the granary, shaking a scatter of grain to fall through the slats to the mud beneath. 'Why doesn't he come for me!'

'You?' Cunovinda paled and her hand made a tentative move towards him only to pause and withdraw to the leveret's fur, as if she feared a rebuff. 'Farann – no! Don't say it. He left us here for safety.'

'We were children then.' He had noticed Rhiannon. His blue gaze slid across hers but it was for her benefit as well as his sister's that he said with youthful pride. 'I'm a man grown now, a trained warrior. It's time I won the Warrior's Light.'

Was he talking of leaving, of going to war? Rhiannon's heart gave a lurch of disquiet at the thought. 'You can't go,' she said. 'You've been elected to the royal guard. You must serve for three years.'

'I'll ask the king to release me,' Farann replied.

'You can't fight the Romans!' his sister exclaimed. 'No one wins against them. Not father, not Caratacus – not all the tribes of Gaul.' Anxiously, she laid hold of his sleeve. 'They offered mercy, Farann. Father doesn't need to go on being hunted. If he gives himself up – '

A jerk of his arm unloosed her hold and his young face set in hard lines as he glared at her. 'He'll never do that!'

Tears bloomed in her eyes and she turned as if to hide them, bending her head over the leveret's long ears.

'He won't!' Farann muttered forcefully, directing the denial at Rhiannon. 'Only a fool would believe Roman promises after everything they've done. Surely you don't believe they'd just open their arms and forgive him, do you, Rhiannon?'

'They forgave Caratacus,' she reminded him. 'Have you forgotten the story that merchant told us? Caratacus was taken in chains to Rome but made such a brave speech that the Emperor spared him, and his family. They live in exile now, but . . .'

'Exile!' His bitter laugh cut across her voice and silenced her. 'Wasn't my father an exile for long enough, waiting to be restored to the home that's now denied him? There's nothing for him but to fight on until death puts an end to it. There's nothing for me, either. I may as well set out to find him. The last of the Trinovante royal blood will stand together, perish together.'

At this, Cunovinda whirled round, tears starting from eyes like bruised violets on a background of alabaster. 'You're more than a Trinovante. You're part Roman, too! Our mother was a Roman! How can you bear such hate against her?'

'Cunovinda!' Awkwardly, he swept his arms about her, bringing her to weep on his shoulder, his dark head bent over hers. Rhiannon saw his face work with dismay and uncertainty, his profile etched in firm lines against his sister's hair. 'I don't hate her! That's not what I said. It's the Roman state I hate – the things they do to people. You don't even remember mother. I do. She was soft, and gentle. She loved us, and we loved her. Father grieved so badly when she died I was afraid he might die, too. It's not her we've turned against, it's the soldiers, the governors, the politicians . . .'

She tore free of him, whipping her head up to cry, 'And what about me? What about me, Farann? Will you leave me here alone? Without you I'll have no one. Oh . . . if you go, I'll hate you. I'll never stop hating you!' Sobbing, she dropped the young hare and ran away, evading their efforts to stop her.

Farann glanced sidelong at Rhiannon, half embarrassed that she had witnessed the emotional scene. She turned away, pouncing on the leveret before it could recover from its surprise and run away. She understood the young man's turmoil, guessed that he was torn between concern for his sister and the compulsion to play a warrior's part, to stand with his father and avenge old wrongs.

'I'll take care of Cunovinda,' she offered, bending to put the hare back into its cage and peg the door shut before she straightened to look at him with sad eyes.

'She'll need someone,' he said. 'She's not strong, like you.'

'Am I strong?'

'You are. Strong as a queen should be.' He hesitated, spots of self-conscious colour burning high on his cheekbones to brighten his intense blue eyes. Taking a deep breath, he straightened himself and began, 'Rhiannon, I . . .'

Hot blood suffused her own face and then ebbed as a chill

of premonition coursed through her. Whatever he was going to say, she mustn't listen. She belonged to the Goddess, was dedicated as Dia's vessel. Clear in her mind she heard a voice that said, 'It can never be.' Was that the Goddess speaking? Were those the hoofbeats of the White Mare that came on the edge of a cold wind? A rushing sounded in her ears and Farann's voice seemed to come from far distances, saying anxiously, 'Rhiannon?'

She saw his face as if through a mist, felt his hands on her, supporting her. Guard yourself against loving, her mother had warned. Shock made her pull away, gasping, 'Don't touch me!'

Farann misunderstood. For a moment he didn't move, but his face stiffened, his eyes darted across her face and she knew she had wounded his young pride as badly as if she had slapped him. He thought she was rejecting him personally. She said, 'Farann – ' but even as his name came to her lips he spun away and strode off.

Shaking her head, Rhiannon struggled with the mist that tried to claim her. She felt sick, and cramps tore at her stomach.

No one had warned her that the onset of puberty might come so swiftly, or so painfully.

Three

It was always dark in Morica's hut – dark, smoky and scented. The priestess seldom opened her window flaps and all the interior of her house was blackened by smoke from the central fire, redolent of the herbs she burned. Tiny lamps were kept flickering around the ledge where dwelt a detailed carving of the Triple Goddess, three figures joined as one – girl, woman and crone. The virgin held a mirror and comb in her hand, representing vanity and heartlessness; the full-breasted woman offered an apple as a love lure; the old woman was impassive, her foot resting on a human skull. Dia knew all;

Dia governed all; Dia gave and Dia took away, as it pleased Her whim.

The house itself was built of sacred woods: willow and hazel formed its wattle walls and roof, its floor was of oak and it stood upon alder piles sunk into the river bank, so that partly it overhung the flowing waters. Here babies were born, and here came girls taken of their first moon-flux, to spend a month separate from the tribe. Their absence was a sign to everyone that they had reached womanhood.

So here, too, came Rhiannon the Maiden, the queen's daughter, to learn from Morica and serve the priestess as a handmaid during her month's seclusion. She was not alone. Pretty Pluma with her shining brown hair had come there a few nights before her, and Erefwen was always a frequent visitor to the priestess.

They were fed by offerings brought down from the fort and left outside. They tended the lamps, brought water, and kept the fire burning bright in the clay hearth. Each dawn they cleansed themselves in the river, purifying themselves by total immersion despite the water's autumn chill, and they walked in the woods with Morica, careful to avoid all contact with other people, while the priestess explained to them the lore of the Goddess and the rites in which they would now be allowed to join more fully.

But some of the training was for Rhiannon alone. On days when Morica deemed it provident, the priestess would garb herself and Rhiannon in warm green cloaks and take the Maiden westwards into the depths of the marshy fenland. The great watery wastes, a land of lush growth, many rivers and streams, and secret islands, stretched from the shores of the Great Bay far into the heart of Albina's Isle. Rhiannon discovered broad meres that reflected the golds and rusts of the trees, and where waterfowl bred in thousands. She saw stretches of wet peat bog, beds of whispering reed, banks of sturdy alder and shimmering willow – ever and always the alder of dark Bran shading the softer willow of the Goddess. This was Her domain, where the wind whispered over the surface of silver waters and a coracle could glide silently between earth and sky, hidden under a roof of lacy branches.

Morica showed Rhiannon the secret channels and causeways. Through oceans of reed, lilies, bulrushes and sedges

Morica paddled a wicker boat covered with taut-stretched hide, or led the way over bridges formed by beaver dams, or leapt from tussock to tussock to each new oasis of solid land where the trees grew tall and the shrubs tangled, and where birds flew up, crying their alarm.

On occasion, Rhiannon would catch a glimpse of another rounded wicker boat, or a figure melting among the greenery of the islands.

'Fenfolk,' Morica explained these puzzling sightings. 'They'll not harm us. They know we serve the Goddess – as they do.'

Deeper in the fens, Rhiannon saw evidence of sacrificial offerings in willow groves, remains of fish and birds or some small animal given to Dia in supplication or thanks by the mysterious dwellers in the marshes. But she saw no sign of their habitations.

'I don't think they build houses,' Morica said. 'I've never come across any. Or perhaps their villages lie hidden deep in the trackless wastes where I've never been. They're a shy people. They avoid contact with the world except when they bring their fish and reeds to trade for ironware. But once in my youth, when I was learning from old Saille as Erefwen is learning from me, I lost my way. One of the fenfolk guided me back. He seemed afraid of me – as if he thought me one of the Old Ones. Such primitive folk have strange ideas of the Gods.'

On one of these forays into the watery wilderness, the ebbing of daylight found them still far from home. Their coracle rode a deep, broad channel, floating from the shelter of overhanging branches into the soft light of a sky washed with the pink of afterglow. Morica skilfully turned the paddle, directing the boat toward a dark hump of land where towering alders grew upon an island. Here the priestess hoisted her green skirts and jumped to dry land, drawing the boat in and inviting Rhiannon to climb out onto the beginnings of a well-marked pathway among the grass.

Rhiannon looked around her apprehensively, disturbed by the silent shadows of the island and the darkening marshes that stretched in every direction, pathless and seemingly without limit.

'Where are we? This isn't the way home.'

'No, Maiden.' In the twilight, Morica's face looked gaunter than ever, her eyes mere glints of knowingness made eerie by the blue tattoos that surrounded the deep shadowed hollows of her face. 'Tonight the moon will be full. Tonight you meet with the Goddess.'

A familiar ripple of awe trickled down Rhiannon's spine as the hoarse words whispered away across the water to meet the oncoming night. The pink had gone from the sky, leaving it a pale washed blue deepening to woad. A heron cried harshly and a white winged form came flapping and gliding along the channel, veering up to disappear over the trees.

'This way,' Morica said, taking Rhiannon's hand to lead her up the pathway. At the heart of the island, a glow of light showed among a thick growth of shrubs and trees, beckoning them along the twining pathway as the darkness thickened.

To Rhiannon's surprise, they came to a clearing where a fire had been built. Flickering light shone warmly on the low, rounded shape of a bower made of willow branches, and on the ground lay a small pile of food – fish and small fowl ready skewered on sharpened sticks for roasting at the fire, a loaf of black bread, and with these things a crude pottery jug brimming with liquid, and two equally ill-shaped mugs. Beyond the fire stood the remains of an ancient tree, weathered down to a broad stump that uncannily resembled a gnarled face with vertical slits for eyes and the remains of a branch for a nose, bearded by the grasses that grew round it. It was darkened by dried blood from offerings that had been laid on its crown, and as Rhiannnon stared at it she saw that some of those stains were still glistening wetly in the firelight. Someone had prepared for their coming with reverent care.

'Who has been here?' she asked. 'The fenfolk?'

'Of course. You're their Maiden, too. Now come, you must be as hungry as I am.'

Impatiently they baked the food, tearing off pieces as soon as they were cooked. After a day of wandering among bewildering pathways, Rhiannon savoured the food and the honeyed drink, whose sweetness failed to cover the bitter flavour of the ivy intoxicant with which it was laced. She drank it gratefully, thinking that it would help her sleep and keep out the damp chill of the marshes. She was familiar with the effects of the drug and no longer feared it.

As they supped, the sky beyond the willows silvered with the rising of the full moon, its light contending with the flicker from the fire until the clearing was almost bright as day. And as the white disc showed its edge clearly over the trees Rhiannon found herself on her knees beside Morica, the drug making her feel light-headed, her mind wide open to the Goddess.

Morica prayed aloud, upturning her thin face so that moonlight washed over it, turning it into a skull masked with blue tattoos as she invoked the Goddess in all her aspects. *'For Thou alone art supreme; Thou, Great Mother of All Living, Lady of Summer, Ruler of Wild Oxen, Life-in-death and Death-in-life, Beloved of the twin Gods; Thou man's mother, sister, lover, friend and mourner; Thou Virgin, Mistress, Pyre-Builder; Thou the White Raiser, Red Reaper, Dark Winnower; Queen of all things, first in the heavens, first in earth, first in the underworld: Threefold, Fivefold, Ninefold Goddess.'*

Watching the remorseless white face of the moon that looked so impassively down at her, Rhiannon felt the hairs of her scalp prickle with a shiver that rippled over her skin and left every tiny hair on her body standing on end. Her senses tuned to the murmur of waters and the sound of a wind moving the trees. The world of night was alive with Her dread presence, Her footsteps whispering, Her robe rustling, Her hair floating with the clouds, and Her voice breathing, calling, *Rhiannon! Rhiannon!*

There, beyond the shadows! A pale shape moving! *The White Mare!*

She felt Morica's hand on her arm, detaining her from starting after the spectre she had glimpsed. Morica's voice came low, speaking, singing, chanting, *'In willow days the hawk will fly to hunt the hare through evening haze and seek the night-dark trees that stand gathered to guard the sacred place. The moon in artless beauty rides twin-horned above the alder blooms, to breathe a sigh among the reeds and whisper, willow, he comes, he comes . . .'*

The Song of the Maiden! Again the prickle of supernatural awareness rolled like a wave along Rhiannon's skin. Every word of the song meant something of significance and slowly she was learning to interpret it. This, then, was the sacred place, and these the night-dark trees. Willow days, the month of the hawk and the sacred hare . . . the time would be the blooming of the year, presumably at the spring rites, when the moon was virginal, twin-horned – a new moon. When He would come. He . . . The God.

'You must prepare for Him, Maiden,' the voice breathed out of the night – Morica's voice? Or the voice of the Goddess? 'Be faithful, and obey.'

'I will,' she vowed.

'Prepare. Keep yourself pure for Him. As She is pure. Albina the White, the Virgin. When the Great Year comes, you will be needed, Rhiannon, Maiden, daughter of the queen. Your life belongs to a Greater Queen. You must be faithful. You must obey.'

That night Rhiannon's dreams were filled with strange and frightening images in which the God came to her in the form of a giant man whose head was made of an old tree stump that dripped with blood. But she had no fear of Him for she was inhabited by the Goddess and, standing apart, she saw herself pale and beautiful, with lips red as berries, hair long and curling fair, gowned in silvered white and crowned with stars. When morning came, only those images remained.

At dawn, Morica roused her and they returned swiftly to more familiar ways, and thence to the river and the priestess's hut, where waited an urgent message summoning the priestess to Oakhillfort. Morica hurried away, leaving Rhiannon and Pluma to their chores.

The drug's heaviness remained in Rhiannon's head, so that she could hardly bear her companion's prattle. Pluma's laughter rang round the hut as they cleared away yesterday's rushes from the floor. She was gaily trying to decide which particular young man she would set her traps for, come the spring festival.

Pluma was delighted with herself, delighted to be a woman at last. She was the daughter of old one-eyed Summac and his second wife – a former slave who in her youth had been as beautiful as the daughter she had given him. Pluma was bright and merry, with brown hair that shone bronze in sunlight, and her figure held the promise of lush curves that would please men's eyes. In every way she was different from her half-sister, pale Erefwen – the one worldly and slave-born, the other cold, warrior-bred and destined for the priestess's mantle. Between them a certain enmity existed.

The hut was dark as always, the lamps sputtering in front of the niche where the Triple Goddess watched over the house. The fire smoked fitfully in its ornate clay hearth, the smoke eddying in a draught, but the wide open door did let a little sunlight filter from the entry passage. A shadow cutting off some of that light accompanied a creaking along the floor and the two girls paused in their work as a slender figure straightened at the doorway, long pale braids falling over a woollen shirt and trousers.

Pluma wrinkled her nose. 'Oh, it's only Erefwen creeping in as usual. Come in, sister. What news from Oakhillfort? Is it Matuac who's sighing for me today, or Farann?'

She was joking, but at mention of Farann a pang of jealousy seared through Rhiannon.

'Neither, if either has any sense,' Erefwen said sourly. 'You're an empty-head, Pluma. All you ever think of is men.'

'Is that my fault, when they stare at me so?' Pluma demanded.

'They stare at me, too,' her half-sister retorted with truth.

'Especially Duihno!' Pluma laughed. 'Everyone knows how he lusts for you – the more ardently each time you rebuff him.'

'His obsession is of his own making! I've done no pouting and wriggling to inflame him – I leave that to others.'

Pluma pulled a face. 'Erefwen the virgin!'

'And proud to be so! I follow the Goddess – the virgin Goddess.'

'Well, *I* prefer Olwen to Albina,' came the pert response. 'For me She's the Queen of Summer, Olwen of the White Track of Flowers, lusty and fecund. And if you don't want Duihno maybe I'll take him myself – if he suits me.' Tossing her lustrous hair, she skipped to the door and ducked out.

It was in Rhiannon's mind to call after her, to stop Pluma from leaving her alone with Erefwen, but the words died in her throat and she continued to strew rushes, resettling them, rearranging the spread across the rough oak planks of the floor – anything to keep herself occupied and away from the young woman whose presence she found so disturbing.

'Where's Morica?' Erefwen asked.

'Gone to the settlement. They sent for her to see Ferna. Her time is almost here. We're expecting them back for the birthing. I must get everything ready.'

'Then I'll help,' Erefwen offered.

Rhiannon glanced at her, saying swiftly, 'That's not necessary.'

'I think it is, since my sister's off amusing herself. She always was lazy. Besides, I know what needs to be done to prepare for a birthing.' Smiling, head on one side, she came nearer to Rhiannon. 'Your face is smeared. Here, let me . . .'

Feeling like a fieldmouse frozen under a hawk's winged shadow, Rhiannon suffered Erefwen to remove a smudge of dust from her cheek, and then to smooth her hair with long pale hands, all the time smiling into her eyes in the gentlest, friendliest way. But when the caressing hands moved to her shoulders, and dared to rest on her breast, Rhiannon jerked away, revulsion choking her throat.

'What are you doing?'

The cool blue eyes rested on her face calmly; then Erefwen smiled and laid a hand along the slant of Rhiannon's cheek. 'I'm only touching you. Adoring you. You're the Maiden, Rhiannon. You belong to the Goddess. Dia moves in me, too. Albina the White has called me to serve Her – and to serve you, as Her vessel. Don't recoil when She offers Her love.'

'No!' Appalled by things she didn't understand, Rhiannon slapped the bold hand away and darted for the door. She was relieved to hear voices as Morica returned, bringing a heavy-bellied Ferna to her second childbed, with Tadia her mother clucking anxiously alongside.

But the child, sadly, was stillborn.

On the day when Rhiannon was allowed to return to her family, an escort of young women brought new clothes for her – a long skirt, heavily embroidered, and with it soft deer-skin boots, a fine linen shirt, and a jerkin of rare, pure white sealskin. A belt of soft leather was accompanied by a jewelled dagger, and there was a cloak of heavy wool, striped in brightest yellow and green and lined with beaver fur. Lastly, on her bright hair was set a wreath of soft, fluttering aspen leaves, for it was the time of the equinox.

Thus attired, with her flint amulet dangling among other

chains and brooches, Rhiannon drank deep from the brimming cup of honeyed herbal brew that Morica brought her.

The Maiden was brought home to Oakhillfort, walking behind an exultant, muttering, gesticulating Morica and her pale-haired acolyte, and with the women around her beating drums and chanting songs of joy. Everyone in the settlement was waiting, lining the pathway to watch the procession and call greetings to their princess, their Maiden, hope of the tribe. Her heart beat fast, out-stripping the rhythm of the drums, and as the drug began to work on her blood the autumn light dazzled her eyes, making everything unreal. Dimly, she wondered what Farann would think of her now.

As they neared the sacred oak, Rhiannon saw the Druid waiting under swaying yellow branches, his beard and hair combed, his half-shaven head painted with woad. He was dressed in robes of flowing green, with his wolfskin cloak slung from one shoulder, and his bright grey eyes fixed on her unblinking as he stood erect with his ash-staff in his hand. Though he had not been seen all summer, she experienced no surprise at his appearance now, at this important moment for the tribe: Eogan knew everything that took place – the birds kept him informed.

Nearby, her mother and the king stood waiting, decked in their best, and with them her young sister Araunah and the elders, and around them the royal guard. She saw Garanhir smiling at her – surely with paternal pride – and Ylas and Matuac, so alike, both looking a little awed by this new, adult Rhiannon. She saw Unthaus and Duihno, Nuadat and his new warrior-wife Deucca . . . Old Summac with his one eye, Coeling and Tadia, and Cauva the nurse . . . But where was Farann?

All through the ceremony of dedication, her mind floated free, as if she were a detached observer. Her heart beat heavily, loud in her ears, echoing the hoofbeats of the White Mare who hovered just out of sight, watching, waiting.

In this state of mystic exaltation, Rhiannon knelt beneath the sacred oak as with ritual care the oak-seer gave to Morica one of Boudicca's tame hares. The priestess slit the animal's throat, catching the blood in a silver cup. She dabbled her fingers in the blood, invoking the blessing of Andastre, and sprinkled Rhiannon's hair and crown of yellow aspen leaves with dark drops before offering her the cup from which to sip of the thick fluid. It tasted strong and sour, and it was still warm with life – the life of a creature sacred to the Goddess, binding Rhiannon ever closer. She closed her eyes, feeling herself borne up as if on the back of the spectral white mare, and the roaring in her ears deafened her to all other sound.

Slowly, reality seeped back into her consciousness, first sound, then sight, then clear thought. The rites were over. Eogan and Morica raised her to her feet, standing at either side to support her as they presented her to the people.

She received the kiss of homecoming from the unsmiling queen, who greeted her as her beloved daughter and set round her neck the symbol of her royal birth – a springy torc of pure gold, crafted with all the guile Annamoris possessed, the two ends shaped like mares' heads whose eyes were red gemstones. She received another kiss from the king, and then the homage of the elders and the warriors – as Maiden and also as future queen. But as the effect of the drug began to leave her she found herself searching the faces around her with growing dismay.

Farann was missing. So, she now realised, was Cunovinda.

At last her mother led her, among a chattering crowd, into the queen's house to be divested of her heavy cloak and the annoying wreath of leaves that tickled her face. Her head ached and she wished the noisy women would go away, except perhaps for her mother and her close friends. Adalma was there, and little Araunah, but . . . 'Where's Cunovinda?' she asked. 'And where's Farann?' Tiredly she swept aside a stray strand of red-gold hair, wondering why none of them would meet her eyes. Adalma her best friend seemed troubled; her kinswoman Cameira darted looks from the corner of malicious eyes, concealing some secret that pleased her spiteful nature, and Boudicca frowned as if annoyed to be reminded of unpleasantness at such a time.

The queen said harshly, 'They've gone.'

The words drove all pleasure from Rhiannon's day, all colour from her face. 'Gone? Gone where?'

The queen gestured brusquely at the others gathered round. 'Leave us! Leave us!' When the slave Ivixa lingered to pick a last yellow leaf from Rhiannon's hair, she received a sharp slap that made her yelp and hurry away while Boudicca hustled Rhiannon past the curtain that guarded her own room. When she turned to face her daughter her eyes were hard, her mouth set.

'They've gone to join their father! He sent word to them – secretly, through Eogan. He was afraid to come himself.'

Rhiannon stared with eyes that were green pools of disbelief and hurt – confirming what Boudicca had suspected the moment her daughter added Farann's name to that of his sister. Furiously, the queen told herself it was well that the boy had gone! Her anger and her sense of betrayal coloured her reasoning, so much that she decided to tell her daughter nothing more. Let Rhiannon believe that Farann and Cunovinda had deserted her without a farewell. Rhiannon must put Farann from her mind, scour him out as Boudicca would scour out her memories of Vindorex.

'But . . . what will they do? Winter's coming on.' Rhiannon didn't yet accept the truth. She had wanted Farann to see her, wanted his eyes to light on her with the same intensity she had seen that day by the granary. She had looked forward to it with fearful anticipation all month. 'Mother . . . I don't understand. Why was Vindorex afraid to come?'

'He thought I would betray him!' Boudicca spat. 'As Cartimandua betrayed Caratacus! By the Gods, his years in the mountains must have turned his mind!' She swung away, her fists clenched as she stared from the low window at a goose that was grazing outside by the rubbish pit. She could hardly believe that the fine warrior-prince she had met at Camulodunon could be the same man as the fear-filled wreck he had apparently become. He must have used his sword to slay a hare – only that would explain his total loss of courage. Now he daren't even show his face in Iceni territory for fear of treachery. Did he really believe that all women were perfidious and that she, Boudicca, would betray him to the Romans?

She remembered how once her thoughts of him had been warm and lusty. For his sake she had sheltered his children, been a mother to his daughter and trained his son as a warrior, and she had often prayed, secretly, for his safe return. Now all that remained was bitterness. Her friendship was returned with suspicion and her foster-children had been wrenched from her side to face a fate only Dia could predict.

Farann would fight, she guessed, and probably he would die an outlaw, without ever winning the Warrior's Light. And what would become of tender, loyal Cunovinda? They would perish in the wilderness. Along with their worthless father.

Then so be it. She hardened her thoughts against them, telling herself she was glad to be rid of the problem they had presented.

It was left to gentle Adalma to give Rhiannon what small comfort remained. Cunovinda had left behind her doll – the crudely carved wooden doll that was all she had left of her Roman babyhood – and with it messages of affection and farewell.

'She said that she couldn't let Farann go alone,' Adalma said, her round brown eyes soft with sorrow as she watched the way Rhiannon held the doll, her red-gold hair falling round her face as she sat with bent head, her silence revealing her distress. 'She wanted to come and see you, but she was afraid you might try to persuade her to stay. She said she knew that leaving without a word to you was cowardly. She hoped you'd understand. She begged you to remember her when you watch the stars at night, and to pray for her to Rhea of the White Track.'

'And Farann?' Rhiannon asked.

She sensed her friend's surprise in the long silence that followed, and the way Adalma eventually queried curiously, 'Farann?'

'Yes, Farann!' Rhiannon snapped, lifting eyes that ached with tears. 'Did you see him? Did he leave a message?'

'Why . . .' Adalma spread her hands, shrugging her puzzlement. 'No. Did you expect one? Rhiannon . . . You shouldn't think of Farann in that way. You're the Maiden. You're not supposed to – '

'I know!' Tears spurted from her eyes as she glared at Adalma, turning her anger and her pain onto the only person within reach. 'I don't need a horsemaster's daughter to tell me my duties! Oh . . . what do I care if he's gone! Let him go! He always was an outsider. He never belonged here. He hated us, do you know that? He always caused trouble. It wouldn't surprise me if he went running back to the Romans – that's really where he belongs. I wish he'd never come here. I wish he'd stayed in Rome!'

Four

The years of Rhiannon's early womanhood proved to be lonely ones. The routine of life went on, woven around the religious festivals, the hunting, the sowing and reaping of grains, the care of livestock – and the constant training for a war that Eogan, when he returned from his wanderings, still proclaimed was coming. Rhiannon's skill with a spear and at the reins improved; she often drove her mother's chariot in practice; she shared the everyday hopes and concerns of her tribe; but she was also the Maiden, and the queen's heir. Her destiny set her apart from her fellows.

She retained her friendship with Adalma, and formed strong bonds of affection with her young sister Araunah, but she missed Cunovinda; constraints remained between herself and her kinswoman Cameira, and the other young women were wary of her. She dared not form close ties with any of the young men; that was forbidden.

Perhaps the Goddess Herself had arranged to remove the greatest temptation – Farann – from Oakhillfort. But where was he? Where was Cunovinda? For their safety, Rhiannon frequently prayed and made offerings to Epona the White-Mare-Moon-Mother.

The wary peace with the Romans went on. Occasional parties of legionaries passed through on patrol, but mostly they were friendly, ready to be diverted and entertained by the quaint ways of their 'barbarian' allies. Sometimes they even joined in the festivals, finding links with their own Gods, and at such times religious fervour led them to couple with slaves – but only slaves; no woman of the Iceni would lie with a Roman. Consequently, a few 'children of the God' with part-Roman blood would grow up in the service of Iceni nobles.

For their part, the Iceni bore with the burden of taxes and the crude humour of the common legionary with gritted teeth. They had no swords with which to fight, but they savoured the thought of the spears they were hoarding, and the swift chariots that had been put out of sight as soon as Romans were reported to be near. Iceni honour and Iceni pride had not been lost, only secreted in shadow to be brought into full sunlight when the Goddess called.

In her fifteenth summer, Rhiannon attended for the first time the five-yearly Solstice festival at the *nemeton* on the cliffs of the north, when adults from all the forts across Icenia gathered with the king's warriors to celebrate midsummer. She joined the moon vigil as the women kept watch through the brief night, and she saw the men return in file to the solemn beat of a drum, with Eogan wearing the bloody maned head and trailing hide of a stallion offered in secret rites at the oak grove.

That year Audagas's oldest son Cadfan was Green King. Twelve young warriors formed his band of companions as the festivities filled the day with horse races, foot races and contests of spear-throwing and stone-slinging. For all his youth, Cadfan's war skills were impressive – almost as impressive as his boasting. Yet even he was silenced by awe of the occasion when he was brought, bound in green branches, up from the beach to where the fires waited, in the ritual that retold in symbol the death of the God. The offering that year was a shaggy bull; it gave up its blood as Cadfan was released from his bonds.

As always at festivals Rhiannon found herself separated from the other revellers by her role as Maiden. Morica or Erefwen stayed near as though guarding her and she felt herself an onlooker, detached from what was happening around her, cool and faintly offended by the lusty behaviour of the young men and women who were her friends. She spent most of the festivals in a drugged haze, under the cold and celibate influence of Albina the Virgin.

But if her body could be made unresponsive her thoughts remained her own and they turned often to memories of Farann and Cunovinda, especially when travellers came to Oakhillfort to attend the markets, and barter for goods. But she heard no news of the fate of the two young Trinovantes, or of their father Vindorex. For all she knew they might have taken ship and sailed off the end of the earth.

And all the time the Great Year drew nearer.

Eogan studied the course of the stars and exchanged observations with his masters on Mona, though the nineteen year cycle had seldom been known to deviate. It would swing round to its end and its new beginning when Rhiannon was in her eighteenth year.

Rhiannon's birth time had coincided with Imbolc, the quickening of the year when winter began to lose its grip and ewes came into milk – the month of the miraculous rowan tree. Imbolc came again, for the sixteenth time since her birthing, and that year there was snow, deep and soft.

Adalma had a head-cold and wanted to do nothing but sit by the fire in the horsemaster's house huddled in blankets while her mother fed her broth. Rhiannon's sister, Araunah, too, was suffering from her usual winter affliction of the lungs, being regularly rubbed with mutton fat, swaddled in wrappings and made to sit in a room where herbs and cobwebs were burned on a brazier. The smoke made Araunah cough until her eyes were red and streaming with tears, but old Cauva studied the bowl into which the girl spat the resultant mucus and pronounced the treatment efficacious.

Tired of being indoors among invalids, Rhiannon wrapped up warmly in her furs and went out beneath a pale sky in which the sun showed through thin cloud, giving little warmth. The sacred oak was naked of leaves but wearing a thin covering of snow which had begun to melt and form icicles that dripped onto trodden snow beneath. All around the houses, along the pathways, the snow had been churned into dirty slush. Women gathered by the well, chipping at the covering of ice to draw their daily water; geese waddled after scraps and dogs sniffed about. It was a time of year Rhiannon hated. For her, spring was always too long in coming.

As often when she felt unsettled, she sought the company of horses, down at the enclosures in the snow-covered woods. Warriors clad in furs and thick hooded cloaks stood guard around the herd, stamping their feet and blowing on their hands, or leaning on their lances among the bare trees. Two of them stood together by the thorn and hazel hedge, and as Rhiannon approached she recognised her kinsmen Ylas and Matuac, the sturdy, fair-haired twins, who were arguing the merits of their respective stallions.

'Let Rhiannon decide,' Ylas exclaimed with his broad, sunny grin as he beckoned to her. 'Come here, cousin. Which do you say is the better horse – my Windspeed, or Matuac's Greatheart?'

She considered, aware of the strong rivalry between the twins. If she chose one horse above the other she would be out of favour with one of the young men. 'Greatheart for strength, Windspeed for fleetness,' she decided. 'If danger threatened, I'd be happy with either one – with either of you astride him, to ride beside me.'

Matuac narrowed his eyes at her, disappointed that she had not favoured him above his brother, but Ylas laughed, his grin showing up the white scar that sliced across his cheek in line with his thick fair moustache. Rhiannon still felt guilty for his scars, but Ylas had recovered his full strength and seemed to have forgotten the episode of the boar. 'A diplomatic answer, cousin! One worthy of your father the king.'

'It was a woman's answer,' Matuac argued. 'Flattering, but telling nothing of her real thoughts.'

'And so worthy of her mother the queen,' Ylas laughed, refusing to take the matter seriously. 'And also worthy of the White Goddess – another enigmatic lady.'

Matuac was not satisfied. He laid a hand on Rhiannon's arm, saying earnestly, 'Yet, if you had to choose, if enemies were after you and you had only those two horses by you . . . which would you ride?'

'The nearest,' Rhiannon said, and slipped away before Matuac could see how his bafflement made her smile. Behind her, she heard Ylas laugh out loud, teasing his brother. There was a thump, and when she glanced round Ylas was flat on his back in the snow, having been felled by Matuac's fist. But he was still laughing.

In one of the shelters, she found Teyrnon tending a sick mare that lay listless on a bed of straw. She stayed with him a while, gentling the frightened horse and savouring the undemanding friendship of Adalma's younger brother.

Since their joint misadventure nearly five years ago, she and Teyrnon had grown closer, though he remained in awe of her. He was also sixteen now, still slight and wiry, but already acknowledged to be a master reinsman. No one among the warriors, male or female, could leap from a chariot to stand on the backs of his horses, or run up and down the yoke pole while at full gallop, not with the athletic ease of Teyrnon, the young horsemaster.

That day he could hardly contain his delight; he had been given permission to accompany his father to the trading of horses which lately had begun to take place each spring at a new trading post the Romans had encouraged to grow at a settlement near a river-crossing. The Romans called the place Londinium.

'The king's going, too,' Teyrnon told Rhiannon. 'He's hoping his Jipshun horses might have arrived.'

'Jipshun?' Rhiannon asked, her brow furrowed. 'What are they?'

'Bigger, stronger horses than ours. They come from . . .' He frowned as he tried to remember, 'from somewhere beyond Gaul, and across an ocean. Somewhere at the far end of the Empire – so Eogan told me.'

'You mean from Egypt?'

His freckled face cleared. 'That's right! The king your father paid a lot of money to the merchant who promised to bring them, and he'll have to pay even more when they get here. A stallion and three mares – for breeding. Imagine it, Rhiannon! With Jipshun horses added to our own, we'll be able to ask whatever price we like at market. Everyone will want an Iceni horse to ride.' He blinked at her, puzzled. 'Didn't you know about this? I thought for sure the king would have told you.'

'No, he hasn't.' In fact, Prasutagus hardly spoke to her except when it was unavoidable.

'I expect he has a lot of things to think about,' Teyrnon said.

She raised a wan smile, grateful for his friendship even though he knew nothing about her relationship with the king. 'Yes, you may be right, Teyrnon. Do you know . . . is Londinium anywhere near the new fort of the Trinovante chiefs?'

He shrugged. 'I dunno. Why?'

'I was just thinking that you might hear news of . . . of my friend Cunovinda. You must remember her. And her brother, Farann. If you do hear anybody mention the Trinovantes . . .'

'I'll flick my ears in that direction and listen, like the horses do,' he promised with a grin.

As the daylight began to wane, Rhiannon took a roundabout way back to the fort, purposely to avoid running into the twins again. Ylas she adored; he was open and uncomplicated. But Matuac disturbed her. He disturbed her in almost the same way as Erefwen did. Both of them seemed to watch her with predatory eyes. Both of them were equally unwelcome to Rhiannon.

Deep in the woods, near a path that led up from the river near Morica's hut, Rhiannon saw Garanhir sitting on a fallen trunk intent on whittling a stick with a knife. As always, her heart leapt when she saw the king's champion – the man she believed to be her father. His figure was bulky with furs, in profile to her with the hood of his cloak flung back to reveal his shaggy fair hair and the long moustache that obscured most of his mouth.

Rhiannon hung back, wondering if today she might dare to ask him the questions that burned in her mind; then she realised that Garanhir was not alone – her mother stood near him in the dusky snow-light, half hidden from Rhiannon by the trunk of an ancient tree.

Once before Rhiannon had spied the pair together like this. Then, she had not understood. Now, all her suspicions were alerted as she flattened herself against a tree and strained her ears to listen.

'I want no wife,' Garanhir said, his knife dashing curls of wood from the stick he was holding, his head bent over it as he refused even to look at the queen.

'It's time,' Boudicca replied in a flat voice. 'It's past time. The tribe needs your sons, and your daughters.'

He did look up then, to fix his eyes wordlessly on her face, and Rhiannon saw her mother's hand clench in folds of her thick cloak. The queen stiffened, but kept her head erect.

'I suggest it for your own sake,' she said. 'Some of our people are wondering why you remain unwed.'

'You know the reason,' he replied.

Boudicca caught her breath. 'Do you want others to guess

it, too? Will you bring shame on both of us for something long past?'

'Past, lady?' The words were almost inaudible. 'Until the wild geese call me . . .'

The queen made an angry gesture, but her voice came low and hoarse, so that Rhiannon had to strain to hear the words. 'It was madness then and it's more than madness now. I have other concerns. You forced me to seek another purpose!'

'Circumstances forced us, not any choice of mine. You were and are my queen. And since the king made me his champion . . .' He shrugged in his furs, his breath pouring out in a cloud as he sighed. 'We had no choice. Either of us. Which is not to say that I have forgotten.'

'Perhaps you should.' The words seemed forced out of her. 'I *am* the queen. And as queen I tell you that my people need strong sons of your loins as future warriors to serve my daughter and my daughter's daughter – and *her* daughter after her.'

He looked down at the stick in his hand and ran a thumb along the edge of his knife. 'Where do you suggest I might find a woman worthy of bearing my sons, lady?'

'I know of several who would take on the task with joy. Adalma – '

His head jerked up and he shot to his feet, every line expressing outrage. 'That child!'

'A woman now,' Boudicca argued, though her voice was strained 'A good, gentle woman, who loves you, Garanhir. Last year, when she was Willow Maid – when she presented the victor's garland to you at the races . . . Didn't you feel it then? Didn't you see it in her face?'

There was a long silence in which Garanhir seemed to be searching for answers in Boudicca's own face. At last he said softly, 'I see no other woman but you, lady. You know that. But if you tell me I must take a wife, then a wife I'll have. Adalma, or some other. It's of no importance to me.'

For another endless time they stood looking at each other, not touching, not speaking except with their eyes, saying things that Rhiannon could only sense from their attitudes; then the queen turned away and made off through the snow towards the hill fort.

Another woman might have been weeping, but Rhiannon

doubted that a single tear dimmed her mother's eye. She had never known her mother to weep – not since her brother Mocuxsoris died.

But Rhiannon's eyes were blurred. She had believed her mother to be a true, honourable queen, a faithful Maiden and then a faithful wife, but now she knew better. To couple in the Mysteries at the command of the Gods was good – all understood that – but when her mother had talked of shame Rhiannon had known there was more to it. Boudicca and Garanhir had been lovers. Boudicca had betrayed her husband.

Although she knew that Prasutagus was not her father, Rhiannon could not discard the affection she had always felt for him in spite of his seeming indifference towards her. He was a good man, essentially a kind man, his thoughts often locked away behind still pale eyes that Rhiannon now realised held sadness – was it any wonder he was sad if he knew that his beautiful queen had been unfaithful with his own champion?

Yet somewhere inside her she felt pity for Garanhir, too. The king was an old man and could not live for ever. Garanhir must have hoped to marry the widowed Boudicca when the time came. It was an outcome Rhiannon herself had hoped for.

What manner of woman was her mother? To make a cuckold of her husband; to thrust off her lover and order him to marry elsewhere; to suggest gentle Adalma as his mate . . . It struck Rhiannon that her mother was without human feeling. Boudicca the queen, Boudicca the strong and sure, had no heart.

Soon, the winter lost its grip and green things began to peer through the muddied snow as it melted. At the manhood of the sun, the spring equinox, furze fires bloomed across the heath in celebration, burning off all the tough ends of the bushes so that new shoots would grow for the stock to browse on. The cattle and sheep were driven out, to be rid of bad spirits in the smoke, and at the oak grove lambs were slaughtered in thanksgiving for the quickening of the earth.

Because she was watching for it, Rhiannon observed the inner torment that Garanhir endured as the weeks passed. At first he seemed withdrawn, but slowly he began to take notice of the young women, especially Adalma. Perhaps for the first time he saw how the girl with her sad-puppy eyes blushed with pleasure whenever he looked at her. But still he hesitated.

Finally, on a spring day just before Beltane, Rhiannon saw Garanhir set out wearing his best cloak and ornaments, with his fine mature body oiled until it shone and his hair washed with lime so that it stood back from the Warrior's Light on his brow like a spiky crest. He made straight for the horse enclosures and a meeting with Vranaun, the horsemaster, Adalma's father.

Driven by a fierce emotion she could not define, Rhiannon ran through the woods and up to the sacred oak grove, seeking answers. But the grove was still, devoid even of the birds that elsewhere sang and mated. Here, beneath a circle of sky, sacred rites were celebrated in due season around an altar formed of a single huge flint. The stone was embedded in the ground, its white surface hollowed into natural cups now darkened by the blood of sacrifices. At Beltane the flint altar would run again in blood – the blood of hares, at Dia's own festival, when the Willow Maid held sway.

And in two years' time would come the Great Year, the season of the Maiden, when Rhiannon must meet with the God . . .

Shaking the thought away, she climbed into the branches of one of the tallest oaks. Poised on a gnarled bough she clung to the tree's trunk as to a lover, her cheek laid to the rough bark for comfort.

Numbly, she stared at the familiar view. Along the knoll, a mist of smoke lay on the windless air, floating from the thatched roofs of Oakhillfort to drift above the steep grassed banks of the defences. Beyond it, the wastes of the marshes stretched dark and forbidding among fronds of mist, a lacework of bare, matted branches so early in the year. Part of her destiny lay there, she knew. The thought of it enticed and yet alarmed her.

To the north lay the slow downsloping of ground towards the shore, with the horse enclosures among the woods, and then the dull shine of the Great Bay, mostly sand banks now with the tide gone far out. On the horizon lay a dark uneven line that was the further coast of the Bay – territory of the Coritani.

'Rhiannon!' Faint and far away came the voice of Adalma, searching for her friend. 'Rhia! Can you hear me?'

Not wanting to be found, Rhiannon lithely climbed down from the crotch of the tree, hanging from her hands before making the final drop to grass where primroses were in bloom. The spreading oaks left little light for undergrowth. The ground beneath them was brown with dead leaves, uneven with gnarled roots worn smooth by the feet that had used them as steps to climb down the side of the hill to the dark pool half hidden under an outcrop of chalky rock.

Rhiannon crouched by the pool, holding her hair back from her face as she bent to peer at her reflection. Faintly at the bottom of the still water she could see the glint of gold, and pale round shapes that she knew were human skulls, the result of human sacrifices – war-captives and criminals offered to the Gods.

'Hear me, Epona,' she muttered between clenched teeth. 'Let him not ask for Adalma's hand. Let him not!'

The surface of the pool shimmered, though no breeze disturbed the calm air under the oaks. Rhiannon's reflection broke into a million slivers and vanished. The Goddess was spurning her prayer.

'Rhiannon!' Adalma was nearer now, her hushed voice betraying her awe of the grove and the sacred pool, and with her was Araunah, her clear voice calling, 'Sister! Sister!'

It was Araunah who found her. Crying, 'There you are!' in delight at her own cleverness, the youngster with her silvery hair and wide blue eyes darted out from behind a holly bush. At eleven she was thin as a reed, with veins showing blue beneath white skin at her wrists and temples, and across her chin. She had never been strong and each winter's chills made fresh demands on her meagre resources; but Araunah remained bright and lovable. 'Here she is, Adalma! I told you she'd be here!'

Slowly, Rhiannon got to her feet, brushing leaves from her seat and from her hands, raising a half-smile as Adalma appeared, out of breath but with joy shining from every pore of her plain face.

'Oh, Rhiannon! Rhiannon!' She flung her arms around her

friend, hugged her and then withdrew, flushing, folding her hands under her chin in an agony of delight. 'It's happened. Garanhir spoke to my father. They've agreed a bride-price!'

'That's wonderful,' Rhiannon forced herself to say. 'I'm happy for you, Adalma.'

Her friend gaped at her. 'Why aren't you surprised? Did you know?'

'I'm the Maiden,' Rhiannon said, deliberately enigmatic. She saw the comprehension – and the awe – that came over Adalma.

'Of course. Yes. You foresaw it. Sometimes I forget . . . Oh, I wish you'd told me! I can't believe it. I really can't. That the Goddess should smile on me this way. I've loved him so long, Rhiannon. Since I was a child. I never dared to hope. He's the king's champion. He could have any woman he wanted.'

No, he couldn't, Rhiannon thought. The woman Garanhir really wanted was out of his reach – the woman he wanted was her mother, Boudicca, the queen. But she couldn't tell that to Adalma. Adalma must be allowed her happiness, though it was based on falsehood. Garanhir had offered for her hand only because the queen had told him to do so. But Adalma would never know that. Boudicca wouldn't tell; neither would Rhiannon. And Garanhir, the most honourable of warriors, would carry out his role as he did most things, staunchly and faithfully. At least he would be kind, which was more than could be said of many husbands. And Adalma would have her heart's wish fulfilled.

Perhaps it suited the purpose of the Goddess to have it so.

Adalma and Garanhir were married without delay. At the feasting afterwards, both queen and king gave gifts to show their affection and their pleasure in the match.

As the sky darkened from evening to night, the young men swooped on Garanhir and bore him bodily away to the roundhouse that had been erected for him. The young women surrounded Adalma, clutching at her to drag her in pursuit of her new husband despite her squeals and blushes. Rhiannon remained behind in the doorway of the great hall, watching the fun, feeling as isolated from it as if she had taken drugged wine. Outside the hall a crowd of people laughed and recalled other weddings, other beddings.

Rhiannon glanced behind to where her mother and the king still sat with the elders, both of them smiling, apparently enjoying themselves. And it was a lie. Oh, it was a blatant falseness!

Unable to bear the torment inside her, she pushed a way among the crowd and sought the shadows. She heard a giant's roar, like a furious bear, muffled by shouts and squeals. The crowds of youths and maidens ran out from the bridal house screaming and laughing, tumbling over one another in their rush to escape the bridegroom's fury at their teasing.

Avoiding all eyes, Rhiannon climbed to the solitude of the grassed banks that surrounded the settlement, where only a couple of watchmen patrolled in the darkness. It was here that Cunovinda used to come when she was troubled, to commune with Rhea of the White Track of Stars. But Rhiannon didn't see the Milky Way; for her there was only the old, waning moon – the moon of Caridwen the White Sow. Rhiannon had begun to believe as Eogan and Morica believed, that all the signs and portents pointed only one way – to doom.

Five

As always, the Maiden was excluded from the pleasures of Beltane Eve, when all the unmarried youth of Oakhillfort went chasing the hare with among them the current Green King and the Willow Maid – who that year were Unthaus and Cameira. The merrymakers returned with the dawn, bringing branches of hawthorn to bestrew the roofs of all the houses, and the day continued with races at which Cameira officiated as prize-giver, wreathed in green willow to symbolise virginity. But after the sacrifices and ceremonies round the fires at the oak grove, the Willow Maid was seen to head off toward the darkening fields hand in hand with Unthaus.

The day following Beltane marked the beginning of the hawthorn month, the month of chastity when all the adult men traditionally left the village, some to the hunt, some to attend the courts, some to occupy guard camps amid the woods and along the shore. That year, Segovax the lawgiver led the party of elders who would sit in judgement over quarrels and grievances among the outlying clans; the king had other business.

Taking with him an escort of warriors, along with Vranaun the horsemaster and his son Teyrnon – the youth bursting with pride – Prasutagus was leading a herd of Iceni-bred horses to the spring trading in Londinium. He would bring back with him, so he declared, a stallion and three mares all the way from distant Egypt.

Cheering children ran with them down the track towards the network of fields and farms in hollows and on hillsides between Oakhillfort and the well-trodden path of the Way.

'I hope they don't run across brigands,' Adalma sighed, thinking of her new husband who rode with the king. 'Oh, blessed Dia bring him safely home, and soon.'

Rhiannon too was impatient; she wanted to see the Egyptian horses. And she prayed that there might be news of Farann and Cunovinda.

A sudden change in weather had brought a sea-mist writhing off the Great Bay on the day the king returned. His approach was hidden from his watchmen by swirls of clammy fog; he was at the gates before the horn blew to alert the village.

Rhiannon was down by the hare cages with Araunah and a new-born litter of pups whose mother had chosen to whelp under one of the granaries. She heard the growing commotion of voices as people hurried to greet the king and his party and hear the news.

'It's father!' Araunah cried, leaping up. 'He promised to bring me a new bracelet!'

Together, they ran to the centre of the village, where the crowd parted to let them through. The leaves of the sacred oak scarcely moved under their veil of mist as Prasutagus rode up beneath the tree with Vranaun beside him leading a strange-looking horse. It was taller than the Iceni ponies and of smoother coat. Grey hairs darkened its mane and tail but the rest of it was white.

Rhiannon stared at the animal as if mesmerised. A white mare! It had to be a sign.

But rather than showing pride in his purchase, Prasutagus was frowning over his grey beard and his scarred eye looked more evil than humorous. Perhaps it was because he had brought only one Egyptian horse and not the four he had promised.

Leaving the horsemaster in charge as people swarmed round to stare at the mare, the king strode away towards the queen's house, where at the doorway his wife was waiting. Araunah ran after him and burst into the house to ask if her father had remembered the gift he had promised her. Usually when he returned from a journey he was pleased to see his younger daughter; he was wont to laugh and pull her hair, demanding a kiss, but now he swung on her with angry words. Her wide-eyed hurt and ready tears made his frown deepen. He glowered at Rhiannon, who had paused in the passageway.

'Take her away, can't you? There'll be no bracelet. I had no money left for baubles.'

Before Rhiannon could move, her sister whirled and pushed past her, weeping.

Prasutagus had turned away and was throwing out his arms in a gesture of frustration, saying to Boudicca, 'One mare. That's all we acquired! I paid that merchant a small fortune on his sworn promise. A stallion and three mares – that was what we agreed. He brings a stallion and one mare. Another mare died on the voyage, so he said. And then the customs officer . . . Proud Belin help us! He sent for the procurator's representative. It seems we're not allowed to import stallions – except at a cost that Nero himself would balk at. I was left with this one mare, for which I was robbed of every last coin in my purse. I had to borrow to pay the import tax they demanded. Do you believe it, Boudicca?! I had such hopes!'

'You were ever optimistic where Roman friendship is concerned,' Boudicca said, pitying him and yet impatient with him. 'Did you really believe they'd allow us to breed better horses? We're Iceni. We're savages to them – less than the flies they flick from their fruit bowls. Vindorex said it. Mocuxsoris said it.'

He lifted a fist as if to strike her. 'And both of them are

dead! Dead!' He stood there shaking with rage, pale eyes glaring into fierce green. She hadn't even flinched. What he read in her face made him drop his hand to his side and his whole body sagged as if he were suddenly aware of his age and the long distance he had ridden. 'Where are the slaves? Get me some wine. Get me some food.'

Boudicca sent a flashing glance at her older daughter and with a gesture bade her leave. In this mood, only his wife knew how to deal with the ageing king.

Stunned by what Prasutagus had said, Rhiannon turned like one in a dream and went outside into the misty air. People still crowded round the Egyptian mare, examining it closely and discussing its merits with Vranaun.

'The king has named her Starbright,' he was saying in answer to questions. 'Yes, of course we can breed from her. I'll get her in foal if I have to lift the stallion onto her back myself!'

The crowd laughed and several voices called bawdy remarks, making suggestions and puns. Rhiannon hardly heard any of it. Vindorex is dead, she kept thinking. The king said it: Vindorex is dead. Then what of Cunovinda? What of Farann?

She walked straight into someone whose arms closed firmly round her waist, holding her against a strong male body. When she looked up in outrage, struggling to be free, she saw that it was Matuac.

'Don't fight me!' he grinned. 'Or . . . yes, go on wriggling. It feels good.'

'Matuac . . . Stop it!'

Her hand connected with his cheek, though not very hard since she was impeded by his closeness. Even so, the blow was enough to make Matuac release her, his eyes gleaming, his strong teeth showing under the droop of his fair moustache.

'You ought to look where you're going,' he said. 'What were you thinking about? Or were you off in one of your daydreams?'

Without replying, she shouldered past him, unaware that his yearning gaze followed her, lingering on the lithe line of her back and the curve of rounded buttocks under the cling of deerskin trews.

Among the crowd she saw Adalma, gazing up in adoration

at Garanhir, who had his arm loosely about her shoulders, though he was listening to the exchanges between the crowd and Vranaun. The sight made Rhiannon turn away sharply, and then to her relief she saw Teyrnon, and with him sunny Ylas, so like Matuac in looks but in nature so different.

They both looked up as she approached, Ylas's grin beaming out while freckled Teyrnon greeted her more shyly.

'A pity you couldn't be with us, Rhiannon,' Ylas said. 'What sights we've seen. The south country's all dotted with stone houses – villas, the Romans call them. And in Londinium there are great warehouses, and temples, and craftsmen of all kinds. And ships crowding the river. You can buy anything there. And so many people! People from tribes I never even heard of. Dumnonii. Armoricans from Gaul . . .'

'Trinovantes?' she suggested.

'Oh, some of them too. Everyone was there.'

'Then you must have heard all the gossip,' she said, a glance at Teyrnon begging him to remember what particular gossip she had asked him to listen for.

Eagerly, the horsemaster's son said, 'The Romans have a new Emperor. Nero, his name is.'

'She knows that!' Ylas chaffed him. 'It's moons since we heard that old Claudius was dead. On the other hand, Rhiannon, you won't have heard the latest on the new governor-general. Quintus Verianus? Appointed last year?'

'What of it?'

'Dead,' Ylas said, his eyes dancing. 'Killed by our rain and fogs, poor man. They're having to send someone else to replace him as commander of the legions, and meanwhile Mona stays safe. Won't Eogan be pleased?'

'Perhaps he arranged the illness,' she said. 'The Druids have strong enchantment. They must have, or Mona would have fallen by now.'

Ylas grinned at her, fondly and teasingly. 'Well, you know more about that than I do, Maiden. But it does mean that the procurator's in sole charge and by all accounts he's greedy as a fat sow grubbing after beech mast. The Trinovantes we met said he's taxing them so tightly to pay for the new temple at Camulodunon that they have to think twice before they make water – they're afraid he'll charge them for the pleasure it gives them.'

'We . . .' Teyrnon began, and chewed his lip, his eyes troubled. 'We didn't hear anything about prince Vindorex. At least, *I* didn't. Did you, Ylas?'

'Vindorex?' Ylas's smile died and his eyes were shadowed as he looked at Rhiannon.

'Cunovinda's father,' Rhiannon reminded him.

'Just so.' His steady gaze stayed on her face. 'Teyrnon's right – we heard nothing. There was nothing to hear. I talked with a warrior from Caesaromagus – a kinsman of Baro, the Trinovante chief. Baro has ruled since the Romans disarmed the tribes and Vindorex fled from Camulodunon. Since then, none of them have had word of him, or of his children.'

'Then they may still be alive!'

Ylas shook his head, saying gently, 'That's dreaming, Rhiannon.'

She understood what he was saying but she refused to believe it. They couldn't be dead, not all of them. If it were true she would surely have sensed it: the Goddess would have revealed it.

'I was sorry, too,' Ylas said. 'Farann was my friend. But after nearly five years . . .' He shrugged expressively. 'Outlaws, wolves, bears, storms, floods, Romans, disease, cold . . . A thousand dangers lurk in the world. You have to accept it. They're gone.'

'Who's gone?' Matuac demanded, thrusting himself into a scene he had been watching with growing irritation.

'Farann and Cunovinda,' Ylas explained.

'Oh, them! Well, they never did fit in. Farann never was one of us. Too quiet. You can never trust quiet people – you never know what's going on in their heads. The girl wasn't bad, though. I might have enjoyed rubbing bellies with her when she grew up.'

Rhiannon turned away in distress and left the three young men, though behind her she heard Ylas say wearily, 'Brother, you're a loose-tongued fool.'

In late summer of that same year, a member of the procurator's staff arrived at Oakhillfort with a small escort of subordinates, retainers and soldiers, apparently on a courtesy visit. Rhiannon saw them coming, but she was riding as part of a hunting party and by common consent the hunters swung away into the woods to avoid a meeting with the Romans. Romans had to be endured but they were not welcomed as friends.

The hunting was good that day. Within a short time they came across a herd of red deer, hinds and fawns – at that time of year the stags kept themselves in separate groups, waiting for the autumn. The dogs roused the herd and soon Rhiannon was urging her pony through flickering shade and sunlight, ducking under branches, her spear poised. Around her her companions shouted to each other and the dogs raced, barking.

The Queen of the Woods favoured their efforts: the chase yielded three hinds and two fawns. Exhilarated, some of the party dragged the trophies to a nearby stream while others retrieved their precious spears, then all of them flopped down in the grass. Only Unthaus was quiet, as was his nature. He lay flat on his back with an arm across his eyes, smiling as Cameira and her brother Matuac argued as to whose spear had made a kill. Ylas boasted that his throw had gone straight to the heart and stopped the doe in its tracks. Rhiannon boasted with them; she had played her part, too.

As the sun westered over the marshes, they came home to Oakhillfort weary but pleased with themselves. Rhiannon rode on down to the horse enclosures to see her mount safely rubbed down and pastured with the rest. She was drawn by curiosity to the new enclosure where the Egyptian mare Starbright was grazing, twitching her elegant grey-shaded tail against flies. *The white mare.*

Standing behind the thorn edge, Rhiannon stared at the animal, her thoughts on the Goddess and Her divine purposes, whatever they might be. Morica said that there was to all things a pattern ordained by Dia. Did this white mare have a purpose, too?

As dusk gathered beneath the trees Boudicca came down through the woods in search of her daughter. Seeing the still figure by the thorn hedge she paused beside the grey bole of an ash tree, her brow furrowed.

'Rhiannon!' the name rapped out of her, spoken in a voice which, though low, held sharp authority.

The girl turned as if startled, and on her face was the fey, wide-pupilled look that Boudicca recognised as an echo of the vagueness brought on by the ivy-drug. Being subject to the drug since childhood had affected Rhiannon, made her dreamy and solitary, as if at times she were inhabited by spirits – or by the Goddess.

Though Boudicca respected the forces that governed such things, as a mother she disliked it. She feared for her daughter. But also she was aware that the balance of the Goddess's favour tilted ever more surely away from herself and toward Rhiannon. Her time was fast passing; she was thirty-five years old, prone to muscular aches and pains, her hair less lustrous than it had been in earlier years, her flesh less firm. In contrast, Rhiannon glowed with the glorious beauty of youth. Her time was yet to come.

Where was the fulfilment the Goddess had promised to her servant Boudicca?

'Mother?' Rhiannon held herself straight, refusing to cower before the queen's frown. 'Were you looking for me?'

'What are you doing here all alone?'

'I'm not alone.' A glance indicated the figure of a guard lounging against a tree – the man looked like Duihno – and Teyrnon and his father, who were visible inside the larger enclosure tending a foal's hoof. 'Besides . . . the Goddess is with me. She's always with me. You should know that, mother. Won't She protect me?'

For a moment their glances locked like the antlers of two stags at the rutting season. Boudicca felt baffled, unable to guess at the thoughts going on behind gold-flecked eyes that stared at her so steadily. It wasn't insolence – not quite – but whatever it was it irritated her. 'Only if She chooses,' she replied. 'Rhiannon . . . I came to bring you news. We're going on a journey. To Camulodunon.'

Rhiannon's eyes widened. Something in the pit of her stomach jolted with uncontrollable hope, vain though she knew it to be; at Camulodunon there might be news of Farann and Cunovinda. 'Why? Is there trouble? The Romans who came today – '

'They came to bring an invitation. The new governor-general wants to meet with us as he takes up his appointment. We'll see how these Romans live in their fancy new town, eh? There'll be a a great feast, and games to watch. Maybe chariot races.'

'I thought you hated the Romans,' Rhiannon said.

A grimace twisted Boudicca's mouth. Her eyes were cold as they focused beyond her daughter's shoulder, seeing imaginary foes, and her hand tightened on the hilt of the dagger at her belt. 'To hunt deer one must know their habits. To catch a boar, one must seek out the forest places where he lives. To defeat any enemy one must study him as closely as possible, while he is off his guard.'

'Perhaps that's their reason for wanting us in their colonia – so *they* can study *us*. You always said the Romans could not be trusted.'

Boudicca nodded, appreciating the girl's astuteness. 'I don't doubt they have some hidden motive. But we'll behave as they expect – we'll gape and marvel like rude barbarians, and watch and listen while we enjoy their hospitality. Hatred isn't enough. One must have knowledge, too. We shall go to Camulodunon, and we shall smile on these Romans who came to liberate and stayed to enslave us. It will be a useful experience for you. A queen should travel beyond the borders of her own lands. The world's growing wider, Rhiannon. You must grow with it, and learn all you can.'

'Yes, mother.'

Smiling, Boudicca reached to straighten a blowing lock of her daughter's bright hair. She felt suddenly closer to Rhiannon than for some time. 'I've been speaking with Adalma. She says she hardly sees you since she became a married woman.'

'She has other concerns now,' Rhiannon said, easing away from her mother's touch.

'Surely her marriage didn't end your friendship?' Noting her daughter's covert withdrawal, Boudicca frowned. 'Or do you envy her happiness?'

'No, of course I don't.'

The queen's voice sharpened with suspicion. 'Tell me the truth, Rhiannon – do you wish that you were in her place? Do you dream of lying with Garanhir?'

The question came like summer lightning, so shocking that Rhiannon's flush turned into scarlet fire. 'No!'

Her mother didn't believe her. 'I've always known you

admired him. Many women had hopes, but . . . Is this why you've been avoiding him and his new wife? You're jealous of Adalma?'

'No!' Clenching her hands into fists, Rhiannon shook back her thick mane of flaxen-red curls. Her eyes and her voice spat defiance. 'I'm not the one who should be jealous. He was never *my* lover.'

Boudicca's face froze, then contorted with anger. Her hand lashed out, to crack across the girl's face. The blow jerked Rhiannon's head back, sent her spinning off balance. She fell against the hedge of the mare's enclosure, crying out as the thorns tore at her hands and clothes, scoring her flesh. Then she fell to the grass and lay there, cooling her throbbing cheek in the lush growth. Her hands stung, her limbs and body smarted in too many places to count. She would never forgive her mother.

From over her head, Boudicca's voice came hoarse with fury. 'You may be Maiden, but *I* am queen yet. Remember that, Rhiannon!'

The grass brushed as she stormed away, and on the other side of the thorn hedge Rhiannon heard the white mare Starbright snorting, her head low, as if she offered comfort. 'Epona . . .' Rhiannon whispered, feeling the clouds gather in her head as she imagined herself leaping up onto the mare's back and being carried away, over hill and fen, forest and ocean. Away . . . maybe all the way to the Glass Castle.

'Lady?' A hand on her arm startled her out of her bitter dream.

Duihno squatted beside her. His hair hung lank, bark-brown, either side of a thin, pinched face in which his eyes were set too close together for beauty. 'Can I help?'

Rhiannon sat up, then allowed him to help her to her feet. The left side of her face felt swollen and hot, the right side was numb with scratches and when she laid her hand there she discovered a thread of blood. But she shook her head, edging away from Duihno. 'Thank you. I'm all right.'

'What did you say to her?' he asked, crooked teeth showing through a shaggy, dirty-looking moustache. 'She was furious. The queen doesn't like to be crossed.'

'That's her right,' Rhiannon said levelly, glancing at him from her eye corner. Ever since he had slashed Farann's arm with his knife she had feared his temper, though towards her personally he had never shown anything but deference. 'What occurs between my mother and me is our concern, not yours, Duihno. Get back to your post.'

'As you say, lady.' He saluted, a fist to his brow, and turned to amble away.

Rhiannon watched him with narrowed eyes, wondering if there had been mockery in that salute. But she thought not. Duihno had no subtlety in him. His emotions and needs were basic – food, drink, sleep, fighting, coupling. He had never found a wife; he sated himself on female slaves. But for years he had lusted after Erefwen, the acolyte priestess. That cold maiden continued to spurn him with a scorn that only inflamed him. Erefwen should take care, Rhiannon thought. Of all the warriors, Duihno was the most unpredictable. His lusts were hot but his temper was hotter.

Reluctantly, her thoughts went back to the queen. Rhiannon was beginning to despise her mother for what she thought of as her coldness: Boudicca cared deeply for no one; all she cared about was being queen. She had betrayed her husband; she had callously discarded Garanhir. Had she ever truly loved?

Between them, the constraint deepened. They were both too proud and stubborn to end it.

Boudicca had been shocked by Rhiannon's insolence and horrified to have her old indiscretion thrown up at her. It was long over. Years past. How had Rhiannon known of it? Could she divine the past as well as see the future?

Since childhood the girl had been granted sight of the spectral White Mare, the visible form of the Goddess Epona. She was known to have the power of prediction. She communed with the moon at night, alone up on the high banked defences of the fort. The people avoided disturbing her vigils. Perhaps it was true what they said – that Rhiannon could talk with the Goddess face to face.

The more Boudicca brooded on it, the more she wondered what manner of child she and Huan had produced. Or had it been in truth Huan, had it been in truth herself? Ritual lore taught that at such times the human flesh of the celebrants was merely an instrument possessed by the life-force of an Immortal.

The Goddess has granted us a true Maiden. That echo from long ago sent a chill coursing up Boudicca's spine to raise the hairs on her nape. 'Comes the next Great Year, who knows what deep magic will be needed?' Morica, too, could foresee the future, as could Eogan. Their warnings sounded ever clearer. The winds of fate were blowing.

But she, Boudicca, would be ready. She had been waiting for it all her life.

Six

Once again a party of Iceni warriors, led by the king and queen and accompanied by slaves and laden packhorses, travelled to a meeting at Camulodunon. This time most of them were mounted and only a few outriders travelled in chariots, wheeling ahead and behind to keep a watch. Rhiannon rode behind her mother and the grey-haired king. She felt tense, sensing portents on the late summer wind, but beside her young Araunah chattered excitedly, relishing the adventure. Her cough had been much improved that summer and there was hope that she might outgrow the yearly winter ravages of her lung ailment.

The queen's family was escorted by several of the elders and their kin, the whole party being guarded by warriors of the royal household, including the twins and their sister Cameira. The trusted champions, Nuadat and Garanhir, had remained behind with their wives, charged with the defence of Oakhillfort.

As the travellers left the forests of Icenia, the first signs of Roman occupation showed themselves in lands formerly held by the Catuvellauni, and before them by the Trinovantes: neat white villas had bloomed in sheltered, defensible spots, and groaning ox-carts brought stones to sweating slaves who were laying a road. These men worked under the eye of burly overseers; they were filthy, rib-thin, covered in sores from their fetters. Their brows were branded with the slave mark – the 'S' that signified *servus* – and more than one bore this badge of dishonour defiling the proud eye of his Warrior's Light.

Most of these men turned away as the Iceni rode by, as if to hide their shame, but one stood defiant, unblinking, his eyes dark with hatred. He was chained to a tree by a fetter round his neck; his wrists and ankles were fettered, too, and his dirt-streaked skin was lacerated and bleeding from lash-marks.

'They make slaves of warriors?' Matuac exclaimed in disbelief, halting his pony not far from the man, calling to him, 'Friend, what have you done to deserve this?'

'Matuac!' Prasutagus's voice warned as the whole party stopped. 'Leave it.'

But the slave was already answering in rapid, bitter words. 'What did I do? Why, friend, I defended my lands. I stood against the pretty Roman scribe who wanted to build his fancy villa in my valley. Next day, he sent soldiers. They raped my wife, slew my baby son . . .' He winced aside as the thin tongue of a whip cracked, leaving a fresh bloody line across his cheek and nose. The overseer strode up, waving his whip, speaking sharply in Latin, evidently telling Matuac to move on. Gestures bade the whole party depart at once before they caused more trouble.

The slave had fallen silent, but his eyes still burned. Slowly, thoughtfully, the Iceni royal party rode on along the straight stone road made by forced Britonic labour.

Rhiannon could not forget the look in the man's eyes, nor the bloody whip marks on his flesh. Around her the warriors of the guard angrily discussed the injustice of the man's punishment. Had the Romans no conception of a warrior's honour? they asked. If that man's quarrel had been with the Iceni it would have been settled with a fair fight, with a clean death to the loser, not the disgrace of slavery – not for a blooded warrior.

'Then you must take care not to risk a similar disgrace!' the king snapped, silencing them. 'Be discreet – especially you, Matuac – and you, Duihno. You're known to be hot-heads. If you make trouble I'll see that you answer for it to the governor-general himself. Maybe a spell in his auxiliary legions will cool your blood.'

Soon the great outer banks and dykes of Celtic Camulodunon loomed ahead. The new Roman road ran straight through the defences, past outlying fields and farm buildings that had a neglected air: they no longer belonged to Trinovante nobles; their masters were retired Roman soldiers whose notion of dealing with serfs was brutality.

Further on rose the hillfort from where the warlike Catuvellauni had once set out to conquer all of Albion, and where Vindorex had come to rule his people on his return from exile. Its palisades were broken and rotting now. With the warriors all removed to Caesaromagus, the former Trinovante stronghold had become the home of artisans and craftsmen, some of them foreign immigrants, all of them serving the new Roman town which was the focus of all roads.

That town had sprouted from the original fort where the Emperor Claudius had sheltered during his brief stay in Albion. It now spread down the hill towards the river, a settlement of outlandish houses with tiled roofs. Approaching the western gate, the Iceni were obliged to ride by a new burial ground with carved marble monuments honouring the dead – not only important chiefs, but all the Roman dead. Their alien dust had become a part of Albion. Their monuments would stand for generations, laying claim to the place.

The sight angered Boudicca. She had not forgotten Vindorex, or his children. Camulodunon should have been their heritage. Though they were dead, some day she would avenge them. This she promised their restless shades – there would be a reckoning.

Another road led southward from the gates, linking the civil capital to the trading post at far Londinium. The road was frequented by messengers on horseback, by laden carts and packtrains bound to and from the port and markets of the Roman colonia. Groups of soldiers marched with the wind fluttering their red uniform tunics round their knees and light glancing off polished armour and helmets. Lines of slaves limped with bowed heads, chained together by neck fetters and driven on by the lash.

Here, too, were chiefs and warriors of Albion, all headed

for the meeting with their new military overlord. They were stopped at the gates, their packs searched for hidden weapons, and then they were assigned a guide of Trinovante origin, who showed them where they could camp and informed them of the programme arranged for their entertainment.

Riding into the town, Rhiannon remembered her mother's idea that they should 'gape and marvel like rude barbarians' in order to befool the Romans. Now that they were here, the Iceni could do little else but gape and marvel, without need for dissembling. None of them, not even those who had been with the king to Londinium, had ever seen anything like the Roman colonia with its paved streets and its white-painted houses, its stone-floored forum and its numerous open-fronted shops giving glimpses of goods never seen in Icenia.

The civil capital bustled with people, riding or on foot, from scuttling slaves to swaggering figures in togas and women dripping with ornament. Everywhere, armed legionaries kept watch.

Along the street came a curtained litter before which all made way. As the conveyance drew level with Rhiannon, a beringed hand parted the curtains. Behind it, a plump face topped by a fringe of black curls peered petulantly out at the Iceni and the man gave a little shudder, his grimace expressing his distaste in the moment before he dropped the curtain back into place.

A prescient quiver ran through Rhiannon. She had glimpsed disdain and cruelty personified. Whoever the man night be, she hoped she would not see him again.

But in the excitement of the town she soon forgot the incident. There was too much to see and wonder at.

Having looked at the town, the Iceni headed out to examine the Temple of Claudius – such a place it hardly seemed credible that men had made it. Crowds of visiting Britons wandered there on that day, staring in awe and amazement at the achievements of Roman architects.

The spacious precincts were surrounded by a wall of solid stone, beyond whose gates spread a courtyard set with marble urns planted with flowers. The temple itself reared against the sky, faced with alabaster and marble, and topped by gold statues on a roof supported by white pillars taller than the height of five men. In front of it stood an altar with channels for the blood of sacrifices to run down into drains, all flanked by gilded bronze statues on pedestals – one a lifesize figure of the Emperor Claudius mounted on horseback.

Broad white steps that felt cool beneath Rhiannon's soft boots led up to the columned portico, and beyond great bronze-studded doors the vast interior of the temple was hushed and shadowed, scented with burning spices. Priests in flowing robes tended the altar and braziers of the inner sanctum.

Standing in that dim-lit place of perfumed smoke, with footsteps whispering on marble and sunlight slanting through in misty beams from high windows, it was easy to believe that Claudius might have been a God. Wide-eyed, Araunah asked in a hushed voice whether they were going to offer a sacrifice. They had seen shops in the precinct where votive gifts and small animals could be bought, to be given to the priests with requests for special prayers.

'Of course we shall offer a prayer,' Prasutagus replied, pale and weary from the journey as he took Araunah's hand.

'Only for the look of it!' Boudicca muttered, her eyes bright in the gloom. 'Tiberius Claudius was no God. I saw him in the flesh fifteen summers past. He was old, grey, bent. He limped. He drooled. The words hesitated before they left his mouth, sticking on his tongue as they came. He was Emperor only because his Praetorian Guard chose to make him so. Vindorex told me that was true.'

'Hush!' Prasutagus cautioned, glancing at nearby strangers. 'Be cautious. We may be spied on.'

Boudicca flashed him a look that spoke her contempt of spies, though she did lower her voice as she turned to Rhiannon and her companions. 'This temple is a device to awe us, that's all. The Romans think us superstitious fools to be duped by outward signs. *You* should know better, Rhiannon. Must you visit a temple to commune with Dia?'

'She is everywhere. No house can hold Her,' Rhiannon quoted, comforted and strengthened by that assurance from the ritual litany. Compared with the Great Mother's willow groves, deep river pools and other sacred places, this manmade temple was a showy sham.

*

They camped that night by the river, posting guards to keep watch. Representatives of other tribes camped nearby, and the warriors met to boast, gamble and drink away the evening. The twins were observed returning, supporting between them a limp Duihno, who had had to be felled to prevent him from slitting the throat of an Atrebate prince. He complained of a headache all the next day.

The following morning, they were directed to the stadium. Along one side of it, a newly-erected tiered stand presided over an open arena whose perimeter was described by low palisades. The stand rapidly filled with visiting chiefs, their escorts surrounding them, though soldiers made sure that a central canopied section was kept free for Roman dignitaries. People from the town streamed down the hill to gather around the perimeter fences and vendors moved among the crowd selling wine, fruit and sweetmeats.

'They'll want to impress us,' Boudicca said for anyone who cared to hear. 'It's their way. Fifteen summers ago it was elephants. I wonder what tricks this new governor-general has in mind?'

A blare of trumpets was followed by a stir at one of the entry gates and an escort of infantry marched into the arena, leading a litter fringed with gold. Behind the litter, on foot, came an entourage of petty officials. The party paused before the central stand, the litter was set down, and out of it stepped a fat man wearing a long tunic and draped blue toga.

He was the same man Rhiannon had glimpsed in the town the previous day. Now she saw that his cheeks and lips were artificially reddened, his lashes smudged with soot, his hair blackened and curled by some artifice she could only guess at. He still gave her a cold feeling of unease.

A thin cheer went up from the ranks of townspeople and the man waved and smiled in acknowledgement as if he were the Emperor himself. A whisper went round, identifying him as the procurator, the civil governor, Catus Decianus.

'Called by some The Pig,' muttered a voice not far from Rhiannon. 'His appetite's never sated. Food, wealth, power he gorges on – and he has more unnatural appetites, too, so they say.'

Catus accepted the cheers as if they were his due, then followed by his entourage he climbed up to seat himself beneath the canopy in the centre of the stand. He waved and bowed unctuously to the gathered chiefs and warriors, all the while holding to his nose a delicate handkerchief – as if he disliked the odour of massed barbarians.

No sooner was the procurator settled than the trumpets sounded again and a corps of mounted heralds rode into the arena to line up and blow a brazen fanfare. In the hush that followed, hearty cheers broke out beyond the gate, the sound swelling to the throats of all the assembled citizens as the governor-general rode in, resplendent in full ceremonial uniform of polished breastplate and plumed helmet, astride a fine black stallion. His escort of four squadrons of cavalry wheeled after him, and behind them came the massed ranks of a full legion, century by century, cohort by cohort, following the standard bearer who carried their gilded eagle.

Those who had been present at the treaty-making fifteen years before were sharply reminded of the parade they had witnessed then. It was the Roman practice to strike awe into subject peoples with a show of might. Evidently this new military governor, Suetonius Paulinus, had thought it time to remind the tribes of Albion what terrifying power he commanded.

Seated on his tall black stallion, controlling it with the ease of long experience, he made a speech, which was translated by a man who, by his dress, seemed to be a member of Britonic nobility, though of which tribe none could have said. He repeated the governor-general's address phrase by phrase in a loud voice that reached every corner of the stand.

Suetonius Paulinus watched the reaction of the crowd with shrewd eyes, and Rhiannon found herself according him an unwilling respect. This Roman was not condescending and dissipated. This Roman was a warrior born and bred, a lean hard man with grey hair, his eyes set under a shelf of brow in a thin face with deep lines scored down either cheek. It was the brooding face of an eagle.

'A worthy opponent,' Boudicca murmured, echoing her daughter's feeling.

General Suetonius spoke of the benefits brought to the tribes of Britannica by his countrymen. He talked of the Pax Romana – the peace brought by Roman rule – of learning that could be shared, of the glories of democracy and the superiority of Roman law. Though few of his listeners comprehended him in detail his message was clear, as was the unspoken message of the ranks of well-drilled legionaries standing behind him, bristling with a forest of spears: Rome was here to stay, with consent or by force – the choice was in the hands of the tribes.

As she bit into a juicy fig, Rhiannon found her attention wandering. She studied the escort of officers drawn up behind the governor-general, her eyes lighting on a young man with handsome features and a square jaw set off by the plumed helmet he wore. He looked healthy, his body strong and well-formed by the Gods. She wondered who he was, what sort of life he lived, if his duties would ever bring him to Icenia – idle, irrelevant thoughts.

The speech ended, drawing her attention back as the Roman commander dismounted and his stallion was led away. He strode toward the stand, his staff officers around him, while the soldiers in the arena marched out with the same impressive discipline which had brought them. The stage was set for an afternoon of entertainment.

Curious, Rhiannon watched the officers of the governor-general's staff as they climbed the steps to their seats. She was perhaps ten paces away, close enough to see the black mole on the thin, lined cheek of Suetonius Paulinus. But her main interest was in the young officer she had noticed earlier.

As though he sensed her scrutiny, that particular officer let his glance roam across the rows of assembled Britons.

The meeting of their eyes was almost a tangible thing. Hot blood rushed up her throat to stain her cheeks. She saw his mouth curve in a smile, then the officer behind him urged him on and broke the spell.

Rhiannon turned her gaze to the arena, her face burning, but as the games began she was aware of that dark young officer in the canopied section. Several times, when curiosity and self-awareness overcame her, she glanced that way and found to her embarrassment that he was still watching her.

There followed contests at arms, single combat between men whom the knowledgeable members of the crowd identified as gladiators. There were horse races and demonstrations of

Roman riding skill. Then two chariots trundled out, one driven by a Roman, the other by a Gaul.

The sight of the vehicles caused some smug amusement among the watching Britons; evidently Roman chariots were constructed for strength rather than speed, with solid platform and curved front, small wheels, the whole decorated with carved, painted wood and fancy bronzework.

Unwieldy, was the general verdict. The vehicles would soon bog down in the damp clay soils of Albion if they tried to enter battle.

'Against our swift wicker chariots, they'd be like mud-stuck oxen chasing hawks,' Ylas said, making everyone laugh who heard him. Maybe these Romans weren't as clever as they thought.

Rhiannon wondered what Teyrnon would make of these lumbering vehicles. Their drivers controlled them by brute force, not the lithe skill that made Teyrnon such a champion among reinsmen. She would enjoy recounting this event to him.

Peering on tiptoe as the race rounded the far curve, Rhiannon hung onto Ylas's arm to steady herself, hearing Matuac behind her yell encouragement to the Gaulish driver who, if not of Icenia, nor even of Albion, did have the virtue of being a Celt.

The Roman was a big man, but the Gaul had the build of an oak. His bronzed muscles bulged and gleamed with sweat as he strained forward to slap the reins. Round and round the vehicles careered, tossing up dust, neck and neck until on the last lap when trumpets brayed the Roman team fell back. The Gaul drew ahead by a nose, passing the finishing point below the canopied stand where the governor general, the procurator and their officers were seated.

Yells and whoops of jubilation went up from the throats of the crowd, but under the noise of cheering Matuac exclaimed, 'The Roman pulled up! He let the Gaul win.'

'Oh, of course he didn't!' Ylas replied. 'Why should he? Would you have pulled up, in his place?'

'No. But he did. I saw him.'

While the argument went on, Rhiannon resumed her seat. She, too, thought she had seen the Roman throw the race, presumably to please the visiting warriors and put them all in a good mood. It was more proof of the superior attitude adopted by the conquerors. Rhiannon had been aware of it since she set foot in the town.

And no doubt that dark young officer of Suetonius's staff felt just as his countrymen did. He probably regarded Rhiannon as simply another nubile barbarian who, given a chance, might provide a few hours' amusement.

She set her mind to forget him.

After the spectacle of the games in the stadium, Rhiannon and her sister, escorted by a few of the younger warriors, explored the town. They wandered down streets lined with buildings and busy with horses and pedestrians, wondering at the sights to be seen and speculating over the names of some of the exotic goods in the shops – fruit such as they had never seen before, both fresh and dried, jars of fish paste, olive oil, seeds of all kinds, spices, perfumes, fabrics . . .

'Look at this glassware, Araunah,' Rhiannon breathed, pointing to a shelf crammed with drinking vessels of clear glass decorated with swirls of colour. She picked one out and stood admiring its delicacy, so different from cups of horn or wood or even silver, while the shop-owner's slave stood anxiously by.

'Can we buy one for father?' Araunah asked. 'Have you got any of those silver coin pieces?'

Before Rhiannon could reply, a cry sounded from the doorway.

'Hold! Wait!'

The voice was Matuac's. When Rhiannon looked, Ylas was restraining his struggling twin, who appeared to want to pursue the slender female figure whom Rhiannon glimpsed hurrying away, pulling an edge of her toga over her hair and face. She vanished among the crowds while the twins argued loudly.

'Don't be such a fool! Of course it wasn't!' Ylas said, still holding Matuac by his tunic.

'It was! I saw her!' Realising that his quarry had escaped, Matuac violently wrenched free of his brother's hands, his face set. But still he insisted, 'It was Cunovinda! It was!'

Rhiannon's hopes leapt, but Cameira said, 'How could it

be Cunovinda? That woman was a Roman. You could tell by the way she was dressed.'

'There are lots of Celtic women in this town who go about dressed in Roman fashion,' Matuac argued. 'A lot of them have married Roman soldiers. Hadn't you heard that? And Cunovinda was part Roman anyway. Maybe she's married to one of the veterans who've settled here.' His face was red. He rubbed the back of his hand across his cheek as if it itched. 'Well, it's possible, isn't it?'

'It wasn't Cunovinda.' Ylas said, touching his twin's arm to comfort his embarrassment. 'There was a likeness, maybe, but that's all. The woman didn't know you. You scared her when you grabbed for her with your great paw. Would Cunovinda have run away from us?'

'She might.'

He turned out of the shop and the others followed, emerging in the busy street as two Roman officers rode by. Glancing up at them, Rhiannon was startled to see the familiar face of the young man who had stared at her during the entertainment in the stadium. His dark eyes quickened with interest beneath the rim of his bronze helmet and on impulse he drew rein, as if intending to speak to her.

But the twins had noticed what was happening. They ranged themselves protectively on either side of her and Cameira stepped in front. All three of them laid their hands on the hilts of their daggers, their expressions warning the Roman that Rhiannon was taboo. In response, a speculative look grew in his eyes. He gravely inclined his head, but before he turned away his expression told Rhiannon that this meeting had only further piqued his interest.

His companion had paused to look back, amused, saying something in a dry voice. As they moved away, she heard them both laugh and her face burned with humiliation.

'Lucky we were here,' Ylas said.

'Yes,' she replied, and her voice was hoarse.

That night, at the behest of governor-general Suetonius Paulinus, a feast was prepared in the forum. Torches flared to give extra light as darkness fell and the scent of roasting meat wafted from numerous spits over fires. Tables were laden with bread, with fruit and other delicacies; slaves poured generous cups of wine from silver jugs, and entertainers performed – men juggling with fire, tumblers girating and whirling, dancers in gaudy costumes stepping and posing to the music of pipe, drum and flute.

Roman and Briton mingled freely, managing somehow to communicate even where language was a barrier, but Rhiannon stayed close to her family, apprehensive of receiving another unwelcome approach from that young officer with bold brown eyes.

The governor-general and the procurator made an appearance, their escort of soldiers parting the crowd as the two men walked across the forum, one thin and grey and dry, the other fat and oily. Attendants with them drew their attention to the various chiefs present and Suetonius exchanged a few words with each of his guests. As they approached the Iceni royal party, Rhiannon saw with dismay that the dark-eyed officer she had seen earlier was with them, his soldier's dress discarded for a white knee-length tunic and a long, dark red cloak edged with gold, which he wore draped elegantly over one arm.

She tried to ignore him, but though she didn't look fully at him she was aware of his eyes on her as Suetonius and fat Catus came closer. She heard the interpreter informing the Roman leaders that here were Prasutagus, king of the Iceni, and his wife Boudicca, with their daughters.

Suetonius, all grave politeness, had forced his hard mouth into a smile before his glance fell on Boudicca and had to lift to her impassive face. He was noticeably shorter than she was, a mediocrity against her doughty magnificence. The great electrum torc of Iceni queens gleamed at her throat; firelight played on her long red hair and danced across the glint of gold thread in her clothes and on the bright ornaments that adorned her person. On her brow blazed the proud tattoo of the all-seeing eye, badge of valour, mark of the blooded warrior. She appeared to be all colour and light.

What was said between them, Rhiannon could never remember; it was conventional, polite smalltalk exchanged through the interpreter. But she sensed the general's dislike of her mother's boldness as Boudicca faced him eye to eye, holding herself proud and tall as if to emphasise the difference in their stature. It was not long before Suetonius moved on, trailing behind him the sweating procurator, for whom this closeness to barbarians was obviously a sore trial: Catus kept mopping his brow and touching his scented handkerchief to his nose.

As they passed, Rhiannon chanced a glance at the young staff officer. He grinned broadly, pleased with himself, as though he had known she could not continue to ignore him. Discomposed, Rhiannon was glad to bend to listen to Araunah marvelling over the skill of a nearby juggler.

The hosts of the feast departed, leaving their guests to enjoy themselves. As the night wore on, the noise grew louder. A scuffle broke out and a table toppled over with a crash, scattering apples, figs and dates across the forum. But whatever had caused the trouble was swiftly settled by the intervention of armed soldiers. Before the threat of their swords, the quarrel dissipated. Slaves in dark tunics moved in to clear up the mess.

It was then that Rhiannon glimpsed what appeared to be a familiar face. The incident of that afternoon had renewed hopes that refused to leave her, and now she was sure she saw Cunovinda among the shadows at the far side of the forum. Slipping away from her family, she wound her way among the throng towards the spot where the woman stood with her back turned. She put out a hand to touch the woman's shoulder, beginning to say, 'Cunovin – ' only to stop, disheartened, as the woman glanced round and revealed herself to be a stranger – not unlike Cunovinda, but still a stranger, one of the dancers taking a respite.

Rhiannon felt sick with disappointment. What use was there in hoping to find Cunovinda and Farann again? 'I'm sorry,' she muttered. 'I thought you were . . . someone else.'

The only response was an unfriendly stare from eyes rimmed with kohl. Rhiannon turned away, edging past the base of the tall fluted column that held a statue of a winged Victory.

Then she stopped, a hand flying to her throat: her way was barred by a man who, as she paused, braced his arm against the statue's column and smiled in a knowing, confident way. She stared at him in surprise and alarm – he was the dark-eyed officer of Suetonius's staff.

For a moment Rhiannon thought she might never be able to breathe again; she croaked, 'Please . . .'

He replied in his own language, unintelligibily, though after a moment when her confusion had ebbed she guessed he was asking her name. His own, so it seemed, was Valerius. He said it again, pointing to his breast, 'Valerius. Caius Valerius Rufinus.'

Rhiannon wished he would let her past, but every way she turned he only moved to impede her. She was trapped, her initial dismay and embarrassment turning rapidly to anger. This man had no right to speak to her, let alone to bar her way. She was the daughter of the queen of Icenia. She was also the Maiden, sworn to chastity. But this Roman couldn't be expected to understand or respect that. A people who worshipped their dead chiefs as Gods might just as well be Godless.

She reached for her dagger but he, anticipating the move, clamped his fingers round her wrist and smiled at her as he shook his head. Still holding her wrist so tightly that it was growing numb, he glanced about him and his eye lit on the slaves who were clearing up the mess of scattered fruit. He snapped his fingers and called out, summoning the nearest of the men, who straightened and looked toward the fluted pillar of the Victory.

The Roman called again, sounding irritated, and with evident reluctance the man left his work and stepped slowly among the pulpy debris of trodden figs. Caius Valerius Rufinus slowly unclasped his hand from Rhiannon's arm and for a long moment their glances locked defiantly. Then the slave paused beside them.

Rhiannon flicked a look at the man. What she saw made her catch her breath.

For the slave was tall, muscular and long-limbed beneath a brief tunic of woad-blue. He had dark hair, cut short after the Roman fashion, and he was clean-shaven. On his brow, the branded S stood out clear above eyes darkened by the flickering light.

But Rhiannon, standing numbed and unbreathing, knew well the colour of those eyes. They were the deep, vivid blue of a summer's evening.

The man was Farann.

Seven

Rhiannon stared at the tall, dark-haired slave, feeling as though she were under the spell of the ivy drug. The man could not be Farann. Yet he was.

For a heartbeat, he looked into her eyes and behind the careful opaqueness of his expression she glimpsed the young man she had once known – the homeless, parentless youth whose pride had been his only real possession; he had used it as a shield against the world, even against friends. Now, that shield had thickened, calloused by whatever evil had befallen him in the years between.

A physical pain darted through Rhiannon as she thought of how it must be for him. He, the son of brave Vindorex, high chief of the Trinovantes, should have worn the Warrior's Light; instead he bore the disfigurement of the 'S' brand that marked him as someone's property.

She tried to convey to him that it didn't matter. He was still Farann, her friend, her foster-brother. But his look shut her out as it always had. He wanted nothing from her. He had, she remembered, gone away from Oakhillfort without leaving a word of farewell.

Staring at a point just over Rhiannon's head, Farann translated in a toneless voice what the young Roman officer had said: 'In the absence of anyone to perform formal introductions, the tribune Caius Valerius Rufinus wishes to make himself acquainted with the daughter of the king of Icenia. Will you tell him your name?'

Her mind still swirled with shock. She said stupidly, 'You know my name.'

'Shall I tell it to him?'

'No!'

Valerius understood the sharp negative. He spoke impatiently, his gestures telling Farann to be more persuasive.

'He asks what harm it can do for him to know your name,'

Farann translated, still avoiding her eyes. 'He knows who you are – the daughter of Prasutagus of Icenia.'

She drew herself up, sending a cold glance at the Roman. 'I am the daughter of Boudicca, hereditary queen of the Iceni. And I am the Maiden, Chosen of the Goddess. Tell him that. Tell him I do not wish for his attentions. He insults me.'

Judging by the expressions that flitted across the tribune's handsome face like sun and cloud-shadow across hills, Farann repeated exactly what Rhiannon had said. The Roman found it amusing, then annoying, then was himself insulted. But at the end of the speech he began to regard her with new respect and his tone held less arrogance as he replied.

'He wants to apologise,' Farann said. 'He didn't intend to be offensive. He asks if you will do him the honour of allowing him to know your name. I think you'd better agree. He's not just any ordinary Roman. He's got influence, both here and in Rome. He comes from a powerful family.'

Rhiannon was not impressed. 'Then tell him, if it will make him go away.'

'Tell him what?'

'That my name is Rhiannon!'

Valerius apparently understood that much. He said, 'Rhiannon,' as though it were nectar on his lips, and smiled with a sincerity that made her look more fully at him. His smile had charm, his eyes were warm and full of admiration. He made graceful gestures as he spoke in that odd, clipped language, using her name now. To her ears it sounded like blasphemy.

'He says you're the loveliest creature he's ever seen,' Farann interpreted. 'He easily picked you out among the crowd at the stadium. Not even Rome has maidens so fair. So he says.'

His voice growing ever more toneless, his gaze fixed on distances beyond Rhiannon, he continued to repeat the gist of the flattery the young tribune chose to pour over her. Valerius had the gift of words, more than any man Rhiannon had met, but the compliments had no power to move her when she was still struggling with the shock of finding Farann again.

He was no longer a lanky youth but a full grown, powerful man, tall and well-muscled with broad shoulders and sturdy frame. He had been worked hard, she guessed. In the flicker of torchlight and shadow she discerned scars on his bare arms and legs. She remembered the slave she had seen with the labour gang building the road. Had Farann been whipped, too, day after day to force his submission? But he hadn't submitted. That much she knew by the still-defiant set of his mouth, even though that defiance was turned now against all the world, including her.

But if he hated his bondage, why didn't he escape? He wasn't chained and fettered like those men on the road-gang. He appeared to be free to come and go as he pleased. Why didn't he run away?

In between his translations of Valerius's overtures, they managed to snatch words of their own.

'We're all here,' Rhiannon said. 'The twins, Cameira – '

'I know. And your hair is the colour of ripe apricots, so he says. The ignorant fool forgets that you've never seen apricots.'

She hoped the tears that stung her eyes didn't show. 'If you knew we were here, why didn't you come to us? Oh, why won't you look at me, Farann?'

'You know why.'

Yes, she knew. He was ashamed of his slavehood, ashamed to be seen by those with whom he had trained to arms as a warrior. And perhaps he still remembered the way they had parted – perhaps he still thought she had scorned his youthful advances.

'What can we do?' she asked hoarsely.

'Nothing.'

Valerius broke in, wanting to know what Rhiannon was saying. Farann invented some lie that apparently satisfied the tribune, who reached to take Rhiannon's hand. When she tried to pull away his grip tightened on her fingers, holding her fast and yet not ungently as he spoke to her in a low voice, his brown eyes caressing her face.

'He says he's the one who's speaking to you, not me,' Farran said. 'He wants you to look at him. He likes it when you look at him. Your eyes . . . No, by the wren! I won't say that!'

She glanced up at him, a cobweb of distress catching in her throat. Was it possible that, underneath his veiled hostility, Farann was jealous of the attention this Roman was paying to her? 'Then say words of your own!' she begged. 'Tell me of Vindorex, and Cunovinda. Where are they?'

'Vindorex, my father, is dead,' Farann said. 'They put out his eyes, and then they cut out his heart.'

Horrified, she saw the harsh lines about his mouth as he looked directly at her for the first time, blue eyes piercing her to the heart, and went on, 'They made slaves of Cunovinda and me. I worked in the fens, digging their pestilential drainage ditches and – '

A sharp word from Valerius stopped him. The Roman had, belatedly, realised that more was being said between them than he understood. He stormed at Farran, then brusquely dismissed him, repeating the order twice with dismissive gestures. Farann bowed with insolent courtesy as he backed away, giving Rhiannon a wry, bitter smile.

She yearned to go after him. She felt saddened so deeply that she wanted to weep. But the tribune was speaking again, taking her arm with gestures that implied he would like to escort her back to her family. She allowed him to lead her. She seemed to have no will of her own. Her thoughts were all with Farann.

He had behaved as though he hated her.

Valerius stopped abruptly, jerking Rhiannon's thoughts back to the feast and the forum. Out of the crowd, Ylas, Matuac, Unthaus and Duihno had materialised, all of them bristling with hostility. The twins formally saluted Rhiannon, fist to brow, as if to emphasise her status among them. Duihno had drawn his knife and looked ready to slit Valerius's throat. But the tribune released Rhiannon's arm, lifted his hands to show he had no weapon, and backed off murmuring words of conciliation. Unthaus and Duihno prowled after him.

The twins converged on Rhiannon, both asking questions at once, demanding to know where she had been and how she had come to be with the Roman. Did she want to be disgraced?

'I've seen Farann,' she said. 'Farann! Oh, will you listen to me! Farann's here. I saw Farann.'

They both stopped talking and stared at her, both saying at the same time, 'Farann?'

'You must have imagined it,' Ylas said.

'As I imagined seeing Cunovinda, I suppose?' Matuac

retorted with satisfaction. 'Maybe she did see Farann. Maybe he and Cunovinda are both here.'

'I did see him,' Rhiannon said desperately. 'I talked to him. About Cunovinda I don't know, but Farann was here not many breaths ago. He's a slave. His forehead . . .' She laid her fingers to her own forehead, drawing there the S shape of the slave brand, and as she did so her tears spilled over. 'Oh, find him for me, Ylas! Find him, Matuac! We can't leave him here like this. We can't!'

She lay awake that night beneath the shelter of a hide tent by the river, with Araunah beside her snuffling and muttering as she dreamed. The twins had gone to find Farann; they had not come back. Rhiannon couldn't sleep for imagining all three young men caught in some nameless horror.

Eventually she rolled out from the shelter and went to kneel by the river. It was tidal here and the tide was high, sluicing past banks lush with the growth of late summer. A slight mist drifted over the surface of the water, silvered by the waning moon. Somewhere a night bird called.

'Epona . . .' Rhiannon breathed the name of the Mare Goddess, but for the first time she sensed no response. She looked up to the moon floating over the tidal marshes – it had grown old; it was the Hag's moon, the moon of Caridwen the White Sow. 'Epona . . .' Rhiannon tried again, closing her eyes to shut out the sight of the old moon. She heard the slide and gurgle of the river, the bird crying, a bat squeaking, and faintly, faintly she defined the beat of the White Mare's hooves. Or was it only her own heart?

It was Epona. She felt sure of it. She refused to believe that for her the Goddess might change her nature from strong Mare to dread Hag. It couldn't be that only sorrow awaited her. It couldn't be!

She removed from her arm a costly gold bracelet, resting it for a moment against her brow as she prayed desperately for the safe return of the twins and for the restoration of Farann. Then she tossed the bracelet into the river. The mist swallowed it; there was a soft plop, a swirl of water . . . The gift was given. Now she must wait and see how it pleased the Goddess to answer.

'Rhia!' the whisper came out of the shadows behind her.

She whirled to her feet, the name of Farann on her lips, though when one of the twins appeared – it was Ylas, she guessed – she was glad she had not spoken aloud and revealed her foolishness. Behind him came Matuac his brother, his mirror-image, his shadow.

'We found him,' Ylas said, catching her arm to support her as she swayed a little, overcome with relief.

They sat with her on the riverbank to recount their tale of searching for Farann. They had looked everywhere about the town until eventually they had discovered where Farann might be found. He had not wanted to see them, but when they refused to leave without hearing his story he told them to return later, to a place where their meeting would not be observed.

'He's working for the procurator,' Ylas said and, when Rhiannon expressed her surprise, added, 'We didn't believe it either, but it's true. He's been in Camulodunon almost eight moons now. Before that he was on a labour gang in the marshes.'

'That much he told me,' Rhiannon said.

Matuac sat forward, the whites of his eyes shining in the dark. 'Did he tell you he killed the overseer of slaves? With his two bare hands?'

Stunned, she shook her head.

'The man was a tyrant,' Ylas said. 'He gave a hundred lashes for the slightest crime. Many died of the whip. He had their carcasses thrown into the fen. Even his own men hated him. So when Farann saw an opportunity he killed the man – throttled him. Of course there was trouble. He was caught, imprisoned, whipped until he wished the breath would go up from his body. But the overseer he killed had made powerful enemies. Their curiosity was aroused and they interceded before Farann could be killed. Then when they examined him they found out he was half Roman, and that he knew Latin.'

'He can read and write,' Matuac said in an awed voice. 'When he was a child he had his own tutor – a Greek slave called Crico, who came from Rome with Vindorex. Did you know that?'

'No.' Her voice was husky. Farann had kept himself so close, so secret, all the time he had lived in the queen's household. How lonely and apart he must have felt, and she had only just realised it.

'Anyway, they gave him a job on the procurator's staff, to help out when a translator was needed,' Ylas said. 'He's not badly treated now. He's free to come and go.'

'Then why does he stay?' Rhiannon cried. 'Did you tell him he can come back with us to Icenia? We could hide him somehow.'

'He won't come, Rhiannon,' Ylas said with a sigh. 'He's got to stay – to protect Cunovinda.'

She stared at him, letting the silence lengthen, waiting for him to explain. Her head ached with tears and her heart seemed to have slowed almost to a stop. She sensed a new tension in Matuac, too. He sat with his head bent, pulling at the grass, no longer taking part in the conversation.

'Vindorex had become a very sick man. He had decided to surrender in the hope of mercy,' Ylas said. 'But as they rode for Caesaromagus they were attacked and taken prisoner by a Roman patrol. They told the officer in charge that Vindorex had been promised leniency if he gave himself up, but as ill luck would have it that particular officer had a young brother who was killed in a battle against Caratacus. The man had sworn an oath of vengeance against all Britons. He was determined that Vindorex shouldn't get the same clemency that Caratacus got. So he ordered his men to put out Vindorex's eyes.'

'May Epona trample all Romans to dust!' Rhiannon said through her teeth, her fist hitting the ground.

Matuac said nothing.

'There's worse,' Ylas went on. 'Farann tried to help his father. He was knocked over the head. When he came to he was lashed across a horse. He saw his father lying dead, along with every warrior of his following, and he could hear Cunovinda screaming.'

'Screaming?' her voice was a breath on the night air.

'They raped her, Rhiannon. All of them. By the time they finished she was half dead. But they bound her, too, and threw her across another horse. She and Farann were taken prisoner to the nearest fort. Cunovinda was sold as a whore to serve one of the garrisons on the frontier, and Farann was sent to dig ditches.'

Rhiannon stared at the silvered mist, feeling cold to her soul as the moon of Caridwen dipped towards its setting.

'Farann heard nothing more about her until the procurator learned the story,' Ylas said. 'He brought Cunovinda to Camulodunon. She's still a slave, but she serves the wife of a retired centurion as a personal maid.'

'The procurator did that – he rescued Cunovinda?' Rhiannon asked, remembering how she had recoiled from the sight of the obscene, painted Catus. 'Then he's not so bad.'

'Of course he is!' That was Matuac, fierce in the darkness. 'He can send Cunovinda back to degradation with a flick of his fat fingers if Farann doesn't do what he wants. And you know what that means?'

'Mat, no!' his twin snapped, seeking physically to restrain him from going on. But Matuac jerked out of reach and leapt to his feet, his voice filled with anguish and fury.

'D'you know what that means, Rhiannon? The Pig likes strong young men. Not just to work for him. No, not just that. He likes to touch them. He likes to have them pleasure him. And he especially likes Farann!'

'Stop it!' Ylas leapt up, grappling with his brother. 'He didn't want her to know!' Fists flew and the two fell together, still fighting, while Rhiannon sat like one locked in a dream, her arms folded tightly round her knees as if by that means she could soothe the pain that speared her breast.

Silent tears slid from her eyes in an endless stream. She was aware of nothing – not the twins enduring their own kinds of agony, nor the cool night sounds of the river. Through a glitter of tears she looked up at the sky and saw the old moon slide further into the mist. The Goddess, when it amused Her to be Caridwen, was pitiless.

Autumn rain drove down, battering leaves from the forest trees as Rhiannon huddled in her thick hooded cloak, her eyes on her pony's crested mane. She was going home to Oakhillfort. She was glad of it, except . . . except that Farann remained in Camulodunon, forced by fear for his sister to endure a life of shame and disgrace.

She rode alone, hanging back behind the main party, not wanting to talk. But occasionally one or other of the twins pulled in beside her. Matuac came with crazy plans to ride on Camulodunon and rescue their friends; he was trying to comfort her, and himself. Ylas rode alongside talking of home and familiar pleasures, sharing her grief in his own caring fashion.

From the edge of her dripping hood, Rhiannon saw another pony draw level with hers and when she glanced up she found her mother watching her worriedly from the shelter of her own hood.

'You're grieving over Farann,' Boudicca said.

Rhiannon hid her face and her swollen eyes. 'And Cunovinda.'

'At least they're alive.'

'In slavery.' She tightened herself against shedding more tears. Boudicca didn't know the worst of it – the shame Farann was forced to endure at the pleasure of painted Catus. He had begged the twins not to tell that part and though Matuac had been unable to keep from revealing it to Rhiannon the three of them had vowed that for Farann's sake no one else should know.

The queen rode in silence for a while, her thoughts coloured with deep anger and bitterness which, when she spoke, made her voice rasp in her throat. 'So much for Roman clemency. Vindorex was a fool to believe in it. But at the last he must have changed. He was a sick man or he would never have taken the chance on trusting Roman promises of mercy. Remember it, Rhiannon. The Roman's word is an emptiness, given at a moment's whim. Lightly given. Lightly broken. They spared Caratacus because it suited an Emperor to appear merciful. But they killed Vindorex. They killed Mocuxsoris. They took our swords! May the curse of Bloody Andastre, Queen of Combat, fall on them.'

When Rhiannon made no reply, the queen went on, 'Did you watch and learn, as I told you? Did you see what slight defences they have? They're so sure of themselves there's hardly a palisade around that town strong enough to keep out a sheep. And soon Suetonius will be gone to the frontier, harrying the north and the west, trying to get through the mountains and destroy Mona. While behind him . . . behind him are we, the Iceni.' She smiled to herself, lifting a hand that she curled slowly into a fist like a closing trap. 'This Suetonius thinks he has us on our knees. He imagines we cower before his legions. But he's wrong. The Iceni are not cowering. The Iceni are only waiting. Give us the right moment. Give us a cause worth the dying for. Give us a sign from the Gods . . . And we shall strike. Strike!'

She raised her fist to the lowering skies and let the rain fall on her unprotected face as she cried, 'Hear me, Andastre! Grant me this! The Iceni shall have their day of vengeance!'

They rode on. Behind the shelter of her hood, Boudicca smiled grimly to herself, relishing her secret knowledge. Her wish for vengeance was not a vain dream. Soon there would be swords enough to arm every noble in Icenia.

After disarming the tribes, the Romans had banned imported weapons and strictly regulated supplies of iron so that the Iceni had scarcely enough to make new tools and hunting spears as they were needed. But from each batch, for years now, Boudicca had made certain that a little had been saved and set aside. In recent years, with the co-operation of Eogan, and with help from her loyal ironmasters and bronzeworkers, Boudicca had organised the forging of new swords that were to be kept hidden away until time of need. Not even Prasutagus knew about it; he might have found some reason to gainsay her plan.

Most of the new weapons had been forged deep in the forests by Druid-trained smiths, master craftsmen who lived and worked in secret places and who understood the tempering of metals in cauldrons of blood; these magical swords were stronger than those of ordinary iron. The queen ordered them to be engraved with runes, so that all of the swords were eager for war; they had been taught to relish the taste of the blood that had made them strong.

When the proper season came, those swords would drink the blood of vengeance.

After they returned to Oakhillfort, when Boudicca had retired to her pallet that night, her husband came to her room for the first time in many moons. He was still fully dressed, the lamplight making shadows on his face, deepening the lines that dragged downward from his drooping left eye. He was almost sixty now, an old, tired man.

He had not come for tenderness' sake.

'You talk of war, Boudicca,' he said, low-voiced and bitter. 'Always you talk of war! Now you would taint your own daughter with a dream of death. More and more your voice has echoes of Mocuxsoris.'

'My brother was raised to be proud of his Iceni blood,' she answered in a furious undertone. 'He and I were warrior-bred.'

'And so was I! But I was also taught the worth of discretion. If you had had your way – Eogan's way – the Iceni would now be a subject people, not a free ally of Rome.'

'Free?' She let out a choked laugh. 'When we have no weapons to defend ourselves? When foster-children raised at our hearth are held as slaves of Roman bureaucrats? When we pay our wealth into Roman coffers? You call that freedom?!'

'It's better than the alternative!' Prasutagus rasped. 'Why are you so blind, Boudicca? At least we have control of our own lives. You've seen what happens to those who resist. Their lands are taken, their settlements burned, their people killed or thrown into chains.'

'They wouldn't *dare* do that to the Iceni!'

'How would you stop them? You saw the soldiers who paraded at Camulodunon. They were only a few of the many that Suetonius commands. And how many warriors have we? How many swords will you conjure out of air? How many chariots could you raise to the call of your war carnyx? You – a woman!'

'More than *you* could ever command!' she answered, her voice hoarse with anger and hatred. 'You're king, by decree of Rome. But *I* am queen by right. By ancient right. By the will of the Goddess. I have not been idle these past years. I have been making plans. And if you have no stomach for the fight then I, Boudicca, shall lead my people as sacred Brecca once led them – to victory!'

There was a silence. When the king spoke again his voice shook with the effort of keeping it low. 'So this is how it will end. I've taught you to be strong, but I failed to reckon on your hot pride. You'll destroy your people, Boudicca. Is that what you want – the end of the Iceni?'

'It will be only a beginning!' she hissed. 'We shall drive the Romans from our shores. I shall gather a great army – from all the tribes of Albion.'

'Is that what the Goddess tells you?' he said, and his voice was thick with bitter cynicism and disgust.

Rage blinded her. How dare he mock the Goddess? She lashed out, her palm landing solidly at the side of his face.

Caught by surprise, Prasutagus reeled, stumbled and caught his foot. He fell heavily to hands and knees, where he stayed, shaking his head as if to clear it.

Boudicca stood over him, her fists clenched. 'Coward!' she spat at him. 'Weakling! *This* is all your wisdom tells us – sit still, do nothing, make no trouble. Let the Romans tramp over us as they will!'

'And what does your wisdom say?' he asked, breathless. 'Fight? Die?'

'Before it ends, we shall all be dead!' she raged. 'Like Mocuxsoris. Like Vindorex. Or in chains – like Farann. Like Cunovinda. Unless we act! Unless we decide our own fate!'

The king got unsteadily to his feet, stroked his hair from his eyes and shook himself before turning on her a look that held both disgust and pity. 'Then I pray that I too may be dead before that day comes!' he said, and left her alone to rage at the fates.

Behind the thin wall of plastered and painted wattle, Rhiannon stretched out a hand to comfort her sister in the darkness. Both of them had heard this latest of the quarrels between their mother and her husband. Which of them was right? Rhiannon wondered.

For her, talk of war and vengeance brought no comfort. For five years she had hoped and prayed that Farann and his sister were safe. Those prayers had been in vain. Both of the young Trinovantes had been cruelly treated, wounded in body and soul. Both were enduring a life of degradation. Why had the Goddess refused to accept the offerings Rhiannon had made? Why had She blocked Her ears to the pleas of Her Maiden?

Unable to find answers for herself, she sought out the priestess at her hut by the river. The hut seemed to be deserted. Leaves drifted from the sentinel alders to lie on the thatch and the door was closed. But it was pegged from the inside; Morica must be at home.

'Morica?' she called. 'Morica, I must talk with you.'

After a moment, the priestess's voice answered hoarsely. 'Not now, Rhiannon. I'm not well. Later, I'll come to the queen's house. Wait for me there.'

'Is there anything I can bring you?' Rhiannon asked, concerned. 'Is there anything I can do?'

In reply there came a whispering – two voices, one amused, one sharp. Laughter came from beyond the door and it swung open to reveal a smiling Erefwen, naked and tousled, her mouth swollen and slack, her pupils dilated by drugs. Red marks showed on her pale skin – on her breasts and her thighs, her stomach. Her pubic hair was as pale as that on her head.

After one disbelieving glance, Rhiannon fixed her eyes on the warrior-priestess's face and saw there a gloating, voluptuous smile.

'Yes, you can do something,' Erefwen told Rhiannon. 'You can come in and join us, if you wish. We're in the middle of worship. Paying homage to Albina.' She stretched out a hand invitingly. 'Join us, little Maiden.'

'No!' Rhiannon stepped back, stumbling on a stone that almost turned her ankle. She didn't fully understand what was happening in that hut but she felt sickened.

'Then go away!' the smile turned into a snarl. 'If you refuse to accept the pure love Dia offers, then go. Go!'

Rhiannon fled, her thoughts in confusion.

Eight

That Samhain, Duihno picked out the glass pebble with the blood-red spot at its heart. Clutching the talisman, he leapt into the air and gave a great cry of joy: he had long coveted the honour of being chosen as Green King. He glanced at the watching crowd, eager eyes seeking Erefwen, as if he hoped the favour of the Gods might make that cold maiden look on him with less disdain. But Erefwen only smiled to herself and turned her shoulder to him.

With Duihno at its head, the boar-hunt was wild and long. Several men returned wounded to the fires and the dance. But at the feast that followed all forgot their hurts as wine and ale flowed and the Green King picked fight after fight, crazed by drink and by boastful pride. So degenerate did the night become that the king and the elders left the younger warriors to themselves in the great hall. With the dawn, many a man suffered from a sore head, blackened eyes and a bloody nose. Such was the Samhain when Duihno reigned.

Winter closed in. The solstice brought bitter, icy weather under clear skies when the stars glittered with frosty brilliance. Then with the waxing of the next moon sudden storms sprang up.

On a night when none could sleep, a tempest raged over Icenia. The skies split with thunder and lightning; rain and hail beat down with the force of iron rods; gales shook at houses and at the sacred oak. Amid the furore of crying children, panicking cattle and shouting voices, Rhiannon heard a crash as one of the granaries collapsed. Even the queen's house trembled before the might of the blast. Araunah was afraid, coughing and weeping in the arms of the king, the two of them huddled in furs as they waited for the storm to subside. Boudicca, disturbed as always by the wind, strode about issuing orders as if she could command the elements with the force of her personality.

Wanting to escape the house, Rhiannon slid into her warmest cloak and ventured out into the night, to stand with her back braced against the gale's buffeting. The rain had stopped. The ground was thick with an icy wet layer of hail stones. Shredding clouds scudded across the face of the full moon. But still the thunder rolled, battering across the heavens. Lightning glared to the north and by its glow Rhiannon saw a clutch of people scrambling amid the debris of the fallen granary. They were trying to save some of the seed-corn from the gale, but the gale was winning. Wheat flew and scattered, sharp as grit in the wind.

In the darkness stood Cameira, her hood thrown back so that the wind streamed in her hair. She stared at Rhiannon, shouting, 'The Gods are angry! What have we done?'

As if in answer, a cracking, tearing sound issued from the

edge of the settlement. Like a great bird, the thatched roof of the death hut soared in the moonlight and threw itself down to destruction with a mighty crash. Women began screaming, wailing in terror and despair, begging the Goddess for mercy.

At that moment a flare of jagged white light pierced out of the sky. It drove through the air direct to the sacred oak. With a crack, the tree split. Blinding light played round it. Flames spurted orange in the night. And when the lightning withdrew, Rhiannon could still see the shape of it etched against her inner eye, a dazzling brightness with at its heart a figure – a distinct male figure, bathed in the bright aura of fire from the sky.

She stood transfixed, her face uplifted as she stared at the tree. The fading brilliance on her retina blinded her to everything else.

She had seen the God.

Slowly, the impression of the darkly etched figure faded into shapelessness along with its vivid cloak of light. Before it was gone, she realised that the storm had ceased.

In the awful stillness, the cries of children sounded pitiful; stunned adults wandered about, peering through the moonlight to assess the wreckage of their homes. Three houses had been damaged, several people injured, and in the total ruins of a fourth house Rivus the leatherworker's wife and child had been killed while he slept beside them. He wandered about the settlement, scoring his knife across his chest to spill his grief-blood as he railed at the Gods for taking his family and yet sparing him.

Torches were re-kindled and several of them bobbed around the sacred oak as people examined the damage to the tree. The lightning had split it at the crotch of one of its branches which now drooped lifeless and charred. The scent of burning wood hung aromatically on the air. A deep blackened furrow drove round the tree's trunk forming a slow spiral – the sign of immortality. Recognising it, Rhiannon felt her flesh tingle as if a million ants crawled under her clothes. Then out of the darkness Morica appeared, giving a great cry as she flung herself to her knees in the wet grass, her arms held up to worship the tree.

'A sign!' she cried in her most terrible voice. 'A sign! Blessed be the Great Mother! The God is come down to us. Behold

His mark – the spiral of everlasting life. It's a sign; a sign of great blessing for the Iceni. Rejoice, people! Rejoice and pray!'

Everyone came running to witness the mark of the God's passage from heaven to earth to bring His blessing. Most people fell to their knees and gave thanks, some prostrated themselves in the mud.

The Immortals had exacted a price for their blessing, but the skies were calm now, the clouds were parting to allow the moon to smile through, low in the sky. All would be well.

Rhiannon looked around, making sure all the people she most cherished were unharmed. They were all there, all sharing the general relief that no worse harm had come to them, all examining the spiral mark on the sacred oak. But she felt apart from them. The vision she had been granted cut her off even from her family.

Unsettled and knowing she would not sleep, she made her way up to the high inner bank, her familiar refuge at times of deep turmoil. The bee skeps were all scattered by the wind, their inmates dead. But more swarms would be caught when wild queens flew with the spring. Honey would be made again. Even now herdsmen moved among the cattle and sheep in their winter pens, soothing them, and down in the woods the glow of torches told of the horsemasters' vigilance over Icenia's equine wealth. The dead would be buried, the injured healed, the damage repaired. Only the scar on the sacred oak would remain.

Tucking her warm cloak round her, Rhiannon squatted comfortably on her heels and watched the moon sail through remnants of cloud low over the wet wastes of the marshes. She stared wide-eyed at the white face of light, opening her mind to the Goddess as she prayed for guidance. She was the Maiden. She was believed to have a special closeness with Dia, but in truth she understood no more than anyone else, except at rare moments when she glimpsed a part of the divine purpose.

But tonight she had seen the God stand in the midst of flame in a burning oak tree.

What was the meaning of it?

Tumbling in bewildered succession came other questions: Why had the Goddess allowed evil to befall Farann and Cunovinda? Why did She stand by and watch Roman influence spread like a canker among Her people? Would Her patience endure much longer? Would there be war, as Boudicca predicted? Could the Iceni win such a war? And what did it mean to be the Maiden? What terrors lay concealed in the Mysteries? What secrets would the Great Year unfold?

No answers came on the still, cold night air. The winter moon shone down impassively. All Rhiannon could glean from the silence was a hint that the time for knowing was not yet. Not yet.

Despairing, she drew her hood further over her hair and bent her head in its shadow, her eyes closed. The Goddess would not be pushed, commanded or cajoled. She revealed only what She chose to reveal, and that at a time that suited Her own purposes. Rhiannon must be content. Be faithful, and obey – that was a Maiden's lot.

A stick cracked not far away. She glanced round, getting to her feet as she saw a man standing there, his back to the moonlight. It was one of the twins; she could tell that by the shape of him, the way his hair fell, and by the hint of light on a fair moustache, even though she couldn't see his face clearly.

Rhiannon peered at him, querying. 'Ylas?'

'I didn't mean to interrupt you,' he said.

'You didn't. I was only thinking.' Sighing, she turned to stare at the silvered gleam of the Great Bay, her arms wrapped about herself.

'Is that why you come up here at night so often? To think?' He came closer, touching her arm to make her look at him. As she turned her head, he said, 'Tell me what's wrong.'

'I can't, Ylas. I don't understand it clearly myself. I just feel restless. Uneasy. Perhaps it's because of the storm.'

'It affected us all.' He laid his arm across her shoulders, drawing her to lean on him. 'I wish I could help.'

'You do, Ylas. Just by being here.' She was grateful to him for his brotherly concern and for the warmth he offered in physical comfort. 'Sometimes . . . sometimes I feel very lonely.'

'I'm here.'

She smiled sadly to herself, rubbing her cheek on the fur that trimmed his cloak. It was no good telling him how confused she felt about the meaning of her life – the way her thoughts turned constantly to Farann and her formless fears about the fate that awaited the Maiden; a man couldn't hope to understand. She could no longer talk to her mother, and Morica's advice was so enigmatic that it only added to Rhiannon's confusion. Be faithful, and obey – the command offered no comfort.

Into the silence, Ylas asked, 'Did the God really come down?'

She looked up at him, surprised by the doubt in his voice. 'Didn't you see Him?'

'Did you?'

'Clearly – as clear as I see you now. He was wrapped in a spear of light. He stood in the tree in a cloud of flame.'

'You *saw* Him?' he asked, incredulous. 'But . . . what does it mean?'

She hesitated, knowing that he expected some sort of answer from her, the Maiden. 'It was a sign – a sign from Dia. The storm came to chastise and warn us; then She sent Her Son, the God, to intervene – He put an end to the storm, didn't He? But it was a reminder of the duty we owe. We must not forget that the Immortals demand obedience. We mustn't fail in our faithfulness. We must perform the rites and the sacrifices as they're meant to be performed, and in return the Gods will see that the seasons turn, the moon and the sun still wax and wane, and the earth bears fruit for us.'

'Do you believe that?' he asked.

'Yes, I do.' Having to put it into words for him had settled her own doubts. She glanced at the moon in gratitude, knowing she had received answers after all.

'Then I believe it, too,' Ylas said, wrapping her in a brotherly hug to which she responded with joy.

Everything was well. Of course it was. How secure she felt now, assured of the rightness of things, at peace with the Goddess, warm and companionable in the embrace of her trusted kinsman Ylas.

For the first time she began to comprehend what it must feel like to be held by a lover. If only Farann were here!

The thought was tabu. It disturbed her. She tried to pull away but his grip on her tightened and when she looked into his face she saw it in full moonlight. She saw the bright passion in his eyes, felt the urgency in his arms and his body. He was not Ylas. He was Matuac!

His eyes gleamed with a feral light as he bent his mouth to cover hers. His mouth engulfed her, hot and wet. She couldn't breathe.

With an effort born of panic, she fought him, twisting her head away. 'Matuac! You must not. You must not! I'm not to be touched! Not like this. You know it. It's forbidden!'

Almost at the first word, he released her, dropping his arms as he backed away. When he spoke, his voice was gruff. 'I only wanted to hold you. I wanted to know what it would feel like.' He glanced at the moon, as if aware of the Goddess watching. Her vigilance warned him of the gravity of what he had had in mind. 'You won't tell, will you?' he asked Rhiannon. 'You won't tell? I didn't mean any harm. I only wanted to hold you.'

'And I allowed it,' she reminded him in an undertone, feeling chilled. 'You comforted me, Matuac. You helped me. Perhaps Dia sent you to me.'

'You think so? Oh . . . yes, I did feel a sort of . . . a sort of compulsion to find you.' Frowning over the memory, he convinced himself he had been called to her by forces outside himself. 'Yes, I was drawn here!'

As he made a move towards her again, Rhiannon backed away, her hands up to ward him off. 'And now I tell you that you must go. You must think of me only as the Maiden, the Chosen One. I'm tabu, Matuac. I must not be touched by a man.'

'Only until the Great Year's over,' he said. 'Then you'll be free. Won't you?'

A shiver ran through her as a cloud sailed over the moon and the light ebbed. Sensitive to the signs of the sky, Rhiannon drew her cloak more closely around her. She wished, for her own sake, that she knew the answer to his question. 'Only the Goddess knows, Matuac. Only the Goddess knows.'

So the year wore on, past the seventeenth Imbolc since Rhiannon's birth. New lambs cried in the sheep pens and the children went out with rowan rods to beat out the winter and waken the earth. More than one youngling came home covered in welts – the rowan rods served to settle childish grievances, too.

The winter had brought little snow that year, but heavy rains had followed the storms and farmers elected to delay their planting. The fields were so muddy the oxen would sink hock-deep, and this year no chances could be taken – the stock of seed-grain had been depleted by the tempests. Rhiannon heard one of the farmers mutter that, whatever blessing the coming down of the God had brought, it certainly hadn't improved the lot of those who tilled the earth.

She confronted the man, startling him as she looked him in the eye, addressing him by name. Words flowed from her tongue without conscious thought. 'The ways of the Gods are not for the puny minds of mortals to question. The harvest will come in, full and fair. First the hay, then the corn.'

The man goggled at her, reddening and awed, stammering, 'Yes, lady. Thank you, lady.'

The whisper went round – the Maiden had predicted a good harvest, without need for runes or reading of portent. Through her, the Goddess had spoken direct. As a result, spirits lifted. Men saw that the winds would soon dry the ground. All would be well. The Maiden had said so.

'Was this a true prophecy?' Boudicca demanded of her daughter as they encountered one another in the queen's house.

Rhiannon replied with a level, unreadable look. 'Would the Goddess lie, mother?'

The queen peered at her through slitted eyes. Since the night of the storm she had sensed a change in Rhiannon, a mystic fatalism that worried her. But Rhiannon had been granted a vision of the God. Of all the people in Oakhillfort, only Rhiannon had actually seen Him there in the lightning.

Aware of her mother's searching gaze – and of the reasons for it – Rhiannon said, 'I know that we're forbidden to speak of the Mysteries, but you must know the thoughts that trouble me. They must have troubled you, too. Mother . . . were you afraid?'

The queen shook her head, answering truthfully, 'I went with joy, Rhiannon. There's nothing to fear. I swear to you – the Maiden need have no fear.'

'I'm not afraid,' Rhiannon said. 'Not as afraid as I was

before the storms. The God showed Himself to me. He smiled on me. When we meet again, I shall know Him.'

'Is that why He marked the sacred oak – as a sign for you?'

'It was a sign for all of us. There may be more blessings yet to come.'

'What sort of blessings?' the queen asked, coming closer to take her daughter's arm. 'A victory? A great victory over the Romans?'

'Is that what you see?'

Boudicca blinked and drew away. 'I believe so. I have visions of battle and mastery. And then I have doubts. Sometimes the Goddess hides behind a veil.'

'For me, too,' Rhiannon said. Her eyes were unfocused, her voice a breathy whisper. Despite her denials, she was mortally afraid. 'I see nothing beyond the Great Year. Nothing. When I meet with the God . . . perhaps He won't let me come back. Perhaps He will make me sail with Him on the ebbing tide, to His kingdom under the sea.'

'No!' Disturbed now, Boudicca caught the girl by the shoulders. 'No, Rhiannon! *He* is the one who must die! *He* . . .'

The word choked off. For a moment the two stared at each other, the queen's pale skin blotched with patches of hectic colour as she stood dismayed, seeing Rhiannon frown in puzzlement.

Boudicca shook the girl, speaking swiftly and firmly. 'You know the lore, Rhiannon. This is how the wheel turns – the eternal story repeating season by reason, Great Year by Great Year. She lures Him, loves Him, binds Him, brings Him death and raises Him again. So the seasons turn. So the year waxes and wanes. So comes the time of sowing and the time of reaping. The God must die. He must die in order to live again. He must die, else the earth will sink under our feet, the skies will fall, the sea overflow.'

'I know this,' Rhiannon said, bewildered. 'It happens every Solstice. A ram is killed, or a bull, as a symbol of the waning sun. And at every fifth year we sacrifice a precious stallion.'

'Just so. Just so.' The queen grasped eagerly at this half truth. 'The God dies. Not the Maiden. Your fears are natural. I suffered the same. But Dia will guard you, as She guarded me. Beyond the Great Year She will reward you. I promise you, daughter of my womb. Only trust in Her. Only obey. She asks nothing more.'

Rhiannon knew her mother was not telling the whole truth but she chose not to probe deeper. This was a pool that should stay unstirred, for in the unknown depths of it there lurked something dread. She was ever more sure of that.

But she had become fatalistic; she had seen the God in the tree. She was the Maiden: she must obey.

On the first appearance of the next new moon, as the rite demanded, men walked the furrowed fields broadcasting grain. The virgin moon looked down approving, a pale silver in the daylight sky brightening as the sunset faded and night poured darkness from the east. Everyone knew that the Maiden was watching too, from her favourite spot on the banks of the fort.

Rhiannon sat alone, aware of the importance of her role in this spring sowing. The people trusted her. The prophecy of a bountiful harvest had flowed from her tongue without conscious thought. She believed that the Goddess had spoken through her, and so she felt compelled to sit here, keeping watch over the sowing to reassure the people. Slowly dusk crept across the land, laying indistinct shadows beneath a deepening blue sky. Dots of moving orange brightness pricked out to show where torches were being lit in the hands of those who stood guard around the fields.

Something thrummed in the night air, like the roll of far-distant thunder. Rhiannon heard a rising wind moving among the bare trees in the woods, and a disturbance among the horses in their enclosures. She stood up, straining her eyes in the uncertain light, her head to one side as she listened intently. It was hoofbeats she had heard. The White Mare was close by. The horses down in the woods sensed it. So did she, who had known the presence of Epona all her life. The Mare Goddess was coming now. Her passing shook the trees. Rhiannon could see a ripple of disturbance among pale moonlit branches, moving through the woods, finding the river and curving round toward the heath and the fields. It drew her attention to a distant knot of torches, like fireflies converging all on one spot near the track that led to the Way.

Faintly on the night wind came the sound of shouting voices. Something was amiss.

As Rhiannon raced down the stepped path into the settlement, the watch-horn sounded and men ran to open the gates, some of them armed with spears and ready to ward off any threat. But there was no threat, not that night. The peasants had been alarmed by the appearance of a man who had stumbled out of the twilight. He was heading, step by slow, painful, determined step, for Oakhillfort. The farmers and their families gathered in a half circle behind him, awed and curious. Some of them ran ahead to alert the fort, but none of them dared approach the stranger. He seemed unaware of his surroundings. All his mind was fixed on the fort, as if he moved in a trance. Even the barking dogs kept their distance.

Rhiannon stood with a curious crowd outside the gates, craning her neck to see what was happening. Several people carried flaring torches that lit the scene with yellow flickers under the thin moon. Then Boudicca pushed through the crowd with Prasutagus a few paces behind.

'What is it?' the queen asked Rhiannon.

'I'm not sure,' Rhiannon answered. 'I think someone's coming, but I can't clearly see. They seem afraid of him. Is it Eogan?'

Slowly out of the confusion of shadows, torchlight drew discernible figures on the night. Peasants formed an excited crowd behind the man. He wavered from side to side of the track, each step a halting agony as he leaned heavily on a rough staff. His will alone impelled him onward. He looked like a wild man. A mass of shaggy dark hair, an unkempt moustache and more than a moon's growth of beard obscured his face. He was wearing a ragged cloak, and a rough suit of skins so badly preserved that the stench of them assailed the nostrils of the watchers.

He had come out of the night, so the peasants said. They had looked up and he was there, as if by magic.

A few paces away from Rhiannon and her mother, the man stopped as if he had only just seen them. He swayed helplessly, supported by his staff, apparently having no strength to speak. Slowly, he lifted his hand, stretching it out towards Rhiannon in a silent plea for help, and then he dropped to his knees as if he could no longer stay upright.

'Lady!' the croak came thickly. 'Lady . . .'

Rhiannon recognised that voice. She felt herself enthralled. The Goddess Herself had passed by to foretell this coming. All her instincts told her the man must be Farann, yet she dared not believe it. Hot tears of relief mingled with terror blinded her, choked her. She was unable to move.

'It's Farann!' That was Ylas's awed voice, from behind her. 'By the wren – ' He stepped swiftly forward, brushing the tangled hair from the man's brow, revealing the branded 'S' burned there. A glance of recognition passed between them, then Ylas turned with flaring eyes to shout at the crowd who stood watching. 'It's Farann. Farann! Stir yourselves before he dies at our gateway. Get him inside. Get him to eat and drink. Hurry, you gaping fools!'

A surge to obey him faltered as Ylas saw the forbidding look in the eye of the queen and swung to face her, throwing out his arms in exasperation and disbelief. 'Lady! It's your foster-son returned to us! Will you deny him hospitality, weak as he is?'

Boudicca was pale, her mouth a thin hard line beneath burning eyes. One of her fists clamped tightly round a ring she wore on a thong about her neck – a ring with a stone of pink quartz. In her mind she saw another stranded man, lying on a beach, thrown up by a storm at the feet of a queen and Maiden who had tended him and rashly learned to care for him, only to see him used by the Gods and slain in spurting blood. Was that song of sorrow to be repeated? Where Huan of the Caledones had gone, must Farann of the Trinovantes follow? No, no! She shook her head, jerking it from side to side, her eyes darkened as if with the ivy drug.

Terrified by the ensorcelled aspect the queen presented, Ylas turned to the king, appealing, 'Lord . . .'

But Prasutagus, too, had his doubts, though he could not meet Ylas's eye. 'If he's escaped from his masters this is the first place they'll look for him.'

The cowardly words shook Boudicca out of her trance. Bitter contempt rose like nausea in her throat. What a weak, fearful man her husband was becoming in his old age. She would defy him. She would defy the Gods. She could not leave Vindorex's son to die.

With a fierce gesture that encompassed the whole crowd, she pointed at Farann. 'Bring him inside! Bring him!'

As one, warriors and peasants swooped to obey, lifting the exhausted Farann high as they carried him through the open gates, until only Rhiannon remained, her face upturned in silent gratitude to the crescent moon. Though she still feared for the fate of Cunovinda, part of her prayer had been answered: Dia had heard. From now on, whatever the Goddess demanded of her, she would do; she would question no more. It was enough that Farann had come back.

Glancing round, Boudicca guessed at the emotions in her daughter's mind. The queen had often thought that it must amuse the Gods to toy with the lives of men and now she knew it to be true. The Gods had returned Farann to Oakhillfort – just as they had sent Huan to the shore of the Great Bay. Perhaps it was so at every Great Year. Perhaps every Maiden was fated to sorrow.

Then so be it. The Gods would have their way.

Nine

Farann lay sick in the queen's house for several nights, torn by a fever that made him toss and mutter in delirium, often crying out wordlessly. In her own room, Rhiannon lay awake listening, every muscle tensed as she willed him to recover. She was doing everything she could: she had made offerings at the sacred pool and at the river; she was forcing herself to stay away from him, remaining obedient to the Goddess. But it hurt her to know that others were tending him.

At last Farann woke with a clear mind, though still physically weak. He had been through ordeals that would not have disgraced a hero of legend and bards' tales. When he was a little stronger, the twins brought him out to the main fire one night as the queen's household gathered for supper. There, propped up on a pile of skins, with furs and blankets to warm him, Farann sank his teeth into the first red meat he had eaten in days.

Rhiannon herself ate little food but her eyes feasted to the full, relishing the sight of Farann and yet troubled by him. He was still full-bearded; his hair fell about his face like a tousled mane; but as she had sensed at Camulodunon there were other differences in him – a hardness, a bitter core of hurt and distrust that left his eyes watchful as those of a wild thing.

As the wine jug was passed round and the dogs settled down to gnaw at the bones, the queen asked Farann to tell his story. Her kinfolk all fell silent to listen – they enjoyed a good tale.

'Two moons ago, storms struck Camulodunon,' Farann said. 'Terrible storms. Thunder, lightning, and a great fierce wind.'

Several voices replied, telling him that similar storms had raged over Oakhillfort.

'The sacred oak was split by a spear of light,' Coeling remarked. 'The God came down. He left his mark as a sign.'

'Rhiannon saw Him!' cried the husky voice of Araunah. Her eyes were bright in her thin, pale face as she coughed raspingly and added, 'Did He come to Camulodunon, too, Farann?'

Farann's glance had lighted on Rhiannon, standing back in the shadows, but now his attention returned to Araunah. She sat close beside him, curled up on an edge of the furs that covered him, her white-fair hair in a braid across one shoulder. The sight of her brought a flash of teeth behind his thick beard as he smiled. 'If He did, I didn't see Him, Araunah.'

Matuac scoffed, 'He wouldn't come down for Romans, now would He?'

'He might,' Farann said. 'They worship Him, too. They call Him Apollo.'

When Araunah would have asked more questions, her mother chided her and the girl subsided. But her excitement had made her short of breath and she kept coughing, hawking up the mucus that thickened on her chest with every winter. Boudicca worriedly wrapped more furs about her younger daughter and bade Farann go on with his story.

The storms that had racked both Icenia and Trinovantia had allied with high seas and freak tides at Camulodunon. A fleet of merchant ships had been caught in the estuary, bringing goods from which the procurator expected to make a huge personal profit. One of the ships had been wrecked outside the river harbour, the others were in trouble in the storm. Catus had ordered all his slaves to be on hand to unload as soon as the ships docked.

Farann described the confusion of wind and rain, the gale howling, the skies split by lightning, men struggling with heavy boxes down heaving gangplanks and along the river wharf. And then a sudden surge of the tide smashed a ship into the dock; wood splintered and cracked, men were tipped screaming into the water. The next huge wave swept Farann off his feet. He found himself submerged, swirling helplessly in a fierce undertow. When he gained the surface he heard voices crying out for help. All around him, men were being swept out into the estuary towards the sea. But the Gods had decreed that he should be saved. An eddy brought him close enough to shore to haul himself from the water and crawl out of danger.

'I must have slept,' he said. 'When the dawn came I woke stiff with cold. I was in the estuary marshes. And I knew that the Gods had smiled on me. The Romans would think me dead, like the others who drowned and were swept away. Freedom lay before me for the taking. My only regret was being forced to leave my sister behind, but if Catus thinks me dead he'll have no reason to harm Cunovinda. And while I'm free I can hope to save her.'

He said little of the ensuing time, when he had been forced to live by foraging off the winter land. He had avoided settlements, for fear of being captured and given back to the Romans, but once when desperate hunger drove him near a homestead he had been discovered by a child whose family treated the wanderer kindly. They were simple peasants eking out a living from hunting and fishing, but they still recalled the name of Addedomarus, Farann's grandfather.

These folk sheltered Farann for a night or two and sent him off with good wishes and the invaluable gift of a sharp knife which had proved the means of saving his life more than once. With it, he had hunted, fended off predators and skinned what he caught to make himself the clothes in which he had at last found his way back to Icenia and Oakhillfort.

Listening, the king Prasutagus stroked a long thumb and forefinger to smooth his grey moustache. 'Can we be sure no search is being made for you?' he asked.

'Not even the Romans would trouble to pursue a dead man,' Matuac said with scorn.

'But he bears the brand!' Tadia breathed. 'The slave's brand. When Romans come, they'll see it and know.'

At this, Farann raised himself so that the furs fell from about his torso, revealing his body to be finely muscled, lean and hard as a wolf's, and striped by the scars left by many whippings. As he glanced at the faces around the fire his eyes too were hard, alight with challenge. He said, 'If I'm unwelcome, I'll move on.'

'No!' Boudicca spoke low and vibrantly as she came to her feet, remembering too clearly how Vindorex had been denied the shelter of Oakhillfort because Prasutagus had feared Roman reprisals. The son of Vindorex must remember it, too. 'No fosterling of mine shall be driven from my hearth! Let the Romans come. We shall defy them.'

'And this?' One sweep of Farann's hand dashed the tangled hair from his brow, exposing the puckered scar where he had been branded. 'Can you remove this?'

'We can change it,' Boudicca replied. 'A tattoo will disguise the scar. You shall wear the Warrior's Light, Farann.'

It was Cameira who objected scornfully, 'When did he win such an honour? Has he killed an enemy in battle?'

Her brothers, the twins, both loudly argued that Farann had done better than that: a slave, and in chains, he had choked the life out of a vicious overseer.

'It's not the same,' Cameira said, but her glance assessed Farann with sharpened interest, considering the power in that strong frame.

He returned her look with a challenging stare that made her toss her hair back and leap to her feet to stand for a moment with her hand on the hilt of her dagger before she spun on her heel and strode from the house. Watching, Rhiannon was riven by jealousy as she sensed the high feeling running between the pair. It was anger now, but that kind of anger led often to passion of another sort.

'He has earned the Light,' the queen decreed. 'He is welcome among us. You are come home, Farann.'

Every member of her household agreed, each adding a voice to the chorus. Even Prasutagus declared the young man welcome, though his tone betrayed reservations; Farann could not be turned away, but if the Romans discovered him here it would go badly for those who had sheltered him; one life was being saved at grave risk to many.

The king felt tired. More and more he found himself outvoted in matters that concerned the tribe. He no longer had the strength, or the will, to argue as once he might have done. For seventeen summers he had spoken out for caution and for peace, but the wheel turned inexorably, the voices that cried conflict grew stronger. It was the way of youth to seek changes. Soon a new leader must accept the yoke of kingship. Prasutagus sensed that his course was almost run.

Nevertheless, in these days of his old age the king unexpectedly found pleasure in the company of his foster-son. As Farann grew daily nearer to full strength he shared the fire with the king and they talked together of many things.

Often frail, pale Araunah would come and sit by them and listen to their talk, as would the twins and Cameira, but Rhiannon stayed at a distance and Boudicca listened only in snatches between going about her affairs with her usual briskness.

As the days lengthened into spring, Rhiannon stood often at her loom at the back of the hall. She was weaving a pattern of bright blue and green stripes cross-threaded with scarlet – blue for Farann's eyes, green for the Willow Maid, scarlet for the Goddess. Though spinning and weaving were still chores she abhorred, the work soothed her and took her mind off a future that loomed dark and obscure, and in those spring days of Farann's convalescence it kept her within sight and hearing of him as he sat talking with the king.

Ever and again his hooded glance slid in her direction, making her flush and fumble with the shuttle. But his thoughts remained hidden from her. She often felt that he still hated her.

Boudicca swept in, pausing a moment to catch the gist of the conversation. To her, these sessions by the fire were yet more evidence of her husband's increasing senility. However, she did derive a certain satisfaction from hearing Farann repeat her own misgivings and doubts about Roman intentions; Prasutagus listened to the young man as he had never listened to his wife.

'They're not to be trusted, lord,' Farann was saying now. 'They give their word lightly, thinking it no dishonour to break it – not when they're dealing with barbarians, which is how they think of us behind their outward show of courtesy. My father always said it was so and now I know it to be true. Though my mother was a Roman, everything I've learned about Roman ways makes me mistrust them. They believe themselves invincible. They believe their Gods have given them a charter to rule the world. They despise all peoples beyond the bounds of their Empire. And too many of them are like the procurator – quick to use their power to increase their personal wealth.' When he spoke of Catus Decianus his voice thickened with revulsion and hate as though the very thought of the man made him feel sick. 'The procurator has gathered around him a band of hard, violent men who have no creed but to advance their own fortunes by doing his bidding. Even if it means murdering innocents.'

Prasutagus, smoothing his beard, murmured something that was evidently an objection, for Farann answered flatly: 'I've seen it, lord. I've heard them boasting of their deeds, and of their rewards. The veterans of the colonia are discontented and bitter. They had hoped to retire with farms in Italia as their reward when their service was done. Now they find that their allotted land is here in misty Britannica. Here they must stay, instead of going home. So with encouragement from Catus they pour their resentment over the people they blame for their exile – the people who are nearest – *my* people, the Trinovantes.'

'Then surely the governor-general will stop them,' Prasutagus argued with more hope than assurance. 'I met the man. I looked into his face and read his heart – a warrior's heart, and full of contempt for the procurator.'

'You read him right, lord. General Suetonius is a soldier above all, with a soldier's mind set on battle plans, tactics, strategy. What does he care about the petty details of administration, of taxes and levies and funding for the Temple? He leaves that to Catus. Even though he hates the man, he knows him to be zealous in pursuit of his career. Suetonius is interested only in his own aims – military aims – to subdue the west and march on Mona, to destroy the Druids. He believes all resistance is led by Mona. Once let him clean out that nest of rats and – so he thinks – Albina's Isle will fall at his feet. Lord . . . for now, it's Catus you must concern yourself with. He holds the fate of the Iceni in his soft, fat, scented paws.'

Noting the loathing in his foster-son's voice, Prasutagus watched him for a moment with pale, thoughtful eyes, saying at last, 'Our fate? What do you mean? There's nothing he can do beyond what he already does. We pay our taxes promptly. We're allies of Rome. We have a treaty. I'm a Roman citizen.'

Boudicca, listening, made an impatient sound in her throat and in the gloom inside the house her green eyes flashed, returning her husband's glance. But the king looked swiftly back at Farann as that young man said:

'Can you live for ever, lord?'

Prasutagus stared at him. 'What?'

It was a moment before Farann answered and then his reluctance to say what had to be said sounded clear in his voice. 'The treaty stands only for your lifetime, lord. This is Roman policy. *You* are their ally. *You* are a citizen of Rome. But when you die the Iceni will lose your protection. They'll become subjects of Rome. Like the Atrebates. Like the Trinovantes. Little more than serfs in their own lands.'

'They must take us first!' Boudicca cried, shaking a raised fist. 'By Andastre, let them come! Let them try!'

Her husband ignored her. He seemed to have shrivelled into himself as he fixed his eyes on Farann's face, seeking to read the young man's thoughts. What he found there gave him no comfort.

'What can we do to prevent it?' he asked.

Farann shook his head. 'Perhaps nothing. But you might forestall the Emperor's greed. He always wants more land, more wealth. If you do nothing, he may take all you possess. But perhaps . . . if you freely give him a half share, as a legacy on your death, he might allow your family to keep what remains. It has been done before. If we couch it in the right language, it might work.'

'We?' the king queried.

'One of my duties at the procurator's office was the copying of documents,' Farann said. 'I can write in the proper forms of Latin, and advise you on the terms you must employ – if you wish it.'

Prasutagus stared into the fire, combing his long beard with his fingers. 'If you think it will save trouble . . .' he sighed.

Across the hall, Boudicca caught her daughter's eye and smiled triumphantly at her; the king was learning to face reality at last.

On Beltane Eve, cold rains dampened the ardour of some of the youth during the chasing of the hare, but Duihno as Green King, garlanded in oak and holly as symbols of the twin Gods, whooped and yelled as he raced away. No maiden was safe from him that night. During the races and feasting of the following day he and several other young men vied for the attentions of pretty Pluma, who that year had been chosen to wear the willow wreath on her shining brown hair.

Obliged to watch without participation, Rhiannon noted the subtle games being played, as they were always played at feasts and festivals among the youth of the tribe. Duihno still lusted after Erefwen, but when she spurned him he made play with her sister Pluma in an effort to stir the young priestess to jealousy; his efforts were vain. The twins, being valiant, healthy, and kinsmen of the queen, had their pick of girls and enjoyed their popularity, though Rhiannon was conscious of sidelong glances directed at her by Matuac. Cameira had this season turned her shoulder to the faithful Unthaus. Cool, quiet Unthaus merely shrugged and turned to the nearest available girl, as if he didn't care.

As for Farann, he remained aloof, a distant observer – more distant now than he had ever been in the past. A charged animosity remained between him and Cameira, unresolved since the warrior-maid had questioned his right to assume the Warrior's Light. Farann's pride had made him refuse the queen's gift of honour until such time as he could earn it beyond doubt and prove Cameira wrong. But despite his apparent disinterest in the girl Rhiannon still felt forces at work between them. She fretted over the deep hurt she sensed in Farann and feared that he might turn to Cameira for comfort. But she herself could do nothing to help him. First came her duty to the Goddess. Farann must wait.

*

Down in the horse enclosures as spring spread fresh green leaves in the woods, Vranaun the horsemaster, with his son Teyrnon, tended the sick Egyptian mare. They had used all their skill, but still Starbright was failing. She lay shivering, twitching as if with ague, her eyes dulled, in a shelter deeply cushioned with fresh hay.

Hearing this news, Rhiannon came down to the woods to share the vigil. She sat by the mare's head, gentling the animal and stroking its soft nose as it lay quietly shuddering away from life. Tears misted Rhiannon's eyes. The Iceni had hoped for so much from this mare. But Great Epona had denied their dream.

'Will you let her die?' The booming bass made all three of them look round to where Eogan was standing in the shelter's opening. They had been so engrossed that none of them had heard him approach. A tingle at Rhiannon's scalp reminded her that the Druid could appear wherever, whenever and in whatever guise it pleased him to appear.

He snapped orders at Vranaun, telling him to fetch certain things – herbs, dried roots, and some things with names unfamiliar to Rhiannon. Vranaun and his son hurried to obey.

Eogan's gleaming eyes fixed on Rhiannon, studying her intently. 'Are you faithful, Maiden?'

She got to her feet, fear making her pale though she held her head high. 'I am.'

'I expected no less,' Eogan said. 'Now let me see this mare.'

He knelt by Starbright, his long fingers gently moving over her. When Vranaun and his son returned, a potion was made, mixed with oil and some of the mare's own blood. Eogan's hands moved over the pot, weaving mystic patterns as he muttered spells. Then he bade Vranaun hold the mare's jaws apart and he fed the mixture to the back of her throat. Very soon, her shivering stopped and she lay still, sleeping.

'Tend her well,' Eogan said, rising stiffly to his feet, tall and gaunt in the confines of the rough hut. 'She will recover now. As soon as she has the strength and comes into season, set your best stallion to her. All the portents are good. The God has visited our sacred oak – there'll be mistletoe growing there for us to cull before long. The right stars are rising in the sky. The sun reaches his proper arching. And soon a foal shall be born to a white mare. It blends. It binds. All things hasten to an ending.'

From a pouch at his belt he took a handful of some fine substance like dust or sand, which he sprinkled over the mare, making magic signs with his free hand. Then he tossed more dust in the air towards Rhiannon, muttering an invocation before fixing her with a look that held her immobile.

In a rumbling undertone redolent with threat, he said, 'Be sure to keep faith, Maiden. On your shoulders rests the hope of your people. Be very sure!'

A swirl of his wolfskin cloak and he was gone.

The wicker shelter held the Druid's mystic aura for what seemed a long time. Then at last Rhiannon was able to move. She shared a troubled glance with Vranaun, who was watching her askance, and then with Teyrnon, whose eyes were wide.

'But how did he know the mare was sick?' Teyrnon asked in a hushed voice. 'How did he know when to come?'

'Eogan knows everything,' Vranaun said. 'It's the way of Druids.'

By the time Rhiannon returned to the fort, Eogan was gone back to his forests. He had visited only long enough to examine the lightning-split oak – to walk round it three times and pray over it, pressing his fingers into the spiral scar that had branded its trunk; he had spoken at length and in private with the queen, and he had visited the new colt. His purpose in coming was as much a mystery as were all his goings and comings.

But one thing was sure – he had saved the life of Starbright.

That midsummer, when the festival of the sun was celebrated at the oak grove along the knoll, Eogan materialised again to cut the throat of the sacrificial ram, sprinkle its blood and intone the ritual invocation. Then along with the king and queen, and most of the elders, the Druid withdrew to the fort as the dancing grew wilder and the wine and ale took its regular effect.

As ever at the summer Solstice, Rhiannon wore a crown of white flowers to signify her celibacy. She joined in the dancing, with Erefwen beside her, but her own urges were subdued by the drugged brew which Morica gave her. When the people about her began to break away and merge with the shadows of night she only felt tired, ready for sleep. Soon she would follow Morica's example and go home to bed.

On the far side of the fire she saw Cameira twisting and stamping, a thin gown clinging damply to her curves. And nearer at hand was Pluma, naked now with sweat gleaming along the contours of her full breasts, narrow waist and broad hips as she swayed in an ecstatic trance. Around her a clutch of half-clad young warriors clustered, hot-eyed and wet of mouth. Among them Rhiannon recognised Matuac.

Her head was beginning to ache and spin. The drums still throbbed and smoke eddied from the horse-shoe fires as a core of celebrants stamped beneath the trees of the grove. They were all caught up in the ecstasy brought by the ritual, all lost in their own way of worship: a trance brought on by dancing to bodily exhaustion, oblivion induced by alcohol, or the frenzy of sexual coupling.

But one dark figure beneath a tree stood apart and apparently unaffected by the rites. It was Farann, watching from a distance as was his habit, with the Iceni but not *of* the Iceni, or so it seemed. Since his return he had hardly spoken to Rhiannon. He attended to his duties among the warriors, hunting with them, practising with spear and chariot, sleeping every night in the great communal hall. He sedulously avoided Rhiannon and yet frequently she found him within sight of her.

She realised that Farann was the object of Cameira's dancing. The warrior-maid's gyrations took her ever closer to him, with her head flung back and her arms writhing out in a defiant invitation that dared him to respond. But in the flickering flamelight Rhiannon could not be sure what held Farann's attention. Was it Cameira, or was it the whirling, naked, sensual Pluma?

Then someone charged into her, pushing her roughly aside, making her lose her balance. She tripped over a clump of grass. As she stumbled to her knees she heard Duihno's drunken, slurring voice say, 'Well? Well? This time?'

He had hold of Erefwen by the shoulders, shaking her violently. She brought up her knee, aiming for his groin, and her hand clawed for his eyes. But he twisted aside and grabbed her leg, spilling her to the ground. As she lay winded,

Duihno brought his heel viciously against her ribs and with shouted curses at her strode away, towards the fire. Shouldering aside the young men who throbbed around Pluma, he grabbed the girl's arm. But she laughed at him and pulled away, and went gaily running into the shadows, pursued by Duihno and several other young men – including Matuac – whose lust demanded assuagement.

Rhiannon saw it all as in a dream, distorted as through a glass pebble. The drug had her in thrall, but somewhere inside her she retained a core of awareness; she noticed that Farann had moved closer to her. He stood poised in firelit shadow, as if he had been on his way to help – but to help whom? Herself, or Pluma? Behind him, a furious Cameira had stopped dancing. When Unthaus came up behind the frustrated girl, she whirled to throw her arms about his neck and drag him to the ground to couple with her openly.

By Rhiannon's feet, Erefwen groaned and began to get up. Rhiannon bent to help, but the pale-haired priestess shook her off. She was bruised but her pride forbade her to admit it.

With a glance to where Duihno and her half-sister had disappeared, Erefwen said, 'He will be sorry. And so will she. The little fool goes with him only to hurt me. Pah! Much I care for either of them! May Caridwen take them and mash their skulls to feed to Her pigs!'

She swung away and made for the safety of the fort, a hand pressed to her sore ribs.

The festivities were dwindling. Bodies slumped in exhaustion about the fire, some of them naked. Cameira and Unthaus lay still violently engaged in passion on the edge of the yellow light. And on the periphery of her vision Rhiannon was aware of Farann still watching, still distant, a tall shadow among other shadows.

Distressed, she turned away and began to walk towards the fort, beyond the grove of oaks to the hawthorns that here edged the chariot track. Slowly she left behind the firelight, until the night was illumined only by the thin greyness of the stars and the virgin moon.

'Rhiannon!' As the hoarse voice came from the darkness a hand fell on her arm, pulling her under a tree. This time, she knew him at once. He was Matuac. She could feel the heat of him, smell his wine-sodden breath.

She fought him, but he was stronger. He pinned her to the tree with his body. She screamed, but he clamped a hand over her mouth, muttering incoherently that he needed a woman, that Pluma had escaped him. 'Throw off your virgin crown!' he growled, a hand tearing the wreath of white flowers from her hair. 'Pay homage to the God now. Now!' He pawed at her body, his fingers catching the neck of her tunic, ripping it with a violence that hurt her neck. 'The God's in all men. Even in me. Pay your homage to me, Rhiannon. To me!'

She twisted for escape, crying out in alarm and revulsion as his hands defiled her and his hot mouth tasted her flesh. Holding her pinned by the throat, he paused to uncover himself. But a roar of inhuman rage split the night. Something thwacked at Matuac's head. His grip relaxed. He crumpled to the ground.

Dimly, Rhiannon saw the figure of another man – a tall man dressed in dark clothing. Her heart knew him even though her eyes and mind were clouded by the night and by the ivy drug. Tears of relief stung behind her eyes as she instinctively reached out for him.

Farann tossed away the cudgel he was holding and grasped her by the shoulders, holding her at arms' length. 'Are you hurt?'

She shook her head, gulping back her distress as she stroked weakly at his tunic, needing contact with him, wishing he would take her in his arms, yet at the same time knowing that it would be wrong. 'No. No, you came in time.'

'He meant no harm,' he said. 'Matuac thinks with his belly, not with his head. Blame the wine, and the smoke. Blame Pluma for maddening him with her dancing, and the Gods for making him as he is. Sober, Matuac would never hurt you.'

'I know that.' A shudder ran through her and suddenly she felt the night chill on the air. One hand clutched the torn edges of her tunic at her throat. 'Don't plead for him, Farann. I won't make trouble for him, even though . . . even though this isn't the first time.'

He was silent for a while, his fingers digging painfully into her flesh so that she sensed the struggle he was having with himself. Then abruptly he released her and stepped back, saying, 'Let me escort you to the queen's house, lady. The Maiden should not walk alone.'

Too weary and befuddled to argue, Rhiannon complied.

In her own room with Araunah breathing steadily close by she lay awake, her mind revolving in slow circles, no thought staying long enough for her to grasp it fully. She thought of Farann, her yearning for him, his strange apartness and his silences, and of Matuac's clumsy importuning – he, too, was suffering in his own way. She thought also of what it meant to be the Maiden. She was being saved, and saving herself, for a meeting with an Immortal who could stand amid lightning and be unharmed, who could take any form He chose – and yet, surely, as the Goddess would inhabit the flesh of Her Maiden at the Mysteries, so the God must borrow human form. Which man would be called to fulfil the rites at Beltane? Which man?

She was startled awake by the alarm call of the watch-horn, a succession of piercing notes that drove through the settlement rousing every living being. The queen's household leaped to answer the call, grabbing up spears as they ran, Rhiannon with them. Outside, grey dawn light showed the fort in furore, warriors streaming toward the gates.

'The horses!' a voice yelled. 'They're after the horses!'

A hand on her arm stopped Rhiannon in her tracks and she spun round to find Ylas holding her. 'Not you!' he shouted at her. 'You must stay here. Your mother commands it.'

Behind him, beyond a scatter of running people, she saw her mother standing wearing a loose night robe, her hair in a single braid across one shoulder, her eyes compelling even in the colourless light of dawn. The sight of her recalled Rhiannon to her first duty – her service to the Goddess. She must keep herself safe and pure for the Goddess.

Frustrated, she stood and watched her friends and companions answer the call to defend the livestock. Ylas ran away, yelling, 'Matuac! Where's Matuac? Mat! Mat!'

For all Rhiannon knew, Matuac was still lying under the hawthorns where she and Farann had left him. And how many other fighting men and women were laid low by the excesses of midsummer?

The raid had been cunningly timed. The attackers were able to drive off numbers of cattle and some horses, though despite the festival the enclosures in the woods had been guarded and most of the valuable herd was safe – including the white mare. But two men had been killed and several people injured, among them Garanhir.

Rhiannon saw men bringing the king's champion in on an improvised sledge; she saw Adalma pale as death, a hand to her mouth and her eyes so wide they seemed to be screaming silently. And then she saw her mother, expressionless, striding by as though Garanhir meant nothing to her. Rhiannon wondered if that were true, or if the queen was also screaming inside herself. From Boudicca's demeanour, it was impossible to guess.

'They were from Seafort – Audagas's men,' Prasutagus said angrily when the council met to debate how they should answer the affront. 'They came after the Egyptian mare. Teyrnon guessed it and called the guard to defend Starbright most strongly, else she'd be gone now. It seems there's no end to Audagas's arrogance. But this shall be the last time he defies my authority. My pouch of patience is empty. Segovax, ride with a message to Audagas. I demand that he meet us. This time, we shall end the blood feud for ever.'

Ten

The king led them in his chariot with Ylas as reinsman while Matuac drove for the queen. Between the two Eogan rode long-legged and uncomfortable on a pony – the Druid much preferred to travel on his own two feet. Rhiannon rode among the warriors with Araunah beside her, both of them eager to witness the fight that would end Audagas's long reign of brutality at Seafort.

Behind them they left Garanhir, sorely wounded with ribs

crushed by pounding hooves. He had fallen in the fight, and been trampled. But Adalma was nursing him and if selfless love and devotion could mend him then he would be well, in time.

As they came over a succession of wooded ridges they saw glimpses of the distant expanse of the sea. They reached a vale dotted with furze and rowan, where shepherds were hastily herding sheep away. And there, on the slope of the further hill, ranged among the trees, waited the warriors of Audagas's clan.

In front of the opposing force, naked but for the oil that glistened on every rippling muscle, stood a giant warrior with a wild crest of hair lightened and stiffened with limewash. His limbs and his massive chest were matted with a growth of brown hair that narrowed across his belly to his groin, so that he resembled a bear with naked upper arms and thighs between which his manhood hung oddly puny in its flaccidity. He wielded a curved axe, and bore a round red shield strapped to his left arm. Patterns painted with woad turned his face into a terrifying mask.

'It's Cadfan,' someone said, identifying Audagas's oldest son, who was said to have the strength of three men now that he had come to full manhood. Even as a youth he had been formidable in contests of strength, and he had boasted that some day he would challenge Nuadat and take his place.

'At last!' This from Nuadat, spoken with deep satisfaction as the gnarled champion slid from his horse and exchanged a speaking glance with his warrior-wife Deucca, who gave him a tight, proud smile and leaped to the ground beside him.

In full view of friend and foe, Eogan stepped forward and began chanting the prayers of purification, asking the Gods to stand witness to the battle and to grant justice. Nuadat stripped off his clothes and allowed himself to be rubbed all over with sacred oil. He kept himself shaven and free of all body hair, in fine contrast to the shaggy Cadfan, the better to enable the holy power of magic to act as his shield. Clothes and hair interfered with the magic: nakedness was necessary to give complete protection.

After the oil, Eogan painted blue patterns on Nuadat's face and body – circles on his face to echo the all-seeing eye he wore on his brow; the spread of branches, signifying the oak, across his breast, and the spiral of immortality down his body. Only his back remained unpatterned: no true warrior ever turned his back on a foe.

At last Nuadat was ready, a finely decorated shield on his left arm, and in his right hand a heavy thrusting spear to weigh against his opponent's axe. Apart from these weapons he wore only a gold torc about his neck and a knotted girdle of plaited leather round his waist. Pausing, he lifted his hands for the blessing of his fellows, who replied with raised fists. Rhiannon clenched her own hand, lifting it high, chanting with the others, 'Nuadat! Nuadat!' as the tribe's champion turned to face his enemy.

Slowly the two naked warriors began to walk to meet each other at the bottom of the hollow where the sward spread thick with wild-flowers, while from the slopes warriors chanted their names to a quickening rhythm.

The fight was fierce and long. Grunts and cries of challenge escaped the combatants. Metal clanged on metal, wood thunked on wood. A shield deflected the thrusting spear. Nuadat dodged a blow from the axe and spun lithely away to make a fresh feint. They circled, closed, struck, parried. Blood began to smear from superficial wounds. Fierce howls and groans came from the throats of the onlookers as the two vied for an opening, sweat streaming from every pore, their eyes glaring hatred.

Then Cadfan's axe caught in Nuadat's shield. The shield split in two. The axe sliced deep above Nuadat's wrist, severing muscle and bone. Nuadat, dodging, slipped and went down on one knee. The axe flashed up again for the final blow. Audagas's warriors raised a shout and Cadfan yelled as he brought down the axe. But the fierce ululation of triumph choked off. Nuadat's spear thrust past his guard, tearing through gut and lungs as it drove for Cadfan's heart. Cadfan's blow faltered. The axe struck the side of Nuadat's face, slicing flesh. For a moment the two were locked together, each weapon drinking the other man's blood. The hairy Cadfan seemed to be leaning onto the spear, bowing as if in acknowledgement of his defeat. He toppled, taking Nuadat with him. They fell as one, their blood staining the bright flowers.

A high-pitched scream broke from Deucca. Wailing, she ran down the slope to fall on her knees beside Nuadat, loosening her hair so that it fell round her face, tearing at her bodice until she exposed her breast. Her cries and shrieks filled the valley. She leapt up, tearing a spear from the sling behind her, lifting it for a throw, screaming at the Seafort warriors to come, to meet her.

Another warrior emerged from the ranks of Seafort folk – Audagas's second son, Erthil. He ran howling down the slope with a spear poised. Running, he launched it, ducking aside as Deucca's spear reached him. His own spear flew straight and deadly. It impaled Nuadat's woman through the chest with an audible thump. Deucca hung there, letting the breath go up from her body in a long gurgling sigh. Afterwards, there were those who said she was smiling, that she had no more taste for life if Nuadat were dead.

Teeth showing in a fierce grin, Erthil took an axe from his belt and swung it round his head. 'Who's next?' he yelled. 'Come, cowards. Who'll meet Erthil, Audagas's son? For my brother's life I'll take ten of yours.'

Several of the royal guard moved to answer the threat, but Farann moved fastest. He was first in the race down the hill, launching himself into the battle with stabbing spear and dagger. The others halted, obeying the rules of honour – no third person interfered in single combat. Rhiannon strained to see past them, her heart unsteady, her mouth dry with fear. But Farann fought like one possessed, with a fury that few men could have withstood. In the end, Erthil staggered and fell. Farann was blooded from superficial wounds but he remained standing with lowered head like a bull about to charge, eager for more blood.

As others started from both sides to turn single combat into general strife, they were halted in their tracks when a stentorian shout of, *'Hold!'* shook the very air. The voice belonged to Boudicca. As everyone stopped, she ordered Matuac to drive forward and all eyes turned to where she stood regal and imperious in her decorated chariot with her red hair drawn back in curls from her tattooed brow and the great electrum torc of Icenia pale at her throat. She rode down into the hollow among her warriors, where Nuadat lay woefully injured with Deucca dead beside him, and where

Cadfan lay in his last sleep with his brother Erthil not far away. Farann stood over his fallen foe, clasping his bloody spear.

The queen's eyes locked with the hard blue ones of her foster-son and then she deliberately turned her head away and looked up at the trees in whose shade the people of Seafort sat waiting.

'Audagas!' the queen called in that low, commanding voice she had learned to summon and project until it sent shivers of awe down the spine of every listener. 'Audagas, I, Boudicca, queen of all the Iceni, would speak with you face to face. Come down. Obey me.'

At first it seemed as though the chief of Seafort would defy her, then slowly he rode out to meet her, kicking at his pony as it trod down the slope. He was a short, stocky man, with a bronze helmet jammed onto his head so hard that his bushy brows stuck out from its rim. He wore his moustache long, obscuring his mouth, the colour of rust now threaded thickly with grey.

He paused a pace or two from the queen, returning her steady gaze with suspicion. 'Lady?'

'You have one more son,' she reminded him in a voice that carried far on the silence. 'Will you have him die, too, for a foolish cause? Must the Iceni continue to war amongst themselves for a few cattle, or a few horses?'

'It has always been so!' Audagas answered. 'Warriors must fight. Would you have us stay at home and learn to spin and weave?'

'I would have you use your strength – not against your own kind but against our common enemy! Shall we lose more fine young men and women in a blood feud among our own kin? Our warriors must fight for a greater cause.'

'Show me that cause!' Audagas challenged. 'Give me a sword in my hand and I'll ride at your side, lady. I, and my warriors.'

Shouts of agreement rose from the ranks of riders behind him. The people of Seafort were eager for a fight. Any fight.

From the advantage of her height in the chariot, Boudicca looked down into the fierce face below those bushy brows and the jammed-down helmet.

'There will be swords,' she vowed in a low voice, and saw

the spark of belief and hope that lit his eyes. 'When the time comes, Audagas, we shall go full-armed into a battle that will send the Romans back into the seas that brought them. I, Boudicca, promise you this. There will be swords.'

The truth of that promise rang in her voice as she thought of the small hoard of sharp swords, forged strong and tempered in fresh blood, that lay waiting in the depths of the forests – waiting only for the right moment to cry battle.

Audagas watched her with narrowed eyes and glanced up at the people on the hill behind her. The king was there, and the Druid Eogan, and the queen's daughter, the Maiden – the power, the magic and the hope of the tribe – all of them backing this red-haired, green-eyed, compelling queen who spoke with such conviction.

He looked again at Boudicca, his expression sullen and defiant before those daunting green eyes. 'Then we'll follow you, lady,' he said. 'When the time comes. But let that time be soon. Let it be very soon. The youth of Seafort were not bred to sit idle waiting.'

Jerking at the reins, he turned his stubby-legged pony and kicked it into a walk that took him back up the hill stiff-backed and proud.

A group of his warriors rode out to collect the bodies of Cadfan and Erthil while others from Oakhillfort gathered tenderly to bear Deucca's body to her horse and to bind Nuadat's grave wounds. The champion was still breathing, but even if his life could be saved he would lose his left hand.

Eventually, with his two dead sons tossed over their horses, Audagas and his warriors melted into the woods, heading back for their homes.

'This was well done,' Eogan rumbled into his beard as his fierce grey eyes swung to Boudicca. 'Well done, lady.'

Messages passed silently between queen and Druid. Rhiannon saw the satisfaction that curved her mother's mouth, and the look of triumph mingled with scarcely veiled contempt that the queen directed at her husband. She saw something else, too – she saw Farann striding back up the slope, an expression of grim determination on his face. Glancing neither to right nor left, he made straight for where Cameira stood, and as he paused before her the look in his eyes was a spear as sharp as the bloody weapon that had drunk the blood of Erthil.

'Do you still deny my right to wear the Warrior's Light?' he demanded.

Cameira flushed, but her mouth remained stubborn. 'You've proved your valour, before us all. That rides with our law. Before today we had only your word. I would always question the unproven word of an incomer.'

'So should we all!' This harsh agreement came from a scowling Duihno. 'We of the Iceni don't grant the Light without proof of its deserving.'

'Enough!' Boudicca's voice cut in sharply. 'If proof of Farann's courage were needed, we've witnessed it in ample measure. He shall wear the Warrior's Light. Aye! And he shall have honour among the Iceni, as one of us. Bear witness, warriors. Bear witness, all of you. I, Boudicca, choose Farann above all others to be my daughter's champion and protector. Maiden's champion from now on!'

Startled, Rhiannon met Farann's glance and found herself captured by the emotions she read there – emotions that echoed her own. She felt breathless with surprise, numbed by dismay. If she was driven into greater proximity with Farann, would it be a sterner test than she could withstand? Was this Dia's way of proving, once and for all, the faithfulness of Her Maiden?

She looked to her mother, hoping for answers, but the queen evaded her eyes. Even Boudicca didn't know why Eogan had suggested that some means should be found to bring Farann and Rhiannon together, or why she had agreed to it. Was it a challenge to the Gods – a defiant, prideful gesture that risked all on a gamble? Boudicca knew well enough the urges that both her daughter and the young warrior were valiantly resisting. Perhaps somewhere deep inside her she was jealous of that. Perhaps she actually wanted them to suffer, as she herself had suffered. Or was it that she wanted them to be together, to steal a little joy before the Goddess, dread Caridwen, Dark Winnower of Souls, Slayer of Dreams, stepped in and demanded her portion of human blood steeped in tears of sorrow?

Maiden's champion, Maiden's guard. It meant that Farann must defend Rhiannon from all danger – from verbal taunts and from physical attack. He was never far away now, near her at feasts and at chariot practice, riding beside her to the hunt. But he kept his barriers taut, his expression closed against her; he seldom allowed himself to meet her eyes directly, and when he spoke to her his words were formal. Rhiannon knew that such self-discipline was worthy – she was the Maiden, not to be touched, not to be defiled in any way before she came to the God – but she was still a young, full-blooded woman and at times Farann's stern distances enraged her so much that she wanted to strike him if only to force a response from him.

He wore the Warrior's Light now, blue on his brow. Morica had skilfully fashioned the all-seeing eye tattoo to blend with the shape of the brand that scarred his forehead, but the disguise was far from complete. Farann would bear his badge of shame to the gates of the Glass Castle, where perhaps gentle Arianrhod would grant him release from it. Bitterly aware of that puckered 'S', Farann had trained his hair to grow long and shaggy, falling over his forehead and almost into his hard blue eyes.

As for Nuadat, he lay mortally sick, more from grief than from his wound. His left arm had been severed above the wrist and no art of Eogan and Morica could grow back the upper portion of his right ear, though the flap of flesh from his cheek was roughly stitched into place. Nuadat was strong enough to survive the mutilation, as had others before him. But with Deucca dead he seemed to have lost his will to live.

Gentle Adalma tended him, bringing him into her house to lie alongside the recuperating Garanhir. Perhaps the long friendship that had endured between the two champions helped to heal both of them, for slowly, reluctantly, Nuadat too began to recover.

On a mellow harvest day of golden sunlight, the warning came on the wind – Romans! Romans approaching, heading along the Way for Oakhillfort! The message was passed on by the cryptic tune of shepherds' reed pipes, repeated by watch-horns from farm to farm. As the musical news reached the fort, where the chariots were at practice, most of the reinsmen halted to let down their warriors before driving their vehicles rapidly away to hiding.

The smooth efficiency of the deception amused Boudicca. The Romans had no idea of the real strength of Iceni chariot squadrons; indeed, they found the Britonic fondness for the flimsy vehicles rather quaint and colourful. It was to cater to what she considered to be Roman purblindness that Boudicca remained in her chariot, with Rhiannon at the reins. She ordered her daughter to drive her out to meet the visitors, accompanied by a guard of warriors walking either side.

Rhiannon obeyed, urging the ponies into a walk, though she felt uneasy. It seemed to her that the air smelled sour. The signs were awry. Lately there had been warnings on the wind, and that morning soon after dawn a trio of whistling swans had flown over Oakhillfort, heading southward, yet it was only the month of the hazel; the birds were a moon ahead of their time.

Now Romans were coming. Her scalp prickled with a feeling of foreboding.

A military escort approached, guarding yet another band of civil servants of the procurator's staff, identified by green and white pennants on cavalry lances. Raising dust as they came, they left the Way and took the winding track to Oakhillfort, among hills where the harvest was under way. Sickles flashed in the fields, workers bent to bind sheaves, and laden sledges were heading home dragged by shaggy oxen with curved horns. As Rhiannon had foreseen, the yield of grain would be a rich one that year.

At the foot of the long slope leading down from the gates of Oakhillfort, Boudicca halted her party and waited, head high and back straight, for the visitors to come near. She knew very well what the soldiers would be thinking; Romans in Icenia seldom troubled to conceal their contempt. To them she was a rude barbarian clinging to an illusion of dignity, a queen of lions whose teeth had long ago been drawn, ignorant, uncultured, savage, the butt of ribaldry in tavern and barracks.

So let them laugh. Let them laugh who knew nothing of war chariots hidden in bushes, of swords buried in forest places, of the secret, burning heart of a queen who had vowed vengeance. Let them laugh. Her day would come.

Rhiannon stood in the chariot, the reins firm in her hands to keep the horses in check. She watched them, speaking to soothe them, making the small adjustments of weight and curb that were necessary. A breeze flipped at her hair, teasing tendrils about her face. As the Romans approached she heard the soft thud of hooves, the jingle of harness, and from her eye corner she glimpsed the bright gleam of sunlight on polished bronze and gilt, the flutter of red cloth, the toss of plumes. The escort of soldiers was larger than usual, and fully armed with swords, shields, spears . . .

The party slowed at a signal from the tribune in charge, and halted not many yards away. The officer saluted Boudicca, a fist over his heart in the Roman manner – a courtesy not often afforded to Britons.

Stunned, Rhiannon stared at the handsome face shadowed by the plumed helmet. Caius Valerius Rufinus, she thought, hot blood rushing up to stain her cheeks. She remembered his full name with shameful ease, remembered how he had looked at her and spoken to her on the forum at Camulodunon. She stared at him in dismay, her thoughts flying protectively to Farann. The tribune knew him! Farann would be discovered, taken back to slavery . . .

This was what the warnings had meant – this was what her prescient sense had foreseen. Caius Valerius Rufinus brought danger, not only for Farann but for herself, too. Because, despite everything she knew in her head, still her instincts responded to the man.

His glance met hers, the smile in his eyes saying that he had expected to see her here, and that he was flattered by her reaction, then he addressed the queen with unusual civility, 'Lady, your greeting honours us. I am Valerius Rufinus, tribune of the Twentieth Legion, attached to the staff of the civil governor in Camulodunum. Forgive the intrusion, lady, but we are conducting a census, by order of the procurator my lord Catus Decianus.'

He had learned the Britonic language, Rhiannon realised as her initial shock lessened and allowed her mind to work again. He spoke it well, if with a strong accent. This time, there would be no need for interpreters. This time . . .

Unaware of her daughter's discomfiture, Boudicca watched the tribune through narrowed eyes, suspicious of his polite manners. But if he intended mockery it did not show in his face. As hospitality demanded, she invited him and his people to share the shelter of her village.

While the Romans conducted their business with the council of elders, Rhiannon sought out Farann, who was down in the woods among the horses, sitting on a stump and oiling harness leathers. Anxiously she begged him to be sure to stay out of sight. If Valerius recognised him, disaster would ensue. She was sure of it, though she consoled herself that his looks had changed since the Romans had known him. At Camulodunon he had had his hair cropped, his face clean-shaven; now his hair was shaggy, tumbling down his neck and into his eyes, and he wore a thick dark moustache that concealed most of his mouth. But he couldn't disguise his height and strength, or the pale whip scars that showed on every uncovered part of his limbs and body.

'He'll not recognise me!' Farann said bitterly. 'Who ever remembers a slave's face? Why has he come – why him in particular?'

'He has his orders. He's attached to the procurator's staff.'

Farann's mouth twisted. 'As I was?' The shame he had endured at Camulodunon was still sharp in his mind. But such a fate would not be meted out to an officer of Valerius's background. No, The Pig wouldn't dare put his fat pink hands on a young man of good Roman family. He only did that to slaves – especially enjoying himself when those slaves were of noble Britonic blood. Farann gritted his teeth, wishing he had killed the man. Or perhaps he should have killed himself, as had others before him, sooner than live degraded. But there had been Cunovinda – and where was his sweet sister now? – and beyond her there had been Rhiannon, and a hope that had never left him.

Guessing at some of the thoughts moving behind his bleak blue eyes, Rhiannon impulsively laid her hand on his arm, hurting for him. 'Farann . . .'

He jerked away, getting to his feet, saying, 'It's no coincidence that Valerius Rufinus is here. He's pursuing you.'

'You can't know that.'

'I know it! I remember the words he spoke to you at the feast on the forum, and the look in his eyes.'

'That was long ago. But if you're right – if he does have

eyes for me . . .' she hesitated, knowing she shouldn't ask but unable to resist the temptation, ' . . . will it trouble you?'

His look was lightning, searing her in the instant before he controlled himself, turning away. 'My duty as Maiden's champion is to protect you from all harm – especially the harm that will follow the attentions of a Roman who cares nothing for our sacred traditions. You're the Maiden. Don't expect *him* to honour that.'

'If he doesn't, *I* shall!' she said, angry now. 'You forget that I've taken solemn vows.'

'I do not forget!' he got out through his teeth. 'Forget?! My head boils from remembering it every time you come near me!'

'And do you think I would let some lusting Roman break my faith with the Goddess?' she cried. 'If he approaches me, I'll repulse him.' She laid a hand at the hilt of her dagger, adding fiercely, 'And if he persists, I'll kill him! And I'll need no help from you, Farann!' She swung on her heel and strode away, stamping each foot to the ground in a fury of rage, hurt and fear – fear because if Farann felt the need to defend her he might betray himself. He must stay out of sight. He mustn't show himself, however much his pride cried against it. If he risked his life on her account she would die of grief.

It was only later, when her temper cooled, that she realised he had come close to admitting his feelings for her. But by then she had other worries.

Returning to the queen's house, she found its doors guarded by sturdy legionaries. The soldiers barred her way with drawn swords, stolidly ignoring her protests until one of the officials appeared in the doorway and apparently ordered the men to let her in.

The inspectors were in the process of counting everything the royal family possessed – jewellery, wine, even clothing. Fuming at her own helplessness, Rhiannon had to stand by while they emptied her personal baskets and sorted through her belongings, one man calling out his findings while the other made marks on a wax tablet. They even made note of Araunah's dolls and the board game she had left lying; then they invaded the queen's room.

Distressed, Rhiannon snatched up a cloak and fled from the house. But as she passed the guard one of them threw out a hand to detain her. He thought she was trying to sneak the cloak away from the inspectors. For a wild moment they tussled over the garment, then the man drew his sword. He thrust its hard hilt under her chin.

Speechless with disbelief, she stared at the man. Was he mad? Was he about to kill her – over a cloak that was hers – a cloak the assessors had already noted?

But a voice interjected – a sharp male voice barking an order that made the soldier come to attention, his sword held vertical in front of his face. The cloak fell draping to the ground and Rhiannon swiftly swept it up out of the dust. Glancing round, she saw Valerius striding towards her, his face all concern.

'Lady Rhiannon . . . forgive this mistake. The man will be punished. He went beyond his orders. Far beyond them.'

'Do Romans *ever* observe limits where barbarians are concerned?' she asked, her voice thick with disgust. 'It seems not, tribune. Or they would not be invading my mother's privacy – and mine – with even more efficiency than usual.'

'The procurator's orders – '

She gathered spittle in her mouth and ejected it at his feet. '*That* for the procurator! May Caridwen feed on his skull!' She thrust past him, leaving him staring after her, his eyes narrowed as he stroked his mouth to hide a smile.

Making for the great hall, Rhiannon saw Farann lurking in shadows under low eaves by the door of the building. Evidently he had witnessed her encounter with Valerius. He had unsheathed his dagger and his face was dark with anger.

She paused, taut-faced, her green eyes flecked with gold sparks. 'Not yet, Farann. Not yet!'

Inside the hall, the council sat in angry session, debating the latest outrage. The Romans had more on their mind than a census of people: they were on a mission to reassess every item the Iceni possessed. The rate of taxes was to be revised.

Grumble as they would, there was nothing the elders or the warriors could do about it.

Accompanied by a small guard of armed legionaries to discourage argument, each inspector set himself to counting – amphorae of wine; brooches, bracelets, all kinds of jewellery; lengths of cloth, hides of tanned leather; pottery, both home-made and imported, glassware, tools, livestock . . .

Segovax the lawgiver went about grim-faced, carrying the marked sticks that were his tallies left from the last assessment. In all cases, it seemed, the accounts were disputed.

All of this occupied several days. The Romans ate and drank of Iceni largesse, but they slept outside the fort. On the heath near the Way, the legionaries had built a marching camp – a deep ditch and sturdy palisade inside which they erected their tents – and there they spent each night. They must have been aware of the resentment their prying aroused.

For the counting of livestock, carpenters erected a set of gates that were carted out to the heath, where the sheep and cattle were herded together and driven through one by one. Then the gates were moved to the woods and Valerius Rufinus himself oversaw the tallying of the horses. He had been warned to look for the Egyptian mare and took care to be certain no foals of hers had yet been born. A special tax would be payable on her offspring, the inspectors declared.

'And what of the census?' Boudicca was heard to demand of the tribune. 'Would you have my people run between gates to be counted, too?'

'Lady . . .' he answered with a gesture of helplessness. 'I regret the necessity, but we have our orders.'

'Pah!' said the queen, and swept away in impotent fury. But in her heart she added one more injustice to the lengthening list of her grievances.

Eleven

When, finally, the assessment was completed, the king invited Valerius Rufinus and other important members of his party to feast in hall that night.

The feast was as splendid as Icenia could provide, with roasts of mutton, pork and venison, fish fresh from river and sea, loaves of rich dark bread, and sweetmeats of honey and seeds mixed with fruit from the woods. Wine flowed like streams, and ale, and mead, while Alvran sang and some of the girls danced to the music of reed pipe and drum. Among them, Pluma seemed the most popular; lithe and curvy with flowers threaded in her shining brown hair, she had always taken sensual delight in her own body.

Rhiannon was aware of Farann far off down the hall, hidden among a crowd of other warriors. She hoped he would stay there and not risk being recognised, though Valerius appeared to harbour no suspicions. Indeed, the young tribune seemed to have nothing on his mind but his interest in Rhiannon herself. Throughout the feast whenever she glanced his way she found him watching her with an intensity that both disturbed and flattered her.

Under the clamour in the hall, Valerius spoke to Prasutagus. Rhiannon saw the king stop suddenly, his teeth sunk into a joint of mutton as he stared at the tribune and suddenly began to choke.

Valerius leapt up to slap the king soundly on the back. Others hurried to help, exclaiming in alarm. Slowly, Prasutagus managed to draw a strangled breath and waved away the group of anxious warriors as colour flowed back into his face. Then he turned watery eyes to Valerius, croaking, 'Loans? Loans?! We were told they were grants!'

'Then there was a misunderstanding, lord.'

A silence spread outward as though a stone had been thrown into a pool, creating ripples at the centre of which sat the grey king and the vital, dark-haired, handsome young Roman. Beside them, Boudicca was glowering, angry spots of colour burning in her cheeks to echo the muted fire of her gown.

'What loans?' she demanded.

Her husband wiped his drooling mouth on the edge of his sleeve and when he spoke his voice was faint. 'You remember, Boudicca – at the signing of the treaty we were awarded gifts of money and goods to – '

'You were given loans,' Valerius corrected. Glancing across the bowed figure of the king, he met the storms in Boudicca's face, before which his own gaze wavered briefly. 'Lady . . . This is the truth of it – certain wealthy citizens in Rome were glad to extend loans to help the Iceni. Now they are calling in those loans, with the due interest. Surely you knew the time would come?'

The queen looked through him, her mind working. Valerius was lying – or perhaps he had been misled by his masters: the word had been 'grants' when the treaties were signed, and there had been no hint that the bounty would one day have to be repaid. It was a trick. An insult! Her temper rose to meet it . . .

But she remembered Mocuxoris, reacting in anger and hot blood, rising to avenge an earlier insult – and dying for it. It must not happen again. When the time came – the real time of reckoning – heads must be clear and cold. All her instincts told her the time was not yet come. First let the Great Year pass, let the rites be celebrated in solemn order. Then – yes – *then* would the great tide of Celtic anger be free to rise and drown the enemy in an ocean of blood.

'Of course we knew,' she said, tossing her head, waving a beringed hand in a dismissive gesture that told her warriors to continue their talk and their enjoyment of the night. 'But we should have been forewarned, Caius Valerius Rufinus. We shall need time to gather our resources.'

'The assessors have drawn up lists, lady. These will be left with you. You will be allowed seven nights in which to gather the goods. But . . .' He looked across at Rhiannon, a significant light in his eyes as he leaned closer to the queen. Though he spoke quietly, Rhiannon's eyes and ears divined his words. 'If the burden of repayment is too much, I . . . I do have a certain influence in Rome. My father is a member of the senate, a respected, wealthy man who is close to the Emperor. I might find some means to lighten the load for you, in return for . . .' again he glanced at Rhiannon as he added, 'for certain favours.'

Boudicca drew a hissing breath. 'My daughter's taboo! For you – for all men!'

His eyes darted to hers, widened by surprise. 'A priestess?'

'The Maiden. Chosen of the Goddess. Dedicated to the God. For moons yet to come. But beyond that . . .' The queen sent a speculative look at her daughter and lowered her voice to a murmur. 'Beyond that, if she chooses . . .'

Rhiannon felt sick. She was being held out as a lure, bartered over like a slave. If she needed more proof of her mother's heartlessness here it was, written clear – my daughter's honour for a few sacks of wool. She got to her feet, her hands clenched, her heart iced with hatred. 'Never!' she spat at them. 'Never!'

As she left the hall, stumbling blindly out into a night lit by a few burning torches along the paths, she was accosted by someone whose hard hand closed about her wrist. It was Farann. He said roughly, 'What did he suggest? What?'

'A bride-price,' she said bitterly, wrenching free of his grasp. 'No – a whore-price. It would hardly be marriage he wanted.'

'I'll kill him!'

'No! Don't risk your life for nothing. Kill him, his soldiers will come. Kill them, the legions will come. The king's right – we can't win against them, Farann. The best we can do is endure.'

'I'd sooner die!'

Heavy breathing behind Rhiannon warned of the arrival of Matuac, who came stumbling out of the hall stinking with ale-fumes. He stopped at sight of them, demanding, 'What's going on? What's the matter? Did that fornicating Roman insult Rhiannon?'

Before either of them could reply, sounds of quarrelling voices came out of the shadows beyond the sacred oak. A man was snarling, a girl pleading. There came a sharp slap, a cry of pain. A slender figure came running across the grass, with a man in pursuit of her. As they passed by a flaring torch, its yellow light revealed the girl to be Pluma, the man Duihno.

With the grace of a deer, Pluma sped on to throw herself into Farann's arms crying, 'Oh, Farann! Help me! Save me! He'll kill me.'

Duihno shambled up, panting hoarsely, to halt as both Rhiannon and Matuac stepped out with daggers drawn to defend Pluma.

'Let me get at her!' Duihno raged drunkenly. 'She's nothing but a whore! Flicking her tail at those Romans – and at the rest of you! I saw her – I saw her sneak out, and that scrawny Roman wax-scratcher after her. He's been drooling over her these past three nights, and she encouraging him.'

'It's not true!' Pluma wept, lifting her tear-streaked face to look piteously at Farann. 'Oh, it's not true, Farann! Is it my fault if men like me? But I wouldn't go with any midget of a

Roman, whatever Duihno says. He's got no right to question me. I'm not his woman. I'm not! I never made any promises to him. He only wants me because he thinks it will hurt Erefwen.'

Matuac let out a growl. His dagger flicked a notch out of the air a mere whisper away from Duihno's face. Duihno backed off, a hand clapped to his unmarked cheek.

'Slave-born bitch!' he flung at Pluma before whirling to stamp off into the darkness.

In Farann's arms, Pluma was trembling like a frightened bird. She clutched at him, whispering, 'Oh, thank you. Thank you. He frightens me so. Farann . . . Oh, Farann, he might be waiting in the shadows. Will you walk to my mother's house with me?'

Farann hesitated, sliding a sidelong glance at Rhiannon, who turned away and, with Matuac at her heels, made for the queen's house. She knew well what reward Pluma would offer for her 'rescue.' Since her father had died, the girl had run wild and her mother, who had once been a slave, seemed to wield no control over her. Pluma enjoyed the delights of the senses. If Farann accepted a gift so freely given, who could blame him?

Valerius Rufinus and his party of soldiers and officials departed early the following morning bound for more tax-gathering duties. They would return after seven nights, to collect the dues of the royal village and its farms.

As soon as the visitors were gone, Boudicca ordered her chariot to be prepared. She commanded the whole complement of chariots to parade with her, to train harder and harder, at the reins, with the spears. Her feelings demanded a release of energy in violent action.

Rhiannon stood at her loom, deliberately deaf and blind to her mother's brisk mood. She herself was restless, taut with a burning anger that made her shuttle jab and catch in the warp threads. Her thoughts were a jumble – Farann and Pluma, Valerius, the loans that must be repaid, and the hints Valerius had dropped – hints that the queen had so eagerly caught up.

'Rhiannon!' Boudicca's voice rang sharply from the doorway. 'Leave that. Come. You're my reinswoman.'

After a delay long enough to infuriate the queen, Rhiannon looked up. 'Am I, mother?' she replied in brittle tones. 'Until when – until after the Great Year, when you trade me off to the Romans in return for your security?'

The queen's brow darkened. She strode back into the hall, swirled her cloak aside as she passed the fire – and stopped. Her mouth stretched in a smile that left her eyes cold as a winter sea. 'How you delight in wounding me. You see so much, yet you understand so little. When the Great Year is over there'll be no more dealing with Romans – except in fire and blood! Do you think I would stand by and see you – you, Maiden, daughter, queen . . .' The words tangled in her throat and all at once her eyes glistened with furious tears. She lifted a fist to the heavens, shaking it in the faces of the Gods. 'Sooner may your blood run red on the altar at the grove! I'd slay you myself before I let any Roman defile you.'

'Then why did you say – '

'I spoke to test you! And you answered me. You answered *him!* Never! Never!'

The sight of her mother's tears dismayed and yet comforted Rhiannon. Her own eyes blurred and she found herself embracing the queen, being hugged in return, both of them choked with emotions for which there were no words.

'Enough!' With a husky laugh, Boudicca drew back, holding her daughter at arms' length. She leaned to kiss Rhiannon's cheeks, first left, then right, and smiled at her, her hands tight on her daughter's slender shoulders though her eyes were unfocused, looking inward. 'You're like him,' she said softly. 'Stubborn, wilful, quick to feel a wound . . . All you lack is his laughter.'

'His?' Rhiannon echoed on a whisper.

Boudicca's look sharpened back to the present. She stepped back, a hand seeking the pink quartz ring that hung at her breast. 'You remind me of my brother,' she said. 'Now come, Rhiannon. The chariots are waiting.'

They had been hunting pig, avoiding the anger of the sacred boars while chasing herds of lean, black, squealing sows beneath the thick oak canopy of the deep forest. Now they were merrily riding home, a group of young warriors with among them the Maiden and her champion Farann.

Slowly, the others drew ahead with the trophies of the hunt. Their voices came back on the mist that had swirled up from the Great Bay to spread across the land and invade the woods with patchy grey veils, drifting and shifting. Now it was so thick that trees loomed up unexpectedly: now it thinned and let bright light from the sky seep through, picking out the gold patches in leaves that told of autumn spreading through the woods. Neither Rhiannon nor Farann made moves to catch up with the rest. Gradually, even the sound of voices faded.

'You never speak of Cunovinda,' she said.

'But I think of her,' he replied, and the look in his eyes was bleak. 'I think of her often, and dream of ways to rescue her. My only consolation is that her mistress was good to her. When last I saw her she was as happy as anyone may be in bondage.'

'I miss her. She was a good friend.'

'And my only kin now.' He watched his pony's ears, leaning to stroke them, then said abruptly. 'We should ride on. The others are out of sight.'

'They'll turn back if they miss us,' Rhiannon said.

'But we should not be alone, lady. You know that.'

From her eye corner she slid a look at him where he rode beside her seemingly aloof. 'No doubt Cameira will come to find you.'

'Cameira?'

'She makes no secret of her desire for you.'

'That's her sorrow, not mine.'

'And Pluma, too. Lately her eyes seem to follow you everywhere. Do you never feel your blood stir in response?'

He glanced at her sidelong, blue eyes veiled by dark lashes. When he spoke, his voice was so rough that it drove the colour from her cheeks. 'Sometimes I do. Of course I do. I'm a man like the rest – whatever you may think!'

She stared at him with wide, pained eyes. She had no idea what had been in her words, or his mind, to prompt such an attack.

Farann made an irritable gesture as if he were sorry to have raised sour echoes. He said, 'Cameira wants mastery over men. She gains it by giving her body and keeping her heart aside. She has eyes for me because I offend her – I'm an outsider – and so her perverse will is driven by a wish to conquer me and then cast me aside. I understand her too well to be swallowed up by her schemes. As for Pluma . . .' He hesitated, unwilling to lie to her. He was what he was. 'All men lust for Pluma.'

'And she for all men!' she retorted, stung into jealousy.

'So she pretends. But she teases. She entices and then runs away.'

'Has she done that to you?'

He hesitated, sending her another glance from his eye corner.

'Forgive me,' Rhiannon said swiftly, flushing. 'My curiosity is born of envy. I wish I were free, as Pluma is – and Cameira.'

'No, don't say that. You are not like them.' Edging his horse closer to hers, he laid a hand on her rein and drew both ponies to a halt. His thigh brushed hers, alerting all her senses to him. Blood rushed up into her face. She daren't look at him but she knew he was studying her hair and her set profile.

Softly, gruffly, he said, 'I often wonder what mischief moved the queen to make me your protector. The lady Boudicca can play the schemer when it pleases her.'

Rhiannon said nothing though she cast a swift, troubled glance at him. The same doubts had been in her own mind.

'She knew that she offered me temptation,' Farann said. 'There was honey in it – but it was smeared on a blade more sharp than a man dare handle. She knows I'll do nothing to break my sacred trust.' He sighed heavily, bitterly. 'She knows me so well. The queen my foster-mother has always read me much too clearly.'

The mist seemed to be closing them into a world of their own, magical, tempting, far from everyday concerns. Such was the tension and excitement in Rhiannon that her chest felt tight; she couldn't breathe properly. She licked her dry lips and turned her head to look into his face. 'Farann . . .'

His expression stopped whatever she was about to say. His gaze caressed her face, a tender look tautening into pain and agony as he lifted trembling fingers and traced the line of her cheek. She felt drawn to him as never before, her whole being yearning for contact with him; her mouth ached, her body longed for the touch of his, for the strength of his arms . . .

'I'm unclean,' Farann said in a voice deep with self-loathing.

'You're the Maiden. You're pure, undefiled. And I . . .' He snatched his hand away from her and turned his shoulder to her, staring off into the mist. 'You know what I am – what I became at Camulodunon. Ylas told me that you knew. How can you ever forget that?'

Viciously he kicked at his pony, startling it into a canter and then into a gallop. He raced ahead with Rhiannon riding after him, just managing to keep him in sight until to her relief she saw him pull up and lead his pony into a walk. She slowed, too, until she was almost level with him and the soft thud of hooves was barely audible on the grass beneath a stand of aspens, shimmering golden in misted sunlight as they rode on quietly.

'It *is* forgotten,' she said at length. 'By me, at least. Now *you* must forget it, too. If it troubles you so much, seek help from the Goddess. Speak to Morica. There is . . .' she hesitated, wondering if she were about to commit sacrilege by revealing the secret, but surely Dia would understand the need. 'There's a pool, deep in the marshes. A deep, clear pool of cleansing water. The Goddess bathes there. In that pool She restores Her virginity. Farann . . . It might cleanse you, too. Go to Morica. Ask her to take you there. If Albina grants this boon, perhaps it will be a sign. Perhaps *you* will be chosen to – '

He glanced across at her, every muscle taut. 'To what?'

'To tread the primrose path,' she quoted softly from the Maiden's Song, watching her pony's ears flick at a fly. Suddenly she felt too shy to meet Farann's gaze. 'Mortal, with footsteps of a God.'

Farann was silent for a while, respecting the awe in her; then he said quietly, 'What does it mean?'

'I'm not sure,' she sighed. 'It's part of the Mystery. If Morica knew I'd repeated it . . .' She looked up at him, words that had burned inside her for months suddenly bursting from her without conscious intent. 'Why did you leave me no message? When you went to join your father – when I was at Morica's hut . . . You went away. With no word.'

'I did leave word – with your mother. Didn't she tell you?'

Rhiannon remembered that day, remembered her own shock and her mother's anger and bitterness. 'No. No, she said nothing. She was distressed that Vindorex your father wouldn't trust her.'

'So she decided that you should forget me,' he guessed. 'Perhaps she was right.'

'I did not forget,' she breathed, but as she looked at him her eyes stung with tears, drowning the sight of him, and she turned her head away to hide her distress. 'Forgive me. We shouldn't speak of such things. It's wrong, Farann. We'll be punished. Please . . .'

As she took a deep breath and blinked hard to clear her eyes, she belatedly registered their surroundings. They were on the edge of the Way. The mist had parted suddenly. In the distance, riding toward them, came a column of Roman cavalry.

'It's Valerius Rufinus!' she breathed in alarm. 'He's a day too soon! Quickly, Farann! He mustn't see you. Ride on, ride on!'

'I won't leave you alone!'

'I'll be with you. Go, Farann!'

More mist drifted across the broad track of the Way, shutting them off from sight of the Romans, but not before Rhiannon had seen the leader of the column spur up and break away from his men. Farann kicked his pony into a gallop. Rhiannon followed, almost lying along her pony's back, as they crossed the Way into the woods on the further side. But soon she heard another horseman coming, charging through trees and undergrowth at an angle designed to intercept them. She veered off her course, toward the pursuer, willing Farann to escape while she delayed Valerius. She could only hope that Farann, when he realised what she had done, would not be so foolhardy as to come back to defend her.

Reaching a place where she was between the two men, she stopped and turned her pony to face the oncoming Roman. She drew her dagger from its sheath, holding its sharp blade ready to attack. Valerius burst out of the mist, into the clearing. Startled by the sight of her, he drew rein so fiercely that his horse reared. He fought for balance, but was tossed loose from his saddle to land heavily among a patch of bright red toadstools.

Infuriated at having her witness his loss of dignity, he clawed to catch the flying reins before his unsettled horse could decide to bolt. A jolt of laughter escaped Rhiannon as his plumed helmet jerked from his head and toppled into the grass. Then slowly, chagrined and red of face, Valerius picked himself up, resettled his leather armour with a grimace of pain, and stood holding his horse's head, quietening the animal.

He glared up at Rhiannon from under a fringe of dishevelled hair. She was smiling to herself, amused by the spectacle he had unwittingly presented, and reassured to think that by now Farann must be well on the way to Oakhillfort.

But she was off her guard. Without warning, Valerius charged at her, catching her wrist to deflect the knife, tumbling her from her horse. His free arm swept about her waist, pulling her in against the contours of his hardened leather armour as his mouth plunged for hers.

She fought him, pummelling with her left hand, clawing for his eyes, jerking up her knee for that place where men were most vulnerable. She barely caught him, but it was enough to make him curse her and spring back, though he still held her wrist. His fingers twisted cruelly. She cried out with pain and the dagger dropped from her numb fingers. Valerius swooped to pick it up, then he released her and stepped away, testing the knife's edge on his thumb. Over the glint of the blade he squinted at Rhiannon. 'Would you have used this?'

'Only give me the chance!' she answered, glaring at him as she eased her aching wrist.

As if remembering something, he glanced about him at the woods where tendrils of mist hung and drifted. Then he fixed Rhiannon with a look, his head on one side. 'Where is he?' he asked.

'Where is who?'

'Your escort.'

'I have no escort.'

'But he was with you – I saw him before the mist closed down.'

'There was no escort.'

He shook his head at her. 'Do you expect me to believe that king Prasutagus allows his daughter to wander unguarded?'

'I am the Maiden – child of the God,' Rhiannon reminded him coldly. 'I go where I choose. None would dare harm me.

As to being alone with a man . . . if you knew anything of our law you would know that's forbidden. I'm taboo, not to be touched. If you're found here alone with me, it will not go well for you.'

'But there was a man who took that risk,' he observed, watching her with shrewd eyes. 'I saw him. Is that why he fled – because he was afraid of discovery? A faithful lover, indeed, who leaves a maid defenceless in the woods.'

In a tree overhead a bird croaked. Rhiannon saw that it was a raven – a bird sacred to Bran, Lord of Annwm. Suddenly the woods seemed vibrant with threat. 'I am not defenceless,' she said. 'I am warrior-bred. I need no man to defend me. And I have no lover. The word defiles me, Caius Valerius Rufinus. I am the Maiden. I am promised. Promised to the God.'

His eyes narrowed. He stroked his smooth chin, his mouth curving in a wry smile. 'A vestal, by holy Zeus! And an Amazon!' Then his manner changed and he threw out his hands in a gesture of appeal and apology. 'Lady . . . forgive this rough foreigner his ignorance. I would not offend you, nor break your sacred law. Do me the honour of allowing me to escort you to safety.'

Still Rhiannon mistrusted him. No man of her acquaintance used words the way Valerius did, guile hidden beneath charm. Or was the charm sincere? She watched him from veiled eyes, seeking to read his thoughts, half of her wondering if she could make a leap for her pony and escape him. No good could come of this, she knew. The air thrummed with warnings.

To her bafflement, Valerius laid her dagger across his palm and held it out to her hilt-first. She glanced from the knife to his face and back again before slowly, tentatively reaching out, suspecting trickery. At the last moment she snatched the dagger and braced herself to ward him off, only to see him lift his chin and present to her his defenceless throat, saying, 'Kill me if you will. If you refuse to trust me, I might as well be dead.'

'Words!' Rhiannon said scornfully, tossing the thick braid of hair back over her shoulder. 'Is that what impresses Roman women – words?'

He straightened himself, his eyes alight with rueful amusement. 'Some of them. The more foolish ones. You're not like them. I knew that from the first time I saw you. I tried to tell you, but language separated us. Why do you think I was so eager to learn this impossible tongue of yours? Why did I volunteer to stay at Camulodunum, when all the fighting and the glory lie in the west, with the legions and my lord Suetonius Paulinus?'

'Well, why?' she asked, watching him narrowly.

'Because I knew that sooner or later my duties would lead me to Icenia – to you, Rhiannon. And now that I've seen you again I know that my heart led me right. My feelings are sincere. Come back with me. I'll build you a fine house – with piped water, and a bath, with marble floors, and slaves to serve you, and a garden . . . A house fit for the wife of Caius Valerius Rufinus.'

Rhiannon stared at him, colour ebbing and flowing in her face as her thoughts veered in wild confusion. 'Wife?' she managed at last.

His expression changed, a frown taking the softness from his eyes. 'What other life would I offer to the daughter of a king?'

'The daughter of a queen,' she amended. 'A queen of the Iceni! Do you think I would marry *you?* Ha! The council would never allow it. *You* could never be high chief to my people.'

'Nor would I want to be. I would take you with me – to Rome.'

Her smile was full of biting scorn. 'Where your family would cast you out for allying yourself with a barbarian.'

'Then I'll change their minds.'

'Not even your Julius Caesar could change the mind of Rome,' she reminded him. 'Not even for the sake of the queen of Egypt.'

This caused him to peer at her curiously. 'Where did you hear that?'

Rhiannon shrugged, remembering that it was a story she had heard Farann tell. 'I heard it.'

'But where? From gossip? Or . . .' Behind dark eyes his brain worked, sharpening his expression. 'Or from the Druids? Are there Druids who teach in Icenia? Is there a Druid at Oakhillfort?'

A chill drained through Rhiannon. She had been enjoying

the verbal battle, enjoying the warm feeling of being admired – even believing that he meant it, however impossible the dream. But now she was reminded of who he really was – a Roman, an enemy of Farann and of all her people, including the Druids.

Looking him squarely in the eye, she said flatly, 'There is no Druid at Oakhillfort. All the oak-seers of Albion are gathered on the isle of Mona – casting runes and weaving enchantments.'

'How do you know that?'

'It must be so. Why can't your vaunted legions break through to the sacred isle? What holds them back from the mountains of the west – what blunts their swords, blinds their spies, turns their soldiers into witless cowards, if not the strong magic of the Druids?'

He looked so furious that she thought he might strike her. Her hand went to her knife, ready for him. If he made a move she would plunge the blade into his throat.

But the singing silence was split by a scream – a woman's scream from somewhere off in the misty woods. The high voice cried, 'No! No-o!' The final note choked off. And with a croak the raven took wing, to vanish in the mist. Gone to his master, dark Bran. Gone to summon dread Caridwen, the Blue Hag. Death walked the woods: Rhiannon felt it like ice on her flesh.

Valerius had turned and bounded to his saddle, wrenching the horse round to point it in the direction from which the screams had come. He was on his way as Rhiannon grasped a handful of her pony's mane and launched herself to straddle the cloth across his back.

They reached the scene almost at the same moment, bursting into the clearing where a shaft of slanting gold pierced the mist. Soft sunlight brightened along the sprawled and lifeless body of a young woman. It was Pluma. She lay twisted on her back, one leg under her, her clothing in shreds, her body torn by numberless wounds. Blood stained her fair flesh and the once-lustrous brown hair that spread over bramble and grass.

And over her, still holding the bloody knife that had claimed her life, stood Farann.

Hearing the horses, he looked up, first to Valerius, then to

Rhiannon. He seemed dazed, but as his eyes met Rhiannon's a shock ran through him. He drew a veil over his thoughts, closing her out. His face set in cold, expressionless lines and he opened his hand to let the murder weapon fall by Pluma's lifeless feet.

Valerius leapt down from his horse, rasped his sword free from its sheath and advanced on Farann, saying over his shoulder, 'Do you know this fellow?'

'Yes.' Cursing the croak in her voice, she tried again. 'Yes, I know him. He's one of the royal guard.'

'Is he, now?' Valerius stepped forward, peering thoughtfully at Farann, who glowered with bright blue eyes from under the tangle of dark hair that hid the scar and the tattoo on his brow.

Even the trees seemed to hold their breath; not a breeze stirred, not a vole scratched.

It had been dark that night on the forum at Camulodunon when Valerius and Farann had last met, Rhiannon told herself. Farann had been wearing a slave's tunic, his hair neat and short, his face clean-shaven. And Valerius had been more interested in paying court to her than in the slave who had acted as interpreter. Now bright daylight surrounded them and Farann was dressed in warrior's garb of wool and leather, with spears slung round him; his hair was long and unkempt, falling into his eyes, and a thick dark moustache obscured the lower half of his face. Why should Valerius recognise him? Oh, sweet Albina, blind the Roman!

'I've seen this man somewhere before,' Valerius mused.

'I told you,' Rhiannon said swiftly, ' – he's of our clan. He was here the last time you came. About the fort. And at the feast.'

Leaning forward, Valerius laid the edge of his blade under Farann's chin as if to see his face more clearly. He frowned over the puzzle, searching his memory. 'He was at Camulodunum, too.'

The breath failed in Rhiannon's throat. She couldn't see the Roman's face but she could clearly see Farann's eyes blazing cold hatred at his enemy.

'In the forum,' Valerius said. 'Yes, that's where I've seem him – he was one of the warriors who came bristling to rescue you from me. I knew I'd seen that glare before.' Satisfied by this clarification, he stepped away from Farann. Over his shoulder, he said, 'There's rope among my kit. Find it, Rhiannon. We'll take this fellow back. Let's see what your law has to say about murder.'

Twelve

Farann refused to speak. No word broke from his lips as he was bound and led back to Oakhillfort, where the council of elders gathered in the hall and warriors crowded in to hear what was said. Faced with questions, Farann closed his mouth, shuttered his eyes, and looked out into distances somewhere halfway to the Otherworld.

Shock and outrage rumbled among council and warriors. Any murder committed in secret was bad – far different from killing in a fair fight – but for a man to hack a woman to death was anathema. Farann must pay for it. With his life.

Those who had loved or lusted after Pluma joined in the call for blood vengeance. Those who believed in law and order demanded the denial of all human rights to the perpetrator until he was brought to trial and sentenced to death. The queen raged, pacing in front of Farann, demanding that he speak, that he explain himself.

'Why did you do this thing? Why?'

Farann stared beyond her, as though he heard nothing. And through her numb distress Rhiannon noted that Valerius was watching everything with critical eyes.

Argument was still raging when Duihno rushed into the hall, his clothes torn, his breast exposed, his hands and nails bloody from clawing at his flesh and scoring it with a knife to shed his grief-blood. Crazed with sorrow and fury, he plunged for Farann intent on killing, but hands grabbed him, dragged him away. From halfway across the village his screams for vengeance could be heard.

Still Farann refused to say anything either in denial or defence.

At last the king got to his feet, his face almost as grey as his beard. 'He gives us no choice. Take him to the punishment pits.'

In the darkness of middle night when the moon swam low behind wreaths of cloud, Rhiannon crept from the queen's house and stood for a moment scenting the breeze; it had a crisp edge of approaching winter in it, causing her to shiver and pull her cloak more closely round her. Once again the moon was waning – the Hag's moon, a reminder that to all things there came an ending in death and decay. It was fitting on this dreadful night when Farann lay a prisoner deep in the stinking punishment pits, awaiting the fires of Samhain.

Under her cloak Rhiannon carried a jug of wine and a shoulder of mutton. It must have been the scent of the meat that drew two or three dogs around her, padding after her with hope in their eyes. On her way to the far end of the village, Rhiannon stopped to shoo the animals away, and when she turned again a figure had loomed up in front of her. She gave a startled cry, swallowing it for fear of waking the occupants of a nearby house, and relief flooded through her as the man said, 'It's only me.'

'Ylas?'

'Of course.' He took her by the elbow, turning her away from her chosen path. 'I've been on the same errand as you. Don't go down there, Rhiannon. He won't talk. All the answer I got was the rattle of his chains.'

A step sounded on the path behind them and both looked round to see Matuac yawning and scratching at his rumpled hair. 'What are you doing?' he asked grumpily. 'I heard Rhiannon creep out of the house, and then I found you gone, Ylas. Where've you been? Or need I ask – to visit the Trinovante, I suppose. Crying forgiveness, is he?'

'Shut up, Matuac!' Ylas rasped. 'You know Farann better than that. I still count him among *my* friends, whatever he's done.'

'He didn't do it!' Rhiannon said. 'Don't say such things! You *do* know him better – both of you!'

Her distress silenced Ylas, but Matuac said, 'We know he once killed a man with his two hands – a big, burly overseer of slaves, so they say. And today he was found standing over

Pluma with a bloody knife in his hand, when everyone knows she's been waggling her tail at him lately. What else do we have to know.?'

'We know Farann!'

Reluctantly, Ylas said, 'But if he won't even try to explain himself . . .'

'Of course he's guilty,' Matuac added. 'He was always strange and secretive. He never did belong here. See what happens when the queen honours an outsider.'

'He's not an outsider!' Rhiannon cried.

'Yes he is!' Matuac returned. 'He always was, he always will be. Maiden's champion! Hah!'

'Oh . . . let me past!' Head down, cradling the offerings she had brought for Farann, Rhiannon charged between them and hurried on down the winding path, past the last houses to the woodyard and the rank-smelling tanning pans. Beyond them, the death hut stood squat and dark, reeking of ill omen. Pluma lay there, awaiting her lawful vengeance. And in front of the death hut were two deep pits where sometimes private offerings were made to the Gods, and where prisoners were kept to await trial.

Rhiannon fell to her knees, setting aside the jug of wine and the meat she had brought as she peered into the pit. The stench of rotting offal assailed her, but no ray of moonlight pierced the black depths of the hole.

'Farann! . . . Farann!'

There was no reply, only the distant lone howling of a wolf – it might have been a dog at one of the farms but to Rhiannon it sounded like a wolf, harbinger of winter and the dread seasons yet to come. Soon it would be Samhain, the start of the Great Year, when the fires would be lit and offerings made. Terror blazed red across her eyes at the thought of seeing Farann die in those fires.

'Farann, please! Talk to me. I've brought you food, and wine.'

Only silence and that nauseating smell of decay came up from the pit, making her cover her nose with a corner of her cloak. How could Farann stand it? She begged, she wept, she ranted and she pleaded, but he refused to answer. Like a mussel, he had clamped his shell down and no one could reach him.

With tears running down her face she sat in the grass at the mouth of the pit and wept, rocking back and forth in her distress. He had killed Pluma – he must have done. She didn't want to believe it but she had seen him standing over the girl's dead body, the knife still dripping blood in his hand. Perhaps he had been driven to it; Pluma's wantonness had enraged many a man. But if he were innocent then why didn't he say so?

A scuffle beside her alerted her. The dogs had sneaked up behind her. One of them grabbed the mutton and ran off, his fellows leaping after him. Rhiannon picked up the jug and flung it after them, hearing the spatter of wine as the vessel fell and smashed. Weeping even more bitterly, she flung herself face down on the ground.

The coolness of grass came against her cheek, but her fingers touched the strands of a nettle hemp rope – the means of ferrying food and drink down to prisoners. Perhaps . . . she felt the rough twist of the rope, calculating its strength . . . enough to hold Farann?

Her hand closed on the rope, but as she started to lift it a sandalled foot clamped hard on the twisted hemp. Stricken, Rhiannon looked up at the tall figure who had materialised beside her. At first she thought it was Eogan, appeared out of air, then she saw that it was Segovax, the law-giver, Druid-trained and just as stern as Eogan might have been. Behind him, two warriors of the guard stood sentinel. She ought to have known the pit would be watched.

Segovax bent and laid a firm hand under her arm, drawing her to her feet. In the moonlit shadows he considered her tear-strewn face with eyes that were not unkind.

'Maiden . . . you know the law. For the crime of murder, a life must answer.'

'He didn't do it!' she breathed desperately. 'He didn't!'

'That is for the Gods to decide,' Segovax replied, a big hand reaching to stroke her head in a paternal gesture of comfort. 'Go to bed, lady. And remember your duty. It does not lie here.'

Numbed by her grief for Farann, Rhiannon stood on the great defensive bank overlooking the gates of Oakhillfort as she watched the final gathering of the goods demanded as taxes, and as repayment of the loans. Finally the long column moved off: soldiers guarded ox-carts groaning under their load of skins and grain, with trained hunting dogs tethered alongside, and behind them trailed the livestock, herded by slaves who were themselves part of the payment. Under a windy sky they wound down the track between outlying farms, heading for the Way.

A horseman in the plumes, armour and red cloak of Rome rode out from the village, slowly leading his horse through the twining entry set maze-like between the high banks. Caius Valerius Rufinus had taken leave of the king and queen and was now setting out to lead his rich prize home – home to fat Catus Decianus, who would no doubt take his cut of the proceeds before passing the rest on to Rome.

Rhiannon watched the tribune from her vantage point, her arms twisted around her to hold her cloak tight against the wind that tugged in its folds. She felt emptied of emotion, cold to the soul with fear and with despair. Truly, for her, the Goddess showed Herself only as Caridwen the Implacable.

Seeing her there, Valerius halted, his head tipped back to meet her eyes as his horse danced under him, restless in the wind. For a long moment their glances locked. Rhiannon allowed herself to think how it might be to go with him – to leave behind the troubles of Oakhillfort and the duties of the Maiden – to go with Valerius and forget . . . Except that there would be no forgetting. If she deserted her duty now, her conscience would not allow her to forget.

After all, the Goddess had never promised that Her burden would be easy. Faithfulness was what She demanded – not for the Maiden's own sake but for all the people, to ensure the continuance of all things. On the shoulders of the Maiden, on the faithful celebration of the rites, depended the whole future of Icenia.

But if I were free . . . Rhiannon thought, and let her mouth twist into a self-deriding smile. Even if she were free she would not go with Valerius. His ways, his language, his thoughts and his feelings were all alien to her, as were his Gods. Her life was here at Oakhillfort, as a servant of the Great Goddess and as the future queen of the People of the Horse.

Unhurriedly, she turned her back on the young Roman,

keeping her cloak close about her for comfort, and walked away, to the steps cut in the inner side of the bank, where the bee skeps were alive with buzzing.

'I shall come back!' Valerius called after her, but she vanished from his sight with no sign that she had heard him. He sat watching the place where she had gone, only half aware of the restless horse beneath him.

A watchman paced along the bank – a tall warrior with a fierce scarred face, carrying a spear and, at his belt, one of the curved horns that were blown to arouse the village at need. He set himself spread-legged on the bank, glaring down at Valerius.

The tribune saluted mockingly, a fist to the breastplate over his heart, then turned his dancing horse and urged it into a gallop to catch up with the slow-moving column.

Bitterly, the Iceni counted the cost of obedience to Rome. That winter would see them short of everything – bread, despite the good harvest, since the Romans had taken a good share of their grain; mutton, since many sheep had been driven off; clothing, since sackloads of wool had been commandeered; and riches in cattle, gold, silver, bronze . . .

'They'll drive us to poverty!' Boudicca said, 'That's what they want – to make beggars of us.'

'More grain will grow,' her husband argued. 'We've game in the forests, fruit in the woods, fish in the sea. Come spring there'll be lambs and calves again – and foals in the enclosures. Perhaps an Egyptian foal next year. Vranaun believes the white mare has conceived.'

'Then let us trust Vranaun is right!' she said scathingly. 'One Egyptian foal will make us rich again!'

Prasutagus watched her storm from the house, his drooping eye twitching, his shoulders bent. His mouth too was twisted now, and often spittle drooled down his beard. He had begun to wonder if he had led his people astray all these years, but he could not imagine himself taking any other course. There had been only two choices: bow to the Romans, or die.

But the older and weaker he grew, the more he thought that death, with honour, might have been preferable to being torn to pieces chunk by bloody chunk, battered on the rocks of his wife's contempt.

He told himself that Boudicca was unaware of the pain she brought him, as she was unaware of the deep love and admiration that had grown in him over the years. Like the old fool he was, he kept finding excuses for her coldness towards him. At present she, too, was sick at heart over their foster-son, though as ever when something hurt her deeply she feigned indifference. The boy had always been difficult – proud, stubborn, given to impenetrable silences – but was he capable of the secret slaying of a young woman?

Araunah had come out of her room, her huge blue eyes washed with tears. She was still small for her age, rib-thin and undeveloped. She was crying because she loved him and hated to see him hurt.

Prasutagus held out his arm to her and she came to huddle against him. He bent his cheek to her hair, grateful for the consolation she offered. She was not his child. No child had ever sprung from his seed, not for his first wife, long dead now, and not for Boudicca. But he had Araunah, the child of Garanhir whom once he had loved as a son – until Garanhir had betrayed him. Garanhir, and Boudicca . . . How very long ago it seemed. How very little it mattered now. Closing his eyes against unmanly tears, he felt that when the bards came to tally him with other high chiefs of Icenia, the song of his life would be a record of failure.

As though the sky itself wept for shame, on the day of Farann's trial a fine, steady rain seeped down from low clouds. The elders of the council gathered in the great communal hall. Two curved and cushioned stools – copied from furniture seen at Camulodunon – were set for the king and queen, who arrived with their daughters, their guard and Morica, with her acolyte Erefwen. Other warriors and their wives took their places, sitting or standing on the sleeping platform around the hall, or leaning on the great oaken pillars, carved with faces and runes and hung with bright shields. Most of the other inhabitants of Oakhillfort tried to crowd in, too, some perforce left outside to crane over heads and peer through the door.

The crush parted and then closed again as Farann was brought through, bound in iron chains, his hair matted, his clothes filthy with mud and offal, and soaked to the skin from the rain. Avid eyes studied the sorry spectacle of the Maiden's champion come to this. Thus he had looked when he staggered up to Oakhillfort only seven moons ago. Many people remembered it. Many said it was a judgement – he should not have been allowed to return among the Iceni.

Rhiannon pressed her hands together to stop their trembling. She was too afraid now to shed more tears. She could see the twins, who both looked grim, and their sister Cameira with that spiteful, smug look on her face. Young Araunah only looked bewildered – she hardly understood what was happening. She stood close to the king now and his arm slipped about her thin waist as he passed a tired hand across his face and wiped his mouth on his sleeve.

Erefwen's expression was pinched, Morica's watchful, sharp as ever, ready to act in behalf of the Goddess to Whom the murder of a woman was the most heinous crime. The man who had committed such an act could expect no mercy from Her priestesses.

As for Boudicca, her face was set and stormy. She had cut Farann out from her affections the moment she heard the news, just as she had excised his father before him – or so she assured herself. She had been wrong about him. Now she was angry with herself for having the weakness to pity him. Look at him standing there so proud and defiant. How she detested his arrogance! But somewhere deep inside her there was bitter weeping. Was there never to be an end to sorrow for the queen of the Iceni?

'Enough!' Though Prasutagus's voice was not strong, still it held authority enough to silence the mutters. He got to his feet with his hand lifted, staring through the smoke in the hall to where Farann stood beyond the fire, erect despite the weight of his chains, his feet set apart for balance, his head high.

Dim daylight seeped in and rain dripped through cracks in the thatch. Torches burned in iron brackets adding extra light but increasing the swirl of smoke, and a faint steam arose from wet hair and clothes, sending a dank aroma to settle throughout the room. Across the spaces that separated them, the ailing king regarded his foster-son with pity.

'Farann . . . you were discovered with the maid Pluma –

she dead from stabbing, you holding the knife. Have you anything to say in your defence?'

'I am innocent,' Farann said in a voice devoid of all feeling.

'And nothing else?'

'I am innocent,' came the stubborn answer.

Seeming too weary to argue, the king signed to Segovax to take over. The lawgiver stepped out from among the elders, calling for evidence from all who had anything to say in the matter.

The arguments were heard from many mouths and with varying opinion – Farann had been seen with Pluma here and there, or watching her with covetous eyes. She had enjoyed her popularity, been generous with her favours. Farann must have been jealous of her flirting with other men. Frustrated and in a temper, a man might lash out without thinking and kill a teasing woman. There were one or two who thought her fate had been inevitable – it had been a question of which man broke first.

Others reminded the listeners of Farann's courage, proven in the battle with Audagas's clan, and of his known honesty. Ylas spoke out loudly for his friend, as also did Garanhir and Nuadat – the latter wearing the stump of his left wrist bound with leather. Farann's blood was noble, they told the elders, and his line was a proud one, tracing itself back through Vindorex and Addedomarus to many famous high chiefs of Trinovantia. Such a man would not commit the act of which he was accused.

'His line goes back through foreigners, too!' someone grunted.

Cameira leapt out to prowl round the fire, and round the prisoner, jabbing her finger at him accusingly. 'Remember how haughty and proud he has always been. An outsider among us! Part Roman, never forget! But still better than any of us – so he thinks! He has never been one of us. Yet he dares to have eyes for the daughter of the queen.' She swung and pointed at Rhiannon, her face contorted into hatred.

Morica intervened, scowling. 'The Maiden scorns all men.'

'Just so!' Cameira crowed. 'And a man scorned by one woman may take his revenge on another.'

'He's killed before!' a voice shouted. 'We all know that. And then he worked willingly for the Romans.'

'Only because of his sister!' Ylas strode out, scanning the crowd for the owner of that slanderous voice.

'He abandoned his sister at the first opportunity!' one of the women said. 'He probably hates all women.'

Cameira lifted her fist, shouting above the growing furore, 'We have the word of the Maiden, and of that Roman officer – Farann was there. He had the knife. He did the deed.'

'No!' Unable to contain herself any longer, Rhiannon sprang into the circle to confront her kinswoman. 'We did not see him kill Pluma.' She swung round, her arms held out in appeal to everyone present. Her only thought was to protect Farann. 'Don't listen to Cameira. She speaks out of hatred. She wanted Farann for herself but he refused her. For that she would see him die – not for slaying Pluma. He did not kill Pluma.'

A murmur ran round the hall – this was the Maiden speaking. She was known to have the gift of prophecy. Could she also divine hearts and minds?

'Then who did kill her?' Cameira cried. 'You say I speak from hatred. Can you deny you speak from love? Or has the Goddess shown you the truth, Maiden? Come, speak. If you know who is *not* guilty then you must know the name of the slayer.'

Realising what she had done, Rhiannon glanced round the room, her mind darting like a trapped bird. She, the Maiden, had spoken out. Now she must prove herself to be more than a woman blindly defending her man. She saw the avid eyes around her, waiting, watching, breathless for more signs from the Gods. And she saw Farann's face, washed with firelight, veiled behind writhing smoke. He understood what she had done and why. He understood the dilemma she now faced. But he didn't believe she could save him.

The hall dimmed around her. All she could see was Farann's eyes watching her. A great calm came to her. He was not guilty. He had not killed Pluma. Dimly she heard the hoof-beats of the White Mare, signalling the presence of Epona, and across her mind came the vision of the God in the tree, standing unharmed in the midst of lightning, a blaze of promise that she alone had seen. *'I am the Maiden,'* she thought with awe and wonder, surprised that she could ever have forgotten or doubted it.

'I *am* the Maiden.' Quiet as it was, her voice had a quality that stopped every breath in the hall. Her eyes were still fixed on Farann's, though she wasn't aware of seeing him. The Goddess had taken her; she felt light as air, and infinitely powerful. She held out a hand. 'Bring me a hare. The Goddess shall give an answer.'

There was a scuffle by the door as someone ran off to fetch one of the tame hares. From the corner of her eyes Rhiannon saw Morica join her on her right hand, and then Erefwen, thin and wraith-pale on her left. No one moved. Everyone waited. Eventually a man hurried in, holding a wriggling hare by its ears. He hurried forward, paused to look questioningly at Boudicca and say, 'Lady . . .'

Impatiently, the queen signed to him to hand over the hare. She was intrigued and disturbed by what was happening. She herself, when she had been Maiden, would never have dared to do what Rhiannon was doing. This daughter of hers had powers that Boudicca could only wonder at.

The man handed the hare to Morica, who held it out to Rhiannon, a knife offered in her other hand.

'Let me do it,' Erefwen murmured. 'Let me read the entrails.' She glanced at Rhiannon, her cold blue eyes alight with excitement. 'I know who *I'd* select for the fires,' she said under her breath.

Rhiannon watched as the two priestesses knelt by her feet, holding the squirming hare, laying it on its back. But her mind was busy, her peripheral vision searching the crowd. It was as though Erefwen's words had cleared a mist and allowed her to see the problem clearly for the first time, without the confusion aroused by her fear for Farann. She felt rather than saw the moment when Erefwen's knife swiftly slit the hare from throat to crotch. All eyes were on it, all throats taut with held breath. Only Rhiannon was oblivious to the portents in the mess of spilling entrails.

She had her answer. She had it in the moment when Duihno looked up and found her watching him. The look of sheer stark terror on his face was enough.

He had killed Pluma – in anger, in jealousy, in lust – and then he had dropped the knife and run. Farann must have been nearby – perhaps returning to look for Rhiannon. He had heard Pluma's screams, had gone to help her, found her dead, picked up the knife . . . Hurt pride had made him silent, because first Rhiannon and then everyone else had believed the evidence of circumstance rather than their knowledge of his character. And Duihno had taken advantage of it, rushing in with his clothes torn, his skin bloody and scratched . . . by Pluma first, no doubt, before he added to his own wounds under the guise of grief.

All this the Goddess made clear to Rhiannon in that single moment when the wretched Duihno lifted his eyes and with horror found her watching him, reading his soul. She knew. The Maiden knew! He backed away from her, found himself impeded. He turned right, and left, trapped by bodies with faces that rapidly turned hostile as people realised what was happening. Knowing that every eye in the hall had turned on him and there was no escape, Duihno ran and flung himself down on his knees before the queen, begging for mercy. The words that tumbled from his own mouth condemned him.

Hands seized him and dragged him away. He was wrapped in the chains that had bound Farann and carried away to be dropped into the punishment pit, there to rot with the rest of the offal – until Samhain.

In the wake of the revelation, people crowded round Farann all eager to say they had never really believed any ill of him. Among them, Matuac was most anxious to make amends. Boudicca raised her voice above the clamour and bade Farann come to her. Though he was vile with mud and the stink of putrefaction, still she called him her beloved son and clasped him to her bosom and kissed him on both cheeks in sight of everyone.

'He should have spoken,' Prasutagus said querulously. 'He should have told us the truth.'

'He did,' Rhiannon replied. 'He told us he was innocent. He wanted us to believe him on the strength of his word. Perhaps he expected too much.' She glanced at Farann, allowing herself to feel irritated with him and his stubbornness now that he was safe from threat. 'He was always the proud one.'

'Still he should have said something before now,' the king insisted. 'It leaves us in his debt. His honour's been stained.'

'One thing can wipe out all memory of these past few

nights,' Farann said, and fell to one knee beside Boudicca, looking up at her earnestly. 'One gift alone, lady.'

The queen glanced at her daughter, hoping that the boon would be one she could grant without dishonour. 'Name it.'

'To bathe in the pool of purification.' Aware of horrified gasps from the women around him, Farann kept his eyes fixed on the queen. 'Lady, only the blessing of the Goddess can cleanse me from . . . from the stink of the punishment pit.'

Boudicca glanced at Rhiannon, hoping for explanations, and Rhiannon turned to Morica, pleading, 'Grant him this. He means no sacrilege. It's important, Morica. I ask it – I, Rhiannon, Chosen of Dia, daughter of the queen . . . Is it so much to ask of Her, when She demands so much of me?'

'I must seek Her advice,' Morica said. 'Albina may grant this request. But if She does you must be led in darkness, Farann of the Trinovantes. Blindfolded there and back. No man may look on the secret places of the Goddess and live. Agreed?'

Farann's head dropped between his shoulders and a great sigh heaved out of him. 'Agreed,' he muttered.

He could feel the marshes around him, hear the ripple of waters and the call of birds as the coracle swayed under him, but Morica had blinded him so efficiently with linen strips bound round his head that he could see nothing. But at least he had been granted his wish. Perhaps the pool could wash away the taint of fat male hands and a thrusting male body that had defiled him in unspeakable ways.

Unclean as he was, he daren't declare his feelings for Rhiannon. To do so would sully her. Other women – slaves at Camulodunon, and willing partners like Pluma – he had used for the assuaging of carnal appetites. But Rhiannon was the Maiden, kept pure from birth. He loved her beyond life. And if he could purify his body, and cleanse his mind of memory, perhaps then he would be worthy of her.

The only thing that troubled him was that Morica had sent Erefwen to lead him through the marshes. The younger priestess made him feel uneasy: she seemed cold all through. She drew from him none of the usual responses he felt towards females; indeed, she repelled him with her bony thinness, her pale hair and her unnatural bleached-blue eyes. How Duihno could ever have desired such a creature was beyond Farann's understanding; she seemed to hate all men.

Here in the marshes, in the realm of the Goddess, she had him at her mercy: unarmed, his eyes bound, sworn to obey her every command. Her silence unnerved him. If he hadn't heard and felt the paddle sweeping through the waters he might have thought himself alone.

Eventually the coracle bumped against a bank and he felt Erefwen step out. She said, 'Come,' and he unsteadily followed, feeling his way with hands and feet, clawing at some growth of greenery as his feet slipped and touched water. Then he was on dry ground, standing with head cocked to listen.

The silence was profound, underlined by the gentle lap of water. It raised the hairs on his neck, made him shiver with awe as he felt the eyes of the Goddess on him. 'How much further?' he asked.

'No further,' Erefwen murmured from close by. 'This is the pool, where you wanted to be, Farann of the Trinovantes. Unclothe yourself. A suppliant bathes naked.'

Feeling oddly vulnerable without his sight to aid him, Farann stripped off his clothes and dropped them to the grass. The air struck cold on his flesh, stirring the roots of every tiny hair on his body. His skin crawled as he straightened, imagining Erefwen's pale, cool, luminous eyes studying every detail of his nakedness.

'You desire the love of the Maiden,' she said, her voice coming from somewhere in front of him. 'Do you think yourself worthy to walk with the footsteps of a God?' She answered her own question with a harsh laugh. 'That's hubris – isn't that what the Greeks call it? You should know – you with your Roman education. Do you aspire to meet with the Maiden on the sacred isle?'

He clenched his hands and his teeth, feeling a muscle flicker and spasm in his jaw. 'I aspire only to the blessing of the Great Goddess. That's all. Is it part of the ritual to taunt a suppliant?'

There was a silence, then, 'Be still.'

She began to walk slowly round him, sprinkling him with drops that he realised must be oil. The drops gathered and trickled down his body, giving off a faintly perfumed aroma. She was chanting softly, calling on the Goddess to hear, to grant the wish of those who came in humility and trust. Her fingers touched his flesh, painting patterns with the oil – the branches of the willow and then the spiral of immortality, on his shoulders and down his spine, then across his chest and stroking down his lean belly, past his navel to his groin. Despite himself, her touch stirred an uncontrollable response and he felt his loins tighten and begin to swell.

He knew that Erefwen had seen the evidence of his rising lust. When she spoke her voice was dry with contempt. 'The pool lies before you, Farann of the Trinovantes. Walk into it. Cleanse yourself.'

She led him to a brink where he could feel the grassy bank sloping away under his feet. Her hands came flat in his back, thrusting him forward. For a moment he teetered, arms flailing, and then fell into what seemed like a bottomless chasm. A yell escaped him, cut off by bitterly cold water that shocked the breath from his lungs and closed over his head.

But he felt its magic, felt it seep past his skin to touch every part of him with its clear, icy purity. Now – now, he might aspire to the hand of the daughter of the queen.

As he surfaced, choking and gasping, he heard Erefwen say, 'You're a fool, Farann of the Trinovantes. Like all men. A witless fool. The Maiden Rhiannon will never be yours.'

BOOK THREE

War Queen of Albion

One

As the ivy moon waned toward Samhain, so Eogan returned, appearing out of twilight. He was at the gates before the watch noticed him, though they had been alerted by the sudden howling of several dogs in the village. The Druid's arrival laid a shadow on Rhiannon's heart, for he had come to oversee the choosing of the new Green King. The Great Year was beginning.

The old Green King still sat chained in the punishment pit. He was heard sometimes railing against the Gods, or sobbing with remorse. The cry of a screech owl sent him near mad with terror, so it was said by those who heard him scream. He had begged his guards for a knife, or poison to end his life. He knew what fate awaited: a new Green King must be chosen: the boar hunt must take place. Every night he could see how the moon waned. Portents of death came on every wind.

This year, more than any other Rhiannon could remember, a feverish anticipation gripped the people as the day of the ceremony approached. The older ones knew the solemnity of it; they spoke of it in hushed tones with significant looks. The younger ones caught the urgent excitement of the occasion. To represent the God was always a coveted duty. Now, with the Great Year, its meaning was deeply holy, tinged with dread – yet eagerly sought by all the young men.

They gathered beneath the sacred oak, all the wifeless warriors of Oakhillfort, and some from other clans who had come to try their luck. Farann was among them, and the twins, and Unthaus – and Kai, the third and only remaining son of Audagas of Seafort – some of the strongest, finest, most lusty young men of Icenia. They formed a circle about the lightning-marked tree, watching as Eogan muttered over his runes, divining truths from the fall of a handful of bones and pieces of flint marked with strange signs.

A drum beat insistently, calling everyone to come and witness the choosing. Slowly, the people gathered. Rhiannon stood beside her mother, with Morica and Erefwen not far away. Her eyes were constantly drawn to Farann and apprehension made a tight fist in her breast. She suspected that the man she must meet in the Mysteries would be the man who this day was chosen as Green King. Would the Goddess grant her wish? Was it too much to hope that Farann might be the man?

From her eye corner, the queen watched the play of emotion on her daughter's pale face. Rhiannon was so young, so tender, so trusting. She had learned that the Goddess could be fickle, but she had yet to understand the depths of Dia's indifference. Boudicca let her hand stray to the thumb-ring given to her so long ago by Huan of the Caledones. She remembered her own feelings of nineteen summers past: she too had thought she understood the Mysteries; she too had innocently willed the Gods to choose the man she most desired: she had willed his death.

The ceremony began. Keeping pace with the drum beat, Eogan moved around the circle offering the wicker bottle to each young warrior in turn, to Ylas and then to Farann, and on past others to red-haired Kai of Seafort. Each man withdrew a glass pebble, holding it fast in his fist as Boudicca held her ring. The queen found herself pitying all those youthful warriors. None of them knew the real end that awaited the Green King at the Solstice of the Great Year. They coveted only the pleasures of leading the boar hunt home, of taking the champion's place at feasts and festivals, of being smiled on by all the girls – and perhaps also they coveted the Maiden whom whispers said might be the prize. The drum beat on. The Druid continued his circle, coming to Matuac and Unthaus. At last each man had taken his chance. Now he held fortune or despair within his grasp.

Striding to stand under the oak, Eogan threw up his arms. The drum beat stopped.

'Now!'

Rhiannon thought her heart must burst with tension as the warriors all looked at the tokens. She saw Farann's disappointment and her heart twisted with his. Across the circle their regretful glances met. Then she heard Matuac yell in triumph and in the same breath Ylas shouted, 'Mine! It's mine!'

There was consternation. Two Green Kings? Tadia made a little moaning noise and threw a hand to cover her mouth. Her husband Coeling steadied her as their sturdy, fair-haired warrior sons both ran to Eogan, each displaying the glass pebble in his hand, each glancing round to discover Rhiannon among the crowd. Both of them had picked out a token with a blood-red drop at its heart. *Both of them.*

Boudicca knew a momentary spurt of disbelief – it should have been Farann! Was Rhiannon to escape the full grief and sorrow that came from being Maiden? Then she saw her daughter's face and her bowels twisted with shame. She was glad, for Rhiannon's sake, that Farann had been overlooked by the Gods. But Rhiannon could not escape her duties. She had yet to fulfil the rites – to meet with the God and to bear a child of His loins, if the Goddess granted it. And beyond that time . . .

Beyond that time, Boudicca thought fiercely, there would be fire and war and bloody vengeance. Beyond that time, Rhiannon would learn what it meant to be a queen.

Again Rhiannon exchanged a look with Farann and saw his eyes slide from her as he turned away, accepting what fate had sent. No man could argue with the choice of the Gods.

'A sign!' Eogan thundered, and turned to throw his arms up in homage to the tree. 'A sign from the Gods! Vron and Bran. Star of Life and Serpent of Wisdom. Oak and holly. Robin and wren! It blends. It binds! The Great Year begins!'

'But what does it mean?' Rhiannon asked faintly as the people cheered and shouted. She turned to her mother, to Morica. 'What does it mean?'

The priestess regarded her with sharp, wolfbitch eyes set deep among blue tattoo marks on her ageing skin. 'It augurs well, Maiden. The Goddess smiles on us. As the twin Gods struggle for her favours, so shall the twin warriors contest one against the other. Ylas and Matuac. Matuac and Ylas. Which one will be supreme?' Morica smiled, showing discoloured teeth. 'Dia will choose for us, Maiden. When the time comes, Dia will choose.'

*

That night all the young men were busy, sharpening their spears and tending their brindled hunting dogs. In the queen's house the excitement was almost tangible. But Rhiannon was subdued, troubled by formless fears of what was to come for her in the spring.

After their initial surprise, the twins both seemed pleased with their fortune. They had always vied with one another; now their sibling rivalry came into full play. Both were also aware of some closer link with Rhiannon. Maiden and Green King led the dance at festivals; Maiden and Green King . . . Ylas and Matuac both dimly perceived some greater significance in this Great Year choosing. They both began to regard Rhiannon with questioning sidelong looks.

'*I* shall kill the biggest boar!' Ylas declared.

'Pah!' his twin returned. 'Yours will be a runt beside mine. You might be the fastest, but I'm the strongest. Isn't that so, Rhiannon?'

She made some answer but what concerned her most was the new light in Matuac's eyes as he let his gaze roam over her. Ylas must have sensed her discomfort; he drew his brother's attention away with more taunting and boasts of victories in tomorrow's hunt.

Their mother Tadia watched them with frightened eyes.

'Both of them?' she said privately to her friend and kinswoman Boudicca, clutching at her sleeve. 'Must *both* of my sons be taken?'

'I think not,' Boudicca replied. 'Only one of them will be called to walk the primrose path. It must be, Tadia. Who knows but that Dia decreed your twins should be born to fulfil this role – as Rhiannon was born to be Maiden. Whichever one of them is chosen, he will go with joy. He will be reborn to new life. It's a sacred trust, an honour.'

'I know that.' She was white to the lips. 'As it was an honour when the Goddess demanded the life of Huan. That did not stop you from mourning him, lady. Which of my sons must I lose? Both of them are dear to me. If I must grieve, what comfort will Dia offer in place of my son?'

The queen drew a sharp breath, her eyes glittering. 'None,' she said with brutal truth. 'None beyond knowing that you have served Her purpose. When the Gods call, mortals obey. There *is* nothing beyond that.'

*

With the cold, frosted dawn the warriors gathered near the sacred oak, their hounds straining to be off as they scented the morning chill and the excitement in the air. The twins were both wreathed with yew. Ylas seemed tense and troubled, Matuac laughed and boasted: both of them were conscious of a sharpening of their rivalry and both kept throwing covert glances at Rhiannon. Wisps of foggy breath clouded out of the mouths of the gathered people as light increased and a tinge of red in the east foreshadowed the sunrise. Rhiannon stood wrapped in her cloak, apart from the crowd but watching and listening, sharing glances with Farann, who stood among the warriors rubbing his hands and stamping his feet for warmth. He must wait. Both of them must wait. After the Great Year, when her duty was done, perhaps then . . .

No one mentioned Duihno, but all knew that the punishment pit was empty: Duihno had been let free. The old Green King – the God of Summer – always led the boar hunt. Soon the dogs would be on his scent. But this year it was no game with merely symbolic meaning. This year, because of his crime, he would be caught and brought back to die. It was part of his punishment to be hounded, to run in gibbering terror from a fate he could not escape: it was the law.

Eogan the Druid appeared, his grey eyes lit with inner fire. In his hand he carried a dirty cloak smeared with blood. This he tossed down for the dogs to get the scent of it as he spoke the ritual words, more meaningful this year than they had been in living memory: 'Hunters, your quarry has fled to the woods. The ancient rites of Samhain demand his death. Fetch him home! Fetch him home to the fires!'

The horseshoe fires were lit below the oak grove. By the time darkness fell the flames were leaping higher than a man, and more wood was being added to stack the blaze.

At last the hunters returned with their quarry. They came in tired, grim of face, carrying their trophies – three massive boar and one human male – all trussed and hanging from poles. The boars were put aside for the feast that would ensue tomorrow; Duihno was brought up inside the circle of stern firelit faces. Now he would pay the price of his secret slaying. He was bleeding from many wounds, his skin flayed by briar and thicket as he fled; he was alive but unconscious – Caridwen had granted him that much mercy.

Ylas and Matuac, having thirstily refreshed themselves with ale, came to where Rhiannon stood on the slope above the fires, the oak grove towering behind her.

'He was already wounded,' Ylas said bitterly with a nod to where the limp form of Duihno was being bound, young willow branches weaving a rough basket round him. 'Eogan speared him through the foot before he let him go.'

'That's the law,' Matuac said, dashing ale foam from his thick, fair moustache.

'We could have caught him without it!' Ylas laid tighter hold of Rhiannon's hand as the drum took up its beat and the three of them paced into the dance, forward and back with the other celebrants following in train, weaving spirals along the hillside as the wicker-clad bundle that had been Duihno was laid in the centre of the blazing horseshoe. Men formed a circle about the fires, with long branches and pitchforks in their hands. At a signal from Eogan they pushed the fires into one central blaze. Fresh flames and sparks writhed high into the dark sky.

Duihno must have come back to consciousness at the last moment as the fire closed round him. A chilling scream shot up to the dark sky, cut off as his lungs roasted.

Rhiannon tried to close her mind to the horror of that death, though she felt sick with pity and with fear. Truly the Gods were remorseless. Her hands were held fast in those of the twins either side of her, her feet pounded the earth, her voice came husky as she chanted with the others, 'Dark Caridwen, Goddess of Death, Queen of Winter, Lady of the Waning Moon. Let not the light die over us. Restore the sun to the world. From death let there be life.'

It was the ancient plea of a people who knew that, without the blessing of the Gods, the dark and cold of winter might never turn to spring.

The snows came early that year, livid clouds swirling down from the north sending a fury of white flakes to bury the land in a thick cold blanket. Food was short – the Romans had taken too much of the grain for bread to be freely baked, and when the warriors went out to hunt they often came in empty-handed; even the game had deserted Icenia, it seemed.

Nevertheless, for the festival of the winter solstice resources were found and if food was less than bountiful at least there was plenty of wood to feed the great fire that roared on the central meeting place all through the night. Flames writhed up to the sky, shooting up yellow sparks, the warm glow lighting the faces of the revellers who celebrated hopefully. For the sun had reached his lowest ebb. From now on he would be rising in the sky again, restoring warmth to the earth. Let the moon wax and wane only five more times and it would bring Beltane.

Troubled by that realisation, Rhiannon slipped away from the feast. She took care to leave while Matuac was occupied; lately he had followed her everywhere, making clumsy jokes and finding excuses to touch her until she felt stifled by his growing hopes. And Ylas knew it; he tried to protect her from the importunings of his twin but every time she met his eyes she saw the questions there. Both of the twins knew, or had guessed, what must happen at Beltane.

Borrowing a torch from its bracket by one of the paths, Rhiannon made her way to the gates, where she told the guard she was going down to the horse enclosures to check on the white mare. The man let her through with warnings to stay close to home.

'Wolves have been seen on the heath, lady.'

'Yes, I know,' Rhiannon said. 'I heard them howling in the night. They're hungry, too. Don't concern yourself. The Goddess protects me.'

Outside the fort, deep snow was trampled into tracks, some leading to the farms, some to the river and some to the woods and the horses. A frost glinted on the surface of the snow, sparkling in the light from her torch as she made for the woods and then veered away through deeper snow toward the river. She hoped the watch on the banks would not see her light heading away from safety. She had to get to the river, to a particular spot she had in mind, and she had to do it without interference.

She stopped, alerted, as the distant wolves howled again. The sound echoed eerily across the frozen wastes of Icenia beneath a sky lit by cold stars. It was the dark of the moon, as it was the dark of the sun, the most dread time when Bran ruled with his wife, mistress, sister and slayer Caridwen, Hecate, Annis – whatever one chose to call her – the Old White One, the Blue Hag, Death-in-Life . . . Rhiannon shuddered from more than cold. If it was her doom to be the toy of the darkest aspect of the Goddess, why did she even hope for an answer to her prayers? She already knew what the answer must be – nothing but despair.

But perhaps her prayers might touch the Goddess's softer selves, sweet Olwen, or sensual Uroica – or swift, strong Epona.

Only the tracks of animals and birds marked the snow as she came to the river and, with the aid of her torch, identified an alder tree and then an elder bush. Setting the torch down, supported against a fallen branch, she took out her knife and from each tree cut a twig. She knelt by the river, where icicles hung over the water and ice was beginning to build near the bank. From a pouch she took a handful of barley – stolen from the grain pits right under the noses of the guards whom Segovax had set to watch the stocks of corn. But Rhiannon was the Maiden; the guards hadn't watched her too closely. Besides, she had taken only a few grains which she had needed desperately – barley as an offering to invoke and placate the Goddess. She tossed it onto the surface of the river, watched it slide away on the sluggish flow. After it went the alder, and then the elder, for the twin Gods.

'Epona . . .' she ventured, but the night was still. Despairing, Rhiannon lifted her face to the stars, whispering, 'Great Mother of All Living! Hear me. If I must meet with the God in the shape of a man, then let it be Ylas. Let it be Ylas!'

'No!' The choked breath came out of the darkness behind her, terrifying her. She whirled to her feet, the bare knife ready in her hand. Who was spying on her? Was it Matuac?

Pale light from the torch flickered over a tall figure thickly cloaked but with his dark head bare. A dark moustache drooped half over his mouth and down either side to his jaw. Not Matuac. Farann. He glared at her out of shadows that, with the light beneath him, turned his face into that of a demon. 'Ylas? You pray for Ylas?'

'Because I must! If it can't be you . . . If it can't be you, then I hope – ' All her fears swarmed up and burst tears from her eyes. She choked his name and ran to him blindly.

This time he didn't hold her off. He opened his cloak and gathered her close into his arms.

'Then it must be Ylas,' he said hoarsely. 'Because if not Ylas it will be Matuac. Yes, I understand, sweet lady. At last I understand.'

Weeping, she huddled against him, soothing her cold hands and face in the heat from his body. Once a man had held her like this and she had dimly known how it might be with a lover, but now with Farann she knew. She wanted no other man but him. She clung closer to him, trembling and afraid, but warmed by a secret glow of painful, guilt-torn joy.

He bent his head, his lips seeking hers. A wordless moan of protest escaped her, but she turned her head to meet him and pressed closer, burrowing against his warmth, clutching at him. For one endless, aching moment she hung there, tormenting herself with the pretence of being like any other woman – free to love as she chose. But the years of training had done their work. She was the Maiden, promised to the God. She could not betray her vows.

She tore away, unable to speak. Through her tears she saw that Farann understood: she saw in him a passion and sorrow that matched her own.

He said, 'But there will come a time for us. When the Great Year is over . . .' He paused, waiting for her agreement, and when she said nothing he shook her a little, saying anxiously, 'Rhiannon? There *will be* a time for us?'

Wildly, she shook her head, bitter tears dripping down her face. 'I don't know. I don't know!!'

She turned and blundered away, heading for the twin fires on the banks, either side of the gates of the fort. Behind her Farann picked up the torch and slowly trudged back through the snow. He did not believe in the Gods as Rhiannon did, though he respected her faith and the long years of her obedience to her duties as Maiden. But he had clung to the hope – to the conviction – that after the Great Year she might be his. Now that dream seemed to be fading. Bleakly, he recalled what the cold warrior-priestess Erefwen had said: "You're a fool, Farann of the Trinovantes. You'll never have the Maiden." If she was right, then his life no longer had purpose.

*

A thaw caused the snow to sink. It filled the river to a gushing brown flood and turned the earth to red mud; then overnight temperatures dropped again and ground that had been rutted mud became like iron, while the river froze across and on the fringes of the Great Bay each tide built higher the wall of ice that was growing on the shore.

Boudicca woke shivering in the deepest hour of night. She pulled down a corner of the furs that covered her to the hair, listening. What had woken her? Had there been a cry? Or was it Araunah coughing? She listened intently but could hear nothing other than the bitter wind moaning about the thatch, and a scratching that was probably mice. Still, she was disturbed enough to gather her furs around her and push out through the curtained doorway.

A red glow from the mounded fire showed her two warriors of her guard nodding over their spears among a pack of sleeping dogs. One of the men stirred, saw her, and shot to his feet, waking his drowsy companion with a start. 'Lady!'

'Put another log on the fire, Nodenir,' she bade him in a low voice, not to disturb the rest of her household. 'Was there a noise? Did you near anything?'

He looked at her blankly. 'No, lady.'

'No, of course not. You were asleep, you turbid toad.' She watched him squirm under her chiding, and she sighed, rubbing wearily at her eyes. 'Perhaps there was no sound. Perhaps I was dreaming. But light me a lamp.'

Nodenir hurriedly took down a small bronze lamp from a niche over one of the inner doorways, and lit it from the fresh flames that licked up around the log he had added to the fire. The lamp's flame flickered wildly in a freezing draught from the roof; Boudicca sheltered it under the curve of her furs, and went to draw aside the heavily embroidered curtain that shielded her daughters' room.

Both of the maidens were asleep under mounds of coverings. Rhiannon's bright hair spilled out across her pillows; Araunah was almost invisible, huddled deep in the warmth of her bed, breathing with the rasp and hackle that worried Boudicca every winter. But it appeared that neither of the girls was in need of her at present.

She backed out of the room and let the curtain drop, sending a wry smile at Nodenir and Licinis. 'A mother's unease, that's all. How I wish the spring would come! This cold saps all our strengths.'

That was true, she thought as she touched the curtain of her own room and paused, remembering that her husband had seemed none too strong lately. Before she went back to bed she would just check on him, to reassure herself.

In the room beside hers, Prasutagus lay flat on his back. In his sleep he had thrown off the top part of his furs, beneath which he was still fully dressed for warmth. Holding the little flame of her lamp up beside her head, Boudicca bent to cover her husband more securely – and saw twin flames reflected in the dull mirrors of his eyes.

Her heart clutched inside her breast. Her legs weakened under her and she sank slowly to her knees, studying her husband's peaceful face, feeling numbed with disbelief. He appeared to be staring up at the underside of the thatch, his scarred brow giving him a quizzical look, but that was illusion. He would never stare at anything again: Prasutagus was dead. Prasutagus, high chief and king of the Iceni, had sent up the last breath from his body. That must be the sound she had heard – the sound that had clamoured along her instincts and woken her – the dying breath of the man who had shared her realm and her life for eighteen summers.

'No.' She denied the truth that lay before her. He could not leave her. He had always been there to steady her. Even when he most angered her she had never been able to ignore his opinions, his steadfastness, his certainty of purpose. From the first she had respected his wisdom.

'No!' She refused to believe that he was dead. He had wanted her to be ready to rule alone, but she wasn't ready. Not yet. Not yet! There was so much to do. So much to learn from him. She felt again as she had at nineteen – a youngling of no experience, needing guidance from someone older. Without him she was adrift.

'No!' Louder this time and, *'No-o!'* louder still until it became a wail of fury, raging against the fates and against the inscrutable Gods, waking all the household and soaring up and out like the cry of a she-wolf echoing across the frozen iron-bound hills of her queendom. *'No-o-o-o-o!!'*

News of the king's death spread swiftly. In response, all the chiefs of Icenia gathered – Audagas from Seafort, Lanaccion from the forests of the south, Dagobit from Eldergroveplace, and other noble Iceni lords, along with their guards of warriors. They came riding across the frozen hills to pay their last tributes to the king, and to attend the great tribal council that would follow the funeral rites.

Boudicca listened to them speculate on who might hold the high chieftainship – perhaps the kingship – in Prasutagus' stead. Their anxious whispering caused her a certain grim amusement, for in this matter she and the Druid were of one mind, one purpose. The next high chief must not be pacific and cautious; nor must he be a hot-head with too much fire in his belly; nor yet a strong-willed man intent on wielding power by himself. The next high chief must gladly concur in the plans that queen and Druid had long been incubating. Yet he must be strong enough to gain the votes of the council. And, not least, he must be acceptable to the queen and her family.

Was there such a man, in all of Icenia – in all of Albion? Queen and Druid had already made their choice, long before the funeral rites commenced.

The pyre had been built at the edge of the heath beneath a sky of frosted blue in which the sun was a pale spectre hovering low over distant forests. All the trees wore a coat of hoar-frost. Every spider web was rimed, every fallen leaf and stalk of grass delicately edged with ice. It was too cold to dig an earthen chamber to bury the body, as was the usual custom; Prasutagus was to be cremated and his ashes placed in an urn in the death hut, to await milder weather.

Eogan led the procession, chanting the funeral dirge, with Morica and Erefwen behind him, their hair sprinkled with ashes, their faces smeared with woad. They lifted their arms aloft, wailing, and bent low as if in pain, pacing in the ritual steps as the drum beat softly.

Members of the royal guard carried the king's body swathed in deep blue linen – the death colour that honoured dread Caridwen – and behind them walked the queen, with her two daughters, all of them bare-headed in the freezing weather, their hair spilling loose and rubbed with ashes of mourning, their faces smeared with woad. Beneath the blue smudges Rhiannon was pale, unnaturally calm, numbed by her grief for the man who had never been her father. But Araunah wept enough for two, clinging to her mother under the edge of Boudicca's cloak, the tears at times turning into a wrenching cough that tore at her slender body and made her turn her face against her mother's breast. Each spasm left her gasping until more tears came, and more coughing.

Boudicca herself might have been as frozen as the ground for all the emotion she displayed, though all had heard her wailing over her husband's body on the night he died. She had herself under control now. The first shock had passed. For nights past she had lain awake thinking, planning, her mind suddenly clear of all uncertainties.

Behind the royal family in a long stream came the other chiefs and warriors, and all the people of Oakhillfort, and behind them again a straggling skein of humbler folk – farmers, fisherfolk, shepherds – come to show their respect for a king whose reign had been notable for its lack of upheaval and strife – a blessing for common peasants however much it had irked the warrior nobility.

The flames of the funeral pyre leapt high, rivalling the cold red sunset and lingering to light the night, with a column of smoke rising high into the still air. Slowly, all that remained on earth of Prasutagus of the Iceni was consumed in the blaze. But he had been a king. He would be granted rebirth, in common with other chiefs and heroes.

The customary feast took place in the great hall. Chieftains and warriors of Icenia recalled the valorous deeds of the dead king; Alvran the bard had made a song for him, and out of respect there was as yet no official discussion of the future – that would come in council tomorrow. Even so, there was talk enough for people to form their opinions.

Next day the chiefs and elders gathered again in hall, with Boudicca the queen and Eogan the Druid at the head of the circle. What should be done? they asked. Who was to become the new king? Was the queen to be allowed her own personal choice? The law said that the high chieftainship was given only through alliance in marriage with the queen. Was Boudicca ready to marry again?

Each faction had its own ideas. One or two of the chiefs were wifeless and coveted the prize of power; some were willing to put aside their present wives in favour of the queen; others put forward names of their sons or their warriors – old and young alike. It was plain that each man, in some way, sought his own advantage.

For the first time, Boudicca began to sympathise with queen Cartimandua of the Brigantes, who had found herself yoked to a fiery young husband who disagreed with her at every turn. Such a fate might embitter any woman.

In the queen's house, away from the furore in the great communal hall, Rhiannon sat by the fire watching over Araunah as she lay sick, weakened by the demands of the past days. Araunah was grieving inconsolably for the man she had called father, even talking of wishing to follow him into the Otherworld. Troubled, Rhiannon hushed her and told her such talk was foolishness. Why, she was only just approaching her thirteenth summer! She had not spent her puberty month at Morica's hut yet. She mustn't even think of dying when the joys of womanhood lay ahead of her.

Araunha smiled gently, sadly up at her. 'What joys, Rhiannon? Joys like you have, and mother?'

Before Rhiannon could find a reply she was distracted by the arrival of Adalma, who came bustling in wrapped in a warm cloak of intricate pattern and colour. She was bringing a bowl of broth for Araunah.

'Made by my own fair hands,' she laughed. 'Made just for you, Araunah.'

She settled by the younger girl, feeding her mutton and barley broth from a horn mug and in between sips stroking the silvery blonde hair from Araunah's blue-veined brow, talking cheerfully of nothing of consequence. Adalma's hands *were* fair, Rhiannon thought – white and plump, and softened from constant contact with the natural oils in the wood she loved to spin and dye and weave. Adalma had a talent for making cloth that brought the highest prices in market. She was happy with her household chores, and with being a wife to Garanhir.

Conscious of her own hands, calloused and hardened from days spent at the chariot reins and wielding a spear, Rhiannon watched her friend tend Araunah with endless kindness and patience. After a while, Adalma even brought a genuine smile to the sick girl's lips.

Rhiannon smiled too, saying, 'If you need an example of

the joys of womanhood, sister, you have it here beside you. Adalma has been disgracefully joyful for as long as I've known her. Why, she's so contented she's even growing fat when the rest of us have gone hungry this winter!'

To her surprise, the teasing made Adalma go bright red. Above cheeks of fire, her seal-pup eyes widened into orbs of embarrassment and soft delight. 'That's not fat, Rhia. I . . . I'm to have a child.'

The news startled Rhiannon, but the next moment she wondered why. Her mother's involvement with Garanhir was long over. Why should the queen care if Garanhir's wife was carrying a child of his loins – hadn't that been the object of the marriage?

'That's wonderful!' Araunah breathed, her wan face lighting. 'When will it be born, Adalma?'

'Oh – moons yet. Morica thinks it will be in early summer. The oak month, perhaps. Morica wants it to be a girl.' She laughed at the thought. 'Morica wants every baby to be a girl, had you noticed? But I think Garanhir should have a son. A fine boy with curly golden hair. And perhaps after that a daughter.'

How very odd, Rhiannon thought, that Adalma could gaily speak of the future when for herself everything seemed to stop at the barrier of Beltane. Beyond that time – beyond the Mysteries – her own life seemed to trail into thick mists of nothingness.

'Ho, Rhiannon!' The call came from Matuac as he hurried in. 'Quickly! Come! Something's stirring among the council. They're all gathering outside, and Vranaun's gone to bring up the white mare. They're going to decide on the new high chief. Come and see. Come!'

Two

Around the oak, certain of the chiefs and warriors stood in a wide-spaced circle at some distance from the tree. They were all, Rhiannon saw, more or less eligible candidates for the role of high chief. Some strutted confidently; others glowered about them as if to fend off any detractors. Boudicca looked on with her usual aura of assured authority, and perhaps only her daughter was capable of detecting the covert glow of satisfaction and anticipation that hovered on the queen's face.

Rhiannon wondered why her mother was so pleased. Had she some particular man in mind? Her thoughts flew to Garanhir and she saw him standing to one side among the guard. His face was set in its usual lines of gravity, but beneath them Rhiannon glimpsed his pain.

As the news spread so people came hurrying to see what was happening. The explanation rippled from tongue to tongue – there was to be a choosing of the next high chief; the white mare, most sacred of all beasts to Epona, was to make the choice. Eogan had consulted the stars, and the stars had told him to settle the matter in this way – by decree of the Mare Goddess.

The Druid himself squatted under the oak, casting his runes. His breath made clouds on the cold morning as he chanted in a low rumbling voice that seemed to run words all into one long thread which he took and conjured into patterns in the air. His long, bony hands wove mysteries. His voice sent ripples of awe down many a spine.

Eventually the crowd parted to allow Vranaun through. He was leading the white mare. Starbright was visibly heavy with foal, and she was blindfolded, trusting the horsemaster to lead her. The two came into the circle, up to Eogan, and then at the Druid's word Vranaun led the horse three times about the oak.

'Uncover her eyes!' Eogan commanded.

It was done, the blindfold untied. The mare stood tossing her head, her ears twitching, her eyes rolling as she orientated herself and saw the circle of waiting men around her. She scented the air, and pawed at the ground.

Vranaun stepped away from her. So did Eogan. The chiefs and warriors in the circle all held out their hands and began to call to entice the mare to come to them.

'Great Epona!' Boudicca prayed in a sweet, carrying voice. 'Choose for us! Queen of the Winds, grant guidance.'

The mare's ears twitched and soft nostrils quivered. Slowly

but surely the horse walked forward – between two of the candidates – straight to where the queen stood.

A gasp went up from the watchers, and then an awed hush descended. The queen laid her hand on the proud arched neck as Starbright nuzzled at her waist, and then as though it were making obeisance the horse knelt before the queen. The Goddess had made Her choice.

Boudicca lifted her face to the sky, raised her fist, and cried, 'Blessed Andastre! Epona! My thanks!' Then smiling with fierce eyes she gazed around the circle, daring anyone to gainsay the choice of the Goddess. 'So shall it be! I, Boudicca, queen of the Iceni – queen and high chief! From this day, *I* shall lead you.'

It had been done by trickery, Rhiannon knew, though only an initiate in horsemastery would guess it. Boudicca must have visited the white mare in secret, bringing sweetmeats and special treats that the horse had learned to associate with her, with her scent and with the sound of her voice. So out of all that circle Starbright had known the queen to be a friend, had answered her familiar call and been drawn by the inviting scent of the substances she had secreted in her pouch – barley cake sweated under her armpit and flavoured with sweet oils, with fennel, strawberry, elecampane root, or whatever pleasant-scented herbs the queen had trained the mare to know. After that, making the mare kneel was a simple matter of touch and word.

But if it was a ruse then it had been connived at by Eogan, and by Vranaun the horsemaster. Perhaps the Goddess Herself had approved this scheme. Who could say it was not meant to be?

When the council convened again in the great hall, some among the chiefs and warriors expressed misgivings. It was many years since the Iceni had been led by a woman. But with Eogan standing beside her, casting his baleful grey glance on every objector, and with Boudicca herself so strong and sure, using the physical power of her presence and speaking in that compelling voice, sweetly cajoling or scornful at need, so in time the objections died to mutters and faded away.

For a long time now, the queen had been taking more and more authority to herself – at festivals, in council, and most notably in the battle with the Seafort clan. Her people had become accustomed to listening to her speak as a leader. They knew she was not merely a figurehead but a personality of considerable power. Not least of the arguments was the fact that the white mare had picked her out; only a very bold man – or a great fool – would dare to doubt that the Goddess had signalled Her favour toward Boudicca.

She was after all, so they reasoned, hereditary queen in her own right, descended by direct bloodline from sacred Brecca, the first and greatest of all Iceni queens. Not only that – she was a leader at the chariots and a proven warrior with sword and spear. She had won the Light by her own courage in battle. And she was experienced in dealing with Romans. She had been present when the original treaty was made; and now her warriors recalled how even the governor-general and the procurator had cowered before her when they met at Camulodunon.

When it was put to a vote, queen and Druid had their way.

Exhausted and yet elated after the nervous and emotional strain of the past few days, Boudicca sought the quiet of her own house and the company of her daughters, while the rest of the gathering continued to celebrate with yet more ale and rousing bawdy songs of war and of love. The queen saw Araunah safely asleep, then she sat by the fire, allowing Rhiannon to comb out her long hair. The motion of the comb soothed her and she eased her aching neck, reconsidering her memories of the day.

It had been a day of great triumph, but she had also learned that a few of her older chiefs still leaned towards the opinions of Prasutagus. If she called for war too soon, before the proper cause arose, some of her people might refuse to follow her.

She sighed and closed her eyes, and for the first time Rhiannon noticed the signs of ageing in her mother's face. The thought distressed her. She felt at once afraid and protective. 'I'm glad there'll be no stranger intruding among us,' she said. 'But you mustn't tire yourself, mother.'

'I'm not tired,' the queen answered at once. 'I doubt that I shall sleep at all, my blood is pounding so. All my life I've waited for this, Rhiannon. To be queen in truth. It's what the

Goddess promised to me, many long summers ago. She did not forget. She does not forget her faithful Maidens.'

The reminder made the comb pause in Rhiannon's hand. The wheel had not stopped turning with the king's death; it rolled inexorably on. Soon the winter would be over, the spring would come, and the time of the Maiden be at hand. Rhiannon had always awaited the coming of spring with impatience; this year she wished the winter might linger. But she daren't ask her mother any questions. By common consent the subject was taboo. Be faithful and obey.

'Lady! Lady, pardon me . . .' The door guard outside had been given orders that the queen was not to be disturbed. Now he showed his face, agitated. 'Lady, Farann of the Trinovantes is come. Shall I let him in, or . . .'

'Of course let him in!' Boudicca snapped. 'You're a fool, Licinis. I didn't tell you to bar the door to my family.'

The guard withdrew and Farann appeared, seeming wryly amused by the fellow's zeal for his task. His eyes gleamed, a glint of blue showing in the firelight as he shared a speaking glance with Rhiannon and hunched down to warm his hands.

'Why are you here?' Boudicca asked fondly. 'No more ale?'

'Ale flows like rivers in warriors' hall tonight. We have much to celebrate!' he assured her, then his expression changed with a frown and he stared at the fire. 'Not that I'm in any mood for drinking. Lady . . .' He looked up again, earnest now, his eyes meeting hers. 'Lady my queen and foster-mother, may I speak my thoughts?'

Her gesture bade him go on. She loved him as a son, but still this dark young man with his unnerving blue eyes disturbed her; he had caused her disquiet ever since they first met, when he had been no more than seven-summers-old. Was it only a woman's imagination – and latterly a mother's concern for her daughter – or was this feeling truly foreknowledge of some role that Farann had to play in her life?

'I have a great fear,' he said. 'When the roads are open again and the news of the king's death reaches Camulodunon . . . Then the Romans will come. If I'm right – if they intend to bring Icenia fully under the shadow of their red cloaks, then . . . Then they may forbid a woman to rule the tribe. They may appoint a chief of their own choosing – a man who will be obedient to their ways. Like Baro,' the name made his lips twist, 'Baro who thinks himself leader of the Trinovantes now.'

Boudicca let the silence lengthen. A log shifted in the fire and a little tongue of flame licked out across the clay hearth, as if a snake hid among the embers. The queen reached to still Rhiannon's combing, and glanced round with a slight smile to thank her daughter. Rhiannon backed off, sending a troubled glance at Farann.

Without haste, the queen rose to her feet, smiling on them both. 'Then let them come,' she said quietly, but her voice had an edge as sharp as the ceremonial sword that hung now from the carved beam above the door of her room. 'Let them tell me to my face that I am not the queen. We shall see whose word is law in these lands.'

After the cold came rains, beating down from grey skies as slowly the days lengthened. And as the first winds of the ash month sighed damply across Icenia, Vranaun the horse-master, with his son Teyrnon, tended the gravid Egyptian mare and anxiously awaited the birthing of her foal. It was a secret matter, a mystery to be shared only with initiates of the craft; all people were forbidden to come near the shelter where the mare was kept. But when all the signs were good Vranaun sent word to the Maiden Rhiannon, who came eagerly to witness the beginnings of the new breed.

She was in time to see Vranaun skilfully guide the foal free of its mother. It slid onto the hay, glistening with blood and mucus. Almost at once, it began to kick strongly. Starbright turned her head to look at it with pride as the foal struggled to stand upright on wobbly legs. It was mostly brown but with a white blaze down its face. The promise of its mother's elegant lines and long mane could be seen mingled with the sturdy strength of its father.

'Will it help us, Vranaun?' Rhiannon asked.

He squatted in the straw, watching the foal, evidently thinking that one small colt was a tiny step towards the breeding of a whole new strain that might one day bring wealth to its creators. But eventually he said, 'Perhaps so. If he lives. It may not be for me to see, but perhaps for Teyrnon, and for you . . .'

She exchanged a look with the slight, wiry young man

beside her, who grinned shyly, showing gapped teeth. 'I'll breed the best horses in Albion for you, lady.'

But the hope that sparked inside her was damped at once by the sound of watch-horns blaring. There were Romans coming – coming to settle the future of Icenia in the wake of the death of Prasutagus.

Breathless from running, Rhiannon ducked into the queen's house and whipped off her wet cloak to shake it. The fire hissed as drops flew across it. Most members of the household were there, and some of the guard, all grim of brow, while at the back of the hall the queen, apparently unconcerned, was weaving at her loom.

Glancing at her daughter, Boudicca asked, 'What news of the mare?'

'The foal's born,' Rhiannon said. 'A colt. A fine colt. He will sire many others.'

'If Epona smiles on us,' Boudicca murmured.

The news of the colt might, at any other time, have been of joyous welcome to the warriors; now it scarcely touched them. They were restive, squatting by the fire, standing up to stretch their legs, pacing the hall. Closest to the queen stood Nuadat as if ready to protect her with his life. The right side of his face was raked by livid scars left from his battle with Cadfan; his ear looked as if it had been chewed off by rats and his left arm ended in a stump, but his right hand was clasped firmly on the hilt of his knife. His face was set in grim lines. He, who had always been so merry, had not been seen to smile since Deucca died.

Garanhir was there, too – the king's champion come to add his strength to the queen's guard, and Farann stood in the shadows by the door. But the twins were not in the house. Ylas and Matuac, being the queen's nearest male kin, had been sent to meet the leader of the Roman visitors and bring him with all due respect into the house of mourning.

The twins returned together, pausing to salute the queen with fist to brow and announce the arrival of an envoy from the procurator at Camulodunon – an envoy in the shape of Caius Valerius Rufinus. The identity of the messenger caused Rhiannon no surprise, though a stir of disquiet moved inside her. Valerius had warned her that he would return.

The Roman entered with an arrogant swirl of his wet cloak. For a moment he stood letting his eyes adjust to the gloom, his gleaming helmet tucked under his left arm as he raked his fingers through his cropped dark hair. He saw the warriors of the guard seated or standing about the fire, with among them Rhiannon – to his eyes fairer than ever; she met his look with a proud challenge that made his blood stir afresh. Near her was her sister Araunah, and in the depths of the house the queen stood quietly at her loom, guarded by two mature, glowering warriors.

Boudicca presented the aspect of a grieving widow, a woman alone now and helpless, vulnerable. Unfortunately, Valerius knew better; he had felt the keen edge of her temper, seen her aroused. The death of old Prasutagus was hardly blow enough to quench the proud fire of this queen's spirit. Nevertheless he silently applauded her attempts at deception as he saluted her and told her of the procurator's deep sorrow on hearing the news of her husband's death.

'King Prasutagus was a valued ally of Rome. A wise leader of his people. We share the grief of our friends the Iceni.'

'Return my thanks to Catus Decianus,' Boudicca replied softly. 'It was good of you to come so far with his message, Caius Valerius Rufinus. You must be in need of refreshment. Araunah . . . pour wine for the tribune. Cameira . . . have Ivixa bring some food. And see that his men are fed and sheltered.'

These orders brought bustle in the house as everyone moved to obey, to make room for the visitor and see him comfortable as hospitality demanded.

'Lady . . .' Valerius said, his mouth curving in a wry smile at her attempts to deflect him from his purpose. 'I did not ride all this way in such haste, and through your inclement weather, only to bring you condolences. The civil governor wishes to ensure the continuance of peaceful co-operation in Icenia. Obviously there is need for a new leader at Oakhillfort. When he comes to be chosen – '

'He?' The sharp word cut across what he was saying and silenced him. Leaving her shuttle wedged among the warp threads, Boudicca moved further into the light, revealing that though her face was pale and marked with the blue woad-smudges betokening grief, her eyes were just as bright and

perceptive – and as glittering hard – as ever. 'You're mistaken, tribune. We have no need for a new leader here. *I* am queen of the Iceni – hereditary queen, as was my mother before me and her mother before her – back through countless generations to Brecca herself. My husband the king is dead, but I the queen remain to lead my people. You may go back and inform the procurator he has no need to concern himself. The future of Icenia is already assured.'

Seeing that he had been unprepared for this answer, she contained her triumph behind an ingratiating smile. 'But we have not forgotten our debt to Rome. My husband did leave a will. I think the Emperor may not be displeased with its terms. Rhiannon . . .'

Rhiannon turned aside, stooping under the curtain that shielded her mother's private quarters. There on a shelf, rolled up and tied with sacred scarlet thread, lay the parchment so carefully drawn up by Farann in the hope of assuaging the Emperor's greed. She took it out to Valerius and gave it to him, looking no higher than the kerchief he had bound round his throat to prevent the rain from dripping down his neck.

Valerius untied the thread, saying, 'Forgive me, lady, but I must see that – ' He stopped, seeing the neat script that marked the parchment. Startled, he lifted his eyes to the queen's and found them flat green lakes of absolute calm, telling him nothing. 'This is written in Latin.'

'Of course,' Boudicca said.

Valerius swiftly scanned through the will, frowning over it. In the correctly formal, effusive language of bureaucratic Rome, the document declared half of the late king's considerable estate of coin and jewellery, lands and livestock, as a legacy for the Emperor, the rest 'between my daughters equally to be divided.'

'This will have to be taken to Rome,' he said. 'It will need the Emperor's approval.'

'Then take it,' Boudicca replied. 'But first, tribune, accept the hospitality of my house.'

Belatedly, Valerius realised that he had underestimated this woman. Barbarian she might be, but she did not lack intelligence. She had cunning, and boldness. He must warn his superiors to be wary. Though she ruled a small, insignificant tribe, yet she might stir trouble at an inconvenient moment.

It would look well on his record if his report helped to neutralise that threat.

He sat by their fire, sharing their food and drink, aware of the warriors' eyes on him, sharply alert for any wrong word. They were suspicious, and they resented his presence among them. Briefly he wondered how far away his escort was, and whether he should have brought more than a handful of men. But Oakhillfort offered no overt threat. These Iceni were not fools. They would not dare to harm an official representative of Rome.

Rhiannon avoided him – avoided being near him, looking at him, even speaking to him. When he addressed a remark directly to her, her mother answered for her. But he kept finding himself watching her. No Roman maid was like her. She was bright, beautiful, seemingly shy and yet capable of savagery. And mystic – that was what intrigued him most – the aura of otherworldliness when her eyes looked dark and haunted as if she saw visions. An added lure was the fact that she was still a virgin: they called her the Maiden and said she was promised to the God – the thought excited him.

'I might ask for permission to take this will to Rome in person,' he remarked to the queen. 'If I were to speak for you, Nero might be persuaded to look more favourably on the terms of the will. The dividing of the estate is a device often applied by wealthy citizens. I congratulate your spies on discovering it.'

Boudicca arched her eyebrows in surprise. 'Spies, Caius Valerius Rufinus? Every merchant who passes by has gossip to tell, and my people visit your town and trading posts. We need no spies to learn what turns the wheels of life in Rome. We need only eyes and ears.'

'Even so,' he said. 'It will not be an easy task to persuade the Emperor to accept the will without question – or to concede your right to rule, lady.'

The hiss of her indrawn breath was audible through the house as she dropped all pretence of politeness and let her eyes flash with anger. 'I need no permission from your Emperor to lead my own people!'

'But it will go better with you if you seek his goodwill,' Valerius reasoned. 'Perhaps I should take with me an ambassador from among your people – perhaps a member of your own family. Someone who might appeal to the Emperor on your behalf.' His eyes had strayed again to where Rhiannon sat back from the fire weaving red and green thread into a braid.

Rhiannon sensed his glance, or perhaps she sensed the sudden tension that gripped the hall; she looked up as the queen said in a low voice, 'You mean my daughter, tribune?'

Finding the tribune watching her, Rhiannon flushed – not entirely with displeasure. Valerius was a strong, youthful, handsome man and she could not pretend that his interest did not flatter her, even though her heart rode fetterfast elsewhere. She also had to admire his boldness in pursuing his suit when he was so much at a disadvantage. He had courage, this Roman. His desires were vain, of course, but . . .

'She's not for you!' Matuac leapt up, brandishing his knife. 'Filthy Roman! You insult the Maiden!'

'Enough, Matuac!' Boudicca cut him short with a gesture as she rose to her feet imperiously and pointed to the door. 'The meeting is over, tribune. Go back to Camulodunon. Tell Catus Decianus – and Suetonius Paulinus – that they need have no fear for us. *I*, Boudicca, rule here. All is well with Icenia.'

Around her, her warriors were alert, hostile eyes on the tribune, hands hovering over ready knives. He made a little mocking bow, saluting her and then Rhiannon, before spinning on his heel to stride out. But he stopped suddenly, a hand flying to his sword, jerking it half out of its sheath as he peered through the shadows at where Farann stood.

'You!'

Farann returned the glare with cold eyes. 'I.'

Valerius turned, appealing to Boudicca, 'Lady . . . Do your laws permit a man to commit a secret slaying and go free? This man – '

'This man is my beloved foster-son,' the queen answered. 'He was proven to be innocent of the killing.'

'Is this true?' He frowned, looking to Rhiannon for an answer.

But his expression revealed other thoughts, including a growing puzzlement as he glanced again at Farann. He was newly questioning his memory of the warrior's identity, wondering where they had met. Seeing it, Rhiannon's heart jerked with alarm and she said swiftly, 'The Goddess Herself revealed the truth. The real slayer has answered for his crime.'

'Indeed?' His brow furrowed as he stared at Farann. 'So this man is again a member of the royal guard – your foster-son, you call him, lady?'

'And Maiden's champion!' Rhiannon said, her chin held high, her eyes defiant above cheeks where sudden spots of colour burned.

Valerius considered her, thoughts moving behind shrewd brown eyes. He was recalling that Rhiannon had been alone in the woods with one of the warriors, back last harvest time; he had seen the man from a distance. And later this tall, grim warrior had appeared, standing over the dead girl. Valerius had been distracted at the time but now he recalled the tension he had sensed in Rhiannon, as he sensed it again now. She cared for this dark warrior who dared to show his hatred in his eyes.

The two men locked glances, sparks of enmity and rivalry flying between them.

'Your name?' Valerius asked.

Rhiannon held her breath, hoping Farann would lie but knowing with despair that he would not.

'My name is Farann,' he said, and after the slightest hesitation he straightened himself even further, lifting his head. Pride flowed through him as he added, low but clear, 'Farann, son of Vindorex, son of Addedomarus, of the Trinovantes. But I was born in Rome, tribune. My mother was Julia, the daughter of Marcus Saturninus.'

This news made Valerius's eyes narrow even further. 'You were born in Rome? Can you read and write? Was it you . . .' He touched the pouch at his belt, where he had placed the king's will for safety.

'I wrote the will at the command of the king,' Farann said.

'I see.' Valerius glanced about him, thinking that there was more here than he had guessed. The procurator would be most interested in what he had to report.

He swept a bow in the general direction of the queen and strode out to call his men from wherever they were resting. He would start back for Camulodunon at once.

Behind him in the queen's house, incredulous voices demanded whether Farann had lost his senses. Valerius might not remember him yet, but only let him make enquiries and he would soon discover that Farann of the Trinovantes was an escaped slave, and the son of an avowed enemy of Rome. The procurator would demand his return; the queen would be called to answer for it.

Farann looked at Rhiannon, and at Boudicca, his eyes bright and steady. He said, 'I was not bred to play the coward. Too long I've skulked craven in shadows when Romans appear. Lady . . . If you ask me to leave, I'll go.'

'Go where?' Rhiannon demanded, torn by panic and dismay. 'You can't go, Farann. It's too late for that.'

'The Maiden speaks,' Boudicca said with a wry smile. 'And she is right, Farann. This danger is not new, only sharpened. but Valerius Rufinus has many other things on his mind. He may forget that he saw you here. If not . . .' Her voice trailed off as she stared into the future and wondered if this was what she had envisaged ever since she first saw the boy Farann – would he supply the spark that would light the flame to spread the blaze of victory across all Albion?

Three

The Queen of Spring had laid white blossoms and a fresh veil of green among the trees of the woods and across the heath. Nightly Rhiannon watched the moon fade from the full to its waning. For one thing she was relieved – there had been no further disquieting visits by Romans, nor any word of trouble from Camulodunon. Perhaps Valerius had gone to Rome; perhaps he had forgotten to make enquiries about Farann. But somehow she knew that it would not end there. The foresight with which she was blessed – or cursed – gave her no comfort.

Now again Eogan appeared to take his part in the festivities of Beltane, and as always among the young people anticipation rose toward the night of the hare hunt. But as Beltane Eve drew near, the Druid decreed that this Great Year demanded the added ritual of a contest between the twin Green Kings, symbolising the annual struggle between the twin Gods – Vron of the Waxing Year, Bran of the Waning Year – for the favours of the White Goddess, Queen of All.

'The race for a bride!' someone exclaimed.

Hearing the words, Rhiannon's breath caught in her throat. Now it came. Now. She knew that Farann had glanced at her but she daren't look at him, or at the twins her kinsmen, both of whom were tense with anticipation.

'Not a foot race!' Matuac said. 'That wouldn't be fair – Ylas is faster than I am. Everyone knows it.'

'Nor a contest for length of spearthrow,' Ylas put in. 'His arm has the edge in strength.'

'Chariots,' Eogan said. 'Both of you to choose a vehicle that pleases you, and ponies the same. Go now. Prepare.'

They were to race down the track from the Way. The finishing line would be the edge of the chariot track around the fort, and in case of any dispute Eogan would judge the winner. All the inhabitants of Oakhillfort gathered to watch the race, some of them lining the end of the track, others grouped on the banks to get a farther view.

Under the guidance of Morica and Erefwen, Rhiannon was wreathed in a crown of willow and white hawthorn. She chose her own vantage point from which to watch the race, on the high grassed bank near the gate, where she had often stood or sat thinking, observing, or praying, but never so tensely as she did that day, with Farann on one side and her mother on the other.

The air was clear and fresh with promise. Beyond the curves of the hills Rhiannon could just see the line of the Way and near it the cluster of figures that must be the twins and their chariots, with the companions who had gone to see a fair start under the eye of Segovax the law-giver. Eogan waited among those near the fort, to judge the finish.

Time seemed to stop, yet it flowed too fast for Rhiannon. She felt the pounding in her blood that signalled the nearness of Epona. Her head felt light, her hands clammy, her stomach churned. Let it be Ylas. Blessed Epona, let it be Ylas. Ylas she could bear if she must. But Matuac . . . even her thoughts recoiled from images of lying with Matuac; surely her body would reject him utterly.

But perhaps she would not recognise the man who came. The God could assume whatever form pleased Him. Perhaps He would come in a blinding light, as He came to the tree, so bright that she would not see or know whose flesh formed the vessel. Blessed Epona . . . she was mortally afraid!

Dimly, she saw that the race had begun. How slowly the chariots seemed to move, crawling towards her with their twin drivers stripped to the waist, fair hair flying, indistinguishable one from the other, both wielding whips, yelling at their ponies, wheels rattling and leaping, first one in front, then the other straining level and passing . . . Which was which? Both were striving, using every muscle, every mote of skill, every curse of voice and bite of whip.

And then a flight of screaming swifts, returning to their summer breeding places, swooped low across the track. One pair of ponies balked and pulled aside. One pair of wheels jumped on uneven grass. One chariot fell back. Its driver had it under control and on the track again. But too late. His brother had reached the finish. He was wheeling his ponies in a crazy arc that set the chariot up on one wheel for an instant before the driver shifted his weight and came safely to a halt.

Breathless, his body dripping with dust-streaked sweat, he raised a fist and looked up to where Rhiannon stood. His grin showed white through his shaggy fair moustache as he yelled his elation loud and long, while his twin pulled up alongside him, red-faced with anger and humiliation. Only then did Rhiannon see the scars on the loser's body – the whorls and slices of a boar's curving tusks. The loser was Ylas.

Matuac had won the Maiden bride.

Later, when they came face to face as children merrily danced about the sacred oak, Matuac's grin was confident, his eyes gleaming.

'So the waiting's over,' he said. 'I shall be the one – not some Trinovante outsider, nor some high-born Roman with fancy ways. Not even my brother Ylas. The Goddess sent her birds to stop him, did you see! *I'm* Her choice. *Me,* not Ylas. Tomorrow night, Rhiannon . . . Tomorrow night I'll show you how it feels to bed with a God.'

As required by the rite, the Maiden came that evening to the gates of Oakhillfort with a wicker cage containing a hare. All the youths and maids had gathered, chattering excitedly, pushing and squabbling in their eagerness, under the leadership of the twins – Ylas wreathed in holly, Matuac in pale leaves of young oak. Rhiannon saw Ylas watching her, but when she looked fully at him he grinned as if his only thought was to enjoy himself; whatever his real thoughts were, he hid them well.

When the hare was released, the twins headed after it with their companions following in a laughing crowd to hunt the hare until dawn and return to strew the roofs of all the houses with boughs of white blossoms to welcome the summer. Rhiannon watched them go. She was immersed in blessed numbness, as she had been all day, feeling as though she was surrounded by water that deadened sound and distorted sight. It was always so when she walked close with the Goddess. She felt someone place a soft cloak around her, and hands came on her leading her down towards the priestess's hut by the river, the women coming behind, chanting softly, singing the Song of the Maiden. *Furze fires quenched by ivy dew; White, and scarlet, and midnight blue . . .*

From his post up on the high banks, Farann watched the Maiden's procession wind its way down to the river. A muscle worked in his jaw as he ground his teeth, and the hand that held his spear was locked so tight around the shaft that it burned with cramp. He had volunteered to stand watch rather than take part in the revels of Beltane Eve. Tonight he had no stomach for lusty tumbling in the woods.

Matuac, he thought. Matuac the foolish, the hasty, the good-hearted, the hot-headed. It would have been easier if he had been able to hate Matuac, but he couldn't. He was fond of both twins as if they were his brothers; Matuac was not evil, only too inclined to think with his belly. His gut reacted before his mind did. He had not arranged his own choice as joint Green King, nor had he won the race unfairly. The Gods had ordained it, for whatever reason moved those inscrutable Entities. But such thoughts brought him no comfort: he had seen Rhiannon's face when Matuac came in the winner. And, whichever man had been chosen, still Farann would have known this same sick fury of outrage and jealousy that was building in him.

Must he lose everything he held dear? First his mother, then the familar life of Rome, then his grandfather, his home at Camulodunon, his father, his sister . . . The Gods had taken everything. Weren't They satisfied yet? Did it amuse Them to rob him of his woman, too?

Erefwen had said it – "You will never have the Maiden." But Erefwen might be wrong!

Rhiannon was woken at dawn. In the company of Morica and Erefwen, she travelled deep into the marshes as had her mother before her, to the pool of purification where she rested before bathing in the cold waters. The two priestesses towelled her dry by a fire they had built, stroking perfume into her body and onto her hair as they combed it out and let it dry into a soft cloud of curling golden-red.

Now, as they prepared her and dressed her in the loose white gown and cloak threaded with silver, they told her the last details of her duties. She was given the long ritual knife with its hilt of dark blue quartz – the knife with which to mark the God as a reminder that the Goddess could take his life if She wished. Rhiannon felt the knife hang heavy between her breasts as she sat by the fire and sipped the drink the priestesses gave her.

Beyond the fulfilment of her duties the future lay dark. But she had passed through fear to calm waters of acceptance. If she was fated not to survive this night then she was content to die. Only one regret remained – that she might never again see a certain man whose image would not hold still in her mind. She knew him to be dark and tall, with blue eyes, but he was separated from her now by Mystic barriers no human could penetrate. She had gone beyond him. The rite, and the ivy drug, swept her to meet her fate.

It was almost dark when the two priestesses pushed the coracle out onto the waters. Pale ripples marked the flow beneath the boat, carrying the Maiden to the sacred island. She saw it towering darkly ahead of her against the glimmering sky, where tall alders shaded gentler willows, and now she saw the glow of a fire at the centre of the island. In her mind's eye she pictured the clearing where the tree stump altar was thick with dried blood; she had been there many times. She came now with fast-beating heart, her mind fixed on what must be done. Though she was still afraid, her fear was overlaid by excitement induced by the drug. She felt herself glowing. She was filled with the aura of the Goddess – the familiar drowning of her own human self in the will of the supernal Female, who surely tonight was as lusty and full-blooded a woman as only She could be, a Virgin ready for Her mating.

If only She had not chosen Matuac!

The boat bumped gently against the shore. Rhiannon climbed out and tethered it securely, obeying instructions she had learned by rote. She must walk now up the path where shy primroses slept in the grass, where mist crept up with the night, towards the fire that beckoned among the trees.

He had heard her coming. He was scrambling to his feet, to stand naked before her, staring at her with eyes she could drown in. A tall man, dark-haired . . . Tears of joy and gratitude dazzled her sight as she let fall her cloak and gown and opened her arms to him. The God had after all been kind: He had taken the shape and form of Farann.

Farann had been waiting for her, calm now and conscious of no regrets. Ylas had been right – they had been forced to act. They had tracked the Druid and Matuac into the marshes, had heard Eogan's instructions and seen him persuade Matuac to take a deep draught from a silver cup. Then the Druid had left and Matuac had paced up and down impatiently, muttering to himself, his words growing ever more slurred as the drug took hold. Then he had begun to throw off his clothes as if they irritated him.

He had not heard Ylas and Farann creep up. He had hardly made a sound as he fell unconscious. They had dragged him to the far side of the island, bound him hand, foot and mouth and left him sleeping under a bush. Then they had looked at each other in the fading light.

'Well, go!' Ylas had exclaimed.

Farann had hesitated, torn between his sense of honour and his desire for Rhiannon. 'You are Green King.'

'Chosen by Eogan to increase the awe of the rite – because Mat and I are twins. It means nothing.'

'Rhiannon believes,' Farann said. 'She expects Matuac.'

'She'll have been prepared – as he was.'

'Drugged?'

'Of course! How else could they persuade her to lie with Matuac? It's all trickery, Farann, to keep us in awe. I don't believe the Gods care which man it is. Rhiannon's giving the gift of her virginity as an offering to the God. So go and accept it and stop being a fool. You love her, don't you? As she loves you. The Goddess will understand that. I'll stay here and keep Mat quiet if he wakes.'

Now Farann, in Matuac's place, sat naked on the bed of furs that had been prepared. He felt the night alive with whispers, questioning what he had done – he had interfered in the rite, defied the Gods. So be it! he raged in silent answer, remembering Cunovinda his sister. The Gods punished faith and innocence. Might They not reward sacrilege?

At last he saw a pale shape among the trees and as he got to his feet Rhiannon appeared, clad in shimmering white with her bright hair flowing above her. She peered at him in the firelight, blinking as though her eyes were misted, her apprehension giving way to a glow of joy that made a physical pain of tenderness and longing stab through his gut as her clothes drifted about her feet. She stepped free, pale and softly curved in the firelight. His for the taking. His alone. He knew that, whatever happened, nothing would make him regret this night. He swept her into his arms, felt her sweet soft trembling against the ready heat and fire that swelled in his loins.

Words tumbled out of him as he carried her to their bed of furs. 'My love, my love . . . Sweet love . . .' His hands caressed her, trembling over her breasts and her belly, his concern for her battling with the surging demands of his own body.

Sensing his fear of hurting her, Rhiannon twined her arms about him. Her womb jerked, spasmed and flowed molten with desire as she pulled him to her. She felt him pierce her body with sharp pain and soaring joy. The God moved in her. The Goddess showed her how to respond, how to pleasure Him as He pleasured her until the mounting sensations lifted to the skies and crashed back to earth leaving them both gasping and exhausted.

'Forgive me,' he muttered against her mouth as he kissed her feverishly. 'Forgive me, love. I had to come. I had to.'

His words made no sense to her. 'Hush!' Rapt in remembrance of her instructions, she stilled his lips with her fingers and, rolling away from him, stood up and went to find the silver jug that stood behind the tree-stump altar. The fenfolk had been there. The blood of a sacrifice buzzed with flies, but Rhiannon saw it only as a holy thing. All was well. She was still faithful. She would obey to the last.

Moving as if through a mist that slowed her limbs and clouded her mind, she returned to the firelight and offered Farann a drink.

'Poisoned?' he asked wryly.

'It will make you sleep. You must sleep. I must leave.'

Pushing aside the cup, he reached for her. 'I don't want you to leave. Not yet.'

'But I must! I must! Only first . . .' She reached for the knife that had hung about her neck. It wasn't there. Stupidly she stared down at her naked breasts. 'The knife . . .'

'This?' He produced it from among the tumbled furs, only just beginning to understand that Rhiannon was under some strange enchantment. She hardly knew what she was doing. Her face was pale, her eyes wide, the pupils eclipsing green irises. Momentary alarm touched Farann's thoughts. 'Must you kill me?'

She shook her head, drawing the wicked thin knife from its sheath. 'I must mark you. It's the rite. I must. Be still.'

While he knelt in front of her, watching her face with troubled eyes, she laid the sharp blade to the base of his throat. Its first cold kiss made him wince and draw away, catching her wrist. 'No!'

'But I must!' Through the cloud that dulled her thoughts she saw the blood trickling from the cut she had inflicted, and as if from some vast distance she seemed to hear her mother's voice saying, '*He* is the one who must die. *He!*!'

She backed away, shaking her head, a hand over dazzled eyes. The cloud was thickening, threatening to pull her into oblivion. She scarcely felt Farann's hands on her, helping her to dress, looping the knife's thong about her neck, guiding her to the coracle.

'Can you find your way?' he asked anxiously. 'Rhiannon, are you sure you must do this?'

'I must! I must leave! Let me go!'

The last she saw of him was a vague shadow fading among

other shadows as drugged mists finally claimed her and she slumped unconscious into the bottom of the coracle as it floated free on the waters of the marsh.

Slowly, Farann returned to the clearing and began to dress. Now again he felt the chill of the marshes. The Goddess had long ago hidden Her pale sickle behind clouds as though disdaining to shed Her light on the profanation of Her Mysteries.

A movement behind made him whirl, dagger in hand ready to defend himself against anything. But the fair-haired warrior who stood on the edge of the light offered no threat. Farann relaxed with a sigh: until that moment he had forgotten Ylas was nearby.

'She's gone?' Ylas asked. 'Is all well?'

'I think so. If she knew me, she felt no surprise.'

'If she knew you she probably believed the God had favoured her with a happy fantasy. Rhiannon's faith is strong.'

'I know.' That fact troubled Farann – that he had deceived not only the Druid and the priestesses but Rhiannon too. But he thrust the thought aside. The act was committed. 'We'd best hurry and bring Matuac up here. When Eogan comes he'll expect to find him sleeping. The wine in that jug . . . I think it's drugged.'

'Yes, that would seem likely. But I'm the one who's staying here, not my brother.'

'You?'

'Me. You're going to untie Matuac, put him into the boat we came in and set him adrift. He'll be safe. No bear or wolf comes this far into the marshes. If he gets lost the fenfolk will guide him back.'

Farann frowned at him. 'Why? If we just leave him here . . .'

Smiling a little, in a way that was sad and knowing, Ylas reached to smear his thumb in the blood that still seeped from the cut in Farann's neck. 'Because of a warrior I once knew when I was a youngling – a man called Huan – a prince of the Caledones from the north. Do as I say, Farann!' All at once his voice was harsh. 'You'll ruin everything if you keep arguing. See my brother safely adrift, then you vanish too –

before Eogan comes. Or do you want to take another look at the bottom of the punishment pit – without hope of escape this time?'

After a moment's hesitation, Farann left.

In the clearing, Ylas stood listening for a while until every sound had faded. Then slowly he stripped himself naked, sat down among the tumbled furs and took out his knife, watching for a moment as firelight played on the blade. The wind struck cold and he shivered as he lifted the knife on his palms, holding it up to the sky, where he saw the clouds part and the new moon briefly show.

'For Thee, Dia,' he made the solemn vow. 'My life for Thee, and for love. Of a brother, a maid, and a friend.'

Swiftly, before his courage could fail him, he drew the blade of the knife in a light semi-circle about his throat. He sat for a moment, feeling the pain bite and the blood begin to run from the thin cut; then he wiped his dagger clean on the grass, sheathed it at his belt and reached for the jug of drugged wine, welcoming the sweet, herb-scented taste in his dry mouth.

It made his head swim, took away his fears. He drank more, until the jug ran dry and he tossed it away, laughing out loud over the follies of humankind as he lay down, rolled himself in the furs, and slept.

The song of a bird somewhere very close by woke Rhiannon to the bright light of noon. She blinked away the bleariness from her eyes and saw that she lay in the shelter of a bower of branches. She remembered what had happened – but through a glowing haze that made nothing very clear. When she moved, a pain shot through her head and she moaned aloud.

Someone scrambled into the bower, making the singing bird start away with a frightened flurry of wings. Morica bent over Rhiannon, her eyes glittering with a feral light.

'Was it done? Was it well done?'

Rhiannon moistened her lips, whispering, 'Yes. Yes, it was all done as you told me. He was there. I lay with Him and I marked Him, then I left and He slept.'

The priestess lifted the object she held in her hand – the thin knife with its hilt crusted with blue quartz, unsheathed, with a rim of what looked like rust along the blade. Her mouth stretched in a wolfish smile. 'Yes, you marked him. Albina the White has awakened again to womanhood. Blessed be the Great Queen!'

With a start, Rhiannon realised that what showed on the knife was not rust but blood. She remembered cutting the man – cutting Farann, watching his blood seep from his skin. Farann. Again she tried to move and again the pain shot blackly through her head, making her lie back with a whimper. It couldn't have been Farann! The man had only had the appearance of Farann. She had been granted a kindly illusion. That was the only thinkable explanation.

Morica pressed a cup to her lips, saying, 'Drink this. It will help to clear your head. You must rest, daughter. We shall stay quietly here in the marshes during the hawthorn month. You must rest and pray – pray that the Great Mother of All Living will grant us a child of this coupling. A girlchild, daughter. A girlchild for Dia.'

It was peaceful in the marshes with the call of birds, the lap of water, the patter of rain among new leaves. Rhiannon rested and slept, and rested again, though she was not contented in mind. Unease stirred the watery wastes. Little flurries of wind came unexpectedly to shiver across the surface of the water and raise the hackles of her skin, and ever and again in the night some water bird shrieked an alarm that woke her to lie with pounding heart. Portents everywhere warned that all was far from well.

It troubled her that she couldn't clearly remember what had happened on the sacred isle. Her memories were all hazed in obscurity, not to be trusted. She had met with the God, that was enough. But she began to understand why her mother, questioned about the identity of the man *she* had met, had insisted that it was the God. Perhaps the Maiden never knew for sure which man she had lain with. The man Rhiannon remembered had been so very like Farann, even to the odour of his body, and the whip scars that marked him.

Several nights passed. Rhiannon didn't count them; she had to remain in the marshes a whole month to ascertain whether her moon-flux would come or not. The moon would darken again before she could be sure.

Then, while the moon was still waxing toward the full,

Erefwen came paddling in haste with news from Oakhillfort. There was trouble. The Maiden must go back at once. Neither of the priestesses would tell Rhiannon what was wrong but they whispered together and as they rode back through the marshes they signed to each other in the strange language that Rhiannon had never been able to interpret – with one finger, or more than one, slantwise against nose or shin, numbers of fingers and angles of slant obviously meaning something that only priestly initiates understood.

Eogan knew that sign language, too. Rhiannon detected him using it as he stood waiting grimly by the river, watching for their return – he was there, despite the fact that in the hawthorn month he should have been in the forests with the young men. Her mother the queen stood by him, looking pale and angry.

They took Rhiannon to the priestess's hut where a fire burned and smoke hung in the gloomy room. Lamps flickered around the carved statue of the Triple Goddess, so that the three faces seemed to be moving, changing expression – girl, woman and crone. Rhiannon's head swam with dark mists of dread.

Boudicca knelt by her daughter, shaking her shoulder and saying urgently, 'You must tell the truth, Rhiannon! Which twin did you lie with? Which one? Was it Matuac, or Ylas?'

Rhiannon's eyes had widened with the dimness until she seemed to be in a trance. 'It was Matuac. Matuac was chosen.'

'But Ylas has the mark!'

'Ylas?' Her mind seemed to spin, confusing her further. Had it been Ylas? 'Matuac was chosen.'

'Matuac was waylaid!' that was Eogan's threatening bass. His eyes glimmered in the gloom and his shadow behind him wavered huge on the wall, turning him into a terrifying figure.

'You must know which of them it was,' Boudicca said. 'You saw him naked, Rhiannon. You lay with him. Was he scarred? Badly scarred? Was it Ylas?'

'Scarred . . .' She closed her eyes, pressing her fingers to her forehead in an effort to make the memories come clear. Yes, the man had been scarred, but by whip marks, not the gougings of a boar's tusks! Distraught, she looked into her mother's face and saw there tears to mirror her own. 'You ask me for the truth, mother. This is the only truth I know –

that I can't say which of them it was because I don't know. All I saw was . . . the God. You know how it was. It was the same for me as it was for you. Mother . . . it was the God!'

Boudicca could not refute that, nor reveal to Rhiannon the truth of what lay in her own memories – not with Eogan and the priestesses listening. Besides, Boudicca could see that her daughter was telling the truth as she recalled it; all of them could see the fear and bewilderment in those wide green eyes. Perhaps, for Rhiannon, the God had really come. She had always been a very special Maiden.

'It is enough,' Eogan decided dourly, his deep voice vibrant, his eyes pale and bright. 'Whatever deceit was practised, Ylas bears the mark.'

'The earth must have blood,' Morica muttered. 'Whose blood, She cares not.'

These allusions troubled Rhiannon, but she could not interpret them. At the last Great Year Garanhir had been the man, had he not? Yet Garanhir had survived. Ylas would survive too. Ylas . . . she could not conceive of his challenging the Gods, but it was easier to believe that he, rather than Matuac, had been the tender lover she had met on the island in the marshes. Did he remember it, or had he too been under a glamour that blinded his eyes to the truth?

As Eogan understood it, Ylas had followed his twin, laid him unconscious and set him adrift on the marshes before taking his place. And in the morning when the Druid went to wake him Ylas had made pretence of being Matuac. He had been able to continue the deception for days, until Matuac himself had stormed into the forest camp with his own version of the story. Only then had Eogan realised that an exchange had taken place. and by then it was too late to amend it.

Perhaps it was as Dia willed. Only She knew why Ylas had acted as he had. But indeed it was Ylas who bore the mark of the knife. It was Ylas who would answer for it. Bowing to the enigmatic ways of the Gods, Eogan departed to his forests and the company of the young men.

At last Rhiannon was allowed to leave the priestess's hut and go home with her mother to the queen's house – 'She'll be as safe with me as she would in the marshes,' Boudicca vowed. 'No man will dare come near during the month of chastity. If she's with child, then she's with child. The child is what matters most.'

Four

Only a few nights after her return from the marshes, Rhiannon lay awake in her room at the queen's house, disturbed by a fresh wind that eddied around the thatch, and by an unease that drove sleep far away. The moon had set. Soon dawn would come. What was amiss? A faint sound came from somewhere outside – a sound she could not identify. She eased herself up on her pallet, listening, but apart from Araunah's snuffling there was nothing to hear . . .

. . . Until the night was split by the urgent call of a watch-horn. A fast succession of notes sounded an alarm. Rhiannon leapt from her bed. The alarm call ceased, choked off as if the blower had been struck in the throat. There came a sharp cry, and then a long, fading scream. Rhiannon ducked under her curtain. In the hall the women were springing up, grabbing weapons from the wall. Rhiannon, too, grabbed a spear and ran out with the rest to face whatever threatened.

It was barely dawn, the eastern sky tinged with a faint grey, but the village was waking to danger. Women ran from their houses, some carrying crying babies. Rhiannon heard the sound of male voices shouting from near the gates, and out of the night a troop of Roman cavalry came thundering into the village. Dogs ran barking to attack them. Children cried in fright. Women fled, screaming, from a storm of flying hooves.

The raiders swept up to the queen's house. Several of them rode straight at Rhiannon and her companions. Huge and fearful they looked in the half light. She loosed her spear at one, saw it glance off body armour. He was on her. She spun aside from the charging horse. The rider's cloak enveloped her as he threw himself from his saddle. She fell, with his weight on top of her, the breath knocked from her. Around her the other women screamed, men cursed, horses plunged and whinnied. Rhiannon struggled with her attacker. She drew her knife, slashed at him – and reeled back from a stunning blow to the side of her head. Her brain exploded with pain, her sight flared red. She lay dazed and helpless.

It was over very soon. Surprise had been the attackers' best ally – surprise, and the unexpected fortune of finding the women alone. A small force had scrambled over the steep double banks and silenced the watch. Once inside, they had opened the gates for their comrades. Another section had neutralised the male guards in the woods; some of the men had been killed, others were being herded together and brought in under the threat of cavalry lances. Women and children were dragged out from hiding places and forced to join the rest.

Rhiannon's hands were cut, her ribs bruised where she had fallen on the sharp stones of the path. She felt hard hands picking her up, thrusting her forward to where in the grey dawn light other women had gathered in groups under the sacred oak, some bearing the marks of violence, some cowed and weeping.

Her mother was there, standing defiant with Araunah beside her, both of them tousled from sleep. The queen wore a tunic and breeks, with her hair fastened in a loose braid; she had had no time to don a cloak and her only adornment was the thong with her horsemaster's amulet and the ring with its stone of rose quartz. Yet she looked regal, imperious, her eyes glittering and her mouth set. Other women and children were still being brought up, casting frightened glances behind them as they were driven on by horsemen with lances, or soldiers afoot with drawn swords.

'Where are your menfolk?' one of the sergeants demanded.

'Men do not remain in Iceni villages in the month of chastity,' Boudicca answered coldly. 'Your presence insults our religion. The governor-general shall hear of this outrage.'

One of the soldiers said something, asking what the queen had said; the sergeant told him and most of the men laughed, some making ribald remarks that turned the laughter bawdy. But a new voice, speaking sharply, silenced them. The men stiffened to attention as an officer rode up. Rhiannon saw that it was Valerius. His glance slid across hers, wavering under the withering hatred in her eyes as he paused to confront Boudicca, saying, 'Lady, I regret – '

'Save your speeches!' Boudicca spat. 'You've been a guest in my house, Caius Valerius Rufinus. Now you come sneaking like a brigand in the night. For what? Were you afraid to face my wrath in daylight?'

He nudged his horse closer, his handsome face set in stern, cold lines as he looked down at her. 'You should consider it a compliment to your cunning, lady. This is a truth-seeking mission. Given warning, you have time to lay too many deceits.'

'So what do you intend?'

'I regret I must ask you to wait here. The procurator wishes to speak with you.'

The procurator?! Rhiannon exchanged a startled, questioning glance with her mother, who made a little gesture of negation. The queen had no way of guessing what this meant, except that it boded no good.

While they stood waiting the sky lightened and sunrise spread pastel shades of grey and blue and yellow among soft wisps of cloud. Merry birds sang from the sacred oak and the high points of thatched roofs. Rhiannon looked about her at the groups of unhappy women, old men and tearful, frightened children. She caught sight of Adalma, big with pregnancy. As their eyes met, Adalma started forward as if to join the queen's family, but the nearest soldier threatened her with his spear and she drew back, a protective hand to her swollen belly.

Cameira and others of the guard returned Rhiannon's glance. They felt as she did – helpless, angry, apprehensive. Morica and Erefwen glared with narrow tattooed eyes. The few men, too, looked grim with frustration. The Romans had rounded up every man they could find in the woods and the enclosures. They stood together in a knot a little apart from the women. Among them, Rhiannon saw Vranaun, with blood oozing from a wound in his scalp.

Behind and around each group there were soldiers, some still mounted, others standing guard on foot: tough, hard-looking men, veterans of numerous campaigns. To them, this attack on a village of women was no more than a morning's amusement.

Out of the past Rhiannon seemed to hear the echo of Farann's voice, saying to Prasutagus, 'The procurator has gathered a band of hard, violent men who have no creed but to advance their own fortunes. Even if it means murdering innocents . . . Catus holds the fate of the Iceni in his fat, scented paws.' The memory sent a shudder through her, and at the same moment Araunah said, 'I wish father was here. What will they do to us, mother? Mother, I'm afraid.'

'Don't be.' Boudicca clasped her younger daughter more tightly and lifted her chin as she stared directly at the sergeant. 'They won't harm us, my love. They wouldn't dare!'

A movement among the houses drew Rhiannon's attention to the track leading from the gates. Valerius was returning, and beside him, looking ill at ease in the saddle, rode the portly figure of Catus Decianus. They were accompanied by another section of cavalry riding in twos with pennants flying from their lances.

A dog ran out, snarling and snapping, making the procurator's horse dance nervously. Catus clutched at the horse's mane, fearing a fall, but one of his escort spurred up and skewered the dog on his spear. It yelped once and then fell silent as the man shook it loose and left it lying. Catus composed himself into a semblance of haughty disdain and rode on to the central meeting place where his men held the queen and her women.

As they halted, Valerius and the escort dismounted; the fat procurator remained in the saddle, looking down his nose at Boudicca with an expression he might have worn if he had passed by the stinking punishment pit. He murmured something which Valerius repeated as a rapped order. Soldiers moved among the captive groups, forcing them back at spear-point, away from the queen and her daughters.

Again Catus spoke in a low voice. Valerius listened, his eyes flickering expressionlessly from Rhiannon's face to Boudicca's. He said, 'His excellency bids me inform you that you appear to have misunderstood the meaning of being a client kingdom of Rome. The terms of the treaty applied only while king Prasutagus was alive. His death changes many things. The Emperor will decide on the governing of the Iceni. You may not set yourself up as queen without leave.'

'Set myself up?!' Boudicca repeated in disbelief, and put

Araunah aside as she stepped forward and tipped up her proud head to stare into the procurator's face. 'I was queen long before the coming of Rome. The women of my house have been queens since the Gods dwelled among us. I need no leave from Rome!'

'You do, lady,' Valerius argued. 'Under the treaty – '

'Rot the treaty!' Her hands clenched as she took another step nearer to Catus. In response, two soldiers moved forward to protect the civil governor, swords angled to Boudicca's breast. The threat only caused her to regard the men with a contempt which after a moment she threw up at the procurator. 'Do you fear an unarmed woman, Catus Decianus? Ha! But swords will not protect you, nor yet a full legion. Hasn't your puppy dog,' with a gesture at Valerius, 'told you that I can kill with a look?'

Valerius stiffened, insulted by that 'puppy dog' taunt, but a flicker of unease crossed the fleshy face of the procurator. He muttered something that made the two soldiers back off a little, though they kept their swords ready. In response, Boudicca smiled scornfully to herself, enraging Catus. Angry colour surged up his neck as he spoke again in clipped Latin, gesturing Valerius to translate.

Valerius did so, glowering, 'The procurator has no time to argue with you. The matter is decided. The king is dead. His estates belong now to Rome. We are to come to collect Rome's due.'

'No!' The queen's cold glare turned onto the tribune. 'One half. That was what the will said – one half.'

'All of it! Now!'

'And if I refuse?'

'You can't refuse.'

Boudicca drew herself up, her eyes green orbs of outrage in a face gone pale as death. 'Do you know who I am?'

'You're a foolish woman who should hold her tongue if she values her life,' Valerius said under his breath.

From the folds of her tunic she drew a knife. Its blade glittered in the early sunlight as she thrust upward with it. But Valerius was too quick. He twisted aside. His hand fastened on her wrist. One wrench and with a little cry of pain she dropped the dagger as her arm was forced up behind her. The two soldiers converged on her, laying hands on her.

Crying out in alarm, Rhiannon darted forward, and Araunah beside her. A soldier slung an arm about Araunah and lifted her off her feet. She struggled there, screaming, kicking. Rhiannon lunged for the face of one of the men holding her mother. He slapped her aside and other soldiers caught her, hitting her when she struggled. She saw her mother being forced toward the sacred oak, writhing furiously but helplessly at the centre of a group of men. Catus watched them, a smirk twisting his full red lips.

A high-pitched cry came from Morica. 'May the curse of Caridwen be on you! May your eyes burn in your heads! Your blood congeal, your entrails – ' She was stopped by a blow from the hilt of a sword that made her stagger and fall senseless.

Some of the other women were crying out in protest, but the weapons of the soldiers held them impotent. Araunah's screams had turned to coughing. The man who held her threw her aside and she sprawled to the ground, lying there, sobbing and choking.

Through eyes misted with fear and disbelief, Rhiannon saw men bring ropes and lash her mother's hands together. Boudicca fought them, but against so many not even the strongest warrior could have prevailed. They tossed the rope up over a thick branch of the tree and tied it so that Boudicca hung half suspended under the spread of tender young leaves.

'We must, I fear,' Catus said in a purring voice, using the Britonic language he employed only when necessity demanded, 'make an example of her.'

He glanced at Rhiannon, a slight cruel smile playing about his lips and crinkling the corners of his eyes. She felt sick, not only for what he was doing now but for her memories of what he had done to Farann. The man was a monster, vile and depraved. And Valerius was acting as his confederate in this outrage. His guilt was just as deep.

Knowing an appeal for mercy to be hopeless, she returned the procurator's glance with a cold stare. He would not hear a princess of the Iceni beg for favours.

Catus's smile deepened the dimple in his cheek, though it left his eyes iced. He gestured towards the queen, the merest flick of wrist, but enough to make one of his men step forward to where Boudicca dangled from the branch with only her toes reaching the ground. The man fastened his hand in the neck of her tunic and wrenched it, making her cry out in pain. He wrenched again, and again, until the fabric ripped. Another jerk and it fell free, leaving her bare to the waist. The man lifted her thick braid, pushing it over her shoulder to fall in front of her; then with a glance at Catus, who nodded slightly, he took a knife and cut the waist cord that bound her breeks. She hung there, naked, as a man stepped out with a whip curled in his hand.

'No.' The word choked out of Rhiannon, strangled with horror. 'No. Please. Don't, *don't!*' She screamed aloud as the whip cracked. A crimson line painted itself across the queen's white back. Boudicca moaned once. It was the only sound she made. Later they found that her tongue was bitten through.

Through eyes that felt dry – too dry to allow for tears – Rhiannon was obliged to watch as her mother was flogged without mercy, until shreds of bloody flesh flew from the whip and blood ran in red streams down her back, down her legs, and formed pools among the grass under the sacred oak. Long before Catus ordered them to stop, Boudicca had fainted. Rhiannon squirmed against the hands that held her, but they held too tightly, bruising her. She glanced up at the man closest to her and saw his eyes glazed, his mouth open as he watched the whipping of the naked queen. Many of the men were aroused by the sight. They had begun to look at the women with lecherous eyes.

A woman cried out in anguish and broke free of her group, darting away among the houses. The others had caught her panic. They turned and fled, with the soldiers after them. Some made only a few steps before hard hands seized them and threw them down, beating them and tearing at their clothes. Screams and pleas for mercy mingled with curses and coarse laughter.

'Will you allow this?' Rhiannon cried, looking to both the smirking procurator and to Valerius, who watched the scene with a face like stone. 'Are you men or monsters? Isn't it enough that – ?' The words broke off as Catus flicked his hand at her, as if brushing away a bothersome fly.

The men who held her laughed and swung her round, one on either side forcing her to stumble along between them, cuffing her when she pulled against them. She fought with all her strength, but still she was dragged into the queen's house and tossed to sprawl on the floor by the fire. The men were talking, apparently arguing about who should have her first. Rhiannon glanced about the house, seeking a weapon, and saw a cauldron chain dropped in a corner. She scrambled for it, grasped it and sprang up, facing her assailants.

They came at her either side of the fire. There was no escape. None. She swung the chain at the man on her left; the man on her right lunged and caught her round the waist. His weight sent her toppling. The chain was wrenched out of her hand. She fell against the curtain that guarded her room. Her hands gripped at it, tore it down. She fell with the man on top of her, groping at her, grasping her, tearing her clothes.

'Hold!' The order snapped from the doorway. Valerius stood there. He looked cold, haughty, evil. He spoke to the men, ordering them out, his tone of voice conveying his meaning to Rhiannon – that he wanted her for himself. When the men protested he reminded them brusquely that there were other women for them. He was their superior. The queen's daughter was *his* prize. He reinforced his claim by drawing his sword.

Clearly unconvinced of his right to deny them their pleasure, the two soldiers backed out of the queen's house, grumbling.

Rhiannon got to her feet, glaring hatred at the tribune. 'Here's the truth! Your tongue drips honey but your belly's hot with lust. It was words. Only words!'

He didn't answer at once. He seemed to be trying to control some fierce emotion and when he spoke his voice was hoarse and low. 'I spoke the truth!'

'Then let me go! Let me go to my mother!' She moved to dart by him but he swiftly barred her path and she backed away, fingernails ready, muscles poised to flee or to fight.

'You're safer here,' he said.

'Safe? With a man whose only thought is to use me for a moment's pleasure?'

'That's not so! I offered you marriage! It was you who scorned my protection. Will you take it now? Will you change your mind and come with me?'

Incredulous laughter shook out of her. 'With you? After what you've done to my mother?'

'She had to be taught a lesson, before her arrogance overcame her! The Emperor is not a fool to be tricked by a woman's cunning. In future she will remember that.'

'You stood by and watched them kill her! Monster! Monster!' She leapt for him, clawing at his face. He caught her wrists. Rhiannon spat full in his eye, screaming insults at him, hating him more murderously with every moment. She felt the fire of anger growing in him as she continued to strive against him. Her kicks and jabs hurt him, her words goaded him, but she rejoiced in the pain she was inflicting. 'Bastard Roman! Toad spawned in putrid mud! Procurator's puppy dog!' Seeing that gibe bite deep at his pride, she expanded the insult. 'You do his errands. Do you also rut with him, puppy dog? He likes young male flesh. Go out and grovel for him. Let *him* share in this day's rewards!'

His face contorted and a blow snapped her head to one side. She sagged in his grasp, dazed and gasping. 'He will have his reward,' he said through his teeth, his hands bruising her arms. 'I shall return your beloved, the Trinovante, to his tender mercies. How will that please you, lady?'

Rhiannon stared up at him, her anger turning to sick panic and fright. 'No . . .' She shook her head desperately. 'No. Please . . . Not Farann. Please! If you spare him, I . . . I'll go with you. I'll go willingly. Wherever you want. As your wife. As your mistress . . .'

'For him!!'

Jealousy and frustration exploded inside him. He threw her against the wall. The jolt jarred her whole body, splintered agony inside her head. Her legs sank under her and she slid to the ground, half fainting. Valerius knelt over her, teeth clenched as he tore at her clothes. Feebly, Rhiannon fought him, but her strength was ebbing while his seemed increased. Lust and anger drove him on. The air cool on her nakedness as he fell upon her, his hands brutal, his mouth hot and wet. He forced her thighs apart viciously, his body invading hers without pretence of gentleness.

She lay helpless under the onslaught, pride and dignity torn and scattered in pain and sick revulsion. Her mind went spinning, seeking escape from the insults he inflicted on her unresponsive body as he violated her. She felt herself to be an empty shell – a thing of no worth – a thing that he used to staunch his own feelings of anger and frustration.

'Barbarian bitch!' he grated into her face as he at last withdrew from her and stood up to straighten his clothing. 'You were no virgin! Who has had you? Farann of the Trinovantes? Then if you have no qualms about lying with slaves you should find no shame in being a whore for legionaries. Let's see who'll have you next.'

He was gone. Bruised and sick to her soul, Rhiannon dragged herself to her feet, holding onto one of the carved pillars. The fire was a mound of ashes, smoking fitfully, and from outside the sounds of screams had turned to muffled sobbing. She felt the sticky trickle of semen running down her thighs. Nausea retched at her stomach. Defiled by a lying Roman, when not many nights ago she, the Maiden, had lain with the God! Her own body disgusted her.

She would not be raped again, she told herself. Sooner she would die. She took the ceremonial sword down from the wall; it was heavy, but her arm was strong from years of practice at the reins and with spears. Since her own room's curtain was torn down, she retreated to the queen's private room. She sat in a corner wrapped in furs with her back against the cool wall. The sword's hilt fitted comfortingly to her hand and the deadly blade was hidden under the blanket that covered her. The next man who came she would kill.

She heard voices of men coming into the house – several men. But now they were not after women; they had turned their minds to booty. They searched the queen's house, looting it of everything of value – jewellery, furs, even the enamelled parade shields from the walls. When they came to the queen's room they ignored Rhiannon as they rooted through her mother's belongings, taking her chains and gold brooches and armlets. She sat and watched them, feeling cold and numb, waiting for the first move towards her person. Let one of them so much as touch her and he would die for it.

Perhaps they sensed her murderous thoughts. They left her alone.

Only when the men had gone did she realise that she had unwittingly prevented them from finding the royal treasure of the two great torcs, and the small store of gold that lay hidden in a pit beneath a board over which the queen's pallet was stretched. The men had been in too much of a hurry to search well. Perhaps the Goddess had distracted them.

At last the soldiers moved off, laden down with booty. As the sound of the horses died away into the distance, Rhiannon staggered to her feet and, with the sword heavy in her hand, walked stiffly out into bright morning sunlight. Bodies were sprawled everywhere, some beginning to stir and weep, a few who would never move again. Erefwen sat in the dirt, her clothes hanging from her, her pale eyes like knives of ice as she cursed all men with words that might once have made Rhiannon shudder.

Then she saw Cameira bending over the supine body of Araunah. Cameira's clothes were torn and she was weeping, but not for herself. As she looked up, Rhiannon saw the blood on her young sister's naked thighs. She too had been raped – a sick thirteen-year-old not yet come to puberty.

'Is she alive?' she asked.

Cameira nodded. 'Yes, but – '

'Take care of her.' She straightened herself, took a firmer hold on Craver's hilt and forced her legs to move towards the sacred oak where the body of her mother hung limp – limp, but not yet lifeless.

Morica was with the queen. The side of the priestess's face was swollen, her eyes half shut. She said, 'Help me, Rhiannon. She's still alive. Help me get her down.'

Other women came to help. They concentrated on tending the queen. They avoided each others' eyes, for their eyes were terrible.

They placed Boudicca face down on her pallet. Her back was shredded, the flesh torn and crusted with dried blood. Morica tended her, bathing her with warm water and herbs, muttering prayers mingled with curses. Knowing that her mother was in the best hands, Rhiannon did what she could to help others.

Araunah had been brought in. Cameira was looking after her. The girl was quiet now, gone beyond tears and even beyond coughing into a netherworld where no sound seemed to reach her. But she wasn't asleep; her eyes were open, staring inward onto horror.

Outside, women stumbled about in shock. They had all been raped or beaten. Some of their children had been taken – dragged off into slavery. A few men were left, most of them wounded and dazed. Every house had been looted, pottery and glassware broken, buckets and cooking utensils spilled out of doors, looms overturned, belongings scattered. As she walked among the devastation Rhiannon saw the old horse-master Nemmon kneeling over the body of his son and weeping aloud. Vranaun lay sprawled on his back with flies eagerly buzzing around the gaping wound in his chest. She stopped to stare at him, unable to believe that he could be dead. Wise, steady Vranaun . . . his children would grieve bitterly for him – Adalma, and eager Teyrnon.

'Lady! Oh, lady Rhia, please . . .' The voice, hoarse with weeping, called to Rhiannon from the doorway of a house where she saw a young slave girl beckoning. The girl's clothes were torn and thick with dust, as was her tumbled hair, and her mouth bled where her lips had broken against her teeth.

Inside the house, amid a scatter of cooking utensils and ashes, Adalma was in labour. She had crawled across the floor leaving a trail of blood. She clung now to one of the posts, her cheek against the wood. Blood pulsed from between her legs in terrifying spasms and her eyes were sunk in shadows that gave her face the appearance of a mask, death-pale and tinged with blue. Her pallid lips stretched in a faint smile of welcome and her hand groped out as Rhiannon fell to her knees beside her.

'Save my baby,' Adalma breathed. 'Save my baby, Rhiannon. For Garanhir's sake. Please . . .'

Rhiannon glanced at the slave. 'Get Morica. She's with the queen. Tell her the most urgent need is here. Run, girl! Run for your life!'

She had never felt so helpless as during the time she sat by Adalma, holding her hand, smoothing tumbled brown hair from a face cold with sweat. She wanted to talk, but no words seemed adequate. Why ask what had happened when she knew all too well – Adalma too had been raped, and probably by more than one man. No, not men – filthy, worse-than-animals who cared nothing for the woman they had abused and even less for the precious child she carried. It seemed to Rhiannon that she herself had been lucky; Valerius had saved her from the worst excesses that his men had inflicted on others. But she would gladly have endured all that Adalma had endured if it would have saved her friend. She stroked the cold soft hand, murmuring words of comfort that both she and Adalma knew were lies, but Adalma smiled, her brown eyes soft with sympathy as if she pitied Rhiannon the distress she was suffering.

After endless ages, Erefwen came. But she took one look at the blood that still pumped from Adalma and the bleak light in her eyes told Rhiannon there was no hope.

'Save the baby,' Adalma said faintly. 'Just save . . .' Her hand twitched in Rhiannon's. She gave a little sigh.

'The child,' Rhiannon whispered through strangling tears.

Erefwen knelt by Adalma, a hand on her mounded belly. She felt the shape of the child, bent and listened with one ear. At length she straightened and covered Adalma's nakedness. 'It's dead,' she said coldly. 'So perish any Roman-gotten bastard in *my* womb. Come, Maiden. The Goddess will welcome Her own. We must tend the living.'

Erefwen went out, but Rhiannon sat for a while beside her friend, holding the still, cold hand, rocking back and forth as tears came seeping from deep inside her and drew forth racking sobs that shook her being. She fought with her grief, but soon it overwhelmed her and she got to her feet, tearing at her hair and clothes. Tears poured down her face as she ran out under the bright spring sky and stood raging up at the heavens.

'Laugh, Caridwen! Cackle, Old Hag! Here's more chaff to fly from your winnowing basket. More souls to gobble and crunch. Laugh, Old White One! But tell me why! Why?! I have been a faithful Maiden! Why have You allowed this to happen?'

A dull panic seized her as she heard the thud of hooves. Were the Romans coming back? But as the horsemen burst into sight, some of them already leaping from their mounts, through her drowning eyes she saw that they were Iceni – all the men who had been away in the forests hunting. Someone had got word to them, though they came too late.

They let their horses trot loose as they ran about the village asking questions, seeking their own loved ones. Farann arrived, sawing at his reins as he saw Rhiannon. The horse reared, but he leapt lithely down and thrust the pony aside as he stared at her with a mixture of horror, relief and apprehension.

'Rhiannon? Are you hurt? Rhiannon . . .'

Her sight seemed to dim through a scarlet haze. She recalled the sacred island, the sweet passion she had known there – but with what man? The memory was mixed up with the horror of that morning, with Valerius grinding his body into hers. She threw up her hands as Farann ran towards her and he stopped, his agonised glance fixed on her white face and flaring eyes.

'Don't come near me,' she whispered. 'Don't touch me!'

She saw the surprise and disbelief in Farann's face. She saw the hurt in him, but at that moment she felt nothing. She was locked behind gates of ice, a prisoner of shock and sick terror.

Garanhir came running, saying, 'Adalma? Where's Adalma?'

Someone directed him to the house where his young wife lay.

Ylas and Matuac rode up, both of them halting as they saw Rhiannon standing there. Her torn clothes, her bruised face and dirty blood-smeared hands, allied with what they read in her eyes, made them hesitate.

'Where's Cameira?' Ylas asked.

'And mother!' said Matuac.

Behind her, Rhiannon heard Garanhir's voice raised in a great roar of grief and pain. He walked stiffly out under the sun, carrying the bloody body of his wife in his arms. Tears glittered on his face.

'She was so young,' he said hoarsely. 'So young and so gentle. And the child . . . Why, Rhiannon? Explain this, Maiden. Why did the Goddess allow this?'

Rhiannon shook her head. 'I know nothing. Nothing. The ways of the Gods . . . I know nothing.'

Something in her manner made his look sharpen as if he saw her clearly for the first time. Shock hit him and he swayed as he stood, saying almost inaudibly, 'The queen! Is she – '

'She lives,' Rhiannon said. 'They whipped her until her blood became a libation to the earth. But my mother is strong. She lives, Garanhir. And now . . .' A fierce emotion filled her as she lifted her fist to the sky and felt herself transformed by a Godlike fury and wish for vengeance. In a voice that stilled all movement around her, she cried aloud: *'Hear me, Caridwen! Dread Spinner of Fates . . . Now shall Bloody Andastre wind the horn that cries war! Now . . . now has Boudicca found her cause!'*

Five

Pain was Boudicca's constant companion. She drifted in and out of consciousness, lying face down on her pallet, feeling cooling hands and unguents tend her lacerated back. Sometimes she was alert enough to understand the voices around her; the things they said showed her the full picture of what had happened. Semi-conscious, she swam in dreams where she talked with the shade of her husband – ah, Prasutagus, can you see what your allies the Romans have done? What say you now, old man? Your wife whipped near to death, her daughters raped, your people abused, slain, their children taken to slavery, your royal village looted . . .

When she woke she felt calm, and clear of mind. Her anger was no longer hot but ice-cold, gone so deep it was rooted now at the core of her existence. She knew it would remain with her for the rest of her life. This was no light insult to be avenged in a moment's loss of temper. The War of Boudicca's Vengeance would require cunning, strategy, and much cool, concentrated thought. When the rising began, its impetus must be enough to destroy everything that stood against it. This time, there could be no end but total victory.

Rhiannon concentrated on nursing her mother and sister, shunning the society of men. By her orders, female warriors now guarded the queen's house and men were excluded – the only exception being Eogan, who spent long hours in private talks with Boudicca. When Farann came Rhiannon refused to see him. Even Coeling and his twin warrior sons were made to sleep in the great hall with the others.

'The fault did not come from our own menfolk,' Boudicca

said one day as Rhiannon bathed her back. 'Blame the Romans, daughter – not the men we shall need to ride beside us to war. Not Farann.'

Rhiannon made no reply. She preferred not to think of it, not to face it. Not yet.

'I intend him as your husband,' the queen said, and felt the bathing hands pause in their work, betraying Rhiannon's emotion. 'He's a fine warrior, of fine stock. The council will gladly accept him as high chief. This will ride with your own choice, daughter, as once I promised.'

The silence seemed to last for a long time before Rhiannon said, speaking with difficulty as though near to tears, 'Perhaps.'

'Perhaps?' Awkwardly, Boudicca turned her head so that she could see her daughter kneeling beside her. She winced as a spasm of pain shot down her back. 'Rhiannon, this outrage makes no difference! The son of Vindorex is for you, you for him. I've planned it for a long time. Eogan has read the signs – the match augurs well for the Iceni. Why do you think we made Farann your champion? It was ordained by the Gods. From the first time I saw the boy, I knew his fate was bound up with ours. It's fitting you should marry him. Iceni and Trinovante have long been in alliance. Let us make it permanent.'

Gently, Rhiannon laid a hand on her mother's shoulder. 'Lie down. Lie still. You'll open your wounds again.' She went on cleaning the dreadful lacerations, her mind elsewhere. How could she think of marrying Farann? How could she think of marrying anyone when the very thought of being touched by a man, in any way, made her feel sick with revulsion?

Parties of furious warriors came from every hillfort across Icenia: all had the same story to tell – soldiers had come in over-whelming numbers and taken by force all the valuables they could carry, claiming them as the Emperor's share now that Prasutagus was dead. The chiefs were outraged by the treatment they had received at Roman hands, though it seemed that nowhere had there been quite such carnage and rapine as at Oakhillfort.

Boudicca herself tried to attend the council, but the pain

from her back was too great and when she moved fresh blood stained her bindings. She refused to let her chiefs see her carried into hall face-down on a pallet. Instead she sent Rhiannon, her daughter and heir, with Eogan the Druid to stand by her side.

Rhiannon sat on her mother's carved and cushioned stool, feeling no emotion as she listened to the argument rage. She was aware of Farann among the throng, but she did not acknowledge him. Today she was her mother's surrogate. She knew what was in the queen's mind and that of the Druid; she hoped she could play her part adequately in persuading the chiefs of the wisdom of the plan, but for herself she cared little. Since the day of the Roman assault, her soul had felt dead inside her.

From all sides voices demanded answers. What did the queen intend to do? Were the Iceni to stand helpless and let their lands be looted, their women abused, their warriors turned into slaves of Rome?

'The queen promised us war!' Audagas shouted. 'War to drive out the Romans!'

'We go to war!' The cry from Eogan put an end to argument and brought an answering roar of approval. The Druid lifted his arms for silence. 'But not yet! Not yet!'

'Why not?' a voice demanded. 'We're ready to ride now!'

'Aye!' shouted others. 'Why wait? We go now!'

'Hold!' Eogan thundered, and gradually the noise subsided again to mutters. 'This is no skirmish to recover a few cows!' the Druid cried. 'This must be a war to ring down the ages – a war to be sung by bards from Mona to the Great Bay, from Dumnonia to the lands of the Caledones – a war when Albina shall cast off her virgin cloak and rise gowned in crimson as Bloody Andastre.'

'When?' Audagas demanded. 'Tell us when!'

'With the spring!'

This pronouncement brought a brief shocked silence, then a great outcry arose as voices began to protest that it was too long a time to wait. Nine or ten moons? What did the Druid take them for – cowards and fools? Argument arose from all sides until the sound beat up against the thatch in deafening waves.

Now Eogan again spoke up with all his powers of voice

and reason. He strode about the hall making strong gestures with his beringed hands and arms, the animal tails on his wolfskin cloak whirling out when he turned. Under the penetrating glare from his pale eyes the protesters fell silent.

'The Romans struck at our queen and her women,' the Druid said. 'They intended to subdue her to their will by fear – and through her to make cowards of you all. Then let our foe believe he has succeeded in his purpose. Let him send his spies and find us meekly obedient, working to feed and clothe our children, and to gather our harvest. But cold winter winds will drive these Romans back to their firesides. When Samhain is past, they will come no more to our lands. Then in secrecy we may prepare our vengeance.'

Mutters and then growing shouts broke out from scowling men who still had doubts. They were angry *now;* they wanted vengeance *now*.

Stepping out, Rhiannon lifted her head and unflinchingly faced the eyes that were suddenly fixed on her, the Maiden. Her clear voice rang out sweetly as a blackbird among crows: 'Let us not act in haste. The Great Year is with us. The rites must be observed. Let us woo the Great Goddess and seek Her aid, that She lend us the might of Her anger when we march. The Romans are strong. To win victory, we must prepare. We must prepare with great care.'

As she finished speaking, a silence began, starting from the door and spreading outward. Noting it, Rhiannon saw her mother walking stiffly in, her face pale, her eyes sunken in blue hollows, every step bringing her agony; but her head was high, her eyes fiery with challenge. Around her neck she bore the weight of the great electrum torc of Icenia.

With her came Tadia and Morica, both watchful and anxious, and some women of the guard. Then out from the crowd stepped Nuadat to walk by the queen. Garanhir moved to join her, too, his gaze fixed on her face to drink in his first sight of her since the Roman attack. Their eyes met, briefly, exchanging what messages Rhiannon could only guess, and then her mother came on, pride overcoming pain, sweat beading her upper lip. Not an eye in the hall could help but admire her courage, not a heart failed to swell in rage against the Romans.

Rhiannon stood up, though she guessed her mother would

not take the seat of honour: Boudicca could barely walk upright, let alone sit and stretch the broken flesh of her back and buttocks. The queen exchanged a wry look with her daughter, then as she turned to face her people her aspect changed; she donned the aura of regal authority as a veil for her pain, and lifted her hands until every last sound in the hall was stilled.

Then she spoke, strongly and clearly. 'I understand your rage. I welcome it. It is the good rage of worthy warriors. But it is the rage of men – the rage of my father Antedios, and of my brother Mocuxsoris – a rage swift to rise and swift to vent itself in action – swift to seek death . . . But those who are dead cannot savour their victory!' She paused, looking around the hall, and when she spoke again her voice was low and charged with a rising passion.

'Learn now the more deadly rage of a woman. Women are weaker in body, you say – yes, that's true. And because of it we are slower to rise, slower brought to violence. But when need drives . . . then beware! For a woman's rage is deeper, and colder, and stronger, and longer to endure. It does not explode in heated blood. It lies quietly brewing, and it thinks – with brain, not belly. It plots, it schemes. It examines every path, in order to sweeten the taste of vengeance when at last the time is right and we *strike!*'

On the word, everyone in the hall gasped. A glitter flew from the queen's hand and embedded itself in a wooden pillar, where it was seen to be a knife whose hilt glinted with gold and green enamel.

Even Rhiannon's heart thudded with startlement, but she moved closer to her mother. The effort of throwing the knife had brought out beads of sweat on the queen's brow and tinged her skin with the livid pallor of physical agony. She brought her arm down very carefully, her teeth set against the pain. Her strength was almost done.

'And how shall we wage this war?' Lanaccion demanded. 'Our spears against their swords? Our puny slings and stones against Thracian arrows? If we had our swords we might sing a different song.'

'The queen has promised that there will be swords!' Audagas cried. 'Lady, my palm itches for the feel of an iron hilt again! Where are those swords? Where?'

With a flourish, Eogan stepped out from behind the queen, whipping from under his cloak a great broadsword, honed to an edge that might cleave an enemy's head from his shoulders before he could blink. The shimmering blade caught the slant of torchlight and made every man in the hall hold his breath. Suddenly, every eye was fixed on that sword, and nearly every heart beating with renewed hope.

'Here is a sample,' Eogan said. 'Behold him. Blood Craver. Forged in fire. Tempered in blood. Honed in stone and spark.' He turned and knelt, offering the sword's hilt to the queen. 'Take it, lady – Boudicca, queen and high chief. Take the Craver, first of his breed. Where he leads shall his bond-brothers follow.'

Despite her pallor, Boudicca took the sword and held it out before her. She was tall and fine with the great electrum torc of Icenia about her throat and her hair a bronze waterfall behind her. Chiefs and warriors rose to their feet, lifting their fists in salute – to the queen and to the sword in her hand – a sword that held the promise of honour restored. Pieces of chaff drifted down, shaken loose from the thatch by the force of that great cry of acclamation.

'Boudicca! Boudicca! Boudicca!'

The chiefs and their warriors departed, to train more fiercely now that they had a real goal ahead. Though they had cried against the delay, the arguments of queen and Druid had convinced them that the time could be well spent. At Oak-hillfort, too, the warriors returned with fresh vigour to chariot and spear – and to wielding the great swords that Eogan now produced after journeys into the forests.

But Boudicca still lay prone on her pallet, tended by her older daughter. Her appearance at the council had served to open up her wounds afresh, but she counted the pain well worth the result: she had helped to sway her chiefs to her will.

Hearing a disturbance in the house – anxious whisperings of women, and the deeper note of a man's voice – Rhiannon swept out from her mother's room to confront her guards, who were having no success in persuading Ylas that he must leave. He stood with a stubborn set to his face, a shaft of sunlight through the roof opening high overhead slanting down to gild his fair hair and the long ends of his moustache.

'All men are forbidden this house,' Rhiannon said.

'By whose order?' Ylas demanded. 'This is the queen's house, lady, not yours – not yet. Does the queen forbid me to come inside?'

'The queen's not strong enough to decide. Ylas . . . what do you want?'

'To speak with you.' His glance swung around the women in the hall. 'Alone for preference, but if you force me I'll speak out in front of these. Unless you'll come outside and walk with me.'

Rhiannon's eyes sparked, but she saw he meant what he said. After a moment she gestured to her guards. 'Leave us. But don't go far.'

While the women set aside the work they were engaged in, Ylas regarded Rhiannon with a bright, critical gleam, and as the last warrior ducked out by the door he said, 'Why are you afraid to go outside? Do you think Farann might accost you there? Lady, you should know him better.'

'Is this what he sent you to say?' she asked.

'He did not send me!' He took a stride towards her and she blanched and backed away. Ylas stopped, a swift frown of concern furrowing his brow. 'Rhiannon . . . it's me. Ylas. I'll not hurt you.'

As he moved, so the gold torc about his throat shifted. She had a glimpse of a thin red mark trailing across his skin, where a superficial cut had recently healed. It looked to be much longer than the cut she remembered making on the man she had met on the island, but perhaps her memory was playing her false in that, too.

Seeing where her eyes and her thoughts rested, Ylas touched his fingers to that scar. 'I remember nothing,' he said quietly. 'It's all dark mists. What about you?'

'For me too. A dream. All misted.'

'I know I did wrong to take Matuac's place.' His face betrayed nothing. His eyes were steady on hers. 'But I too was Green King – and I too have loved you all my life.'

She stared at him dumbly. She had never guessed at feelings he had hidden well.

He shrugged. 'I did what I did. It's done. This is another

day. Rhiannon . . . I'm come to plead for a friend of both of us – a man we both know is too stubborn to plead for himself. How long do you expect him to wait? You know his pride. He's waited too long already. He's been patient, out of respect for your duty to the Gods. But now that's over. Yet still you refuse to see him. Your women send him away.'

'So he sent you to beg for him?'

With a little sorrowful smile he shook his head. 'Not he. The idea was all mine. But I can read his thoughts. His pain troubles me. He begins to believe you have rejected him. He's been told the identity of the Roman who violated you. He broods over it alone and in silence. Now I hear that he talks of going to Camulodunon with murder in his heart, of seeking Valerius out and – '

'No!' The thought made her head spin with terror.

'Yes, Rhiannon! And he'll do it, unless you give him reasons to stay. Please. Meet with him. Talk to him. Tonight the new moon will shine. And at the next moon . . . at the next moon it will be midsummer. Do this for me.'

Rhiannon scanned his face, trying to make sense of the turn of his thoughts. Midsummer, yes, when the Great Year rites would be held at the *nemeton* on the cliff. But to Ylas it meant more than that: mentioning the festival, his voice had dropped to a whisper. '*He* must die,' came the echo of her mother's voice. 'He, not you.' But she shook the thought away. Her mother had been speaking symbolically.

'Farann must not go to Camulodunon,' she said. 'Valerius knows who he is. He swore he would give Farann back to The Pig. He mustn't go, Ylas!'

'Then you convince him of it,' Ylas said.

That night she met with Farann alone for the first time since Beltane. She waited for him up on the inner bank, a cloak wrapped round her for comfort and protection even though the night was warm. But Farann seemed to understand her reluctance to let him near her. He kept his distance and they spoke in low voices.

'You must not go seeking Valerius!' she said. 'To walk into such danger would be foolhardy. He knows you. He may be watching for you.'

'Am I to let him go free after what he's done?'

'There'll be a time for vengeance, Farann. But not alone. Not at such risk for yourself. Wait now. Wait and ride with us to war.'

'Wait again?' came the murmur. 'Always must I wait for you! For how much longer?'

'I don't know! Nothing is clear to me any more. I've lost my way, somehow. The Goddess turns her back on me. Perhaps I've angered Her. On the sacred isle . . .' Her head felt so tight it wanted to burst and it seemed that words broke from her lips of their own need rather than hers. 'On the sacred isle I saw no man but you. There was no Ylas – not even the God – only you, Farann. Perhaps for that the Goddess is punishing me. Perhaps my love for you is so strong that it overcomes my loyalty to Her. For me She is Caridwen – Caridwen the Unforgiving.'

'No, Rhiannon!' He could not hold back. He swept her into his arms, felt her stiffen but not otherwise resist him. He held her tight against him, on fire with a fierce need to protect her. A longing was on him to tell her the truth – to confess that he had been the man – but such was her state of mind that he feared what the truth might do. Rhiannon's belief was much stronger than his: he had been raised in Rome, amid a conflict of Gods that had left him cynical; she had been trained from birth to faith and obedience. If she knew he had interfered with the most sacred Mysteries she might never forgive him.

After one brief moment she pulled free, lifting her head to stare up at him, her eyes wide as bruises in a face whitened by starlight. 'There is no hope for us! The Goddess has no mercy. How can I come to you with Roman filth upon me? Perhaps with a Roman child inside me! I can never come to you, Farann. Never!'

Sobbing, she turned and fled from him. He let her go, his thoughts turned black with shame and self-disgust. He had mocked the Gods. Now They were exacting Their price. 'You will never have the Maiden,' Erefwen had said. It seemed to him now that she had spoken truth. Rhiannon was lost to him.

As the thought came he drew himself up and his resolve hardened. His presence here brought danger to his friends; since he had rashly – out of stubborn pride – revealed his identity to Valerius, soldiers would return sooner or later, looking for him. Honour demanded that he leave Icenia. If Rhiannon was denied him, another purpose waited: he was still a warrior, a prince of the Trinovantes, Vindorex's only son. Too long he had lurked in cowardly shadows. Now he would claim his true heritage. Now, at last, he was free to heed the call of destiny.

Only a few days later, Boudicca began to miss the company of her kinsmen and the male warriors, and of Alvran the bard. The women sang sweetly enough but the queen had a taste for songs that related the true tale of the history and valorous deeds of the Iceni. She rested now by the fire, still lying on her stomach, propped up on a mounded bed of straw covered in one of the few furs the Romans had not taken, and with a cloak laid gently over her.

So the men of the guard returned to stand their turn at watch; the two champions sat again by the fire to sup, with Coeling and his sons and some of the women. Eogan did not come – he was off about some errand elsewhere – and Farann too was absent. Rhiannon noticed it at once, but it was some time before the queen lifted herself on an elbow and said: 'Where is the son of Vindorex, the Maiden's champion?'

No eye would meet hers. Rhiannon guessed that Farann's stubborn pride had kept him away and the others were afraid to tell the queen the reason for it. Then she saw her mother's face and knew that the queen already suspected the rift between them – Rhiannon's moods and silences, allied with the women's gossip, had been eloquent.

'Is he on watch?' the queen asked.

The men glanced at each other, hiding some secret among them. It was Matuac who eventually burst out, 'He's gone, lady.'

Rhiannon's heart clutched with fear inside her.

'Gone where?' the queen asked sharply.

Garanhir answered, 'He said that his presence here endangered you, lady. The procurator will be seeking him. Honour demanded that Farann should leave.'

Honour, Boudicca thought; Garanhir would understand such a reason, of course. 'Did he leave no hint of where he was going?' she asked.

Again there was a stubborn silence, and again it was Matuac who broke it, saying, 'He's gone on a mission for Eogan.'

Catching her breath, Rhiannon whispered, 'To Camulodunon?'

'No!' Swiftly, Ylas stilled that fear, though the truth was no less hard to hear: 'He's gone to his own people – to the Trinovantes at Caesaromagus, where Baro is the chief. He's gone to persuade them to be ready to rise with us.'

'But if I know him,' Matuac added with a dark glance at Rhiannon, 'he'll also find some reason to get to Camulodunon. He has hopes of finding Cunovinda, and also that dog Valerius Rufinus. And if he doesn't kill that Roman then I shall, one of these days.'

Rhiannon stared at the fire, seeing its brightness dazzle behind a mist that dimmed her eyes. The mission Farann had undertaken would have been a dangerous one for any man, but for the son of Vindorex it was almost certain death.

As Eogan had foreseen, Roman spies kept watch over Icenia. Troops of soldiers patrolled, harrying farmers and peasants, demanding tribute from travellers. Centurions behaved like great lords, taking whatever they wanted. Once or twice a warrior reacted with anger, but each time the retaliation was brutally put down. For the most part, the Iceni remembered that their time of vengeance would come. The queen had been right: the waiting added savour to the anticipation of eventual victory over these arrogant foreigners.

The nights progressed towards midsummer and the Great Year festival. Rhiannon felt restless: she missed Farann and she was conscious of a weight of dread lying on her heart as she wondered what the Solstice would bring. Deep inside her, she sensed that the Gods might demand a special sacrifice, but she refused to believe what logic told her. She assured herself that the heavy cloud that hung about her was caused by her fear for Farann, and by the fact that she was with child.

Though Boudicca was far from fit, she insisted on attending the rite on the clifftop. She rode there, bravely hiding her physical torment, astride the mare Starbright, at the head of a long column of men and women riding or striding along the Way to the gathering at the *nemeton*.

As she kept vigil with the other women, under the pale sickle of the virgin moon, Rhiannon felt the vibrations in the air. Her skin ran with sweat, but she felt cold. The Gods were neither cruel nor kind; they were simply indifferent. They demanded obedience. That was all. But in return what did they offer? Not happiness. Not personal reward. Only a continuing of life bound round with the rhythm of the seasons and the circle of sun and moon.

So the God must die, as the sun must wane, as the harvest must be culled – so that a sleep might ensue, a rest refresh Him, and He might rise again, in the sky and in the fields, with the spring. It had always been so. The God must die – in the shape of a lusty male animal – a bull, a stag, a stallion . . .

With the dawn, the men returned from their sacred grove, with Eogan wearing the bloody head and skin of a sacrificial stallion, and on the clifftop the twins Ylas and Matuac, dressed only in twining branches of oak, knelt to kindle the need fire.

Rhiannon found no joy in the day. The usual contests were held, meat roasted over cooking fires, ale poured foaming from jugs into horn mugs. But Farann was not there, and Ylas . . . Ylas was merry with an elation that she suspected came from some potion mixed by Eogan and Morica. He was sole Green King now, lord of the feast; he bore the Maiden's mark about his throat. His laugh was too loud, his exuberance more like Matuac than Ylas. When he danced about the fires he breathed deep of the acrid smoke issuing from branches of green oak until the scent crazed him.

He came running to Rhiannon, to grab her hands and dance her away, whirling her until she was dizzy. As her head cleared she found herself in a hollow rimmed with hazel bushes. Ylas panted beside her, sweat dripping down his scarred body, his face reddened by exertion. But in that face his eyes were intense as he took her chin between his hands. The drug had had little effect on him. Underneath his mantle of gaiety he was perfectly cognisant of what was to come.

'Just once before I die, Rhiannon,' he said, and bent to kiss her lustily. 'Remember me.'

'Don't say that!' she gasped. 'It can't be so, Ylas! The Green King survives. The sacrifice is only symbolic!'

'No,' He stilled her protests with his fingers over her lips. 'Not in the Great Year. But I'm content. I understand why it has to be. And I'll come back – this service to the Gods is rewarded with rebirth.' His grin beamed out with wry humour. 'I'll persuade them to let me return as a hero – a great warrior chief. So don't mourn for me. But remember me sometimes.'

'It can't be so!' she breathed.

'But it is.' Smiling, he glanced down the length of her body and back to her face, saying, 'Will there be a child?'

She nodded, clearing a knot of distress from her throat. 'Yes.'

'A girlchild for Dia,' he smiled. 'Isn't that what Morica says?'

'Or a bastard for Rome,' Rhiannon choked.

'No. No.' He smiled again, but the smile failed to reach the depths of his eyes where she read the sorrow in him – sorrow but not fear; he went to his doom unafraid. 'I foretell it now – I, Ylas, Green King of the Great Year, soon to be a rider on the wings of the north wind . . . I prophesy . . . a child of love.'

She searched his face, wishing she knew the truth. Suddenly this fair kinsman of hers seemed very dear to her.

'Farann's child.' Ylas spoke the words very low but they hit her like a blow from a cudgel, robbing her of breath and speech.

She shook her head wildly. 'No . . . No!'

'Believe it, Rhiannon,' he said softly. 'It was Farann you met. Farann . . . who loves you, as you love him.'

'But the mark . . .' She touched the thin scar at his throat, knowing now that she had not made so long a cut. Her memories of that night were true, not illusion.

He grimaced, smiling. 'I gave it to myself. You hardly touched Farann. Your tender heart must have quailed at hurting him. Don't blame him for it. When love is the reinsman, a man goes where he is driven. I helped him, I chose to stay in Matuac's place. I don't believe it matters to the Gods; they don't care who pays the price, so long as They have Their portion of our joy and sorrow. And Farann doesn't know the meaning of the Maiden's mark. Neither does Matuac, I never told him what I knew.'

Her fear returned, she clutched at him, saying, 'It's only a reminder – another symbol. Of the time the Goddess was angry and slew Him, taking His head . . .' The expression of gentle pity in his eyes terrified her. 'It can't mean death, Ylas! Elsewise, how is Garanhir still walking alive?'

'Garanhir?'

'He was the man for my mother. I sprang from his seed.'

'It was not Garanhir,' Ylas said.

The conviction in his voice and his eyes seemed to freeze her brain. Had she misunderstood? Had she believed a falsehood all this time?

'I was only a boy, but I remember the man clearly,' Ylas said. 'I liked him. Huan was his name; a stranger among us – a prince – Huan of the Caledones. I remember noticing that he had the cut round his throat. He laughed about it and made some joke. Then he didn't come back after Solstice, and the queen seemed sad. And then . . .' As he hesitated his eyes became unfocused, looking inward onto dark memory and darker anticipation. 'I saw the ceremony at the pool below the grove. I hid among the trees and I watched. It was Huan's head; I knew it by his long hair. They gave it as an offering to the sacred pool. Rhiannon . . .' He saw her again and now his fingers kneaded her shoulders with fond urgency. 'I go gladly, believe it. But it will be hard for Matuac. He hasn't let himself understand yet. When it's over . . . he'll need your help. If nothing else, do this for me – be kind to Matuac.'

Before she could find an answer or ask any of the questions that whirled in her head, several of the young men, led by Matuac, pounced into the hollow to drag the Green King back to the revels, to take him singing down to the beach to purify himself in the sea.

They returned chanting and stamping in rhythm to the throb of drums as the sun was sending golden light to drench the underside of clouds and from the east the shadow of night crept on. The young men carried the Green King over their heads, bound now in green branches that turned him into a bundle. They were laughing, most of them drunk, none of them questioning the rightness of what was about to happen. Ylas's fair head hung down between their arms as they approached the fires where Eogan waited.

As she stamped in the slow rhythms of the maze dance, Rhiannon found her mother beside her.

'It must be,' Boudicca said, low-voiced. 'As has been, as is now, as shall be again; that the seasons may turn. A life – and in return, a child to be the new hope of the tribe; as I bore you, to be Maiden.'

Sick as she felt, Rhiannon couldn't tear her eyes away from Ylas. He seemed to be smiling even as the knife flashed down.

She squeezed her eyes shut and heard the cry that went up from many throats as Ylas died in a fountain of blood. She turned away, breaking from the line of dancers, stumbling blindly to a place where she could be alone. Her stomach churned and erupted, wrenching her whole body as its contents spewed out in the grass. Her brow felt clammy with sweat; she shook uncontrollably.

Hands came on her and she found her mother beside her, with Erefwen and Morica. And from somewhere behind them the voice of Eogan was lifted in the ritual cry:

'Thus dies the God, to be born again; that the seasons may turn, the earth be fecund, the people faithful. Thus He dies, to ensure continuance until the next Great Year – and to bring us victory over our enemies. Caridwen take Him, Arianrhod guard Him, Latona give Him rebirth.'

White clouds descended on Rhiannon; as she sank into them the hoofbeats of Epona drummed in her ears and through the mist she saw the toss of a brilliant white mane. The Mare reared, and now on Her back was a rider, all clad in shining white with the evening star on his brow – and it was Ylas, waving to her, his grin bright and merry. The Goddess Herself had come to carry him away. Slipping into oblivion, Rhiannon was comforted by that assurance. The Gods, too can be faithful: all is well, all is well.

Six

As the Iceni rode home to the noise and bustle of the midsummer markets at Oakhillfort, Rhiannon stayed a little apart. Her stomach still felt unsettled – perhaps because of the child she was carrying – and her thoughts were unhappy companions. Ylas was gone. Only now did she realise how much she had cherished his friendship. Others too were grieving: Tadia and Coeling rode side by side for mutual comfort, and somewhere Cameira was walking with Unthaus, her hand fast in his as they led their horses. The last Rhiannon had seen of Matuac, the previous night, he had been sitting alone seemingly intent on drinking the contents of an entire skin of wine.

Even as she thought of him, she found Matuac beside her. Dark circles showed under eyes still swollen and bloodshot. He was subdued, riding in silent misery, not even looking at her.

Pity welled up inside her and she reached to lay a hand on his arm. 'Don't grieve, Matuac,' she said, her voice husky with sorrow. 'He went gladly.'

'I know.' He slid a look at her but snatched it away at once as if he couldn't bear the look in her eyes. 'But it should have been me. *That's* why he changed places with me. Because he knew. He died for me. And now . . .' A tear trickled down his cheek into his thick fair moustache. He didn't even try to hide it or wipe it away. 'Now I feel like half a man. I miss him – as if I'd lost my sword arm. He's always been there beside me. Ylas and Matuac. Matuac and Ylas. Now there's only Matuac, I don't know what I shall do.'

'You'll live – to honour his memory.'

'Yes.' He took a breath and when he spoke again his voice was hard. 'And when we ride to war I'll fight for him! Two swords in my hand! Two enemies falling with every blow! If his life isn't enough for the Gods They might as well have mine too! It's useless to me.'

'Don't say that,' Rhiannon pleaded. 'No life is useless. The queen needs you – your strength, your loyalty. And . . . I need you, too, Matuac. I have always needed you as a kinsman and a friend.'

'Yes,' He sighed, and fell silent, his head sunk on his breast in gloomy thought.

Rhiannon glanced at the people ahead. Her mother rode uneasily because of her lacerated back, but only an occasional shift of her seat showed how the lashing still pained her as she bestrode the white Egyptian mare. Eogan rode beside her, and under his cloak he bore a bundle wrapped in linen. Rhiannon had seen him secrete it there as he mounted; she might not have guessed what it was had she not remembered Ylas's words about the head of Huan. Now the Druid was carrying another head, to offer at another secret ceremony at the pool below the oak grove on the knoll.

The thought made nausea rise in her throat. She was beginning to wonder if the Romans were right – if her people were in truth barbarians. Did the Gods really want human blood to flow in Their honour?

'Matuac . . .' she ventured. 'Who was Huan?'

He seemed not to have heard but eventually he lifted his heavy head to blink at her. 'Huan?'

'Huan of the Caledones.'

He thought about it, frowning against the day's brightness. 'It means nothing to me. Why do you ask?'

'Ylas mentioned him. He said Huan was the last Green King – in the last Great Year.'

'That's nineteen summers ago. We were only . . . five, six . . . I don't remember it. Children are kept away. Nobody tells them what . . .' His fist slammed against his thigh; his face was contorted in sorrow and futile anger. 'But Ylas knew, didn't he? If I'd known I'd have made Eogan take me instead! It should have been me. It was me the Gods chose.'

'But it was Ylas they took! It's done, Matuac. Who knows why? The ways of the Gods are a riddle to us. We must be faithful. We must only obey.' Farann did not obey, she thought with a sharp pang that she thrust aside at once. 'Ylas went willingly. He was smiling as he rode away. Epona carried him. I saw them, galloping away into the sunset, toward the Glass Castle.'

He stared at her narrowly, hopefully, remembering that she had been granted other visions of the Gods. 'Is that true?'

'Yes, Matuac.' She spoke with sincerity, her eyes steady behind a sheen of tears; it was what she believed. 'I saw him go. He was happy and greatly honoured. He will be welcomed among the heroes.'

That seemed to comfort him a little, though he continued to brood as they rode on. At last, as if to turn his mind away from grief, he said, 'I'll offer myself for this mission to Camulodunon. I need a purpose to clear my mind.'

Camulodunon . . . the very name was a lure and a terror for Rhiannon. 'What mission is this?'

'An idea of the queen's – and Eogan's. Just a small party, perhaps disguised as traders.'

'To do what?'

'To spy out their defences. And to rouse the Britons of the town to our cause. Whoever goes, they'll need a strong arm in case of trouble. I shall offer myself, in memory of Ylas.'

Romans came to the midsummer markets at Oakhillfort. They were allowed inside the gates with a show of cringing reluctance, as though the Iceni feared what reprisals a refusal might bring. The soldiers sneered. They swaggered as they strode among the throng, elbowing aside people they now considered to be utterly cowed and defeated. These Iceni had been taught to know their place. Catus Decianus had seen to that.

In the queen's house, Boudicca rested after the strain of the journey to the clifftop. Araunah sat beside her, her face even paler than her hair, with empty eyes. She had not spoken since the day she was raped. Nothing moved her. Sometimes it seemed that she could neither hear nor see, though at other times a flicker of expression showed her response. Rhiannon watched the child worriedly. She was sick now in mind as well as in body.

Without warning, a hard-faced centurion with grey hair showing under his helmet pushed his way into the house. The queen's guard protested, and Rhiannon leapt to her feet to defend her mother as behind the grizzled centurion six legionaries entered and began to search the rooms.

'The Trinovante!' the centurion said curtly. 'Farann, son of Vindorex. Where is he?'

'You won't find him here,' Rhiannon said, her throat thick. 'He's gone.'

'Gone where?'

'I don't know. Fled away. Please!' as baskets and belongings scattered in one of the inner rooms. 'My mother's unwell.'

The centurion glanced down to where Boudicca lay weak and pale by the fire. 'Sick, is she?'

'She was flogged!'

'I heard.' His eyes flickered over Rhiannon as if he was remembering what else he had heard about the atrocities at Oakhillfort.

Perhaps he had even been present that day; the thought made her feel ill. 'Get me some food,' he ordered. 'And wine – good Italian wine, none of that sour muck from Gaul.'

Rhiannon signed to the women, who sullenly moved to fetch refreshment for the centurion and his men. The intruders settled down in the queen's house to eat and drink, throwing orders at Rhiannon and the women of the household as if they were slaves.

Eventually, the centurion wiped his mouth on his sleeve and, picking his teeth with the point of a knife, looked again at Rhiannon. 'So the Trinovante's gone? He had warning, did he? From where?'

'From the tribune Caius Valerius Rufinus,' she said clearly.

'Oh? And why should the tribune do that? Are you accusing him of being a traitor?'

'He let slip the information.'

'When was that?' The expression on her face made his eyes flicker away from her. 'Ah, well . . . that probably explains why the tribune's been sent back to general Suetonius at the front.'

'He's gone to the fighting?' Rhiannon asked, unable to quell the hope that rose in her heart. But it died at once as she realised that, even if Valerius was gone, the procurator knew Farann was alive. Catus was not the man to forget an enemy who had escaped him. Wherever Farann was, danger stalked at his heel.

'Flapping tongues aren't welcome at Camulodunum, even when they belong to sons of good families,' the centurion said. 'Though I did hear a rumour that he'd actually volunteered for service at the front before the procurator could send him away under a cloud. Too green to know when he's lucky, throwing up a nice comfortable job at headquarters. Still, there should be plenty of glory for a keen young fellow when they finally break through to Mona's Isle. Anyway . . . you say the Trinovante's not here any more?'

'He left almost a moon ago.'

'In that case . . .' He stood up and tossed a bone negligently in her direction. 'You won't mind if we just make sure.'

Whether she minded or not, he and his men searched the settlement, every nook and corner of it, with rough efficiency. Then they rode away to search the woods and, presumably, to return eventually to the procurator with excuses for their failure.

'So Valerius Rufinus is gone to join the legions,' Boudicca said as if to herself. 'A pity. I had hoped to find him at Camulodunon. I looked forward to watching him die. But I wonder . . . was he sent away as a punishment, or did he offer himself for reasons of his own?'

A shudder ran through Rhiannon. 'I don't care which it was, as long as he's gone. When Matuac and the others go to Camulodunon, it will be a safer place without the tribune there to recognise them.'

She bent her head over the wool she was carding, pulling out the knots and straightening the threads ready for spinning.

'You're thinking of Farann,' Boudicca guessed. 'You're afraid for him.'

'Does that surprise you?' Rhiannon cried. Of course she was afraid for Farann, even though her feelings remained confused in other ways. She could not forget that Farann – and Ylas with him – had broken faith, scorned the Mysteries. Though he had done it out of love of her still she knew it had been wrong. Perhaps it was because of him that the Romans had been allowed to come and ravage Oakhillfort. Dia did not forget. Dia did not forgive. She had taken Farann away and perhaps She meant for him never to return.

The thought brought sudden tears to sting at her eyes and

she closed them tightly, turning her head away in the hopes of hiding her distress from her mother.

'You must put him from your mind, at least for now,' Boudicca said. 'You must think only of protecting the child you bear. The sacred child.'

'Is that what it will be?'

The queen looked sharply at her, seeing her tears, misinterpreting them. 'Yes! Child of the God! Child of the Maiden! *Your* child, Rhiannon.' She made an impatient gesture. 'The man is no longer important. All we needed was his seed. Ylas . . . Matuac . . . even the Roman . . . The Goddess made the choice.' She closed her eyes and laid her head down, feeling exhausted by too much talking, too much thinking. Her hand slid beneath her for the comfort of the touch of the pink quartz ring. 'The fate of the Maiden is sorrow, daughter,' she sighed. 'I learned it early. I hoped to save you from it. I tried to make Farann your shield. But Dia will not be defied. She has taken Farann from us. Now he follows his own fate-ways, as you must follow yours. You have been the Maiden. You will be the queen. You will bear the child and then . . . then we shall ride, you and I, side by side, to whatever fate awaits us.'

Rhiannon sat for a while watching her mother drift into sleep. With the hard lines of her face relaxed, the queen looked almost young again, but vulnerable, tired, her skin no longer fresh and fair but dry, forming lines about her eyes and mouth. 'The fate of the Maiden is sorrow.' Dimly, Rhiannon began to perceive the truth: Boudicca was not heartless; she had been hardened by griefs and had learned to hold her emotions close. But once she had cared: the ring she wore on its thong about her neck – the ring that was so precious to her – was a memento of something that still touched her deeply. Perhaps a man she had loved. Perhaps a man whose life the cruel Goddess had demanded – a man named Huan of the Caledones?

Softly, Rhiannon stroked her mother's hair, noting a few strands of silver among the rich red-bronze. Truly the fate of the Maiden lay through dark pathways, with Caridwen grinning at her shoulder. Now Rhiannon, too, was learning the truth of it.

*

Cameira and her lover the warrior Unthaus had volunteered for the mission to Camulodunon, as had Matuac. Though Tadia questioned the danger to her son and daughter, so soon after losing Ylas, she was a little mollified when Unthaus chose this time to ask for Cameira's hand at last. The marriage celebrations were a tribute to Ylas, both merry and solemn. The couple were bedded with riotous glee, but Rhiannon's feelings of despair led her to drink too deeply of the wine. When she woke heavy-headed, late the next morning, the party bound for Camulodunon had left.

The bridal pair had gone, and with them Matuac, and Teyrnon whose skills at capering and tumbling were intended to attract customers to buy of the goods stacked onto the ox-cart – figures carved from horn and bone, tanned hides and pots of dried herbs. Teyrnon had been eager to go, in some small part to avenge the deaths of his father and his sister. Along with them also had gone Erefwen the warrior-priestess, on a special mission: she was to seek out the most ardent followers of the Great Goddess and enlist their help in a war of fear.

For Rhiannon time seemed to drag like a team of oxen through mud. Most of the time she felt unwell, suffering from the malady of pregnant women that made her sick every morning. She sat with Araunah, who now spent her days weaving braid so loose and uneven that it could never be used. Araunah did not seem to notice. She lived, but her mind was not resident in her body.

'An evil spirit has her,' Morica said. 'She should be cast out into the forests.'

'No!' Rhiannon gasped, and saw her mother's face turn hard.

'She is my daughter,' the queen said. '*I* shall decide what is to become of her.'

Morica's thin lips twisted. 'As you will, lady. But when we march out to war will you then trail an imbecile behind you?'

After hearing this exchange, Rhiannon tried with every art at her command to reawaken Araunah's interest in life. She played games with her, tossed sticks for the dogs to chase, and took Araunah down to the enclosures where the white mare's colt was growing strong and fine. His name was

Starson. Sometimes, watching him kick and run, Araunah could be cajoled into laughing and clapping her hands in the manner of a small child, but mostly her eyes were empty, her being still; she was gentle, obedient. But she was not Araunah.

Many people shunned the girl and thought, as Morica did, that she should be exposed to the wild to fend for herself until the Goddess chose to end her life. But a few were kind. Of these, Garanhir seemed most concerned. Since Adalma died he had grown even more thoughtful and grave, saying little; he was still grieving over his young wife and the child she had not brought to its birthing. But he often stopped to talk with Araunah and bring her small gifts – a doll he had carved, or a flower from the woods, or a pretty stone.

'I believe she knows you,' Boudicca remarked to him one day.

Garanhir straightened and looked at her, saying, 'Sometimes she does, lady. At least, she knows that I'm a friend.'

'Yes.'

In the silence, Rhiannon sensed the pulse of emotions held on a fierce tight rein. Some fate still bound those two. She glanced up and saw them exchanging silent messages as they had so often down the years. Then Garanhir swung away and was gone.

Rhiannon looked at Araunah, but her words were directed at her mother. 'Do you ever think of marrying again?'

'Yes, daughter,' came the queen's quiet reply. 'I think of it.' There was a long silence, then Boudicca sighed and when she spoke again her voice was brisk. 'But my duty forbids it. Though I'm a woman, I'm also a queen, and the queen's thoughts must be for her people, not for herself. Destiny binds us. I'm a child of Andastre, Blood-Red Queen. When my people are safe from oppression – when the Romans are destroyed or driven from our shores – then, perhaps, fate might allow me to turn my mind to my own desires.'

As the summer month of the holly drew on towards the ripening of crops, the cramps and sickness that had bothered Rhiannon began to ease and once again she turned for comfort to the horses, and to the chariot reins. The queen and Morica both warned her against too fast driving, for fear she overturn and harm herself or the child, but she took some part in training and occasionally drove Araunah out for a ride. Her sister had neither the strength or the confidence to stand on the platform, but she sat happily enough behind Rhiannon, clinging on to the woven wicker sides as Rhiannon guided the ponies for a gentle outing across the heath.

She drew rein, straining her eyes against the sun as she saw dust rising in a low cloud along the Way. But whoever was travelling there moved slowly and the shepherds among the hills piped tunefully rather than with warning. The shape at the front of the dust revealed itself to be an ox-cart and as it drew nearer Rhiannon recognised the people walking alongisde it – Matuac and his sister Cameira, with her husband Unthaus. Teyrnon was driving the cart, with Erefwen beside him.

Rhiannon raised her own dust cloud as she drove across the sandy heath to meet the party, who all greeted her tiredly but cheerfully. It seemed that their mission had been successful. She fell in behind the cart and Matuac came to walk alongside. He was sweating profusely in the heat, but through the smeared dirt on his face his blue eyes were bright as they had not been since Ylas died.

'No one suspected,' he told her. 'We blended in with the crowds, minded our manners, and no one even noticed us. The Romans think they're safe. They can't seem to imagine ever being in danger from the likes of us. It's unbelievable, Rhiannon. We can take them with hardly any losses. Isn't that so, Unthaus?'

Unthaus looked round, his scarred face expressionless. 'It may be so,' he said.

'Of course it's so!' Cameira exclaimed. 'Why, we five could have done it ourselves!'

'Aye, so we could!' Matuac said. 'But it'll be easier with a whole army, and with allies inside the town. Especially when the garrison's scared spitless with rumours of death and portents of disaster!' He laughed aloud, 'Erefwen's been busy.'

From her seat up on the board of the cart, Erefwen turned and glared at him with cold eyes. 'Hush, fool! Don't speak such things aloud, not even here.'

Matuac pulled a face at her and walked round to the back of

the chariot, saying, 'Hello, Araunah,' to the girl who crouched there. Stepping over her, he climbed up to the platform and stood balanced with one hand lightly on Rhiannon's shoulder as she guided her ponies at the plodding pace of the ox-cart.

Very quietly, he said, 'We met Cunovinda.'

Her hands clutched on the reins. The ponies halted. Staring unseeingly at the receding cart, Rhiannon forced her lungs to draw breath. 'Oh, Matuac! You met her? Is she well?'

'Very well. It *was* her I saw that time in Camulodunon, but she didn't realise who I was until it was too late. She was frightened. That's why she ran off. She, er . . . she's married now.'

She looked over her shoulder, her eyes round with surprise. 'Married? To whom?'

'To a retired centurion. He bought her as a maid for his wife, because he fancied the look of her. Then his wife died. The man offered Cunovinda freedom if she married him, so . . .' He shrugged. 'So she did.'

'Is she content?'

'Is anybody?' he countered. 'She's grateful to the man. He's not unkind to her. She said I must tell you she hasn't forgotten. She prays each night for you.'

'And . . .' she could hardly force the words out, so tense with fear and hope was she, 'And Farann? Has she word of – ' She stopped, seeing the answer in his eyes even before he spoke.

'Only that she knows he's alive, and is being hunted. She's seen him just once.'

'She has? Oh – '

Matuac smiled wryly. 'If he was not my friend I could hate him for that look in your eyes, though now that I've seen Cunovinda again my loyalties are split. She's become a beauty. Her skin is pale as moonlight, her eyes like violet lakes . . .' He paused, sighed. 'But you wish for news of the Trinovante. Very well . . .

'It seems that The Pig was furious when he found out Farann was alive. He tried to vent his wrath on Cunovinda. But by then she was a free woman, and married to a Roman citizen. Her husband defended her. Then early in the summer Farann came to her house in disguise. She was able to give him food and learn his news. He said he was on his way to Caesaromagus – to see the Trinovante chief there.

'Since then she's heard nothing. But she's afraid for him. She says Baro is a weak man, and jealous of his position. He may well give Farann up to the Romans rather than risk being displaced as chief by the son of Vindorex.'

'I see,' Rhiannon said through chilled lips. The news did nothing to ease her mind of its fears for Farann. The wheel of fate rolled on. Like the White Goddess, it was inexorable.

So the seasons turned in that fateful Great Year, through harvest to dark Samhain and the choosing of a Green King who would not be required to die on the clifftop, though his life might be asked of him in the war that was to come. Many lives would be asked, but none of the warriors quailed at the prospect. They had been born to fight, trained to fight, and now at last their honour as blooded Iceni warriors was to be restored.

As the winter closed in bringing bitter rains and long nights, so everyone worked in the cause. Much wood was chopped and brought in to feed the forges as ironsmiths worked to fashion swords, spears and knives. Every piece of iron not essential for some other purpose was employed, melted down and remoulded. Buckets were dismantled, their iron hoops replaced with willow bindings, and when the iron ran low bronze was mixed with it – from torcs, brooches, anything that could be found. Meanwhile too the chariots were checked and repaired, their harness kept oiled. Carpenters worked as hard as smiths. Teyrnon and his grandfather, with others of their craft, worked among the horses, readying them for battle. Every daylight hour was full of clanging of hammers, sparking of white-hot metal, acrid smoke, sounds of sawing. But always a sharp watch was kept for spies.

No spies came. The Romans slept easy in their towns and winter quarters, thinking the south secure and the west only one last push from defeat.

As the winter passed, so the child grew inside Rhiannon. She made offerings at the well and the river, hoping for a sign to tell her whose child it would be. But the Goddess had turned Her eyes away from Her Maiden. Often Rhiannon wept in cold and despair, alone but for the dumb pity offered by Araunah. Boudicca remained aloof. She had walked similar fateways herself and knew that Rhiannon must endure; she herself had other concerns, going about among her people to keep them on edge and in readiness.

Imbolc approached again – the time of the birthing of lambs, the lactation of ewes – the time of Rhiannon's own birth, and now the time for her babe. For all the portents to be fair, the child must be born before the sixth day of the new moon. Morica and Erefwen hovered about Rhiannon, watching and waiting, bidding her give them a girlchild for Dia. If the birth threatened to be late they were ready with potions to make the womb expel its occupant. Rhiannon began to hate their glittering, tattoo-framed eyes.

The birth pangs started on the last night of the old moon, when the Hag hung like a shred in the cold sky. Easing her aching back, Rhiannon laughed bitterly to herself. This child would be a child of the dark of the moon. Caridwen's child in truth, like her mother, and her mother before her, and perhaps like every Maiden down through the ages. Caridwen's child, doomed to sorrow.

Amid a cluster of anxious women, Rhiannon was led down to the birthing hut, where the fire smoked and the gloom was red. Her mother had stayed at the fort, waiting for news, but Tadia was there as she had been for Boudicca. Her face was more careworn, her hair streaked with grey, but her hands were just as firm in support when the contractions strengthened.

The women stripped Rhiannon and put her into a short birthing robe. Hot on one side from the fire, cold with winter on the other, she squatted over a mound of blankets and skins, bearing down as the pain gripped her womb. The women made a circle round her, swaying and chanting, but dominating them all was the figure of Morica, waiting with avid eyes for another girlchild – another Maiden fated to sorrow.

'Epona!' the gasp broke from Rhiannon's soul as her mind reeled. She dared not pray to Caridwen, not at this moment. She remembered Adalma, dying in blood; Ylas, too, taken by the Gods; and Farann . . . Farann . . . Her longing for him was unbearable agony. She was birthing his child. Farann's child, or the child of Valerius . . . which would it be? A girlchild. It had to be a girl.

'Epona aid me!' she cried again as her aching muscles tensed again. This time the pain crescendoed until she screamed aloud, and then moaned in relief as the strain eased. The child was crying as its head broke through. The women sighed in hope and awe. With another push the child of the God parted from its mother and lay wailing lustily.

Morica bent to lift it up and examine it, and through the sweat that stung her eyes Rhiannon saw the start the priestess gave. Her eyes narrowed to slits. Almost she threw the squalling baby down in her disappointment.

'A boychild,' she said, staring at Rhiannon accusingly. 'A boychild!'

Exhaustion overcame Rhiannon and she let Tadia guide her down among the skins to await the coming of the afterbirth. Through weary eyes she watched as Morica wiped the child clean and swaddled it before bending to lay it in Rhiannon's arms. The priestess turned away, no longer interested.

But in the firelit shadows Rhiannon looked at the wrinkled, screwed-up face of her tiny son and with a sweet pain she found a new kind of love as her heart swelled to welcome him. So small, so helpless, so dependent on her. She loved him as she looked on him with tender, tear-filled eyes. She was fiercely glad that he was not a girl. Let someone else take on the Maiden's cloak when the wheel of the skies turned around to another Great Year. This child was hers, safe from the clutches of the Goddess and her followers. *Your* child, Boudicca had said.

Tadia knelt beside her, peering to see the baby, smiling. 'A fine sturdy boy. Like my Ylas.'

Pity wrenched at Rhiannon; whoever had fathered the child it had not been Ylas, but let Tadia believe so if it comforted her.

Then cold Erefwen came to bend over them. She too looked at the babe and a sneer twisted her mouth. 'I knew it! Look – he has dark hair, dark eyes . . . Expose him to the frost and let him die! Or will you raise a misbegotten Roman brat in the queen's house?'

Seven

When spring came, Suetonius Paulinus made his plans for the final assault to subdue Mona's Isle and destroy the nest of Druids who worked against him there. He was hampered by rains and mists that shrouded mountains and clung to coasts, as if the Druids had called up their last desperate enchantments. But week by slow week his forces advanced in a three-pronged attack through the tribal lands of the Deceangli, along the coastal plain of the west and north, and through the mountain passes.

The tribune Valerius Rufinus rode hard to keep his commander in touch with the captains. His fortitude and bravery won him honour among the legions as he came with messages to and fro, risking storm, flood, and furious assaults from tribesmen who lay in wait among the hills. Often he dropped exhausted into a sleep from which he was roused only to climb to the saddle again for another long day. But he welcomed the task: it gave him no time for thinking.

Thus the minds, eyes and all the efforts of the military governor and his forces were set firmly towards the north west, while behind them in the east rebellion gathered.

Once again the Druid Eogan strode up to the gates of Oakhillfort to confer with queen and council, warning them that the signs must be right before they marched. He would watch the skies day and night, scenting the turn of weather, divining the path of stars. All must blend, all must bind, before the march could begin.

As the wet spring days lengthened the winds arose to dry the land. Boats began to be seen across the Great Bay, heading for Iceni shores, bringing warriors of the Parisii and the Coritani. Other allies made their way through the marshes. From the Brigantes came a war band sent by Venutius the estranged husband of Cartimandua, and chiefs and warriors from across

Icenia began to gather. Their camps filled all the valleys around Oakhillfort.

Daily the queen sat in council with arriving chiefs, moulding them into one unit with her strength of purpose, her inborn eloquence, and the fire that smouldered in her green eyes. Vengeance she sought and vengeance she would have, with their aid. This tall, strong woman with her flowing mane of bronze hair inspired them all with a belief in themselves.

Aware of the growing expectation and impatience in the hum of activity around her, Rhiannon spent what time she could with her son. He was nearly four moons old now. She was suckling him herself, finding that he grew more precious with every day. He had learned to laugh and to know her voice. She had called him Nion, for the ash tree, and at the ceremony of his naming she herself had claimed him as a child of the God – *her* child.

The babe had downy dark hair – which proved nothing, so women said; dark children had sprung from fair parents before and Nion might well have been sired by the Green King Ylas. But there were those who believed his colouring was proof that the child was Roman. Rhiannon forbore to join in the arguments. She alone knew that Nion could not have been gotten by Ylas and she was almost sure he had not come from the lust of Valerius, either. She had only to look at her son and see Farann gazing back at her: the baby had deep blue eyes.

Nion was almost asleep at Rhiannon's breast when Boudicca swept in, her eyes alight, her movements brisk. She said, 'We march tomorrow at first light.'

Rhiannon held the baby closer, relishing his small warmth in her arms. 'Tomorrow is the Eve of Beltane,' she murmured. Only a year ago, little Nion had been conceived in the Mysteries. Now his dark hair felt feather-soft to her lips as she brushed a kiss on his head.

'Just so,' the queen agreed. 'But Eogan deems the signs to be right. The trackways are dry now, the summer lies ahead . . . Come, Rhiannon. I've ordered my chariot to be brought. You'll be my reinswoman.'

'Now?' Rhiannon lifted her head. 'You said tomorrow.'

Boudicca laughed and tossed her hair. 'We leave with the dawn. But tonight, daughter, you shall drive me among the camps. I want all the warriors to know what their war chief looks like. I want to speak to every man. If they see me, they'll follow me. When a woman leads, what man dare lag behind? Come . . . clothe yourself for the part – you're to be my reinswoman – reinswoman of Boudicca, queen and high chief of the Iceni – war chief of all Albion!'

It was as she said: the sight of her, and the sound of her stirring speeches, lifted the hearts of all. As she drove among the camps, men and women came running to see and hear her, with children hanging on their cloaks. Tall she stood in the chariot, with a spear in her hand, and slung behind her on a cross-belt hung the sword Blood Craver in a bronze sheath finely enamelled and decked with gleaming red stones. She wore her favourite red – trousers, slit tunic and fur-lined cloak – with her long hair flowing loose behind her. In front of her hung her horsemaster's amulet, alongside the ring she cherished, and at her throat she proudly bore the great electrum torc of Iceni queens. The Romans had robbed her of most of her other jewellery, but she needed no more. Her own vivid personality would have marked her out as a queen even if she had been naked.

Cheers and shouts greeted her arrival, growing louder when she had spoken and was moving on. Every man felt his strength increased, his hope renewed. Many of them felt they loved her. All of them swore they would die for her. Brave queen, tragic queen, scourged and trodden down but rising now to answer all insults. She outflamed the sunset as she rode among them in her chariot.

At the reins, her daughter stood, guiding the ponies with expert hands. To many of the younger warriors the younger woman was more impressive even than her mother: Rhiannon, once the Maiden, queen's daughter and future queen, erect and solemn in her green cloak, like a slender flame with bright hair and pale, beautiful face. She was in need of a mate, so the young men whispered. When the battles were over, some hero might well be rewarded with the hand of the fair Rhiannon.

That night was born the war cry that was to ring so far afield and chill so many hearts. The queen's name, a name that stood for Victory: *'Boudicca! Boudicca! Boudicca!'*

*

With the dawn the great army set out, a straggling horde spilling across the heath either side of the Way. Birds scattered overhead as if amazed by the sight and the sun rose to reveal a blue and white sky of early summer, with clouds streaked by a wind that raged high above the earth. A good day; a day of high portent: Beltane.

Scouts on horseback rode far and wide ahead to report any danger that might threaten. In the first ranks of the army the queen stood erect and poised, tall in her chariot with Rhiannon as reinsman. The white Egyptian mare, Starbright, was led on a tether behind. Eogan the Druid rode nearby, and behind and to either side came the warriors of Oakhillfort, men and women side by side: Nuadat led the riders with Matuac at his left hand; Garanhir commanded the chariots. Companies of warriors, of the Iceni and of other tribes, came behind under the command of their own chiefs, some riding, some on foot, and behind them again walked peasants armed with spears and farm tools, and others with staves and cudgels. And there were the dogs – savage brindled hounds bred to kill in the hunt or in battle.

Among them, tending to fall back because of their slowness, rumbled the ox-carts bearing the gear and the families, the wives and children, with their slaves to serve them. Somewhere in that throng Morica travelled, and grey-haired Tadia drove a cart that held Araunah and little Nion, tended by Ferna who was there with the two children left to her: several of her offspring had perished and her eldest had been taken to slavery by the Romans. Ferna was thin and hardened now, but she too had a baby to suckle, and would act as wet-nurse to Nion should Rhiannon be unable to tend him herself.

Behind them, dipping out of sight behind the swell of the land, Oakhillfort was left deserted but for a remnant of the sick and the old with a few slaves to attend them. And in the homesteads of the valleys some peasant women would toil with their children until their men returned.

The pace of the advance was slow but it was steady and purposeful. Ever and again voices broke into song recalling other battles and earlier heroes. Parties of hunters went out foraging. Places in the line changed as warriors mingled, some falling back, others moving ahead, and as they moved on their ranks were increased by parties of warriors coming from forest or marshes.

They travelled as long as daylight allowed, and at night made camp around cooking fires. For the queen's family hide tents were erected, where in the peace of evening Rhiannon fed and cared for her tiny son. He slept beside her, a warm and tender bundle content in the shelter of her arms.

For two days their journey was leisurely, but for a brief skirmish when a company of scouting Romans was sighted. Nuadat laid an ambush for them and the entire troop died before they could recover from their surprise.

On the third day the camps stirred at first light, before even the birds had woken. Rhiannon saw her mother and the Druid standing in deep conversation, two shadows under the darkness of the forest canopy. But Nion had begun to squall and as Rhiannon set him to the aching fullness of her breast she saw messengers go out to bring all the chiefs to a nearby clearing. Then Eogan made sacrifice of one of the tame hares that had been brought among the baggage. Prayers rang out to the brightening sky, asking the aid of the Great Goddess in her incarnation as Andastre, Queen of Combat, Red Reaper of Souls and Lady of the Full Moon.

When the ceremony was done Eogan took leave of the queen and strode away into the forest, heading westward.

'He's been called to Mona,' Boudicca told her daughter. 'The Druids are in need of him. The Romans are at their threshold and he must go with haste, but we've no real need of him now; the task before us is for warriors, not for priests.'

How Eogan had been called was never questioned. He had just known he was needed, as he always knew. Perhaps he scented it in the wind. Perhaps the birds and creatures told him. It was the way of Druids.

Fighting units broke their fast in haste. Today they would leave the sheltering forest and come to the first villas, and the road the Romans had built. Once they showed themselves, news of their coming would fly before them and alert the Romans. So the fighters would move ahead, and the ox carts must follow at their own pace.

Swiftly now they moved on, coming soon to the broad road of packed stones where the chariots' wheels rumbled and hooves clopped. The road was deserted, with no sign of the traffic that had passed along it when last the queen of the Iceni had visited Camulodunon – evidently rumour of the uprising had gone before her.

Rhiannon concentrated on conserving her horses, aware of the flood of vengeful humanity behind and around her. Riders went out among the valleys to raid the neat white villas, to slay any enemy they might find and to destroy the houses that grew so alien on Albina's soil. Occasionally people were seen running, pursued by warriors who cut them down. Smoke began to rise from behind white walls. Parties of local Britons appeared to welcome and march with the Iceni.

And at last they came within sight of Camulodunon.

From a vantage point on the great earthen banks built long ago by Britonic Celts, Boudicca and Rhiannon, along with some of the chiefs and nobles, watched the battle progress. The advance guard of the army swarmed across the fields below, destroying the outlying settlements and the old Catuvellauni hillfort. Fires sprang up among the houses, screams rang out. Still the Iceni and their allies pressed on, rampaging through the marble tombs of the Roman cemetery.

'Yes! Yes!' Boudicca cried. *'On! Ride on! Destroy them all!'* Still more of her warriors crowded the plain until the land was a mass of moving bodies. Light glittered on their spears and swords. The first wave had reached the gates of the town and met a fierce resistance, but soon flames were licking around palisade and watchtowers and the defenders fell back, into the town itself.

Where was Cunovinda? Rhiannon wondered, watching the army swarm into the town. Blessed Albina protect her in this danger! Then a plume of smoke caught her eye, away on the river. 'See!' Pointing into the distance, she drew attention to where a ship had suddenly burst into flame. Movement there resolved itself into the shapes of another band of warriors approaching from the south, driving back all those who had thought to escape at the last minute along the river.

'More allies!' Boudicca laughed. 'Let us go and meet them. We'll worship together at the Temple of Claudius. Come!'

Reaching behind her shoulder, she drew the Craver and leapt up to her chariot to lead the charge along the last stretch of road to gates that now stood open before her. The army streamed in ahead of her and around her, crying her name in joyous greeting: *'Boudicca! Boudicca! Boudicca!'* Before her everything fell.

Warriors with drawn swords ran among shops and courtyards, killing and looting, setting fires to blaze. Flames roared up through warehouses, melting glass, scorching pottery, destroying tons of grain and running in rivers of oil. The attack had been too swift, and more deadly than the Romans had anticipated; few reinforcements had been sent to aid the town. And the morale of the inhabitants was already low: they were a superstitious people and had been terrified by soothsaying women who had lately taken to running about the streets crying of blood in the sea and ghostly bodies washed up along the shore; then the statue of the Victory had fallen, smashing itself on its face across the forum – a terrible sign of impending defeat. Finding themselves attacked from within by their own slaves and formerly peaceful Britonic neighbours, a small core of hardy defenders made for the temple and barricaded themselves there, while the fires of vengeance blazed brighter as night fell.

Anxiously watching for a sign of Cunovinda, Rhiannon drove her mother to the centre of the crowd around the temple. The huge white colonnaded building was sturdy, built of stone; it would not burn. But the environs could be destroyed, the outer wall hacked at and pulled down, the altars desecrated, the statues battered. Already men were at work to lay the courtyard in ruins. A warrior had climbed up onto the gilded statue of Claudius on horseback and was hacking at the bronze head. It toppled at last, and bounced off among cheering warriors who fought each other for possession of the souvenir.

Of the procurator Catus Decianus there was no sign. It was discovered that at the first hint of trouble he and his staff had removed themselves to the safety of Londinium.

'Safety!' Boudicca exclaimed. 'There's no safe place for Catus Decianus – no thicket strong enough to hide and protect that Pig, not in all of Albion.'

Leaving the temple under strong guard, the queen rode on to look at the prisoners who had been herded into the stadium. There were Romans among them, soldiers and civil servants, some merchants, and many Britons, including women and children. They looked on with terror as the queen of the Iceni rode up, like a flame herself in the glow from the burning town. Some of them cried out to her, begging for mercy, but Boudicca's face was set like stone. Beside her, Morica and Erefwen screamed curses, demanding vengeance and blood.

'Collaborators!' Boudicca cried. 'There is no mercy! Not in this world! Bloody Andastre take you all!' She signed to Rhiannon to drive on, out of the stadium, while behind them the screams and cries grew hideous as the Celts moved to obey the command and, under the glittering eyes of priestesses, to extract the greatest pain and terror to placate the Goddess.

The queen went down by the river and ordered a camp to be made there for her, within sound of the torture that had been let loose among the prisoners. The light in her eyes was cold and bright, approving of the slaughter: her enemies were being punished, now let them discover what pain and fear felt like.

But Rhiannon had begun to feel sickened by all the blood and cruelty she had seen that day. To kill and be killed in battle, for a righteous cause, that she could comprehend, but to maim and torture for the joy of it was truly barbarian. And in the midst of it, somewhere, her friend Cunovinda must have perished.

She dare not protest, though she did ask leave to go back and find her son; her breasts were full of milk for him and she wished to assure herself of his safety.

'You stay with me!' the queen's answer came at once and those glinting eyes swung on her, reflecting the leap of burning buildings on the rise. 'Tadia and Ferna will see to the child. I want you here beside me to savour my vengeance.'

A commotion in the darkness drew their attention along the river. A rider was coming, fending off a crowd who seemed to be trying to deprive him of the bundle that lay across his lap. He beat at them with the hilt of his sword, finally slashing in rage with the blade, cutting a face open to the bone. The wounded man fell away with a scream and his companions too backed off, allowing the rider free passage. He came on. Whatever he carried across his horse was wrapped in pale flapping draperies and as he reached the queen it slipped from his grasp and fell heavily to the ground. It was a body – the body of a woman. A pale arm flopped out, braceleted in gold.

'Ha! What have you brought me, Matuac?' The queen stooped to take the bracelet, but the rider leapt down and to Rhiannon's horror he threatened her mother with his sword. Boudicca drew back, herself astounded.

Recollecting himself, Matuac relaxed his stance, saying, 'Forgive me, lady, but I won't have her harmed, not after risking death to save her. She was among the captives in the stadium. Don't you see who she is? It's Cunovinda, Cunovinda, the daughter of Vindorex!'

With a little cry, Rhiannon knelt by the woman and brushed aside the edge of cloth that covered her face. Her heart saw past the years, past the make-up and the elaborate hair style in which the dark hair was dressed – Cunovinda. Cunovinda, Farann's sister, grown into the full beauty of young womanhood. Even as Rhiannon stared down at her, kohl-blackened lashes fluttered and lifted, showing huge eyes darkened by the night. For a moment she stared up dazedly, then her eyes widened even further with joyful recognition.

'Rhiannon? Oh . . . Rhiannon!'

Clasping her friend in her arms, Rhiannon closed her eyes against the hot tears that came flooding. After the horrors of the day she had never expected a blessing such as finding Cunovinda alive.

'I have thought this day would never come!' Cunovinda sighed as she and Rhiannon sat by the river under a sickle moon. 'How often I've prayed that I might go free, and see you again. It's been so long!' She reached for Rhiannon's hands, held them and lifted her face to the skies where the Milky Way laid its starry arc. 'But She has been with me – Rhea of the White Track. When despair held me in thrall, I had always the night skies. I've sat often watching them, wondering how you fared, and Farann, and all my friends at Oakhillfort.'

'I, too,' Rhiannon said. 'Thinking of you. Many nights.' She studied Cunovinda's profile, thinking that her friend was blessed with great beauty despite the life she had led. 'I'm so glad they didn't brand you as they did to Farann.'

Cunovinda smiled bitterly and slipped her tunic from one shoulder, turning to show Rhiannon the scarred 'S' brand on her back. 'They brand their whores more carefully – not to spoil their attractions.'

'I'm sorry,' Rhiannon breathed.

'It no longer matters,' Cunovinda said, covering herself. 'That life is over for me now. I learned long ago to detach mind from body when necessary – to pray to Rhea and feel her bear me up among the stars; it has armoured me against many blows.'

For a while they sat silent, their hands entwined, understanding flowing between them. Both had faced horrors; both knew that further terrors waited before the war was won, but here for this moment they had quietness and leisure to enjoy their reunion under the gentle light of the new moon, the Virgin Albina.

From nearby came the sound of laughter and singing: Alvran the bard entertained the queen and her lieutenants around a campfire where joints of meat were roasting on sticks. They had rescued plenty of food from the flames, and there were cattle and sheep in the fields, more than enough to feed the vast horde that now camped around the burning town. The ox-carts and the families had stayed out on the heath, away from the carnage for the present.

Cunovinda spoke of her life as a slave of Marcus Terentius – being a maid to his wife Lupulla and mistress to the retired centurion.

'He knew my past,' she said. 'I could not refuse to lie with him, and at least he was only one man instead of many. But I was ashamed of my life: when Matuac glimpsed me in the street that time, I . . . I fled in shame, not wanting you to know.'

'I understand,' Rhiannon assured her.

'And then,' Cunovinda went on, 'when my mistress Lupulla died and Marcus Terentius offered me marriage, I agreed. It seemed my only hope of gaining a kind of freedom.'

'Where is your husband now?' Rhiannon asked.

'I don't know. When I last saw him he was fighting near the temple; perhaps he's there with the defenders, perhaps he's dead.'

'He might have escaped.'

Cunovinda shook her head. 'No, not Marcus. He would fight to the end. He's strong, and takes pride in his craft as a soldier, though he's no longer as young and able as he was. He would wish to die with a sword in his hand.'

'Will you regret that?'

'Perhaps, a little. He was not unkind to me, and I had no one else. My father was gone, and you and your family were far away. Even Farann . . . They had told me Farann was dead after he was lost in the storm. When he came back – alive, and strong, and wearing the Warrior's Light – I could hardly believe he was real. But since then . . . I've heard nothing.'

Their hands clung tight in the darkness as they shared their fears for Farann.

'But I know if he's alive then he's working for our cause,' Cunovinda said. 'As I have been, with other Britonic women here who still worship the Great Goddess. We've been busy preparing our people for this day. We raised rumours of evil portents; some of the women roamed the streets crying out that doom was coming; they said they had heard howlings, or whispers, and seen ghostly bodies dripping blood. It made the Romans angry, but it also made them afraid. Even Marcus, though he scorned to show it, turned pale one night when a soothsayer screeched warnings at our door. And when news came of the Iceni advance . . . there was panic.'

'Then you've done well,' Rhiannon approved.

They talked together until weariness overcame them and they fell asleep, lying where they were among the grass under the trees. In the night, someone spread a blanket over them.

When Rhiannon woke the early sun was peering through a mist over the river. Her breasts felt sore, being swollen to overflowing with milk. She went to her mother and begged leave to find the cart where Nion would be in need of her.

'Oh, Rhiannon!' Cunovinda exclaimed, following her. 'A baby? You have a child?'

'She met with the God,' Boudicca said.

'Of course. The Mysteries.' Cunovinda turned her wide violet eyes on Rhiannon. 'You didn't speak of that last night. Is it a girl?'

'A boy,' Rhiannon answered. 'And if I don't feed him soon my breasts will burst. Mother, please . . .'

Boudicca summoned horses, and an escort to ride with her daughter to the camp of the families. Matuac led the escort, and Cunovinda went with them, unwilling to be parted from Rhiannon.

Now, in the daylight, they could see the results of their first battle. Camulodunon was a charred skeleton. A crowd of warriors still surrounded the temple; they were trying to find some way to get fire up to burn the high roof. Others pounded with logs on the great bronze doors, but as yet the defenders remained protected. And everywhere bodies lay, or hung on stakes and crosses. Most were dead, some horribly mutilated, some still had enough life to moan and plead for water – no one listened.

Seeing Rhiannon shudder as they rode past the evidence of rage and hate, Matuac said, 'It was necessary. We have to teach these Romans a lesson – Albina's Isle is for Albina's children. We must inflict such damage that they will never come back. When they leave our shores they must leave for good. Don't falter now, Rhiannon, this is only the beginning, we must follow it to the end.'

'I know.' She was remembering what the Romans had done to her mother and her sister, to Cunovinda and Farann – and to those they had killed – Mocuxsoris, Vindorex, gentle Adalma and Vranaun and the rest. Violence and cruelty were a part of life. She remembered Ylas, too. If the Gods Themselves demanded violence and blood what hope had humanity of learning mercy? But was that any excuse for what she could see all around her – small children with their throats cut; women naked and mutilated in unspeakable ways – barbarian – the whole world was barbarian.

Among the fields and copses that surrounded the civil capital the carts had drawn up in groups. The women had shared campfires and food; now they were busy preparing for another day, tending their children, grinding corn, butchering meat. Rhiannon found her own kinfolk in the shelter of a copse. Around them children played war with sticks for swords. Araunah was stringing daisies in a chain, singing to herself; Ferna was feeding her own baby, while Tadia paced about trying to pacify a screaming Nion. She greeted Rhiannon with relief, handing over the child, then recognising

Cunovinda drew her into the circle and with many exclamations and questions they began to exchange news.

Rhiannon settled with her back to a tree, the baby greedily sucking at the tip of her swollen, blue-veined breast. She smiled at him, crooning to him, stroking his soft hair – how she had missed him, how she loved him. Would there ever come a day when she and he would live at peace back at Oakhillfort, with the sound of the sea shushing on the shore of the Great Bay?

'I'd best go back,' Matuac said, surveying the domestic scene wryly. 'You'll be safe here. There are guards set around the camp, and watchers at all the ways. If the Romans come we'll know in time to go out and meet them.'

His eyes lingered on Cunovinda until she looked up at him and smiled, saying softly, 'Thank you, Matuac.'

'It's good to have you back with us,' he muttered, and left.

For two days the defenders in the temple held off the onslaught while the Britons razed the town stone by stone, wall by wall, house by house. They tore down the monuments in the cemetery and defaced the carvings. And finally the temple, too, fell beneath the onslaught. The defenders fought to the last man. Among them was Cunovinda's husband, the centurion Marcus Terentius.

That night there was great rejoicing and feasting, and honours given to those who had won most glory. They sang songs and danced around the fires, making sacrifices of animals and of the captives who had been kept for that purpose. Rhiannon and Cunovinda had stayed with the women and children, but now the queen summoned them to join the victory feast.

A great fire blazed on what had once been the precinct of the temple. Around it, chiefs and warriors sat chewing on slabs of beef and mutton, seating themselves on fallen masonry. The queen herself was enthroned on part of a marble column. She was still wearing her red clothes, and now around her neck were looped many chains of gold; golden bracelets covered her arms and clasped her ankles, and all her clothing was heavy with brooches. From piles of loot the adoring warriors had brought gifts of jewellery to their queen and still had plenty left for themselves and their women.

Through firelit shadows, the queen smiled proudly on her daughter, throwing out her arms. 'Behold the Maiden! Rhiannon, queen's daughter! Child of the God, reinswoman to Boudicca. We'll ride again, daughter. There shall be more victories: I, Boudicca, prophesy it!' She drank deep from a golden chalice full of rich red wine, while warriors brought up other goblets for Rhiannon and Cunovinda. 'Come, sit with me!' the queen invited. 'One on each side, daughter and fosterling – reunited!'

The noise around them went on, the chiefs laughing and boasting of their bravery in the fighting. Audagas was there, and Lanaccion, and Rhiannon glimpsed Cameira, her face still smeared with blood and dirt. Garanhir and Nuadat sat not far away, and Matuac came nearer, lured by the presence of Cunovinda; he watched her with eager eyes and it seemed she did not object.

'Is the babe well?' Boudicca wanted to know. 'And Araunah?'

'Both well,' Rhiannon said. 'Both happy. But then . . . neither of them comprehend what's happening.'

'What's happening is our long-awaited vengeance!' Boudicca cried. 'Eat. Drink. Tonight we celebrate the beginnings of our victory.'

As the evening progressed, a messenger came to inform the queen that the war chief of the south had returned from a foray into the surrounding countryside where he and his warriors had been rooting out last pockets of resistance. He was coming now to report to her.

'Ha! Good!' Boudicca sprang to her feet. 'I've been expecting him. He must join our feast. Rhiannon . . . here's a warrior you must meet. A great leader, one to rival Caratacus: war chief of the Atrebates, the Cantiaci . . .' The man was coming now, a tall figure cloaked and helmeted, with a sword slung about him, striding through the crowd about the fire and into the flickering light, ' . . . And of the Trinovantes,' Boudicca concluded, smiling as though she herself had conjured him out of air.

Cunovinda cried, 'Farann!' and threw herself into her

brother's arms, weeping for joy. He held her close, but over her head his eyes met Rhiannon's.

Gladness leapt inside her: relief, pleasure, love that pierced her heart. But with another breath she remembered all that lay between them: the deceit at the Mysteries; the memory of Valerius; the death of Ylas; the way Farann had left, without a word to her; and the long months when she had needed him and he had not been there . . . The barriers were too broad, too high to be surmounted in a moment.

'Now!' Boudicca cried. *'All of us together at last! It blends! It binds! We go on! On to victory!'*

Eight

Suetonius Paulinus and his legions had reached the Straits and gazed across the narrow water to the sacred Isle of Mona. On the far shore fires leapt amid rolling mists, Druids could be seen chanting spells and waving their ash staffs, while around them wild-eyed women bearing flaming brands screamed curses that turned the legionaries pale. To them, Mona looked like an island of devils.

But at the command they all set out to make the short crossing, some on rafts and improvised craft, others swimming with their horses. Though the inhabitants of the isle fought fiercely and bravely, the numbers of Romans swamped them: the sacred isle fell to the invaders.

Benath the shade of a scarlet tent, Suetonius prepared his report to go to the Emperor: at last Mona was vanquished. With the Druids and their oak groves destroyed, he was confident the rest of the province would be brought to heel with another season or two of campaigning. Britannica would be his – it was a proud moment. For nearly twenty years, general after general had struggled in futile campaigns here in the west, hampered by damp weather, mountainous terrain, and stubborn Celts. Now he, Suetonius Paulinus, had succeeded, and at an age when many of his rivals had thought him finished. He foresaw a great Triumph, with trumpets blaring, the strewing of flowers, maidens dancing and singing, and lines of prisoners walking in chains to sale in the slave market, Druids, priestesses, chiefs . . .

A disturbance outside interrupted his daydreaming. He looked up to see a mud-spattered Valerius Rufinus push his way past the guards, a dispatch in his hand. Behind him, officers of the general's staff came in exclaiming at his intrusion, but Suetonius quietened them with a word and asked the meaning of Valerius's haste.

Sketching a salute, Valerius thrust the message into the general's hand. 'Sir! It's from Cerialis, Legate of the Ninth. Sir . . . there's trouble in the south. A rebellion. Cerialis has gone to the aid of Camulodunum, but – '

'What?! They wouldn't dare!' He snatched open the seal, unrolled the parchment. 'What tribe is strong enough even to think of attacking Camulodunum?'

'Sir . . . It seems that the Iceni are at the centre of it.'

'The Iceni?' Suetonius scanned the message, finding its contents incredible. 'But their king's dead! Who's their new leader? And why wasn't I informed the man was dangerous?'

Valerius hesitated, knowing how the news would infuriate the general. 'They're under the command of Prasutagus's widow. Their queen, sir. Boudicca.'

'Boudicca!' Suetonius spoke the name under his breath, his eyes narrowing in his eagle's face. He remembered the woman he had met on the torchlit forum, standing tall and proud in all her barbarian finery, towering over him and glaring arrogantly at him. She had dared to raise a rebellion – *she* had dared – just when fame and riches were within his grasp!

He crumpled the dispatch in his hand, imagining it to be that woman's neck. She would pay for this effrontery: she would pay dearly.

As the Britons prepared to leave Camulodunon and begin the march on Londinium, they were warned of the approach of Cerialis and the Ninth Legion. Boudicca dispatched her strongest forces to deal with them – Nuadat and his spearmen, Garanhir and his chariots, Farann and his mixed warband from southern tribes. They laid an ambush in the forests and charged out upon the Legion on the march, destroying all but a section of the cavalry, which escaped under the leadership of the Legate, Cerialis. Him they chased halfway back to his fortress headquarters before they turned to rejoin the queen's force.

On swept the march, rolling slowly but inexorably, like a wave building to smash itself on a beach. Those along the way who would not join the tribes died by flame and sword, counted as collaborators and traitors. Boudicca and her armies moved on, heading south, as the summer days passed, towards the bustling, affluent trading post at Londinium.

Learning of the fate of Legio IX, Suetonius all but choked on his rage. That woman had dared to decimate one of *his* legions. Such was his fury that he abandoned all cool strategy and, leaving the bulk of his troops to organise themselves, he rode in haste from the west down the new road that sliced across the country, with only a detachment of cavalry. He found Londinium in uproar; everyone who could or would was leaving; there was only a small garrison. And the Boudiccan army was rapidly approaching.

Suetonius fled in disarray at the head of a straggling horde of people fleeing the Icenian queen's fury.

Londinium suffered the same fate as Camulodunon: its fine new warehouses and temples, its houses and shops, were burned to the ground, its inhabitants slaughtered by any means that the devious minds of the priestesses and the furious warriors could devise.

While her army and its scattered tail of ox-carts regrouped to tend their wounded and forage for food, Boudicca sent out scouting parties to search for Suetonius Paulinus. He could not be found. She learned that the procurator, Catus Decianus, had fled to Gaul. The Pig had eluded her, but the governor-general was still in Albion. She would find him. Sooner or later, she would find him, then would come the reckoning.

Amid the confusion, Rhiannon found comfort with her son. She spent every spare moment with him in the shaded camp that blossomed along the banks of the river Tamesis. Cunovinda too had joined the women; she had never been trained to arms. Now she went among the families helping where she could, and at night she found company and mutual comfort in the arms of Matuac, though whether she loved him or was giving herself out of pity Rhiannon could not decide. However, both Cunovinda and Matuac seemed happy and for that Rhiannon was glad.

For herself, loneliness was her companion. Many nights, when the baby slept peacefully beside her, Rhiannon would lie awake and watch the skies, waiting for some sign from the Goddess. Nothing came. She was unable to decide whether Dia was still angry or whether She had simply shrugged and turned away. Rhiannon knew an aching sense of loss.

She seldom saw Farann; he kept himself occupied on forays and excursions, with such energy that men had begun to speak of him in awed tones, as they spoke of magical heroes of legend: Farann, son of Vindorex, prince of the Trinovantes, war chief of the south . . .

Often a tear would roll down Rhiannon's cheek and into her hair as despair seized her. She was adrift on seas of uncertainty. Every time Farann rode out she knew he might never come back; the war went on and many must yet die; and still she could not bring herself to go to him. He was armoured from her by his own stubborn pride, and now by demands of battle and leadership. Would there never be a time of peace between them?

After a while, the inaction began to pall on individuals among that vast army. Quarrels broke out as various tribes and factions had time to remember old enmities; some of the peasants began to drift away heading back to their farms and their womenfolk, to hay that must be harvested and the corn that was ripening. The chiefs, aware that they were losing their hold on their men, demanded a move to restore morale and offer an incentive to the falterers: more booty, more destruction, more blood.

The town of Verulamium became their next objective. Here lived the present chief of the Catuvellauni, who had thrown in his lot with Rome and lived a Romanised lifestyle in his villa outside the town – a valued ally of Catus Decianus. A traitor!

Once more the horde gathered and the surge forward began, north and west this time. Once more Rhiannon drove for her mother, in the forefront of the rag-tag tide of humanity whose hatred of all things Roman drove them on.

Verulamium fell in flame and blood.

When this rage too had passed, restlessness came with renewed force. The call of the harvest now grew urgent for men who lived by the soil, and even some of the warriors hankered for their homes and the enjoyment of their spoils. They had conquered too easily and grew bored. It seemed that the Romans were afraid to show themselves in force; surely that meant that the war was won. With these arguments, and the natural longing of humankind for its own homelands, splits began to appear in the fabric that comprised Boudicca's army.

She held them together with the force of her eloquence and that of her most able lieutenants. She rode about the camps haranguing them: 'Victory has been ours! Great victory! But the war is not won! Not yet! We have the Romans at bay! Only a short while longer and they must stay and face us! Then shall the last battle be fought, the enemy vanquished. Let us pursue him! Overcome him! Destroy him!'

But where was the enemy? they asked. How could they pursue if the Romans refused to show themselves? Rumour began to spread that the legions had embarked for Gaul without making a fight of it. They must have gone. Why else couldn't they be found?

Then one evening as twilight set in, Farann and his warband rode into the queen's camp with news that Suetonius had been sighted. The Romans had been in confusion for a while; messages had been misunderstood, summonses for help ignored by nervous commanders, but now the main force from the north-west was well on its way to meet the Boudiccan threat. Suetonius was hurrying to join with it.

Clenching her fist, Boudicca rose to her feet and cried in a great voice, 'Andastre! Slow his feet. Send mists to hinder him. Let not the Roman reach his armies. Now, now, we go! Now we follow! We shall catch this Suetonius and destroy him. We go with the dawn! To the final victory! We go!!'

'Aye!' came the answering roar from all who heard her, spreading out among the camps until the woods rang with it. 'We go! We go! To victory! *Boudicca! Boudicca! Boudicca!*'

Suetonius and his forces fled before them up the Roman road. They found traces of him as they went – signs of hurried overnight camps and the ashes of fires, bones tossed about, fly-ridden pits that had served as latrines. Boudicca urged her forces on, faster and faster. The signs grew fresher. They were overtaking the governor-general; she could feel it in her bones. And at night the skies flamed as if all the land to the west was burning. So it would burn, she vowed, with Suetonius beneath it, roasted to ashes on the pyre of her fury.

Towards the end of another weary day, Rhiannon concentrated on nursing her tired horses as they toiled up yet another long slope between swathes of heath and woodland. Purple heather was already fading, bracken turning brown at its tips, leaves on aspens shimmering yellow. Summer itself was dying, turning to autumn. Four moons had waxed and waned since the march had begun. How many more moons would shine down before this turmoil ended?

'Stop!' Boudicca gripped her daughter's arm in hard fingers as she glimpsed riders ahead. They appeared over the horizon, urging their weary horses to a last desperate effort. There were only three of them left out of an advance scouting party of twelve, and even as they approached one man dropped from his horse and fell lifeless. One of the others was clutching his arm, from where blood poured.

'They've met their reinforcements!' the remaining man gasped as he slid to the ground and fell to his knees more in exhaustion than homage. 'They've halted. Up ahead. We ran into an ambush of Gaulish mercenaries armed with axes. They're waiting for us, lady – a huge force of them. Legion upon legion!'

'Good!' Bouddicca cried, countering the hopelessness in the man's voice. 'At last comes the day we've all been waiting for! Make your camps here. Tonight we rest. And tomorrow we conquer!'

More scouts went out to assess the Roman position and set a watch on the enemy overnight. They rode under the command of Farann, who volunteered for the task as he had volunteered for so much, as though he sought danger for its own sake. Almost inured by now to the fear and worry she had endured for so long, a weary Rhiannon made her way back to where the ox-carts were still toiling behind. They camped on wooded slopes where fires danced like will-o'-

wisps among the trees. The harvest moon rose round and white and full. The Goddess, too, had thoughts only for war.

Shaded from the moonlight by a clump of white willows, Rhiannon lay listening to the breathing of her small son beside her. Not far away, Araunah snuffled and muttered as she dreamed her lost-soul dreams. Most of the people round them seemed to be asleep, but for Rhiannon fears of tomorrow crowded too insistently. She could no longer read the future: she saw only a misted nothingness.

Perhaps there was no future.

Someone was moving nearby. As Rhiannon sat up, a woman's figure crouched beside her and the voice of Cunovinda came out of the shadows, saying, 'Hush! It's me. Farann has sent one of his men to find you. He wishes to talk to you, Rhiannon. Will you go?'

'Am I his servant to be summoned?' Rhiannon asked dully.

'He could not come to the women's camp.'

'Why not? Matuac does – and others beside.'

'But my brother is a chief now,' Cunovinda reasoned. 'A war chief. Please . . . go to him. Talk with him. The man is waiting to guide you. I'll stay here with Nion.'

Though Rhiannon's pride stung, her heart told her this was no time for obstinacy. She crept out of the camp to where the warrior of Farann's personal guard was waiting.

The man led the way across the wooded slope and into a valley whose rim was guarded by silent men merging into shadows under trees. Here a rill chuckled over stones, following the land down in shallow steps and tiny waterfalls to a clearing where bracken was banked. Moonlight robbed the world of colour, turning it to shades of grey with deep black shadows, and on the edge of the stream Farann stood, a tall chieftain with broad shoulders and long limbs, wearing only leather breeks and a cloak slung across his shoulders. His spears and sword were laid aside; he was armed with only the knife at his belt and by the stark expression on his face, which in the moonlight might have been cast in bronze.

The messenger saluted him, fist to brow. 'Lord . . . the lady Rhiannon.'

A gesture dismissed him. Farann hardly looked at the man; his eyes were fixed on Rhiannon, seeking to read her through moon-shadows.

Her heart beat erratically, unsettling her. 'You sent for me.'

'I sent to ask if you would come,' he amended. 'We may talk privately here. My men are on watch. And I've given orders that we are not to be disturbed, short of an attack by the enemy.'

Rhiannon inclined her head, saying, 'You're grown so high, lord. Farann, son of Vindorex, prince of the Trinovantes; war chief of the south. It has a fine ring to it.'

'Other women have thought so,' he replied.

Jealousy wrenched through her, paining and goading. 'Then send for one of them and let me go!'

She heard him catch his breath in anger and his voice revealed that he was holding his temper on a hard rein. 'Had we time, we'd play this game out to its end, lady. But there is no time. I would speak plainly to you tonight. I believe you know why I asked for you. More lies between us than a fever in my blood. Others may soothe that fever – for a moment, for a day. But only you have the power to ease my spirit too. Have I waited long enough? Will you come to me now?'

She lifted her head, staring at him through misty tears. She could hardly believe he was saying such things, unshielding his heart after so long. 'I thought you had forgotten.'

'I have been afraid to approach you.'

'Afraid?'

'Afraid of being rejected again – for a third time. My own heart I know beyond question. Yours I can no longer read.'

'Nor I yours.'

'A man has his pride.'

'You have always had too much of it,' she said.

'And you have not, daughter of the queen?'

'I came to you tonight.'

'Once you vowed you never would.'

'I was hurt. Confused. You were the one who went away!'

'You gave me no reason to stay!' he returned, and striding forward took her by her upper arms and swung her round, turning her face to the moonlight so that she squinted against white brightness. 'Is this how it is to end, Rhiannon? With petty argument between us? Beyond tomorrow's dawning we may never meet again on this earth. Shall we part like this, squabbling like children?'

'No . . .'She shook her head. The thought of losing him

made her mind swim with panic. Unable to see his face clearly, she lifted her hand and encountered the vibrant warmth of the flesh across his ribs. 'Farann . . .' Her fingertips drank of him, sweet intoxication flowing from her hand to her heart to fill her whole body with longing.

The touch ignited too the fires that smouldered in Farann. He pulled her into his arms, his mouth seeking hers as he drew her into the shade of the bracken. All thought receded, all barriers melted between them. In mutual need they coupled fiercely, punishing each other and loving each other, oblivious even to thoughts of the coming battle. Tonight was all that existed for them. Perhaps tonight would be all they had.

Finally, exhausted by the storms of passion, they lay naked together beneath his cloak and slept, wrapped in each other's arms as the moon sank to her setting.

Rhiannon woke with a start. The moon had gone and the night was dark, with that stillness that presaged the coming of dawn. From beyond the shoulder of the hillside a child was crying plaintively and faint stirrings sounded across the camps.

'It will soon be dawn,' Farann said softly, drawing her head down to his shoulder. 'Rest while we may, love.'

She moulded herself to him, pressed her soft fullness to the hard lean lines of his body and closed her eyes, shutting out the future, thinking only of this moment, warm with him as she had never been before – as they might have been for life if only the Goddess had been kind. But the Goddess was not kind. Who knew that better than a Maiden, doomed to sorrow?

His hands caressed her, finding the aching fullness of her breasts. Gently he laid her on her back and bent over her, a black shape against the greying sky. 'You kept the child.'

'Yes.'

'A Roman brat.' His voice was deep with distaste. 'Yet you kept it. Erefwen told me you refused to expose it, such tender love you have for the bastard sired by Valerius.'

'Erefwen.' She lifted her hands to trace the contours of his beloved face and imbue her memory with the reality of him. 'Did you believe her? She hates me, Farann – and through me you and all I care for. It suited her spite to call the child a bastard of Rome simply because he dared to be a boy – and because he has dark hair, as Valerius was dark, while Ylas was fair as the sun. But . . . you, also, Farann, are dark of hair.'

His hands came up to clasp her wrists and his voice was a hoarse whisper. 'I?'

'The child is yours,' Rhiannon told him. 'Ours. He has your eyes, your hands . . . But only I know it. Only I know who it was that came to the willow isle . . . but of himself, not in guise of the God.'

He fought some deep emotion, and in the growing light she saw his eyes filled with pain. 'You remember?'

'Yes, I remember. But I thought it was an illusion of the drug until Ylas . . . Do you know what came to Ylas?'

'Matuac told me,' he said gruffly. 'I wish I had understood. It was savage, Rhiannon – a waste.'

'No, not a waste!' she denied. 'The Gods required it. He went gladly, willingly, knowing it was necessary.'

'Even the Romans don't offer innocent human lives any more! They know it's a pointless waste. Ritual murder!'

'Don't say that! Don't say that!' Distressed, she scrambled to her knees in front of him. 'You can't believe that Ylas died for nothing!'

'I *do* believe that!' he answered fiercely. 'We shall need his sword today, but he is not here to fight with us. On the field of battle his sacrifice would have been worthy. On the altar at the clifftop it was superstition! Why is Eogan different from Duihno, except that he slew an innocent in full view of the tribe, and was praised for it, while Duihno killed in secret and died in the fires!'

Rhiannon was shaking, chills and fever running through her. 'You deny the Goddess?'

'I question whether She demands human blood!'

'You deny Her! You defiled the Mysteries. You – and Ylas.'

'Out of love for you.' As if wearying of the argument he moved away, gathering her clothes. 'Come, get dressed. I've work to do. We shall both have work to do before the day is old.'

Rhiannon scrambled into her clothes, feeling cold now. Joy was finished for her and reality was the war that must be fought. But a part of her was still shaking. Farann did not believe. What was worse, he had stirred the core of her own doubts, too.

He accompanied her back to where the carts were ranged in camp. There he paused to greet Cunovinda and Tadia. The baby, Nion, was awake, crying with hunger. Rhiannon picked him up and sat him on her arm, cuddling him, thinking how he had grown. Eight moons old now, a strong, sturdy child, dark of hair, blue of eyes. Over his head, she met Farann's glance as for the first time he looked on the child he had sired.

He drew her aside from the others and touched the baby's hand. Nion looked up at him wonderingly, snatching for the brooch that pinned the tall man's cloak.

'Perhaps,' Farann said quietly, watching his son, 'I shall this day be required to pay for my sacrilege, as Ylas paid. If we never meet again, lady . . .'His eyes met Rhiannon's and in them she read his resolve, his pride, and his love for her, 'then know this – I have only one sorrow, the parting from you. Take care of my son.'

Not caring who might see, he took her and the babe both into his arms and kissed her with passion and sorrow, then turned on his heel and was gone.

Rhiannon watched until he was out of sight. A heavy weight lay on her heart. It seemed to her that in that moment she was allowed a glimpse into the future: after that day, she would never see Farann again. He would die – or she would die – perhaps both of them. For she was Caridwen's child and the Hag took Her pleasure in tears.

Boudicca's army gathered for its last brief march to face the Romans. The chariots moved first, over the rise and down into a dip, then up a further heathered hillside to a crest from where, as they climbed to the top, Rhiannon saw the vale beyond open out in front of her. A long shallow slope ran down cloaked with heather and bracken to where a stream meandered. Beyond it, folded hills rose to dark forested tops. And against that slope, the Roman force was drawn up in battle array, a huge block of legionaries in the centre, flanked by battalions of auxiliaries and squadrons of cavalry.

A shout of laughter escaped Boudicca as she saw how the

enemy had arrayed himself. 'They'll be trapped – between us and the hills, with nowhere to fall back. Suetonius is a fool. See how he waits for us to close the trap on him.'

Behind and around her the chariots jostled and companies of warriors on foot seethed over the crest, thousand upon thousand of them. Some of them were naked, champion fighters clad only in the magical protection of sacred oil. They beat their swords against their shields, shook their spears, blew horns and shouted as they milled about the slope yelling defiance and threat at the waiting Romans. The Celtic horde outnumbered the Romans by far; they swarmed over the hill-side like ants. They foresaw that the day was theirs already.

From the ranks of the legions a trumpet blew and a figure on horseback could be seen riding out with an escort under banners and plumes, to parade in front of his troops. The breeze brought a thread of sound to Iceni ears: Suetonius was making a speech.

'Drive out!' Boudicca ordered. 'Drive out and let me speak to my warriors!'

Whipping up the prancing ponies, Rhiannon guided the chariot about the slope, among companies of cheering warriors who had spread on a wide front along the hillside. The queen raised the sword Blood Craver and spoke to rouse her forces to their greatest effort. 'Today we put an end to them! Today at last. Too long have they insulted us. Robbed us. Spat upon us! I, Boudicca, queen of the Iceni, cry vengeance! I am warrior-bred. My spears shall fly far. My sword shall drink deep of Roman blood. Will you fight beside a woman, to the death, or do men prefer to run cowards and live in slavery? Follow me! Follow me! To victory!'

The ox-carts containing the families came lumbering up, ranging themselves along the crest to watch the battle. Women brought out wicker cages and released the hares they contained. The animals sprang free and went running down the hill amid shouts and whoops. The hares had magical powers; they were sacred to Andastre, hunted only on Beltane Eve, and if any of the Romans swung a sword at one of them his blood would turn to water and he would turn coward.

'Andastre aid us!' Boudicca cried as the hares ran towards the enemy. 'Now is the time! Attack! Attack!'

With Rhiannon as her reinswoman, the queen led that first

swoop down the valley, as far as the river where she loosed her spear toward the ranks of unmoving Romans. Around her more spears flew to crash against the wall of Roman shields. Rhiannon wheeled the horses, guiding them with expertise amid a mêlée of other chariots and running, yelling warriors who came charging behind to cross the stream.

'To the hill!' Boudicca cried, pounding her daughter's back. 'We must let them see us there. It will hearten them.'

But before they reached the vantage point the first wave of the attack had come with in range of a sudden storm of javelins; many men fell under that deadly rain – another flight felled even more – still the Britons swarmed on. Chariots darted, each warrior loosing spears until all he had left was his sword or a stabbing spear; then he dismounted and his reinsman drove back to wait while the warrior made on foot into the fray. More and more men flowed down the hill, until the valley floor was thick with them. And then the Romans moved.

The central block of legionaries marched forward, behind their tall shields, thrusting with short stabbing swords. Step and thrust, step and thrust, like some monstrous killing machine. Before them, the Celts fell in hundreds. And from the flanks the auxiliaries closed in with their variety of weapons, while the cavalry swept wide like enfolding wings.

Rhiannon was unaware of time passing. Her whole mind was concentrated on the battle being fought in the valley. Now and then she glimpsed a face she knew. Many of them went down beneath the pound of Roman boots, the stab of Roman swords, the charge of Roman horse. Where Farann was she didn't know.

The moment came when she knew that defeat was the only ending. The ruthless efficiency of the Roman fighting man was crushing the less disciplined Britonic attack. She could see it happening: the brave fight was ending in disaster.

Boudicca too could foresee the end. Her face was pale, her eyes glittering as she drew the sword Blood Craver and held it high, crying, *'We go, daughter! To join the battle! Victory or death! Victory or death!'*

Caught up in the moment, with no thought but to do her part, to die or to win, Rhiannon slapped the reins and pointed the horses to where her mother directed – to the edge of a fight where Roman cavalry had surrounded a group of warriors and were slaughtering them one by one. Other chiefs followed the queen. A Roman died under the sweep of Blood Craver's blade. The chariot raced on.

'Turn them! Go back! Go back!' the queen ordered.

But as Rhiannon fought to turn the horses her mother clutched at her arm and sagged at the knees. 'Take me back to the battle!' she said through her teeth. 'Let me die. Don't let them take me wounded!'

From her eye corner, Rhiannon saw the arrow that was embedded in the queen's thigh. Now she thought only of getting her mother to safety. She wielded her goad mercilessly, driving the ponies on through the battle, back towards the hill, passing friend and foe. Roman horsemen were driving their enemies back among the carts. Already some had reached the women.

The oxen were being slaughtered where they stood; the carts blocked the way; Rhiannon could not get through – a crush of people behind her threatened to overwhelm her. Then she saw Garanhir, astride the white mare Starbright. He rode up, calling to Boudicca, leaning to scoop the queen up across his lap.

'You, too!' he yelled at Rhiannon.

'No!' she replied. 'Take her! Save her!'

Knowing that if he delayed they would all perish, Garanhir wheeled the white mare with its precious burden. Rhiannon saw him making for a narrow gap in the line of carts.

Around her the women and children were fleeing. Nion! she thought. Nion . . . Behind her, someone called her name. She caught sight of Farann, fighting his way towards her. Even as she watched he went down and was lost amid a tangle of struggling bodies. She stared at the spot, transfixed with horror.

Then something caught her head a heavy blow, the sky turned to blood. Rhiannon fell into darkness.

When night came, the moon swam up in a clear sky over the field where the mass of the defeated Celtic army lay sprawled and silent. The Roman dead had been removed, the wounded taken to care. Now a detail of legionaries moved among the fallen Britons, looting the bodies of jewellery and weapons, and killing all in whom life still flickered. Stray horses were being rounded up, and on the edge of the battlefield soldiers laboured to dig a funeral pit for the enemy dead. Already men were dragging corpses away.

Two of the looting soldiers, exploring the slopes near the hilltop, paused to listen as a thin, muffled sound came to them. A baby was crying somewhere among the mounded dead that clustered most thickly around the line of upturned carts. Human bodies, male and female, young and old, were slumped against dead oxen and broken wood. Here a wheel protruded, there a spear, there again the curved horn of an ox. There was a stench of death, blood and excreta.

Following the sound of the crying child, the two men found a cart completely overturned, half buried under a pile of bodies. The baby was underneath it. They cleared the dead away, heaved at the cart. It creaked as it lifted and they pushed it until it toppled. They discovered the baby unharmed and still crying weakly beneath the cart. One of them lifted his sword to silence the noise.

But something moved alongside the child. The legionaries both sprang back, their superstitious souls stricken with terror, as a pale wraith rose from the wreckage of household belongings, a thin ghost with moon-pale hair and staring eyes. She held out her hands to them and spoke in words they did not comprehend.

One of the men let out a cry of fright, turned and ran. The other held his ground, but when the wraith moved towards him he too fled.

Araunah watched them go, uncomprehending. Then as if she had only just heard him crying she bent and picked up the babe, shushing him as she had often heard Rhiannon do. 'Hush, baby. Hush, my darling boy. Mother's with you. Mother loves you.'

She looked around her, not understanding what she saw. Where was Tadia? Where was Ferna, and the children? And the queen her mother? She must find them.

Carrying Nion in her arms, she began to pick her way across the debris of carts and bodies, making for the top of the hill and the woods beyond. Clouds across the moon aided her flight.

Nine

Rhiannon existed in a half world of delirium, hardly knowing what was hallucination and what reality. For her, day and night were the same: her half world was dark – she had been blinded.

Hands forced her on, stumbling through bracken and briar despite her exhaustion; sometimes she was carried, sometimes she lay bundled across a horse, sometimes she was thrust roughly down and held still, her mouth covered by a hard hand to silence her while riders came by. Those same hands tended her, fed her on berries, roots and water, led her to relieve herself and washed her hands and face. She heard voices around her but was unable to distinguish what they said or to whom they belonged.

Often tears seeped from her sightless eyes and she begged her tormentors to leave her alone. Her breasts hurt; they were hard and engorged, and her nipples wept milk to soak her clothes. Where was the baby who should have been feeding on that milk? Her breasts and her arms ached for him. He was dead; she knew it. She wished only to be allowed to join him – to die in peace.

Then at last she was allowed to rest. She slept, drifted in limbo, and slept again, to awake one day to awareness of being in the marshes; she recognised the cool lap of water and the call of duck and heron. The air felt cold on her face, but her breasts felt less tender, and when she opened her eyes the blackness that had hooded her was hazed with grey. She closed her eyes again as clear memory brought grief flooding. Lost, all was lost.

'She's weeping!' a voice exclaimed.

Someone hurried to her side and bent over her. Fingers touched her cheek and the voice spoke her name.

'Rhia . . . Can you hear me?' It was the voice of Cunovinda!

Overjoyed, she reached out and found her friend's arm

then her hand, clutching it as tightly as her weak muscles allowed. 'Cunovinda . . . where are we?'

'Safe. Safe in the marshes.'

'How long have we been here?'

'It's almost two moons since the battle.'

'Two moons!' Rhiannon could hardly believe it. As she thought of it her mind swam, oblivion threatening again.

'It took us a long time to come here,' Cunovinda said. 'We had often to hide. The Romans were everywhere, searching for survivors.'

'Who else is here?'

'Why . . .'Cunovinda hesitated, then spoke with a brightness that did not deceive Rhiannon. 'There's the queen your mother, and Matuac, Garanhir, and Nodenir. Morica – and Kai, Audagas's son . . .' She named a few others, some from Oakhillfort, some from other settlements across Icenia, perhaps a dozen and a half in all.

'Only these?' Rhiannon breathed.

'Only these,' Cunovinda sighed. 'Your mother directed us to come here. The fenfolk welcomed us and led us far into their realm by secret causeways. The Romans will never find their way here. We have shelter, and food . . . Here we'll rest, for a while. The others may be doing the same, in other hiding places.'

'Yes . . . Yes.' But Rhiannon knew that hope of finding anyone else alive was thin. They were all gone, all the folk with whom she had spent her life. Lying dead in a valley filled with heather, where their blood stained the earth. The chiefs and warriors. Her kinfolk. Her sister Araunah. Her baby son. And Farann . . .

She turned onto her face, her hands over her aching eyes, and wept inconsolably until exhaustion took her back into black havens of forgetfulness.

When next she woke her mind was clearer, if numb with grief, and the light was brighter to her eyes. She had been hit a glancing blow across the temple, and as she fell had stunned and temporarily blinded herself. But now that the wound and the bruising had healed so her sight was slowly returning. She felt very weak, but she was aware of hunger and guessed that she would now survive. Caridwen continued to taunt her, keeping her alive when most of those she loved had gone.

'Where is my mother?' she asked.

'Not far away,' Cunovinda replied. 'Our bowers are small, but they're weatherproof. Morica tends the queen.'

'Tends her? Ah . . . she was wounded!' She sat up, clutching at the arm of the vague shape she could see. 'Is she hurt badly?' When there came no reply, she tightened her grip, one hand groping to Cunovinda's face as if by that means to read her expression. 'Cunovinda, tell me!'

'The queen is dying,' Cunovinda said sadly.

'No!'

'The arrow was too deep to be cut free. The wound is festering. The poison is in her blood.'

Rhiannon shook her head, feeling the hot rush of tears in her useless eyes. 'Can't Morica help her?'

'Morica has done all she could. No one could have tried harder. She's been far and wide through the marshes, often soaked to the skin and shaking with the cold, to find the herbs she needed. But none of her arts, or her prayers, prevail. The queen has fought bravely. For a long time she was more worried for you than for herself. But even her strength is failing now. I fear she is beyond mortal help, Rhiannon.'

'I must go to her. Help me, Cunovinda.'

'Wait. I'll call Matuac. You can lean on him.'

Matuac came, and after greeting her with affection and sadness he lent her his strong arm for support, with Cunovinda on her other side. They led her out of the shelter where she had been lying and by an overgrown pathway to another sturdy bower in whose shadows Rhiannon could just make out a figure propped up beneath rough blankets.

'Daughter!' Boudicca's familiar voice greeted, with an odd breathiness that told of her pain. Their hands met and clasped, and Rhiannon sank to her knees.

'You're hurt, mother. If I'd known . . .'

'How could you know, when you were sick yourself?' the queen replied. 'You've grown so thin, daughter. You must care for yourself now. You'll be queen when – '

'I don't care about that!' Rhiannon snatched up her mother's hand, bringing it to her cheek, where it felt limp and already cold. 'Are you in pain?'

'Not much,' the queen denied. 'Except from knowing that I led my people to defeat. Was I wrong, Rhiannon? Was I wrong to seek war?'

Rhiannon had never before heard that note of uncertainty in her mother's voice. It frightened her more than anything else. 'No, mother! No! After what they did . . . We had to fight. We had to try!'

'And we failed!'

'We showed them that Britons are not to be treated as dogs. We won great victories, mother! Camulodunon, Londinium, Verulamium. We cut down a legion and set its remnants to flight – it was not failure – you united the tribes; no one else has ever done that.'

'I united a few clans from some of the tribes, for a brief span of time,' the queen contradicted with a sigh. 'Where were the rest? What will the bards sing of me, daughter? Perhaps Prasutagus was right. Perhaps there was never a hope of winning.'

'At least you tried!' Rhiannon wept, cursing the veil that dimmed her sight. Her mother had given up; she could sense it.

A man's hands came on Rhiannon, helping her to her feet. She heard Garanhir's voice say close to her ear, 'The queen your mother grows weary, Rhiannon. Let her rest. You must rest, too. When you're stronger, things will not seem so black.'

She looked round, blinking through the grey mist, seeing only a shape. 'You'll stay with her?'

'Yes. I'm here. Rest now. Cunovinda will go with you.'

He had been faithful for so long, she thought with a stab of pity that brought more tears to distress her.

Rains came, and with them cold mists to haunt the marshes. The streams swirled with dead leaves from the trees and hunger made the remnants of the Iceni fear the approach of winter. There was fish to eat, and at first nuts and berries to be found, with roots and herbs, and occasionally the fenfolk brought a loaf or two of rough barley bread, but it was clear that living through the winter would be hard. Realising it, Matuac organised the men for a foray out of hiding in the hope of finding help of some kind, perhaps another axe or two for chopping wood, or some blankets, or even a store of grain in some abandoned homestead.

As her sight began to improve, Rhiannon sat with her mother employing herself in plucking the small fowl that the hunters caught, or cleaning fish. Boudicca watched her, saying little but evidently blaming herself for having brought her daughter to this.

'It doesn't matter,' Rhiannon said. 'I want to help, since I must eat, too. And it's only while the winter lasts. When the spring comes we'll move out of here. Maybe we'll go back to Oakhillfort and start again. Who knows, perhaps some of our people are already there. Matuac will bring news.'

From the corner of her eye she studied her mother's face; thin and shadowed with pain. Boudicca's staunch spirit was still fighting, but her bodily strength had reached its limits. Sometimes she slipped into fevered dreams when she muttered to herself.

Often in those periods of wandering, Boudicca remembered her father Antedios, dying of a putrid wound from a spear-tip. She was destined to follow him in the same way. She knew it. Not that she cared much, not any more. She had followed the Goddess of War and the Goddess had led her to defeat; Boudicca had always know that She was fickle.

She drifted into waking dreams of childhood, remembering her mother the queen Veda and Mocuxsoris her brother. She thought of Huan, reliving the first days of their meeting. Dreaming, remembering, some long-ago merriment bubbled from her and woke her up. She found Rhiannon watching her with troubled eyes.

'How like him you are,' Boudicca said. 'Like him, and yet not like. If he were here . . .' Tears welled in her eyes and one overflowed to trickle down her cheek. She brushed at it weakly. 'How different my life might have been, if he had lived.'

'Then why did he have to die?' Rhiannon asked in a charged undertone. 'Why, mother?'

'It was necessary. The Goddess – '

'But what good did his death do? Or the sacrifice of Ylas? The Romans still came. We are still defeated! Where was the Goddess when we needed Her?'

'She does not always answer as we wish!' Boudicca said. 'She chooses the path, not we!'

'Then why do we practise the rites?! If the Gods don't listen – if They still follow Their own whims . . .' She broke off, hearing a step on the path, fearing that Morica might be near. Belatedly she saw how her mother was weeping, clutching the rose quartz ring that still hung at her breast. Lately, tears were never far away from the queen's eyes and the sight of them always distressed Rhiannon. Her mother had never been one to weep; it was a sign of her growing weakness. 'Forgive me, mother,' she begged, taking the queen's hand. 'I'm not myself. Tell me, please, about . . . about Huan of the Caledones.'

Boudicca closed her eyes. She did not question how Rhiannon had heard the name of Huan. Rhiannon had always seen and known more than she should. Slowly the haze in her mind cleared and she was young again, riding with Mocuxsoris and a group of other young hunters, coming to the shore of the Great Bay.

Reminiscing, she recounted the history of Huan, from the day she had found him on the shore to the day he died at the Solstice. More tears flowed down her face as she sorrowed afresh, for him and for herself as she spoke freely of her love for him. He had been the first man for her, the only man who had meant so much. After him, her heart was armoured against all others; she had discovered how love could hurt; she did not like to be vulnerable in that way. Even with Garanhir she had held off, fearing to have him come too close. And perhaps she had grown too fond of the power she held as queen; perhaps she had been unwilling to share it, even with Garanhir.

'But Huan gave me a gift beyond value,' Boudicca said, her eyes soft as she gazed on her daughter. 'He gave me you, Rhiannon.' She drifted into sleep, one hand held in Rhiannon's, the other locked around the rose quartz ring. She was smiling a little as she dreamed.

A movement behind her made Rhiannon jump and she turned to find Garanhir there. She knew that he had heard her mother talking. Sadness lurked in his eyes, but he smiled and said, 'I'll sit with her now. You must rest, Rhiannon.'

'You knew?' she asked.

'Yes.'

'Yet you still loved her?'

'And always shall. I made her a vow, long ago when it began. Until the wild geese call me . . .'

'Then what of Adalma?'

'There are many kinds of love, Rhiannon,' Garanhir said.

'And all of them are painful.'

'No, not all of them.'

'Once I believed that *you* were my father.'

He smiled a little. 'I should have been proud to own you. But the only child of my loins is lost now. There will not be another.'

'Adalma's child?'

For a long moment he watched her, considering his answer, then with a glance at the sleeping queen he said simply, 'Araunah.'

'Ah.' The sound was almost inaudible. So many things were suddenly clear.

Voices called across the marsh and with a swish of paddles three coracles emerged from a thick bank of reeds: Matuac and his foraging party had returned. They had found some ragged blankets and begged a little grain from a fisherwife, but what pleased Rhiannon most was the fact that they had found Teyrnon, thin as chaff but still able to beam his gap-toothed grin.

But the news he and Matuac brought was not good. Icenia had been ravaged by Roman troops bent on destruction. They had burned the crops in the fields, destroyed farms and forts, slain people and animals . . . Such was the fury of Suetonius Paulinus that he had refused to waste time in winter camps but instead had kept his men in the field, searching for Boudicca and any of her warriors and allies who were left alive. He had vowed to eliminate all trace of the queen who had ruined his moment of victory and made him look a fool. He had sent for reinforcements from Germany, mercenaries who were roaming the countryside killing and burning. No Briton was safe anywhere in Icenia. It had become a land of ghosts.

For safety, the queen and her small band of followers must stay in hiding.

The worst of this news was kept from Boudicca, but when

she talked of leaving a legacy of failure Rhiannon was able to recount how other tribes had risen with her – tribes in the north and the west of Albion. Teyrnon had heard tell of it. The strength of the Druids was broken; the rebellions they had encouraged had been crushed by the might of Rome; but Boudicca's dream had almost come true. She had raised the war carnyx; she had blown the first defiant blast, and in response most of Albion had stirred. For the first time in history, separate tribes had briefly discovered how it might feel to be one nation.

'The day will come, mother,' Rhiannon said, 'and when it does the bards will sing how you were the first to unite the tribes to a single cause. You, a woman – Boudicca, war queen of the Iceni!'

The thought comforted Boudicca as she sank into delirium and drew near to death. She would welcome peace after her long struggles. Huan was waiting there in the Fields of Heaven, and with him Mocuxsoris. She would gladly ride with them through the days of eternity. In a period of lucidity, she gave Rhiannon the ring that had belonged to Huan. 'I shall need it no more. No, don't weep, daughter of my womb. I go with a quiet heart. People I love are waiting for me. And . . .' Her eyes shone with gladness as she confided, 'The Goddess is with me again. I saw the white hare last night, as I used to see it in my youth. It stood by that thicket, on the edge of the moonlight. It is my sign from Dia. She has come to lead me away.'

She slipped once more into unconsciousness. Rhiannon sat beside her, with Garanhir nearby and Morica by the queen's feet. They watched as night came and the moon rose frosty in a sky full of stars. A wind rose from the north, bringing the threat of snow.

Deep in the night, Boudicca of the Iceni, queen and Maiden, high chief, war chief, leader of Britons, died of wounds got in battle with the foes of her people. Her life had been filled with passion and grief, but peace cloaked her ending.

They had built a boat for her. Nowhere in the marshes was there a suitable burial place for such a queen, and they feared the wrath of Suetonius might desecrate her grave if ever he found it. So they hollowed out an alder tree and shaped it as a boat. They filled its belly with a pyre of kindling and laid her there with the sword Blood Craver clasped at her breast and her long hair combed about her shoulders. Around her throat they left the great electrum torc of Iceni queens: Rhiannon could not countenance removing it. It belonged to her mother, the last warrior queen.

Into the boat they put their offerings of objects carved as she lay dying – a tiny chariot to bear her to the Glass Castle, horses to draw it, and bowls for her food and drink. It was little enough for a great queen, but it was done with love and honour; Brecca herself could not have asked for more.

Riding in coracles they drew the funeral boat through the marshes to the shores of the Great Bay one chill evening as the full flooding tide began to ebb, when the calm sea rolled with a silent swell. Some of the fenfolk went too, out of respect for one who had been both a queen and a Maiden. The mourners paddled out with the alder craft until she was safe from shore, then Garanhir stood up, a flaming torch in his hand. As last champion of the tribe it was his privilege to light the pyre, but he hesitated.

Through eyes that ached, Rhiannon saw him draw himself up. His gaze was fixed on the queen's peaceful face; his own face ran with tears. He could not bear to part from her. Instead of throwing the torch, he stepped with it into the funeral boat, causing the coracle he left to rock dangerously. Its occupants cried out in alarm.

'Come back!' voices called to him. 'Come back, Garanhir!'

But he set the torch at the prow of the boat and took up the paddle that lay beside the queen. Its blade dipped into the winter sea and the boat began to move away. When he was clear of the frail coracles, Garanhir took up the torch, saluted the mourners with it, and thrust it into the kindling before once more taking up his paddle.

'She will need a reinsman to guide her,' his voice came floating back to them.

Through glittering tears Rhiannon saw the flames begin to lick around the pallet on which her mother lay. Still Garanhir continued to paddle, strongly and unhurriedly, uttering no sound as the hungry flames found him. The burning boat headed out into the coming darkness, where soon it became a flickering glow floating between sea and night.

*

Now Rhiannon knew her time of deepest despair. The Iceni were a mere handful of people hiding in the marshes as winter dragged on, wet, gloomy, cold. They were constantly hungry, constantly shivering, all of them grieving for those they had lost. Boudicca seemed to have taken all hope with her; several of her followers succumbed to disease once the queen had left them. Among those who died was the priestess Morica, another link with the old ways.

Rhiannon wept for her people, but she herself had no reserves of strength left to help them. She lay awake at night shivering under thin coverings and listening to her stomach grind in hunger while she ached for the warmth of her baby beside her. She tried to comfort herself with memories of the night before the last battle, when she had lain in Farann's arms. At least they had been granted one night. But it was poor relief when she needed him, and Nion, now.

Many times she brooded on their quarrel. Had he been wrong to take Matuac's place in the Mysteries? Was it because of his sacrilege that so much sorrow had come?

But if the rite had gone as foreseen then Matuac would have died at the Solstice. Yet it was Matuac who had now become the strength of his people. He led foraging parties and brought back all manner of wildfowl and animal to eat. Often they supped on beaver steaks, and once Kai and Teyrnon managed to trap and kill a bear; it served as meat, however tough. Matuac found work for them all, to keep them occupied and stop them from thinking of their discomfort. Matuac told tall tales round the fire at night, and made them sing the old songs – he gave them hope.

'More and more he reminds me of Ylas,' Rhiannon said to Cunovinda as they worked with aching fingers and shards of flint to scrape the last flesh from the bear's skin, which would make a fine rug. 'It's as though the two of them exist now in one body.'

'Perhaps they do,' Cunovinda said, her violet eyes wide and misty as she gazed across the wintry marshes. 'Who can tell the ways of the Gods? You question too much, Rhiannon.'

'Farann questioned, too. Perhaps the Gods do have reasons for Their actions. Perhaps it is all for the best in the end. But if Dia follows Her own vision of eternity, does it matter what we do? Do our struggles to please Her make any difference?

Must the Green King go on dying at every Great Year? Is the Maiden eternally fated to sorrow? Why, Cunovinda?'

'I don't know.' She was silent for a long time as they both struggled with their thoughts and the work that kept them warm: then she said, 'The Romans have many different beliefs, but one thing they find vile is the taking of human life as a sacrifice to the Gods. Their laws made an end to that custom among their own people.'

'Aye . . .' Rhiannon sighed. 'Farann said the same.'

Cunovinda paused in her work to survey her blistered fingers and frown over a memory. 'I heard talk once, from a friend of Marcus Terentius who came to visit us, of a new belief. This man was a poet, a traveller. I didn't hear all the conversation but he was telling about a new band of preachers who say that . . . that not long ago a Maiden in a far land bore a Child of the God – a Son Who in His turn became a King, like our Green King, I suppose, and Who died bound to a tree . . . a final sacrifice, to end all others. I think that was the meaning of it. Marcus's friend said the cult was spreading even in Rome.'

'To be free of human sacrifice would be a blessing,' Rhiannon sighed. 'I've seen enough blood, enough sorrow – and to what purpose? I spent my life following my duty: I was faithful, I obeyed. And in return Dia has taken everything I cared for.' She looked up to where in the dusk the moon was rising, bent and old over the dark wastes of the marshes. 'For me She is Caridwen the Cruel. See how She stares down on us, cold and distant. If we all die tomorrow still She will wax and wane and accept the tribute of other fools.'

'Don't say that,' Cunovinda begged. 'She has not forsaken us. Nor is She always Caridwen. The winter is passing. The spring will come. We are still young and strong. We can build again.'

Rhiannon looked at her friend, wishing she could share her optimism. '*You* might. You have Matuac.'

'There are other men,' Cunovinda said. 'The queen of the Iceni will need a husband. Perhaps Kai. He often watches you.'

Queen of the Iceni. Rhiannon turned away, unwilling to face the thought of a future empty of all she had loved. She was not strong as Boudicca had been. As yet she could not think of any man but Farann. 'I always knew I must marry for the sake of the tribe,' Boudicca had said once. And she too had loved, and lost, and yet still gone on. Perhaps Rhiannon would take the son of Audagas for a husband. Was it the fate of queens, to be denied quietness of heart?

Incredible though it seemed to Rhiannon at the time, the winter did pass. New green began to spread among the trees of the marshes and when a scouting party went out it returned with the overwhelming news that there were people at Oakhillfort.

'What people?' Rhiannon demanded.

'*Our* people!' Teyrnon cried.

'But not many,' Nodenir amended. 'Twenty or so, that's all.'

'They spent the winter in the forests,' Teyrnon said, his freckled face alight, 'but since they went to Oakhillfort a few more stragglers have joined them. There'll be enough of us to start again.'

'But who are they?' several voices cried, anxious for loved ones.

Teyrnon and the others began to list names of those they had recognised. Among them were none that Rhiannon most wished to hear.

'And Erefwen's leading them,' Teyrnon said.

Erefwen! Rhiannon thought with an odd lurch of her heart. Then the old ways would go on. She realised she had been thinking that, with the Druids gone, and both priestesses dead, perhaps there could be a move towards less fear of the Gods. But if Erefwen remained she would make sure the old rites were followed. She was more fanatical than Morica had ever been.

But despite her misgivings Rhiannon was comforted to hear several other familiar names. Every survivor was precious and welcome. Even Erefwen.

Ten

Slowly, they made their way out of the marshes and as they came to the final river Rhiannon saw the bulk of the knoll rising against the sky. Her eyesight had never fully recovered after her injuries and distances now were blurred, but even so the proud rise of the knoll and the defensive banks brought joy to her heart. Perhaps all was not lost. Not quite.

People ran out to greet them, hurrying down the slope with cries of joy to surround Rhiannon, calling, 'Lady!' Seeing how tired she was, some of the men lifted her high and bore her on their shoulders. But, as they went, Rhiannon saw the bitter truth.

The knoll remained, but what her hope and imagination had seen as sturdy defences were in reality shallow piles of bare earth. The steep grassy banks where she had sat so often had been torn down, their debris scattered across the hillside and the chariot track. The great gates of the fort had been burned: only two charred stumps remained. Between them, Erefwen stood, gaunt of face with her long pale hair straggling about her shoulders. Wordlessly she saluted Rhiannon and turned to lead the sorry procession into the fort.

Through aching eyes that stung with tears, Rhiannon saw the devastation that awaited her. Where granaries and work-sheds and houses had been only a few rough shelters now stood, recently built of wicker and mud and hasty thatch. The queen's house was gone; nothing remained but charred wood and trampled ashes. The great hall no longer raised its curved roof to the sky. All had been burned and the remains pulled down and scattered. The sacred oak had been reduced to a hacked stump. Even some of the trees in the sacred grove along the knoll had been cut down; the flint altar had been dug up and shattered into shards. And the pool on the hillside had been desecrated, filled in with mud and broken branches.

Suetonius's fury had blazed fiercest here at Boudicca's homeplace.

Numbed, Rhiannon stood in the centre of the blackened ring of earth where the queen's house had been. This bare ground had once held all that was dear to her; now there was nothing. She could see the hole that had been the treasure pit under her mother's room. It was empty, of course. The gold coins of the royal treasure had gone, and with them the owl-headed torc of Iceni high chiefs.

'So Boudicca is dead,' Erefwen said from behind her. 'Then you are queen, lady. Command us.'

Rhiannon looked round, feeling as though her head was swimming. Erefwen's pale eyes burned with a cold fire. She was rib-thin like the rest, her once-beautiful face gaunt. As Morica's had been, Rhiannon thought. The glittering eyes were like Morica's, too, the pupils widened by some drug of toadstool or ivy, but in Erefwen the fanatical gleam was now accompanied by an open hatred directed at Rhiannon.

'Or shall I do it?' Erefwen asked. 'I am Dia's priestess now. I can read the signs. I know the rites. With the Druids gone, you may rely on me, lady.'

Rhiannon contained a sigh. As she had feared, the old ways would go on with Erefwen as priestess. Erefwen possessed an icy intelligence and an ambition which might have led her to believe she could lead the tribe – if Rhiannon had not survived. The two had never been friends: now it seemed they must be enemies.

As if to establish her claim to power, Erefwen said, 'Tomorrow is the spring equinox. There shall be furze fires on the heath, and a sacrifice to give thanks for our survival. There are yet sheep among the hills, and a few cattle, and our hunters saw horses one day, running wild. We shall rebuild, with Dia's help.'

'Yes,' Rhiannon agreed, though the task looked long and wearisome to one who had so little strength left. The devastation at the fort had crushed her. 'We must rebuild.'

Matuac stepped up beside her. 'Food first,' he decided. 'We'll send out a hunting party. Kai – you lead them. Teyrnon, go with him – and keep a watch out for these horses Erefwen says are nearby. You're still the horsemaster. You need to make a start on our new herd.'

*

All Erefwen thought of was the celebration of the equinox come the morrow. The Goddess demanded Her due, she kept saying. They had survived. They must give thanks, and make sacrifice to ensure the continued blessing of Dia in their work. Her insistence depressed Rhiannon.

The hunters returned with a deer. Soon it was prepared and cut into joints which were skewered on sticks and set to roast around a great fire whose sparks shot up into the twilit sky. The scent of the meat heartened everyone.

Then: 'Riders!' the call came. 'Riders coming!'

'Romans?' Matuac demanded.

'I can't tell. They're too far away yet.'

Drawing swords, grabbing up spears, the men ran to the edge of the knoll telling the women to make ready to flee into the woods. But the riders appeared to be Britons, a party of warriors and a couple of carts pulled by mules. They offered no threat but rode steadily up the slope until they came within hailing distance and stopped, seeing the defenders outlined against the sky.

By that time, curiosity had drawn Rhiannon and Cunovinda to Matuac's side. He held a sword; the two women were armed with spears. Around them other members of their small group stood tensely.

'Hail, Iceni of Oakhillfort!' the voice came out of the night – a familiar voice that to Rhiannon sounded like the sweet singing of heaven – if it were not a ghost from the Otherworld. 'I bring news, and food, and friendship.'

'It's Farann,' Rhiannon breathed and the spear fell from her nerveless fingers. 'Oh, sweet Albina . . . It's Farann. Farann!!' Of their own will, her feet took her flying down the slope, all weariness forgotten. She ran towards the group of mounted men, seeing one of them leap to the ground, and hesitate. He said, on a note of incredulous joy, 'Rhiannon? Great Gods! . . . Rhiannon!' and came striding, running, his arms opening wide to catch and hold her.

She had never known such joy. She clung to him, weeping, twining her arms round his neck, kissing his clothes and his neck and then finally finding his mouth waiting for hers. He held her so tightly it was painful, yet the pain was joy. She could never remember exactly what was said in those moments; it was all one glory of hugging and weeping in joy at a reunion neither had dared to hope for.

Around them the others had arrived, cries of greeting ringing out. Cunovinda came weeping to greet her brother, men slapped backs, some recognised friends of battle days.

Farann had brought a group of warriors and some of their womenfolk, with a supply of food, tools and household goods that to the Iceni were of greater worth than gold.

'Come, ride in the cart,' he suggested to Rhiannon. 'See – here's Lucca, wife of my sound fellow Pryderi.'

'I'll walk with you,' Rhiannon said, clinging to his arm.

Farann laughed down at her and swept his arm more firmly about her. 'So you will, through all the days to come. But see here . . .' He leaned over the cart and drew back a corner of a blanket that was laid across a cosy sleeping nest where three children slept – a youngling with maybe four summers behind her, and two babes. In the darkness Rhiannon could only make out the shapes of them but her heart skipped painfully and she forgot to breathe as she dared to hope.

Farann leaned over and picked up the older of the two babies. The child stirred, but as Farann laid him in Rhiannon's arms he settled back into slumber, a warm heavy weight, more than a year old.

'Greet your son,' Farann said gruffly.

She stood holding the child, weeping helplessly with her head bent over him, until Farann's arm came warmly round her and he led her back to the settlement and the firelight.

The few children were laid to sleep in one of the huts. Rhiannon stayed with her son, still finding the miracle of his survival hard to believe. Even when the food was ready she was reluctant to leave until Farann came to fetch her, saying that he too was in need of her company; and, unlike their son, he was wide awake.

'Araunah saved the boy,' he told her as they ate with the rest around the fire. 'She saved me, too, as the Gods would have it. I was wounded in the battle, left for dead, but when the night came my senses returned – just as the Romans were looting the bodies. They would have killed me, but Nion's crying diverted them and gave me time to get to cover. When they found the babe under an overturned cart, Araunah rose up beside him. In the moonlight they thought her a ghost or an evil spirit. They ran off. Araunah and I escaped together, and eventually came up with some of my people – including Lucca, who suckled Nion along with her own child.'

'And Araunah?' Rhiannon asked.

Farann's expression altered as he sighed. 'I'm sorry, sweet lady. Her strength was all gone. The winter took her.'

The flames of the fire dazzled beyond her tears as she thought of Araunah, and all the others who had perished. 'It took my mother the queen, too,' she said.

'Aye . . . Matuac told me. For that I grieve deeply. She was a fine lady. But you are queen now. Will you choose a husband soon?'

'My husband is already chosen,' she assured him, laying a hand possessively on his arm. 'By me – and by the Great Goddess. She fated us for each other. Who can doubt that now? So you will be high chief. Or . . . have you other responsibilities among your own people?'

Smiling a little, he shook his head. 'Baro is still chief in Caesaromagus. I've no wish to battle with him for the honour. For a while I was war chief, but when the war ended the role ended. These men chose to remain with me. They are all I have to offer as a bride-price.'

'They are a handsome gift,' she replied. 'I accept them, and their women and their children. And as my dowry for you . . . I bring nothing but the prospect of toil and hardship, Farann.'

He took her hand, lifting it to his lips, watching her over it. 'And yourself, sweet lady. The only dowry I could wish for.'

As hunger was for the moment dealt with, voices began to demand to hear news from the rest of Albion. Farann rose to his feet to tell it.

'The news is good. Suetonius has been recalled. There is a new governor-general who wishes to restore peace. The devastation wrought by Suetonius has shocked even the Emperor – as has the news of Catus's attack on the queen and her women, and his robbing of Iceni nobility. The Emperor seeks reconciliation with all the peoples of Briton. And we, my friends, must accept his offer. The Romans are here to stay. We must find a way of living beside them in peace.'

'We?' Kai, the son of Audagas, rose slowly to his feet, his red hair and beard glowing in the firelight. 'You speak like a chief, Trinovante. There are others here with a claim to that role. I am the son of Audagas, son of Sovio, son of Tegid, chiefs of the Seafort clan, of pure Iceni blood. If a high chief is to be chosen, then my name must be on the list for consideration by the council.'

Matuac laughed derisively, saying, 'What council? Everything has changed. There are no elders. The choice must be left to the queen.'

'She cannot choose an outsider!' Kai exclaimed.

All eyes turned to Rhiannon, waiting for her to speak. She wondered how her mother would have faced this crisis and as the thought came the new moon showed behind fitful cloud and it was as though Boudicca stood at her shoulder, whispering advice.

Slowly, drawing grace and dignity about her despite her ragged clothing, Rhiannon got to her feet. 'The law is the law,' she said. 'The council sits in judgement to choose the husband of the queen, for the man will become high chief of the tribe. We have a council – we have ourselves, all of us around this fire. *We* are the council of elders of the Iceni. And we have two candidates for the hand of the queen. Two . . . unless any other man wishes to add his name.'

She looked around the faces of her audience. None of the men spoke or made signs of wanting to be included, though as her gaze met Matuac's he smiled wryly to himself. Once he had had ambitions, but the wheel had turned and his time had passed.

Rhiannon drew a long breath. 'Then I ask you to choose. There is Kai, son of Audagas, a brave warrior, a fine hunter, known to you all. And there is Farann, son of Vindorex, prince of the Trinovantes, war chief of the south, whose name and fame in the recent war you all have heard. For him speak the voices of our dead. He was my mother's choice as high chief, and also the choice of Eogan the Druid. He is my choice, too. From these two I ask you to decide.'

Little discussion was needed. All voices spoke for Farann. And Kai, seeing that the vote went firmly against him, accepted with the best grace he could summon. He was Audagas's son but his temper listened to his reason.

To celebrate the betrothal of Rhiannon the queen and Farann of the Trinovantes they broached the skin of wine that had been carried on one of the carts, and though the spring wind blew cold around them their hearts were warm with contentment and hope.

'Albina!' Erefwen cried aloud, drawing all eyes to where she stood by the broad flat stump of what had once been the sacred oak. She threw back her head to stare at the virgin moon, lifting her arms in supplication. Cold light slanted along the knife she held in her hand. *'Blessed Albina!'* her voice rang out, silencing talk and laughter. *'Thou hast heard the prayers of Thy people. Thou hast brought new life among us. We thank Thee. Now we pray, let the dawn come, and with it the warming of the sun, the true beginning of spring, new life to the earth, new vigour to the crops and the herds . . .'*

The prayer went on, but Rhiannon heard no more of the familiar words. She had heard a child whimper in the arms of one of the younger women who was walking now to join Erefwen. The woman knelt by the tree stump, placing the child there, unfastening its wrappings to expose its pale body in the cold moonlight.

'Accept this offering we give to Thee!' Erefwen cried, taking the knife in both hands, its point poised downward. *'Take back Thine own. Receive the child of the God!'*

Rhiannon's scream froze everyone as she launched herself to save her son. Even Erefwen stopped, the knife poised over Nion's small body as she glanced up, startled. And in that instant a spear sliced through the air and felled the priestess. She was thrown backwards and lay twitching, her hands weakly grasping the spearshaft that protruded from her breast. Then the movement ceased, her arms relaxed.

Matuac ran to stand over her, a foot holding her body while he wrenched his spear free and glared over it at the watching people. 'There will be no more human sacrifice!' he said. 'Hasn't there been enough of death? Didn't the Gods take blood enough in the war? And before it – my brother Ylas. There has been enough! Let Erefwen's blood serve if she believes it to be necessary. She was always full of hate and jealousy. This was her plan to hurt the queen, not to honour the Goddess. Does anyone doubt it?'

Silence was his answer. Rhiannon bent to scoop her son

away from harm, feeling him struggle against her as his cries grew louder; then Farann stepped up beside her, saying, 'No one doubts it, Matuac. This was well done. But let this be the last of it. In future there'll be less of blood and more of sweat. By toil we'll prove our faithfulness. We shall need all our strength not for fighting but for building. Carry Erefwen away. Tomorrow we'll build a pyre for her. We shall honour her. She was faithful – in her way.'

Under Farann's leadership the Iceni found a new will. Their resources were few as yet but each man and woman brought skills to the task of rebuilding, and as it became known that warrior nobles had returned to the fort so a few peasants emerged from hiding to help in the rough scraping of ground and the sowing of what little seed had been left. Others rounded up the sheep and cattle that had escaped the Romans – not many, but some of the ewes already had lambs and a few of the cows were in calf.

The women wove branches of young willow into panels to be fixed between posts that the men had rough-hewn and hammered into the ground. Then the thatch of heather and reed was woven on a network of hazel twigs and slowly a roof took shape. Thick mud was slapped into the crevices of the wicker to keep out the wind, a rough door formed, and behold – another house!

As spring warmed the land and the first green tips of corn showed in the fields, Rhiannon began to believe that her people might have a future. She and Farann – along with Matuac and Cunovinda and other young couples – leapt the fires and spoke the words of a kind of marriage ceremony, but with Eogan gone and both priestesses dead there was less ritual. The Gods did not appear to object. The sun still grew warmer, the birds returned to sing and the land grew green and fresh.

But fear struck again at Oakhillfort with the appearance of a detachment of Romans. Riding in column with pennanted lances, they came trotting up the track from the Way behind a stern-faced officer newly arrived in Britannica. Beside him rode the tribune Valerius Rufinus.

Farann met them, standing on the remnants of the banks

where the gates had been, with a force of his warriors beside him, armed with spears and swords. The Romans rode to a halt below them on the hill.

Across the distance, Farann met the eyes of Valerius and saw that the man had forgotten nothing.

'Who is chief here?' the tribune asked.

'I am,' Farann replied. 'What do you want?'

'We seek news of Boudicca.'

'The queen is dead.'

The Roman officers conferred briefly, then Valerius said, 'Julius Alexianus asks – of what did she die? Where is she buried?'

'She died of her wounds, poisoned by the grief of her defeat. She was given a burial befitting a great queen, but where her grave lies is a secret known only to a few.'

Valerius translated this and his superior frowned, evidently not convinced that Farann was telling the truth. The two officers came on up the slope, with their escort riding behind, watchful and ready to repel any attack. Knowing that the force was too strong to be resisted, Farann signed his men to fall back into the settlement where they took up posts guarding the doors of the huts.

The Roman troop rode in and the two officers halted in the centre of the circle.

'We must see how many are here,' Valerius said. 'Tell the women to come out, with their children.' Seeing the look on Farann's face, he added, 'They will not be harmed, that I swear.'

Hearing this assurance, Rhiannon stepped out from her house wearing a thin cloak with a hood pulled to cover her hair. She carried Nion in her arms as she placed herself near Farann. All the other women and children came out too, to stand by their own menfolk.

Nion was grown heavy; he had several teeth and was nearly able to walk. His great solemn blue eyes surveyed the Romans and he stretched out his arms to Farann, making sounds that said he wanted to go to his father. Rhiannon shushed him, catching his hands, peering up at the soldiers from under the hood of her cloak. Meeting the eyes of Valerius, she felt her flesh turn cold, with remembered horror, with hatred and with fear. He recognised her. But what his blank expression hid she could not tell.

The commander gave an order. Several of his men dismounted and with drawn swords went to search the huts, each man reappearing to report that the house was empty. All the people now remaining at Oakhillfort were gathered on the green.

Valerius leapt lithely down from his horse and without haste studied every Iceni face, walking among them, moving from group to group, ignoring the hostility in their eyes. He came to Rhiannon and looked into her face, then glanced at the child and at Farann. A corner of his mouth twitched in bitter humour as he moved on. When he had examined every person he returned to his horse, remounted and spoke to his commander, who nodded curtly.

'We had orders to arrest any member of Boudicca's family who remained alive,' Valerius said. 'It's fortunate that none of them appears to be here. Am I to understand that they all perished?'

'All of them,' Farann said.

Valerius looked full at Rhiannon, his face expressionless again. 'Then that is what I shall say in my report – the last report I shall make before I return to Rome – that the queen of the Iceni, and all her kinfolk, are dead.' He paused, perhaps expecting a reply. When none came he added briskly, 'From now on, Julius Alexianus will be in command of this area. A fort will be built at the coast and regular patrols will protect you from now on. Do you understand?'

'Yes, tribune, we understand,' Farann answered in tones that said he knew full well that the 'protection' was also a policing measure against further uprisings. 'And we thank you.'

For a few heartbeats the two men stared at each other, their eyes sparking a challenge, then the Roman said softly, 'Farewell, Farann of the Trinovantes.'

The commander lifted his hand and at his signal the column moved off, wheeling around the huts to go back to the gap where the gates had been. Rhiannon watched them go, moving closer to Farann as they watched Valerius depart from their lives.

'He was seeking forgiveness,' she said.

'By this one act, he shall have it,' Farann replied. 'He has given us our lives and our freedom. The future is ours, Rhiannon.'

Only a short time later, a commotion in the woods announced the return of Matuac, Teyrnon and the hunters who had been gone for two days. Whooping and shouting they rode around the settlement on what had once been the chariot track, driving a small herd of young horses. They had found the animals in the forest and rounded them up to bring them home. Most of them were strays from Oakhillfort and other settlements, colts and fillies which had been too young to be ridden to war. Among them, to Rhiannon's delight, was the young stallion Starson, first of the new breed, sire of the future.

In delight, Teyrnon and Matuac rode wildly round and round, driving the horses before them. The beat of hooves sounded good to Rhiannon, the toss of manes made her laugh, and she saw her son's eyes light with pleasure at the sight of the animals. Nion, too, was warrior-bred, she thought as she hugged him and Farann for sheer joy.

She felt the Goddess whisper along the wind, no longer Caridwen but strong, sure, lusty Epona, the White Mare, Queen of the Winds – She Who had guided Rhiannon since childhood. Now She returned in the thud of hooves and the surge of hope, bringing with Her a promise of peace at last.

Rhiannon thought of all her friends – those who remained and those who had gone before. All of them would have a place in the history of Boudicca, last warrior queen of Icenia. The bards had gone, who might have sung her story, but though Rhiannon had few poetic skills she promised herself she would compose the song for her children and their children – a song to be sung around the fires in warriors' hall of a winter's night, that all should remember:

'Let the song be of Boudicca, of her life and of her spirit, which is fled with skeins of wild geese to the back of the north wind; though she dwells in the Glass Castle, beyond the sight of mortals, she remains in burnished memory, one with earth and sky and water; with the Maid, her older daughter; one with Thee, Threefold Goddess.'

THE END

AUTHOR'S NOTE: For Readers who may be interested to know where Non-Fiction (History? Truth?) ends and Fiction (Imagination? Lies?) begins . . .

Very few indisputable facts are known about the queen of the Iceni. Even the name by which we knew her at school (Boadicea) is now believed to be a misreading of an early manuscript and modern historians prefer the spelling Boudicca, or Boudica. Her own people, the ancient Brythonic (Britonic) Celts, left no written records. The chronicles which do briefly mention her were written, years afer the events they describe, by Roman historians. However, there seems to be no doubt that Boudicca did exist and that in the first half of the first century AD she was the wife of Prasutagus, king of the tribe called the Iceni, whose territories comprised more or less the area of England which we know today as Norfolk.

I have been careful to follow the known historical background as closely as possible. In the year AD 43 the Emperor Claudius did visit Britain when his legions conquered the warlike Catuvellauni tribe and certain Britonic chiefs returned with him from exile. Leaders of eleven British tribes came to make treaties of friendship with him and two of them – the Iceni and the Brigantes – were granted the special privileges of becoming client kingdoms. It is not known whether Prasutagus was king at this time, but it is quite feasible that he was, and that he took his wife with him to the great treaty making at Camulodunum (modern Colchester), which was to become the civil capital of Roman Britain. At the time, London was just a trading post; the civic offices were transferred there later.

The disarming of the tribes and the early Iceni rebellion because of it are also historical facts. After that the Iceni seem to have accepted their fate; they retreated into the wings of history for the next few years, during which the Romans were busy fighting Caratacus and trying to conquer the Druid centre on Anglesey.

Boudicca appears in the chronicles as a named personality only on the death of her husband the king in AD 60. Prasutagus had left half of his property to the Emperor, presumably in the hope of placating the greedy Nero (who by then had succeeded his uncle Claudius) but the ruse was in vain.

Roman troops rampaged over Icenia, plundering the king's property and that of his nobles. History records that among other indignities the queen was flogged and her daughters raped. As a result Boudicca raised a rebellion. She was joined by other tribes, notably the Trinovantes, and she razed the *colonia* of Camulodunum (modern Colchester) before marching on to burn London and then St Albans. The Romans were able to stop her only when they were given the opportunity to organise their forces into the formidable battle squares which they had used so effectively to conquer the known world. To date, no one has succeeded in identifying the site of this battle with absolute certainty, but currently the most likely spot seems to be Mancetter near Nuneaton, in central England.

The Roman chroniclers differ about what Boudicca's eventual fate might have been. What is certain is that she did not die in the battle; her body would have been found and the event recorded, had that been the case. One chronicler says she returned to her own country and died; another says she took poison. Tantalisingly, there is a sentence telling us that she was given a magnificent burial befitting a queen – though archaeologists have yet to find the spot, if it exists. In short, no one knows what really happened to her, except that she dropped out of history. What became of her daughters is not recorded, either, but certainly her lands were laid waste by her bitter enemy Suetonius Paulinus, her people the Iceni were decimated and the sorry remnant of them must have accepted the Roman way of life. What other choice had they?

These, then, are the scanty facts concerning Boudicca. More general information is available on the ancient Celtic peoples and their life in the first century AD – gleaned mostly by archaeologists from finds they have made to date. I have made use of all this information in building up my story, but unfortunately evidence relating directly to the Iceni in Norfolk is, so far, sparse and experts differ in their interpretation. However, it's pleasant to imagine that the great gold torc now on view in the British Museum, along with the rest of the wonderful treasure found on the knoll at Snettisham, Norfolk (where I've sited my fictional Oakhillfort) might have been worn by Boudicca herself. Experts have dated the treasure as being some years before her time, but then experts have been proven wrong before . . .

But alas for the scythed chariot of legend: to date no evidence has been found for such a vehicle, and given the way the Celts waged war the scythes would have been more of a threat to the legs of friends than of enemies – according to what we know today. Tomorrow some archaeological dig may turn up just such a vehicle and then opinions will have to be revised again!

As to the religion the Iceni practised, nothing is known but that they were pagan. On many of their coins a horse is depicted and one authority speculates that the name Iceni might mean 'People of the Horse' – which led me to imagine the importance among them of Epona the Mare Goddess, who is known to have been worshipped in Gaul. The rest is purely imaginary, though soundly based on what is known of ancient rites and beliefs, the role of the Druids, etc etc.

In writing this book I've tried to blend factual research with a novelist's imagination, to try to explain what sort of woman Boudicca might have been, and how and why she acted as she did, given the context in which she lived. On occasion I've condensed history in order not to complicate matters unnecessarily, and where authorities differ (as they frequently do about times so long ago) I've taken the line that seemed either most logical to me, or best for dramatic effect. This is, after all, a novel – an entertainment; it claims to be nothing more.

NAMES: When it came to finding names for my characters I gleaned all of them from my researches. Some of them are old Welsh; some of them may have been Romanised – was Prasutagus really called that or was he Prasutag and the Romans added the obligatory 'us'? And what of Caratacus/Caractacus? Was he actually Caradoc, or an early version of that name? No one really knows. My choice has been arbitrary.

As far as the Catuvellauni capital (Colchester) is concerned, it was known as Camulos's Fort (Camulos being a war god) and the Celts called it Camulodunon; they do so in my book. Only the Romans refer to it by its Roman name of Camulodu*num*.

Bibliography

BOADICEA, J M Scott. Constable, 1975.

BOUDICA, Graham Webster. Batsford, 1978.

CELTIC BRITAIN, Lloyd Lain. Routledge and Kegan Paul 1979.

THE CELTS, Nora Chadwick. Pelican, 1970.

CELTIC MYTH AND LEGEND, Charles Squire. Newcastle Publishing Co Inc., USA, 1975.

PAGAN CELTIC BRITAIN, Anne Ross. Routledge and Kegan Paul. 1967.

THE PAGAN CELTS, Anne Ross. Batsford. 1970.

THE PEOPLE OF ROMAN BRITAIN, Anthony R Birley. Batsford.

ROMAN BRITAIN, John Wacher. Dent, 1978.

ROMAN BRITAIN, Peter Salway. (Oxford History of England Series) Clarendon Press, 1985.

TOWNS OF ROMAN BRITAIN, John Wacher. Batsford, 1974.

IN SEARCH OF THE DARK AGES, Michael Wood. BBC, 1981.

THE ROMAN CONQUEST OF BRITAIN, AD 43 – 57, Donald R Dudley and Graham Webster. Batsford, 1965.

REBELLION AGAINST ROME, Plantaganet Somerset Fry. Dalton, Suffolk, 1982.

THE DRUIDS, Ward Rutherford. The Aquarian Press, 1978.

THE DRUIDS, Stuart Piggott. Thames and Hudson, 1968.

THE WHITE GODDESS, Robert Graves. Faber and Faber, 1948.

THE GOLDEN BOUGH, J G Frazer. Macmillan, 1922.

PATTERN UNDER THE PLOUGH, G E Evans. Faber and Faber, 1966.

EAST ANGLIA, R R Clarke. S R Publishers Ltd., 1971.

IN BRECKLAND WILDS, W G Clarke. Robert Scott, 1925.

ROMAN COLCHESTER, Handbook of the Colchester

Museum, Published by the Cultural Activities Committee, 1980.